OF MAGIC AND RUM

BEYOND A CONTEMPORARY MYTHOS

USA TODAY BESTSELLING AUTHOR

CARLY SPADE

BEYOND A CONTEMPORARY MYTHOS

Copyright © 2024 by Carly Spade

WWW.CARLYSPADE.COM

Published in the United States by World Tree Publishing, LLC

Cover and Interior Formatting by We Got You Covered Book Design
WWW.WEGOTYOUCOVEREDBOOKDESIGN.COM

To my younger self, we did it.
We've written a story with mermaids, pirates and mythology.
*And it's out in the world. *fist bump**

ONE

RHODE

ATLANTIS IS DYING. And when I dove to the depths to defend it, the last thing I expected was a portal catapulting me to another place or time. I still can't fathom that the Charybdis followed me. My legs still feel the vacuum of its strong pull, my ears ring with the echoes of its jaws snapping with rows of vicious teeth. It's a creature I can't handle alone, so I did the only thing I could—swam as if my life depended on it. And this island is my savior. Only now, I can't feel Atlantis' heartbeat, nor sense its ethereal thrum.

I've landed on my knees, fingers digging into the wet sand. Now my eyes can't seem to open from fear of what or *who* I'll see. Salty scents laced with hints of coconut greet my nose. A flock of seagulls caw and squawk as they fly overhead. The rolling water hitting against the bank echoes from my left. A gust of wind rustles my soaked dress, carrying murmurs of overlapping voices from somewhere nearby. It's enough to make every muscle in my body tense. But when a man's voice shouts—the distance entirely too close for comfort—my eyes fly open, and I scurry across the sand to seek shade under a palm tree.

My heart pounds against my rib cage, my mind racing and reeling as I take in my surroundings. I'm in some place—tropical? A massive harbor butts against a scattered group of buildings some distance away, and an exceptionally tall ship sails into port.

A tall ship? The modern mortal world has made progress in its maritime vessels, and *that* is no fishing vessel.

My gaze falls to the luminescent blue scales on my arms glimmering with the sunlight, and I slap a hand over my mouth to keep from shrieking. As a sea nymph, water is both my blessing and curse—*if* I wished to be amongst humans undetected. Every ocean, sea, and lake is my home, and I thrive in them, breathe better in them, and swim with the aquatic life. But on land, when water touches my skin, my scales reveal themselves, and there's nothing I can do to stop them.

I remain under the guise and protection of the palm tree with my arms curled around my knees. All I can do is wait for my skin to dry, for the scales to disappear, and pray no one walks past. The docked ship raises an anchor, and blurs of a dozen people on board hurry across the deck, pulling ropes to mount the sails. Another body swings from the crow's nest, effortlessly hopping from riggings and mast like a monkey.

Where am *I?*

I've lived for nearly a thousand years, my father even more so, and nothing has happened like this with Atlantis since its creation. My father wouldn't let it. He couldn't.

I press a fingertip to my forehead. Relief washes over me

when met with smooth skin instead of scaly ridges. And before I rise to my feet to explore, I touch my ears—round and human, not webbed. I'm dry enough to pose as one of them, but I can't risk anyone seeing me in my Atlantean robes. I'll need to find clothes and *fast*.

A sandy path jutting between a thicket of bushes and palm trees leads into the town at the top of a hill. Ducking, I weave through the trees, gaze shifting from behind me and back to the front rapidly. I'm steps away from the town's threshold when a man carrying several wired cages filled with chickens shuffles past me, his attention elsewhere. I leap to the confines of a palm tree, willing the width of my body to mirror that of the tree, but I don't own such magic. Instead, I go still and slowly sink to rest my butt on my heels, my back pressing against the trunk so harshly, its grooves dig into my skin through the dress fabric. To my delight, the Chicken Man scoffs at someone and turns back in the direction he came.

No sooner is the coast clear, I scurry to the next best hiding spot behind a wheelbarrow stacked high with hay. A pair of trousers hang to dry on a rope drawn from a protruding beam of a quaint hut. Without remorse, I yank the garment, thankful it's no longer wet, and duck behind the pile of hay. I tear the bottom portion of my dress away, leaving only my silk linen undergarments on my lower half, and shimmy into the dingy brown trousers. They're too wide and long for me, but they'll make do after several folds at the hips and ankles.

As I keep my head held low and avoid eye contact with people passing by, it becomes more difficult to pinpoint where I am. Humans in a myriad of skin tones, ages, sizes, and features surround me, their numerous overlapping languages and accents bombarding my ears. There are also numerous languages bombarding my ears. Concentrating on the grooves in the skewed wooden planks that make up the walking paths, I let the accents settle against my mind. If I'm to get home, *if* I can get home, I'll need to blend in for now.

Homesickness is already striking nausea in my gut. I may never see my family again—my father and brother.

Rhode. Concentrate.

Pressing a thumb between my eyes, I mumble to myself, picking out the English-speaking accents the most before, finally, a hybrid of British and Irish flutters from my lips. It'll do. It has to. Every man that passes seems to leer at me too long for comfort. Given the few women I've seen wear corsets and skirts with days' worth of dirt staining their cheeks, I must stand out like a sheep in a wolf pack.

I dart to a soil patch with potatoes growing from its bed in front of a nearby house and drop to my knees, digging my fingers into the dirt to cake some underneath my nails and rub it on my cheeks. A man with gray, stringy hair and only one eye, the other covered in a brown eye patch, stops and stares at me.

I run with it because I already look like I'm sailing without a compass. "Pardon me, good sir, but would you mind telling me the year?"

"What?" The man croaks, raising a hand to one ear.

I clear my throat and stand, bits of dirt flying from my knees. "The year," I say louder.

"Aye, it *is* a good year." The man smiles with a singular tooth.

For the love of—

Squinting from the unrelenting sun above us, I dust my hands and move closer. "I seem to have forgotten what year it is." I pull on my sleeves. "I—I can't read either."

The man's face softens, and deep grooves form in his cheeks as he frowns. "You poor child." He presses a pitying hand over his heart. "The year be seventeen nineteen. And it's a good, good year." The man grins before waving and shuffling off, saying hello to every person he passes.

1719. The eighteenth century. The tall ships. The crystal-clear blue waters. The palm trees.

I continue to walk, my mind reeling at the possibilities, so distracted that I gasp when my hip bumps against a rickety wooden sign reading Nassau.

Bahamas. In the eighteenth century. These people. Most of them are—*pirates*. And this is the *Republic* of Pirates.

Immediately spurring thoughts of the violence construed by pirates both by firearm and blade, I splay my hand at my side but pause. The only weapon I can conjure at will is my Atlantean sword—forged with metals that don't exist in the mortal realm and most certainly don't resemble any used in this century. I drop my hand at my side with a gruff sigh. It isn't often I feel so vulnerable despite my powers.

But I can't use my powers in the open and must arm myself. Stealing clothes drying on a line is one thing, but stealing a knife is another matter. Granted, as a child, I'd always steal—mostly from ships on the surface, their crews none the wiser. I hid a chest under some abandoned cargo debris on the shore, filling it with everything I managed to "borrow"—forks, rope, dresses, lanterns, smoking pipes, and the like. My brother caught me once adding a pewter plate, and I swore him to secrecy because father would've harpooned me if he'd found out. Dear old Dad never did find my hoard.

On a ship, everyone is usually distracted by their assigned duties. Land takes a bit more finesse—especially in a port with this much activity and dozens of wandering eyes. My fingers play at the cowrie shell hanging from a piece of twine wrapped around my wrist, and I force myself to stop my nervous twitch. Taking a deep breath, I wipe my clammy palms on my trousers and reach the town's center. As an old friend said, walking confidently makes you far more inconspicuous. In some cases, you could become nearly invisible.

My eyes dart to empty belt after belt with no knives or swords. I'll even settle for a blunderbuss. I can figure out how to use it if a situation arises for it. Finally, resting on a pirate's hip, an unobtrusive accessory to his frock coat, sash, and tri-corner hat, is a dirk knife—small and primarily used for throwing, but with my petite hands, it'll suit fine.

Keeping the cool and calm demeanor I've worked up, I pass the pirate, holding back a gag from the putrid scents wafting from him and another pirate standing next to him—body odor, rotten eggs, and *shit*. I bump my shoulder against him, discreetly slipping my fingers to the knife's hilt and sliding it from its holster.

The weapon is hidden within my sleeve when it scrapes against my palm, and I turn toward the pirate with a hand pressed to my chest. "Deepest apologies. Had a little too much to drink today." I stumble as an extra selling point.

The pirate catches my arm and smiles with a top row of

rotting yellowed teeth. "A pretty thing like you don't need to apologize. Isn't that right, Henry?"

Damn.

A fluttering cackle pushes past Henry's lips, and he sidles closer to me, his apparent underbite cutting into his upper lip, hair a brown oily mess, and dirt so thickly coated on his face it makes his tanned skin even darker. "That's right, John."

"You know, we just got back from four months at sea and be mighty—restless." John's grip tightens on my wrist and he slowly pulls me closer.

Henry laughs again, his gaze glossing over as it unabashedly roams me from head to toe, the tip of his tongue licking his chapped lips.

"I'm sure there's a brothel in town, gentlemen." I turn to pull away, but John twists my arm.

It would be easy to break his arm and kick Henry halfway across the port.

"True. But considering our captain is about as useless as a cuttlefish, we returned empty-handed and are a bit scrapped for payment." John's hand reaches for my chest, and I let the dagger fall from my sleeve into my grasp. The blade is at his throat a breath later, pushing against his skin just enough to draw a thin line of blood.

Henry yelps, aiming his flintlock pistol at my head with a shaky hand.

John's palms fan at his sides. "Now, now. No need to be rash, pretty thing. We're going to get what we want one way or another. Best you make this easier for yourself and spread your legs, hm?"

I couldn't—I *can't* stand here and do nothing. It's not in my genetic makeup.

Glaring at John, his expression morphs from smugness to confusion to terror within several seconds. Saltwater bubbles from his lips before it begins pouring from his mouth. Henry drops the pistol and shrieks at the sight of John grasping his throat.

I could have brought the water to shore and drowned him where he stands, but calling it to fill his lungs from the inside out is far less likely to catch attention. When John drops to his knees, gasping as the water drains from his lungs, gradually returning his breathing to normal, I'm already walking away with extra vigor in my stride.

They make no effort to follow me. Considering the event's outlandish, I'm sure they won't connect me to it. How could they? John will likely assume he swallowed more water at sea than he thought and is now coughing it up. Henry will agree because Henry is a coat-tail rider through and through.

Catching my breath, I find the shade of a palm tree and press my back to it. The dirk's blade has a speck of human blood on it now, and I wipe it away on my trousers before hiding it back in my sleeve. A sigh pushes from my throat, and the familiar sting burns my nose with threatening tears.

Surely, my family realizes I'm gone by now. And I feel far more guilty over their worry for me than any danger this realm can and will throw at me. The thought of my father, most of all, and what he'll do to find me, carves a hole in my chest. He'll search every sea and ocean, visit every powerful being he thinks could help, and run himself ragged because of it.

And here, I can't contact or let him know, at least, that I'm alright—that his only daughter is *fine*.

Anger overtakes me now, and I kick an empty wooden bucket with a subdued growl. I need a ship. I need to barter passage on a merchant ship stopping in port. Swimming my way back, trying to find my way back, is out of the question with the Charybdis lurking. And there's nothing I can do marooned on this forsaken island. Out there—in open water—is my best chance. And despite my ability to materialize tail and fins, the idea of mermaids is an old wives' tale in this time—a mirage sailors have chalked up to deliriousness from starvation or dehydration while at sea for months.

Pushing from the tree, I turn in the direction of the port. As I pass a rickety hovel, the thin wood door flies open. A woman in a bonnet and apron steps out holding a bucket. She tosses its contents toward the street, but instead of the dirty water landing in dirt and sand, it splashes onto *me*.

Gasping at the scales already shimmering over my hands and arms, I cover my face with my sleeve, panic consuming me as I look for somewhere to hide.

"Goodness, dearie, it's just dirty dishwater. Sorry about that, though. Would you like a rag to dry off?" The woman leans toward me, trying to look beyond the guise of my arm.

"No," I yell far louder than intended and startle the poor woman. "Sorry, but no. I'm fine. Thank you. Have a—have a great day."

As I hurry in the direction I came from, I hear the woman mumble something to the tune of, "How peculiar."

I find a vacant alleyway and prop against one wall, letting

the sun warm and dry my scaled hands and arms. My head remains on a constant swivel for anyone passing by, and my leg bounces impatiently, as I wait for the scales to disappear.

It unnerves me to feel this ashamed about them. I love my scales. Adore my nymph form. And in my realm, I'd started to spend so much time in Atlantis that there was rarely a reason to hide any of it. It felt liberating. Like I'd finally been given the chance to be myself—to be who I was *born* to be.

A door creaks open nearby, and my eyes dart to my hands. The scales are gone. Peeking around the corner reveals two men dressed in black, carrying someone on a stretcher from within the house, a sheet pulled over the body. A lump forms in my throat—they're dead. The lead man hitches the handles to readjust, and one of the mortal's arms falls from beneath the sheet, hanging lifeless off the edge—a slender, pale arm that undoubtedly belongs to a woman. The lump in my throat goes coarse.

A burly man in trousers, bretelles, and a white, stained button-up shirt appears in the doorway with his arms folded. He doesn't look to be in mourning or even seem to be sad in any way. I glare at the man's red knuckles, one cracked and bleeding. As the stretcher passes the alley, I note the bruises lacing the woman's freckled arm and the dingy gold band on her left ring finger catching the sunlight. Strands of deeply red hair, much like my own, peek from under the sheet.

My gaze shoots back to the man in the doorway, a matching ring on his left hand, and the sight of it makes my blood boil. I'd love nothing more than to make a scene of this, the undertakers' sheer audacity to simply look the other way when this man beat his wife to death. But I can't do a damn thing. Helpless yet again. But this man's face? I'll *never* forget it.

"Name of the deceased?" A third undertaker asks, holding a small burgundy leather-bound book in his palm, waiting for the answer.

The man in the doorway spits in the dead body's direction as the undertakers cart it away. "Anne Bonny."

TWO

J A C K

PURE, RELENTLESS FREEDOM. If you're cunning enough to keep it. That's why I, Jack Rackham, *chose* a life of piracy. As small as my operation was in England, I'd been a successful tradesman on the seas and didn't care if coins lined my pockets on any given day. But when larger businesses began traipsing through, monopolizing, England gave no two shits about the "little people." They embraced it because it meant more money and power for the country. And London? Forget about it—far too many people and even fewer jobs.

This led me to captain The Revenge, my sloop of war named after the reason I raid and loot the high seas. And life is *good*. *Grand*.

Truffles, my furry Calico cat, bristles underneath my chin, gliding first his spine and following it with a flick of his tail to ensure I give him my undivided attention. The little bastard has the nerve to look at me expectantly when I don't pet him immediately.

"I see you, you insufferable feline," I mumble, indulging him by scratching his head and running my palm down the length of his back several times.

The cat's soft fur always calms my nerves, giving me clarity. This is sorely needed at present, given that I've been staring at this godforsaken map since the wee hours of the morning and have made no further progress. A pirate crew relies heavily on their captain to find the treasures to loot, know the trade routes, and plan for interception. When too much time passes without a decent score, the crew can become restless, vindictive, and in the worst case—mutinous. I've built up enough of a rapport with this current crew that we consider ourselves family, and I don't fear the ones closest to me stabbing me in the back, but I also don't wish to let them down.

Truffles purrs and turns to bump his head against my temple. Sighing, I scoop him into the crook of my arm and stand, moving away from the desk to stare out one of two porthole windows in my cabin. The unrelenting waves crash against the hull, timing with the ship's sway. Stray items I didn't bother to anchor roll back and forth on my desk. The sun blazes above without a cloud in sight, drawing sweat to my brow.

Truffles' tail flicks left to right before curling my arm—his silent way of "claiming" me despite no other cats in sight. I repeatedly stroke his fur from his head to the base of his tail, using my other hand to undo several buttons on my burgundy tunic shirt. We've been at sea for three months and are heading back to Nassau to resupply and take a day's break before heading out again. I'd *never* leave open water if it weren't for petty things such as food and liquids. Solid ground under my feet has become foreign to me.

A knock sounds at the door, sending Truffles leaping from my arms to scurry under my desk and curl up on the pillow I keep for him.

"Yes?" I ask without turning around.

"Captain, your attention is needed on deck," my quartermaster, Ragnar, announces. Danish-born and bred, he makes his Viking ancestors proud.

"What is it?" I snatch the black frock coat hanging from the back of my chair and sling it on.

Ragnar scratches his black beard with streaks of silver and white. "One of the recruits we picked up when last in port—" He leans on the doorway, several strands of his dark hair slipping out of the twine knot, falling over his gaze. "—was caught stealing rations."

I groan and re-button my shirt as I move for the door. "How many know?"

"*For helvede*. The entire fucking crew knows. Word spreads like wildfire on this ship. You know that." Despite the sour news, Ragnar's naturally narrowed eyes squint in amusement.

I *do* know this, but I still keep hoping that by some bizarre, bloody twist of fate, I can handle things discreetly for once. No. He needs to serve as an example—the clueless bastard.

Giving a curt nod, I descend the stairs to the main deck, twisting one of six ornate rings on my fingers. "Where is he?" I make my voice boom, lowering an octave or two.

Bobby holds onto a man struggling to break free of his hold. "Quit your squirming, you blunderbuss."

"We'll take it from here, Red." I interlace my fingers and rest my hands in front of me, glaring at the thief.

Bobby, known to us as "Red," earned his nickname from joining our crew as a former redcoat serving under the British Royal Navy. He sought to escape their hold and still wears the coat but has since smeared it with a white skull matching the skull and crossed swords in the colors we fly.

The thief yanks away from Red, and he lets him with a devious smile. And then the thief's gaze falls on me, his Adam's apple bobbing as he gulps. "Captain, I was hungry. That's all. Didn't mean no harm by it." He runs a hand over the sweat collecting on his shaved head.

"Ragnar," I call out. He appears at my side a breath later. "Who's in charge of the ration portions on this ship?"

"That'd be me, sir," Ragnar answers, crossing his massive arms.

"That's correct. So—" I pause and wave a finger at the thief "—what's your name again?"

"Ham, sir. Short for Abra—"

Holding a palm up, I sneer at him. "I don't care. What I *do* care about is what we're to do with *you*."

Ham's light eyes widen, and his bare feet step forward, but a dozen raised cutlasses halt him. "Captain. Please. I didn't even eat it, the—the quartermaster took it all back."

"Ah, so you were holding it for safekeeping but had no intention of consuming it?" I arch a brow.

Chuckles and profane name-calling echo around the deck.

"I—" Ham goes silent before zipping his spine straight and lifting his chin. "—it was a lapse in judgment at the time, Captain. It won't happen again."

I swivel my hips at my crew, holding my arms out at my

sides. "As long as he's *sorry*, right, crew?"

Objections and more cursing roars from the pirates surrounding us.

I'm now standing toe-to-toe with Ham, towering over him with his nose hovering near my collarbone.

"I thought Calico Jack was supposed to be a merciful captain. Only reason I joined your damn crew," Ham snivels.

Bending into his face, I whisper, "I *am* merciful by comparison, but we here still abide by the code, you selfish ass." Standing tall, I raise my voice for the whole ship to hear. "I could make you walk the plank, or maybe—" I yank the knife from my belt and hold the blade to one of Ham's fingers. "I take a finger as a lasting reminder to keep your filthy paws where they belong."

The color drains from Ham's face, his arm tensing beneath my touch, but he doesn't dare try to pull away. "P—please."

Rolling my eyes, I shove his hand away. "You disgust me." I sheath the blade and turn my back on him, beckoning Ragnar with a single finger.

"Thank you, Captain. Thank you," Ham wails behind me.

Ragnar leans his ear toward my mouth. "Take a finger. Make him scream so the crew can hear, but make it on his non-dominant hand, will you? We still need the cunt able to aim a pistol."

"Aye, Captain," Ragnar says, cracking his knuckles, a glaze forming in his eyes as he brushes past me.

There's no point in looking back. It's not as if violence and bloodshed phase me in the slightest any longer, but to witness his punishment would give him far more clout than he's worth. Ham's cries of agony bounce off the sails, the cheers and whistles from the crew drowning away as I re-enter my cabin and shut the door behind me.

"What's all this?" Duke, our sailing master and resident father figure within the crew, asks. He's sitting in my chair with Truffles curled up in his lap. He pets my cat with one hand while dragging a finger along the routes I've traced on the nautical map for weeks.

Crossing the room in two strides, I grab the captain's log, thick and bound in scuffed brown leather, and toss it in the middle of the map. It narrowly misses Duke's finger.

His brown eyes quirk behind a pair of wire-rimmed glasses, and he reclines, running a hand over the gray beard that falls past his chest. "That secretive, hm, Jack? What are you doing trying to plot routes in the first place? You wouldn't know your way out of a damn bathtub."

"I can navigate fine, old man. But I had to give you a role on the ship, right?" I press a hip on the desk, propping my knee up.

Duke barks a laugh, his long silver hair with streaks of black shifting over his shoulder. "You keep telling yourself that, boy. But you wouldn't last three days without me if you had to change directions more than once. The sea can be a treacherous bitch, my friend."

My navigation skills may not have been the best, but I'd have no place calling myself a captain if I couldn't find our way back home. I've let Duke hang this over my head since we first met years ago, and I'm not about to take it away from him now.

"Tell me about it. Why trouble yourself with a woman

when the sea is *already* a handful, hm?" Smirking, I ruffle my traitorous cat's head.

"What is this really, Jack? Looks like you've found several routes leading in the same direction, but they stop in the middle of the ocean. Not a scrap of land in sight." Duke pushes the book aside and taps his finger to the map.

Staring absently at the spot he poked, I pinch the hair below my lower lip with two fingers. It's because what I found isn't on land but *underwater*. "I've found a treasure, Duke. A jewel. Would make us all filthy, filthy rich."

Truffles stands up, stretching, and decides to knead Duke's portly rounded belly with his claws.

Duke grunts and bats the cat away, but Truffles ignores him and continues to prep his makeshift bed before settling into a ball atop Duke's stomach. Duke sighs. "What's the problem then? Sounds like some profitable gain."

"It's—" Frustrated, I shove away from the desk and rake a hand through my hair. "—it's based on a myth, but—"

"Jack," Duke chastises, dragging out the "a" and flashing me a warning paternal glare.

Magic. Myth. The paranormal. All mysteries of the known world that most people couldn't fathom and didn't believe. But not me. I know with every fiber of my being, most, if not all, of it exists. Who are we to naïvely assume we're the only beings or entities in the universe?

"I know this one exists, Duke." The desk rattles as I slap my hands atop the mahogany. "I. Know. But the crew voted against me every time I brought up going on one of these voyages because as much as they believe in me, they don't believe in *it*."

"I mean, can you blame them? That's a lot of time and effort wasted for treasure existing in myth, Jack." Duke strokes his beard.

"Not this time. I'll have to present it differently. Convince them." I stare into the distance, lost in thought.

Duke appears in my line of vision. "You mean *lie* to them?"

"You insult me." I frown. "Never. I mean more along the lines of—withholding certain information until it needs to be known."

Duke shakes his head and beats a forefinger atop the desk. "And I suppose you want me to back you on this?"

"I'd owe you." Leaning on the desk's edge, I catch his gaze. "This'll be the big one, Duke. Mark my words."

"Jack, you owe me enough favors to last me the rest of my life." Duke scratches Truffles' back, trying to hold back a smile but failing.

I give a lopsided grin. "Then what's one more, eh?"

"Fine. But if this winds up to be some wild goose chase, I'm never doing it again. Understand?" Duke points a stern finger at me.

Still grinning, I hold my hand out to him. "You won't regret this."

We shake hands, and I make my way to the helm to steer us into the port of Nassau.

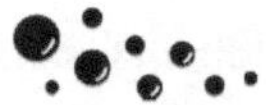

Our boots hit the docks no sooner than most of the crew make their way to the island's local brothel.

I follow in their wake, meeting Omar, the brothel keeper, at the front. After plopping several coins into his palm, I lean against one of the tables. "Whatever they want, yes? That should cover it."

Omar tosses the coins in his hand, jingling them and holding them to his ear. "*Oui monsieur.* But Jack, you don't wish to partake?" Omar's voice is rich with a French accent, and his deep purple jacket is trimmed with gold filigree, which shifts as he swivels, referencing the establishment. "We have a new girl. Scarlet hair like you wouldn't believe. I know how you prefer the red-haired ones, *oui*?"

"You're not wrong, but Omar—" I bow and steeple my fingers. "—I don't have to pay for it."

One of the whores eyes me from across the room, biting her lip and pulling the dress further down to accentuate her tits.

"Trust me," I emphasize.

Omar sticks out his bottom lip, adjusts the powdered wig atop his head, and sighs. "I can't deny that. I swear there's a shift in the winds every time Calico Jack steps onto the docks here in Nassau. You're like a curated fine wine on an island full of years old Sercial."

Blinking, I clap Omar on the shoulder. "I have no bloody idea what that comparison means, but thanks all the same, I believe?"

"A compliment of the highest order, Captain Rackham. I assure you." Omar's obsidian eyes scan me up and down, his fingers playing at the frilly lace peeking from his jacket sleeves.

Giving him a two-finger salute, I turn for the door. "Need

fresh air. I'll be waiting outside. Be a doll and send them out when they're finished?"

"Of course." Omar bows before zipping his spine straight, pointing across the room. "Giselle, it's not been but five minutes. What are you doing out here already?"

Giselle rolls her eyes and throws her hands to her hips. "He fell asleep."

Grinning, I exit into the warming sun, heavy scents of rum and brine in the air. I prop a foot against the building and slip the map from my inside jacket pocket, resting a rolled cigar between my lips. The taste of tobacco relaxes my mind, but I never find it necessary to puff on it.

Rejuvenation should've been a forethought, but my mind is far too occupied to relax. This jewel will put the crew of The Revenge in the history books should we find it. Riches and glory are at our grasp, but I still need to convince them it isn't another one of my "outlandish desires for adventure." I do not doubt that every mythical item I've researched exists. They're more challenging to find than sunken Spanish gold but far more valuable.

"Hi, Jack," a woman's voice croons across the way. She wears a floral print gown, her light blonde hair pulled into sectioning ringlets. She's waving at me with a laced, glove-covered hand and twirling the ivory parasol with the other.

The calluses on my palms scrape the worn leather map, and I offer a tightened smile, irritated by her interruption. A wave is all I can muster. "Good afternoon. Fine day we're having, hm?"

A subtle frown pulls at her lips, but she nods and continues her merry way.

Fuck. I know I'm consumed by something when the company of a beautiful, interested woman becomes secondary to the task at hand.

Ragnar exits first, adjusting his shirt within his trousers and stretching his arms to the heavens. Red soon follows, combing both hands through his greasy blonde locks before securing the dirty powdered wig askew atop his head. Jac Gog, or Glog as we've all come to call him, joins us a breath later, his pale cheeks turned rosy and a sheepish grin lighting his face. Glog became our ship's cook when we were last docked in Port Royal. We didn't often recruit in Jamaica, considering the risks, but Glog came to us saying he wanted to be free after leaving Wales, but all he could offer was a strong back and decent meals. How could we have said no to that?

Sighing, I search the group of men as they arrive, missing one particular crewmate. "Where's Mary?"

I'll never hear it down from other crews about my recruitment of Mary Read. God forbid a woman on board. Most sailors are an overly superstitious lot, but they don't believe in magic. Go figure. Mary is more ruthless and loyal than half the men on my crew, and so long as she swore the oath and did her duty, I didn't mind a woman in our ranks. Besides that, I *love* women.

"Hasn't come out yet. No surprise there," Ragnar said, chuckling.

Ducking back into the brothel, I survey the varying doors leading to rooms on the ground floor and upstairs, with a balcony and additional rooms. "Mary," I shout, waiting for a door to creak open.

Her head pops from one upstairs directly above me, her

chocolate brown hair ruffled, and the sinister grin on her face apparent. "I'm almost finished here, Cap. Promise." Mary's voice is rich with an English accent that is not unlike my own.

"Don't rush on my account." I wave at her, raising both brows as I see two women, one with raven hair and the other blonde, pawing at Mary to return inside. "We're going to the tavern. Meet us at the docks in thirty minutes. And I do mean thirty minutes, Read. Or I'll leave you here."

"Aye, Captain. Thirty—" The raven-haired woman kisses her, cutting her off, and the door slams shut.

Shaking my head, I head back outside. My crew and I head to the local tavern to share a few drinks on solid land before embarking again. Perhaps the Mystic Mermaid offered precisely what I needed to sway them into voting in favor of going after the jewel: alcohol and distractions.

THREE

RHODE

THIRST IS ANOTHER level entirely for a sea nymph. If we're not in the water, we need to drink it as often as possible; otherwise, it feels like a fish out of water—constantly gasping for air which never comes. Only we never die. I clutch my chest, masking my pain and unease as I walk through the first tavern I see called the Mystic Mermaid. The irony is not lost on me—I'm also no mermaid. Mermaids are sequestered to the seas alone with no power to will their fins into legs and walk on land.

Dryness coats my lips and throat, and the fiddler playing a cheery tune in the corner of the establishment does little for the twisted knots my stomach has become. I press my palms on the bar, waiting for the tender to notice me. "Water," I barely get out in a whisper.

"No water here, sweetheart unless you like pissing out your asshole. All I got is ale."

Furiously nodding, I grip the bar's edge and smile when

the tender eyes me warily. He sets a wooden mug in front of me, foam spilling over the edges, and it's in both of my hands within seconds.

After guzzling part of it, I slowly set it down and wipe my sleeve across my mouth. "I'm sorry. I don't have coin."

I can conjure anything aquatic-related, but I have no power to make money appear out of thin air.

The tender, a man in his later forties, tosses a rag over his shoulder, shifts his eyes to the patrons in the tavern, and props on one elbow. "This one is on the house. Looks like you were about ready to die of heatstroke."

That is as good of an excuse as any.

I give a solemn nod and hug the cup to my chest. "Thank you."

"There's a vacant table in the corner if you wish to sit, lass." The tender points and urges me toward it.

It's the perfect excuse to nurse my drink and tune into conversations around me. With any luck, I'll overhear ships sailing from port soon and get off this sandy rock, back to heavenly waters, and on my way home.

No sooner does my ass hit the seat than a man approaches my table. He's stumbling ever so slightly, pulling the red lapels of his frock coat before taking the seat across from me. His midnight black hair catches the light from the dancing flame of the lantern resting on the table between us.

"Don't recall inviting you to sit there," I clip, sipping from my mug as if his presence does little to amuse me. And it doesn't.

The man barks with laughter, his dark handlebar mustache twitching. "See, gents? Told you redheads always spit fire."

Stick around and see what else I spit, you walrus's ass.

Remaining silent, I pluck at the wood of my mug.

The man leans one elbow on the table, props the other on his knee, and flashes me an expression I assume *he* thinks is a smolder but comes across more like a nauseated goat. "Name's Charles."

"Oh? Not Chuck or Charlie?" Lifting my cup for another swig, I quickly scan the room to see if anyone is paying attention to us. Fortunately, the bartender watches us like a mother hen.

Charles sucks on his top row teeth, surprisingly not as yellowed and rotten as I've seen most pirates sporting. "Nah. Charles, my birth-given name, sounds far more prestigious. Wouldn't you say?"

"A pirate concerned about prestigiousness. How innovative of you." My grip tightens on my mug with each passing moment.

Charles chuckles, but not as heartily as when he first sat down. He pulls his chair closer, the legs scraping against the wooden floor, jarring my ears. "I like you. I like you a lot."

"Little old me?" I lean back in my seat. "I'm nothing but a tradesman's daughter temporarily in port for supplies. He should be back any minute now."

Charles's body grows closer, scents of tar and sweat wafting from his clothes. "I'm not proposing marriage, love. I'm proposing for *now*." His hand darts like a cobra, latching to my forearm.

I fake a gasp and yank with dwindled strength. "Let. Go."

An itch courses through me—a desire to defend, snatch my

dirk knife, use my powers, or do *anything*. But unlike before, we're in a tavern with a dozen pairs of eyes who've now all turned their attention to the drama unfolding in the corner.

"That's enough, Vane. Lady says she ain't interested. Leave, or I'll have you kicked out." The bartender claps a hand on Charles's shoulder, jutting a thumb behind him at the exit.

Charles sneers before loosening his grip on my arm and rising. "Hope to see you in port again."

Not if my ethereal life depends on it.

Grinding my teeth together to keep from saying something stupid, I grin at him, glaring daggers into his soul. Charles turns to leave, shoving the bartender as he passes him.

"Thank—" I start to say, but my attention is drawn to the man who just walked in. Several other men surround him on each side like a pirate entourage.

He's handsome. Beyond handsome. Beyond anything I've seen on the island. Tall and tanned with long chestnut hair, a slight wave from the salt water and sun. It hangs just below his collarbone, and a light, well-kept beard courses his chin and surrounds his lips. His smile is a brightened beacon calling for every woman in the bar, not one failing to snap their attention to him—much like me. And how are his teeth *so* white? Several patrons raise their mugs to him, calling out the name "Jack." After he waves, he slips the black frock coat off his form, folding it over the back of a chair. Not only does it reveal a burgundy tunic shirt only half-buttoned, but a toned muscular chest scattered with dark hair and a horizontal slanted scar that disappears into his shirt.

And suddenly, I'm thirsty all over again.

Charles passes him and spits on the floor at Jack's feet. "Best part about Nassau? Peace of mind. The worst? Having to see your sorry ass every few months and not being able to do a damn thing about it."

Jack, unperturbed, runs a hand over the orange sash tied around his waist. "I've missed you too, Vane. How is the—what ship is it now? The—Katherine or The Ranger?"

Charles grumbles something under his breath before turning for the exit. "Go to hell, Rackham."

"I'll meet you there. Perhaps we can plan for tea, hm?" The charm oozing from this particular pirate is enough to send a jubilant zing throughout the room.

No one pays any mind to Charles as he storms out of the tavern, and the music picks up livelier once he's gone.

Jack's gaze turns in my direction for a fraction of a second, causing me to slouch in my seat and pull the hat as far over my face as it'll go. How long his eyes linger on me is anyone's guess because, more importantly, how, in the Seven Seas, can I be drawn to a man like this—a *mortal* man?

Risking a peek, I watch Jack and his crew sit at a circular table. Jack motions for the bartender, and several moments later, the tender returns with two handfuls of mugs, plopping them onto the table.

"Drink up, gents," Jack says, raising his cup. "We've got a voyage to plan."

His words pique my curiosity, and I hide my face with the mug, turning my chair to a better angle to hear their ongoing conversation. They exchange stories about their past hauls—the time Jack got caught behind an island by a Spanish coast guard and they stole a twin prized sloop during the night, how Jack was a privateer for a spell to throw the British off their scent, and countless tales of gold and negotiations at every turn. For every three mugs his crew drinks, Jack only consumes one. And by the fifth, Jack slams his mug down, demanding attention.

"Alright, jolterheads, listen up. I've been researching a jewel in the Mediterranean. A jewel that, if we find it, will make us not only rich but bloody famous to boot." Jack reveals a folded map after reaching into a pocket of his jacket.

My focus is intense now. I'm slanting so far in Jack's direction that the table eats into my ribs.

A man with a dirtied white wig squints a single eye at him. He burps before saying, "This isn't another of your harebrained mythical claptraps, is it, Captain?"

I lean further until *creak*—the table shifts across the floor, making all eyes at Jack's table, including Jack, pop in my direction. The mug shields me again, and I turn to face the wall.

"It is not. This one exists, gents. It's recorded as a massive sapphire with bits of aquamarine surrounded on either side with gold overlay. Supposed to be the size of your fist." Jack makes a fist and shakes it between them.

Is he talking about—no.

Murmuring ensues between them, sloshing sounds of more drinking and guzzling, and then one man asks, "Does it have a name?"

No other jewel appears as he described.

Jack pauses for effect, and I peek around my mug, seeing his palms fly up. "Befittingly—the Sailor's Jewel."

Either he lied to them or has yet to learn the jewel's purpose. The gold pieces are bullhorns, and the jewel—the Tavros Jewel—serves as the guiding light for all supernatural beings who wish to find Atlantis.

Reality hits me like a tidal wave, and I find myself downing the rest of my drink to quench the sand scraping my throat. This crew is going to Atlantis. They're going where *I* need to go.

"This is a chance of a lifetime, boys," a burly older man with a long, peppered beard adds.

The crew goes quiet, Jack's impatience plain from how his knee bounces under the table.

"Shall we vote on it?" The man with the wig asks.

"Aye," the older man instantly answers.

The rest of the men go around the table, voting yes to Jack's idea. Jack slaps his thigh, points at them, and rises. "We shouldn't dally. Let's get to the ship. Get her ready to sail."

"What about Read?" The older man asks, casually running a hand over his beard.

Jack tilts his head. "While I'm sure she'll vote yes, Ragnar, would you fetch her and fill her in before we weigh anchor?"

She?

The man he referred to as Ragnar, with the mysterious squint in his eyes, nods his head. Jack's grin spreads wide. He claps his hands together and swivels on a heel to exit. I stay in the shadows of my corner table, waiting for the last crew member to leave before catapulting from my chair.

"Thank you again," I say to the bartender as I pass.

The bartender offers me a warm smile. "Be safe, lass."

A conch-shell-sized lump forms in my throat at his words.

As I exit, I'm a whirlwind—tucking my hair into my hat, pulling my stolen shirt from my trousers and away from my apparent breasts. A *tsking* followed by a light whistle sounds behind me.

"Miss?" A man with a French accent calls out.

I'm halfway to tucking stray strands of hair into my hat and slowly turn to face him. He's sporting an eggplant-colored ornate frock coat with gold trim and a powdered wig. One arm hangs over his ribs while the other hand is raised, nails clicking against each other. Pretending he couldn't be referring to me, I look around, seeing as I'm not a miss but a sir.

The man bites back a smile. "*Mon Dieu.* The way you were eyeing The Revenge out there, I'm guessing you plan to shove your hair in your hat, ruffle your shirt, and call yourself a cabin boy while stowing away on Calico Jack's ship?"

My heart melts into my boots. "Am I that obvious?"

"Oh, *chérie*, what boy only has the underside of their hair? And those bountiful mounds on your chest can still be seen from a mile away." The man extends his hand but holds it like royalty awaiting a kiss on the ring. "I'm Omar."

Name. Name. I need a name.

"Anne." I slip my hand into his surprisingly silky soft one and shake. "Anne Bonny."

"Pleasure to make your acquaintance, Anne. Come inside. I'll help you disguise yourself a smidge better, *oui*?" Omar's hands fly up, making the lace surrounding each wrist bounce.

I step forward but pause. "What about the ship? They were talking about setting sail as soon as possible."

"We've got time. They still need to raise the anchor. Come,

come." Omar motions me to enter the building, holding back a leather flap.

Gulping, I duck my head, scents of perfume and musk dizzying me. A man plays the flute in a corner, only slightly drowning out the wails, cackles, and screams of pleasure around us.

A brothel. Lovely.

"Right this way, Miss Bonny," Omar places a gentle hand on my forearm and turns me in another direction to a room through a wooden door. He closes it behind us, and my hand darts to the knife at my hip. Omar defensively raises his hands. "I promise you no foul play in my establishment. Not to mention you're not exactly my—" His eyes roam my body. "—type?"

Relaxing slightly, I let my hands rest at my sides. "Why are you helping me?"

"Nassau is an island of opportunity. People come here for various reasons, but everyone has one thing in common: they seek a different life." Omar presses his fingertips together and moves to a trunk at the foot of a four-post bed. "I don't know your reason, Miss Bonny, and I don't need to know, but if you were willing to risk your life sneaking on Rackham's ship, you clearly have an insatiable desire to get away."

He's spot on, and I go quiet.

Omar nods as if I don't need to say another word. "Now, I will need some form of payment for my services."

Still silent, I nod.

"Do you have coin?" Omar's eyes search my hips for a pouch.

Solemnly, I shake my head.

"How about this?" Omar points at my cowrie shell bracelet.

I snap my hand away, protectively holding my wrist to my chest. "Not that."

Omar's eyes bulge, and he blinks rapidly.

Holding my open palm behind my back, I call a pearl from the depths, and soon it rests against my skin. I offer it to him, and his face visibly brightens. "It's a genuine black pearl."

"*Merde*," Omar whispers, taking the petite beauty between two fingers.

"Will that be sufficient?"

Omar nods while staring at the pearl. "And then some. Are you sure you wish to part with it?"

I wrap his hand around it as reassurance. "It's all yours, Omar."

"Let's turn you into a lad then, shall we?"

Taking a deep breath, I follow him to the trunk. Several moments later, I'm wearing baggy-fitting trousers in a more durable cloth, a loose, flowy cream tunic shirt that goes well past my hands, a jacket, and leather boots. He adds a red scarf around my neck for extra protection from the sun after I ask for as much skin coverage as possible, using the excuse of the sun and my pale skin, but in reality—I'm bound for a ship surrounded by water, sea mist, and rain for months.

"And finally, your hair. I don't think there's a need to chop off those beautiful tresses, but—" Omar pulls out sections of my hair to give the illusion of a bob cut. "That should work. But keep an eye out for long strands that might fall out. And on extra windy days, use the scarf to secure it on your head, *oui?*"

"Thanks, Omar. Truly." I shake his hand again before turning for the door but stop with my hand on the iron handle. "You called him Calico Jack. Why?"

"Captain Rackham's nickname. Some say it's because of the Indian cotton he prefers to wear, unlike most captains. Others say it's his Calico cat." Omar snorts and peeks at the black pearl on his nightstand.

"He has—a cat?"

Omar giggles. "Mmhm. And it's a cranky little thing, too. Lives on the ship."

Perhaps I've lucked out after all. What kind of ruthless pirate captain owns a feline?

"Take care, Omar," I finish before making way for the docks.

The crew is busily loading supplies onto the sloop of war Omar called The Revenge. I stare at the mast extending to the skies, the sails still rolled, waiting to be set free for the next voyage. A man carrying several burlap sacks on each shoulder bumps my elbow.

"Stop your gawking and get a move on, boy," the man barks.

Boy. It's working. Hiding a satisfied smile, I pick up the first supply item I see, a short and thin crate, and get in line behind several other men carrying things on deck. A dirtied man wearing only a gray vest and trousers sprints down the ramp, a crate filled with sloshing bottles of rum held above his head. He's cackling into the wind until Jack appears on deck, flintlock raised, and he pulls the hammer back. One shot takes the man down, the bullet lodged into the back of the thief's skull. The man lands in a slump near my feet, the crate crashing to the ground and breaking most of the bottles.

The smoke clears from Jack's pistol, and he stands unfazed and ruthless, a scowl distorting his features. "Salvage the unbroken bottles and throw this piece of shit to the hammerheads," Jack barks before disappearing into the shadows of The Revenge.

I've seen plenty of death throughout my hundreds of years, and I, too, remain undaunted by it. I've grown to accept it as both a cycle of life and necessary for survival. But what has a chill creeping up my spine after witnessing the glint in Captain Rackham's gaze as I willingly make my way up the ramp, a shark into the wolves' den, are the bartender's parting words.

Be. Safe.

FOUR

JACK

"WE—" I PEEL the banana in my hand and take a bite before propping my booted feet atop my desk. "—have a stowaway on board."

Ragnar has just walked into my cabin, more than likely to tell me we're close to shoving off, and I didn't let him get a word in edgewise before spilling that little gem.

"Well, shit." Ragnar eyes me quizzically, no doubt confused by my nonchalance.

With my boots crossed at the ankle, I bounce the top one, eating another bite of banana and smiling. "And I'm fairly certain—it's a woman."

"Twice the shit. Want me to find them? Toss them off the ship before we set sail?" Ragnar juts a thumb behind him.

"You'll do no such thing." I stand and swipe the small bottle of milk I procured for Truffles, snatching his pewter saucer from a desk drawer.

Truffles scurries from his pillow, not caring if Ragnar is in his presence. The cat's eyes grow feral at the sound of metal hitting wood.

"What would you do with her then? Especially if she's a woman?" Ragnar's narrow eyes squint, making one wonder how he sees out of them like that.

Squatting, I set the saucer filled with milk on the floor at Truffles' feet—a coveted snack he gets when we're in port and only enough to last a day because we don't have the means to keep it from spoiling. "Let them stay. They'll be desperate to keep up appearances, so they'll do the chores none of the crew likes doing. If they cause trouble, we toss them overboard. Simple as that." I slap my hands on my knees and rise, grinning like a damn jackal. "But I do *so* hope it's a woman."

Ragnar clucks his tongue and bends sideways to watch Truffles lap at his milk. "Intend to bed her, do you?"

"Perhaps. But I thought more about how much easier it'd be to orchestrate her to our will. It isn't often I can ensure someone won't turn on me from sheer charm." I scratch the coarse hair on my chin.

"Oh, yeah? You mean like you *charmed* Mary?" Ragnar does a snorting chuckle.

"Mary is different. She stood in line for recruitment, and I told her there was no sense in disguising herself. Only after she was on board did the little hellion reveal that meat and tackle weren't her preferred variety of sport."

Ragnar absently stares into the distance. "I swear I'd propose to that woman if that weren't the case."

"Marriage," I grumble, all but gagging at the prospect.

Ragnar nudges me. "You're telling me a decade from now

when piracy becomes but a distant memory, and believe me, it will, you never see yourself settling down?"

Me? A husband? The idea seemed borderline absurd.

Moving to one of the porthole windows, I press my forearm above it and stare at the unusually calm blue water. "The sea is my mistress, Ragnar. And she can be a jealous wench."

"Three pieces of silver says you'll be settled down within two years, conventional sense or not." Ragnar's massive, tanned paw appears in front of me, the brown leather band around his wrist etched with old runes taunting me.

I glare as I turn to face him, sneering at his palm. "You're out of your mind. And do you even *have* that many pieces of silver?"

"What do you care? You're going to win, right?" The skin beneath his left eye twitches.

And this is why Ragnar is my second in command.

"Fine. Agreed." We smack our hands together, shaking right as the ship lurches.

"Better get these *fjolser* working the sails, the lazy maggots." Ragnar pulls his tunic taut, a slight wince pinching his features.

After snatching my frock coat and slipping it on, I exit my cabin with Ragnar at my side.

"Wouldn't it be easier to confront this person? Flat out ask what they're doing and if they're a woman?" Ragnar asks as we make our way toward the helm.

"It's all about giving them a false sense of security." I spy our crow's nest man sitting with his legs dangling from the edge. Pointing at this, I elbow Ragnar in the ribs.

Ragnar grunts but looks up, his entire demeanor changing within an instant. He waves his arms, waiting for him to look down. "Squid, what the hell do you think this is, a tea break? Get your ass moving on those topsails." His words travel across the deck, and he gestures at the topsails.

After Squid focuses on Ragnar's face, he jerks to attention and scrambles across the riggings, his bare feet gripping the wood as he passes.

"False sense of security, Captain?" Ragnar repeats.

Twirling one of the several rings on my fingers, I squint at the horizon. "Yes. Right now, they're probably thinking, I did it. I'm on board, leaving port, and haven't been found out. And if it's a woman, she must feel even more victorious that no one has discovered her."

Ragnar adjusts the twine holding his hair back. "And this is why I'm a quartermaster."

"And a bloody good one at that. Far better than I ever was, I assure you." I ascend the stairs to the wheel, resting my hands on the knubs.

Ragnar gives a half grin and drums his fingers on the hilt of his cutlass. "You also hated Vane as your captain."

I scratch the corner of my brow with a knuckle. "True words, friend."

The oars pull us from port and closer to open water. As the sails unfurl and the crew ties and readies them, I watch intently for the wind to pick up. Once the fabric snaps taut, catching the breeze, I bark, "Pull in the sweeps."

A wide grin graces Mary's lips from nearby as she helps the crew with the rigging before diving into her role as boatswain, directing what each crewmate should do with the lines. Despite her edgy nature, Mary insists on wearing skirts over trousers. She also wishes to keep her skin porcelain with no chance of tanning and wears long sleeves and a brimmed hat to always shade her face.

Memories of the day we recruited Mary Read still surface all these months later. She'd dressed herself in baggy clothes and a wide-brimmed hat, which she pulled over each side of her face. Her hair had been lopped off by a ragged blade and haphazardly shaved in the back, scattered tiny scabs where she'd nicked herself on the back of her skull. With her wide-set, sharp jawline, and thicker eyebrows, she could pass as a young boy at first glance given enough dirt. She'd gone so far as to smear manure on her clothes, masking her scent, but her voice, as deep as she tried to make it, gave her away for me.

She'd become instantly afraid and defensive, pulling a knife on me that I countered with, blocking her arm and hiding the dagger from the view of anyone else. Her fear morphed into surprise, laced with confusion and anger. I'd asked her two simple questions: Can you fight for your life? And are you willing to swear by my ship's code? Given she answered yes to both within seconds, I told her she was more than welcome aboard and that disguising herself wouldn't be necessary. No superstitious nonsense allowed on The Revenge—at least to the point of disrupting the crew.

As soon as she set foot on board, she started to wear the skirts and half-corsets and let her hair grow, rebelliously refusing to cut it even when it got as far as her ass. Mary is a kindred spirit if there ever was one, and her benefit to the crew was on par with at least a dozen other men I could've hired—no regrets there.

"Know which way you're headed, boy?" Duke asks, joining

me at the ship's wheel and patting my shoulder.

I rub one callus against the smooth wood, glaring at the setting sun behind us. "East I'd imagine?"

Duke snorts and spits into the ocean. "That was an easy one."

"Were you able to chart any potential intersecting trade routes?"

"Considering we're crossing damn near the entire Atlantic Ocean, we're going to run into *several* merchant ships on routes from Africa, America, England, and the Caribbean." Duke pulls a small journal from his pocket. "They should be carting everything from rum, iron, gunpowder, and spices. You name it, and it's on these ships. Just a matter of timing and picking up the speed when we can, Jack."

"And that's what I love to hear." Grinning to myself, momentarily satiated by the calming scents of salt and tar lacing the air, my grin widens when the wind rustles through my hair. The sails snap open and taut, hurtling us faster. "Mighty good sailing wind today, hm, Duke?"

Duke closes his eyes, letting the breeze puff his beard. "That it is, Captain."

Ragnar is speaking with our stowaway, pointing in one direction and back to a wooden bucket and scrubbing brush. Ragnar's hands fold over his chest, and the "cabin boy" furiously nods, being sure to keep their chin tilted downward. Ragnar rubs his neck before turning away and busying himself with the next task.

"Keep an eye on the wheel, would you, Duke? And be sure to keep heading due east." I wink at him, ignoring Duke's middle finger blatantly saluting me.

I work my way around the deck, ensuring I'm sufficiently hidden from our cabin boy's view should they risk a glance around. If I were them, I'd assess every crewmate and note who I should potentially stay far away from or, better yet, look for possible allies. But this person is so concerned with shading their face that they scarcely look up from the floorboards. They're on hands and knees, scrubbing the deck with their sleeves pulled over their hands, exposing only their fingertips. When they dunk the brush to clean and re-wet it, they're careful not to get their hands equally wet. Curious. Every time a brisker wind gusts over the deck, the cabin boy stops and covers their face with an arm. Even more curious.

I'm leaning on the mast, hidden partially by a stack of wooden crates and a coiled pile of rope, positively transfixed on our mystery person, when a hand pats my head from above. Either it's Squid or a giant bird. I pray for the former before looking up. Thankfully, it *is* Squid. "Yes?"

Squid blinks rapidly and points to the north, circling his eyes with each hand and pointing again before scurrying back to the crow's nest. Squid hasn't spoken but three words since joining our crew: rum, cat, and rope. We are still unsure if those are, in fact, the only words he knows or if he chooses not to speak because he also can't hear very well. He prefers to be alone and makes one hell of a climber, which suits his crow's nest role.

"Ragnar," I shout, spying the cabin boy, snapping their attention my way, while I look in the opposite direction. "Keep an eye north. Squid spotted something."

"Aye, Captain," Ragnar yells from across the deck.

Cutting my eyes back to the boy, I see them jolting, catching only a glimpse of emerald eyes—very familiar *green* eyes. I edge closer with my hands folded in front of me. The boy lifts a pail sloshing with brown liquid—the latrine bucket. They grimace and struggle to get to the boat's edge, turning their face away as the contents empty into the ocean. If only they accounted for the wind's direction. Some of the liquid mists backward and speckles the boy's shirt. The boy gasps and drops the bucket on the deck, immediately inspecting themselves, pulling the shirt away from their body, but as they turn, the fabric pulls taut along the backside, revealing luscious *curves*. I can't help the devious grin playing on my lips. The boy is not only a girl but a *woman*, after all.

"Captain," Aranck, our crew's healer, beckons from my side. "We have a man who is suffering from severe gout and isn't responding to the normal herbal remedies. We may need to remove his foot."

Aranck's stony features harden, his nose's downward slant accentuated by the frown pulling at his mouth. I'd met Aranck when I sought solace on the banks of America during a trip back from Europe. He's a member of the Cayuga tribe, and I spent weeks with them learning of their cultures and traditions, earning the serpent tattoo circling my left arm, tapped and inked by Aranck himself. When I'd announced my departure, Aranck asked to come along, if only to journey with me for a year. He wished to see the world and couldn't do so within the confines of the land. Given our friendship and the healing skills he learned from his grandfather, I welcomed him with open arms. One year has turned into several now.

I scratch my prickling scalp before answering. "Do what you

must. Tell Ragnar I approve an extra ration of grog for the poor bastard. Keep him below decks until it heals. *If* it heals."

Aranck gives me a solemn nod before disappearing.

In the distance, Mary is between commands, the ship at full sail and charging through open water like the beauty she is. There are blissful lulls in moments like these—when the wind is right and blowing in one direction. And the sky is clear as Caribbean waters boding no incoming hazardous weather. Sailors *cherish* these breaks. I catch Mary's gaze and motion her over.

From here, I can see Mary's lips thin with reservation, but she still answers my plea and walks across the deck until she's standing beside me. "Yeah, Cap?"

"Why don't you go introduce yourself to our new cabin boy?" Jutting my chin at the person now looking around like a lost pup with shit on her shirt, I roll my bottom lip between my teeth, ignoring how chapped they feel.

Mary frowns, and her head flinches backward. "Of course, but seems an odd order. Any reason?"

"Perhaps." I snicker and make a walking gesture with my fingers. "Off you go, then."

I sit back to watch the show from afar, ignoring the well-deserved eye roll from Mary.

Another woman aboard my ship. Jack Rackham, you lucky bastard.

FIVE

R H O D E / A N N E

I TAKE A moment to survey what crew I can before blending in with everyone else. The deck is bustling with activity, and the realization of the melting pot that is a pirate crew has me reeling. A tall, broad man with umber skin and a shaved head leads in pulling a rope. The man behind him, nearly a foot shorter, has sepia-toned skin, and his hair is a mess of tight black curls. Leading the rear is the man in the red coat and powdered wig I'd seen with Jack earlier. An older man in his sixties or seventies hobbles past me on one leg, his ghostly pale skin turning pink in spots where the sun hits most. He exhales deeply, revealing toothless gums on the top and only two teeth on the bottom. He drags a rag over the sweat on his head and neck before continuing.

Pirates are so far ahead of their time, and they don't know it. On a pirate ship, your ethnicity, age, culture, or religion doesn't matter. Because here, everyone ceases to be anything but a pirate, and those around you are your *crew*. Follow the ship's code, uphold your duties—and you're free. And on Jack's ship, it doesn't matter what gender you are either if I heard him correctly saying "she." But I won't reveal myself. I can't. It's far easier to fade into the background as just another pirate boy.

The quartermaster gave me my duties, which, not surprisingly, are peon level. I've scrubbed nearly every inch of the deck, emptied the latrine bucket, managing to give my shirt a revolting poop smell, and now, my throat is throbbing, begging for something to drink. But I know I can't simply help myself to a drink. They ration it as any well-run ship does. But when did they divvy it up?

"*Ehi ragazzo*," a deeply tanned man with stringy black hair yells at me, elbowing the man beside him in the ribs, both laughing. I can't be sure what he says, but the accent is unmistakable—Italian.

Obliging him, I tilt my chin over one shoulder, letting him know I'm paying attention.

"You missed a spot," the other man exclaims, a yellow bandana wrapped around his tar-covered head, a leather patch over one eye that he lifts as he and the Sicilian man start cackling and swatting each other.

A sea of frustration boils in my veins, but I sink to my knees and drag the bucket over. The sun has turned into a hazy halo, The sun has become a hazy halo, its heat scorching my skin through my clothes and making me lightheaded. I drag the brush back and forth across the wood panels lethargically, wondering if my actions are doing anything but pushing water into the cracks.

A fogged bottle with amber liquid appears in front of

me, the imposing form of the quartermaster showing next, blocking the sun and providing blissful shade for a breath. "Your ration. Make it last, boy."

Vigorously nodding, I take the bottle into my hands like a prized relic that might wither in my palms if not held with the utmost care. Plucking the cork from the top, I take several swigs. Energy comes back to me with each drop of liquid coating my throat. I can easily down the entire bottle with how thirsty I've become, but I force myself to stop and store the bottle in my pocket for safekeeping.

Keeping my head low, I continue scrubbing the deck with more force behind the strokes now. Once done, I rise, letting out a breath from the strain that, despite my ethereal blood, is still a harsh reality. Sea mist from a wave crashing against the ship's hull coats my cheek, and I gasp, turning my back on as many of the crew as I can, working my sleeve furiously over my face to dry it. And this is why I've been keeping my head *down*.

Once satisfied that the scales aren't showing, I tentatively glance to see if anyone is staring at me. I catch a glimpse of Jack casually resting on the mast on the other side of the deck and can swear he's been staring at me, but I dash away to not draw attention to myself. Finding a vacant corner of the ship, a feat in itself with how many people are on board, I press my back to the nearest hard surface. Seagulls fly overhead; their squawks, usually not so melodic, are harmonious to my ears now. With a breathy sigh, I shut my eyes and take another small sip of rum.

"Hello there, *boy*," a woman's voice sounds—a deeper register than mine, but still fluttery smooth.

I pop my eyes open, and she's closer than I thought. Four steps and the toes of her boots will be brushing mine. She's several inches taller than me, with wavy chestnut hair below her bustline. Frills of black and deep red skirts wrap around her legs, a black belt with holsters for her flintlock and cutlass resting at her hips. A black half-corset slinks around her ribs, and a billowy white blouse covers her chest and arms. Her wide-brimmed hat shades most of her face but gives her squared jawline harsh shadowed edges. And the smirk playing on her thin pink lips blazes like a bonfire.

When I don't answer, she dips her head to look closer at my face, and I turn away like a fool. "Are you hard of hearing, boy?"

"No. No, ma'am." I press my fingers against the surface behind me. "I heard you fine."

The woman lifts her chin and slides closer. "Then do I not merit your respect? Normally, when someone says hello, you greet them back."

It's hard to tell if the *piratess* is toying with me or—serious.

She's so close now that I can make out her thick eyebrows and eyes the color of the seas we sail.

"Hel—hello, ma'am." Against my better judgment, I still haven't looked at her dead on.

"Please." Rum weighs heavily on her breath, and perfume overlapping with sweat and brine hits my nostrils. "I'm not your captain. No need to stand on pleasantries, darling. Name's Mary. Yours?" She presses a forearm near my head.

Ash coats my throat, and I fight everything in me so as not to make my voice shake. "An—drew."

"Well, *Andrew*." Mary trails a finger down my shirt sleeve.

"You are one of the most handsome lads I've seen on this ship."

This can't be good. This is so not fucking good.

Her lips are on mine before I can process another thought. Mary's eyes are closed, but mine stay open and wide. I stare at her and wonder how, in the Seven Seas, I came to be here in *this* position. My body freezes along with my lips, which have quickly become two dead sardines—unmoving and limp. Mary's mouth moves against mine, her tongue brushing the seam of my mouth. She tastes like rum and smoke, nothing sweet like I imagined *my* lips tasting.

When she realizes I'm not reciprocating, she pulls away with a frown but keeps our faces close, our noses brushing. "I *knew* you were a woman."

"What?" I blurt out.

Mary slaps a hand over my mouth and looks around. "Would you keep it down?"

"Sorry," I mumble against her palm.

She lowers her hand and steps back with her hands firmly on each hip. "There a reason you're hiding it? If you're on The Revenge, you know by now that Rackham doesn't care what you have between your legs."

"I—I didn't know that. I'm new to this—" I flick my wrist at nothing in particular. "—ordeal."

That devilish smirk dances on Mary's lips again. "Stowing away on a ship or piracy?"

"Both?" A strand of my hair falls from the confines of the hat, and I quickly lift a hand to hide it.

"Here." Mary reaches for the tendril and tucks it out of sight with a delicate touch I wasn't expecting.

"I suppose you're going to tell the captain now?"

Mary shakes her head, her callused fingertip absently tracing across the freckles on my cheek before giving me space. "I ain't no snitch, darling. But I can't account for anyone else who figures it out."

The way she carries herself is how I'd appear if not for the need to disguise myself. A woman who knows who she is, the power she bears, and has the confidence to carry it out. I've grown maddening respect for her in a matter of minutes, and I can see us becoming fast friends.

"You haven't asked me why I snuck on board. Why I'm hiding—" Unintentionally, my voice grows louder, and I shut my mouth before alerting anyone.

"Because it's not my business." Mary rests one hand on her saber's hilt. "Everyone on this ship has their reasons, and it's theirs to tell. No one will pry unless it threatens our livelihood. And if they feel inclined to share, we'll be all ears."

Resolute freedom for everyone to be themselves without question or judgment.

"I needed safe passage somewhere. And I won't be a burden to any of you. You won't know I'm here." I bow my head like she's royalty, listening to my plea.

Mary slips a finger under my chin, lifting it so I meet her gaze. "You're impossible not to notice, I'm afraid, even dressed as a boy." Her hand falls, and she lets out a wistful sigh. "And judging by your reaction to my kiss, I assume you prefer the—" She lifts her pinky and wiggles it in front of us.

I bite the inside of my cheek to keep from laughing at her physical analogy. "I'm afraid so, sorry."

Mary waves it off like an irritating gnat. "Don't be. You win some, you lose some. But I assure you. If you want to keep up appearances for more than a week, you'll have to do much better than this, Andr—" She pauses and quizzically eyes me. "What's your actual name?"

"Anne," I answer, smiling and holding out my hand.

Mary shakes it. "Anne and Mary. Resident pirate queens of The Revenge."

"Maybe just you, Mary." Chuckling, I retract my hand and pull the sleeve back over my knuckles.

"Nah." She playfully nudges me. "You'll come 'round. Speaking of. Do you know how to use that thing?" Mary points at my dagger.

Peeling back my shirt, I eye the weapon as if I've only now seen it. "You—stab people with it?"

"Yes, but have you killed someone before?"

Given the company, it feels like a loaded question, but it shouldn't.

"Possibly?" The word comes out slowly, each part enunciated like when learning to read.

"I only ask because you may need to show some of the crew that you're not to be trifled with—that is unless you *want* to be trifled with." Mary gives a playful grin before continuing. "But it's only a matter of time before one tries, and so long as you show them it ain't happening, they'll have no choice but to back down or suffer the wrath of not following the ship's code. Got me?"

"Yes." I nod for extra affirmation.

"Good. I need to get back to work, but Anne, if you need

anything—and I do mean anything—" Mary wraps a hand over my shoulder and squeezes. "Don't hesitate to let me know, alright? Us lasses need to stick together. Especially being surrounded by this many sausages." She snorts and offers a wink.

There's no containing my own quick sputter of laughter. "Thanks, Mary. Truly."

"Any time," she replies while backpedaling. "And you may want to smear some more dirt on your cheeks. Look *far* too pretty for a lowly cabin boy."

My cheeks heat.

Noted.

Days go by at sea with little trouble or interruption. The weather has been holding up with scarcely a cloud in the sky, which makes the sun unrelenting but better for me and my *scales.* We receive food rations daily and watered-down rum every other day. I've quickly learned how much I can sip to make it last throughout the day. I'd done as Mary suggested, coating my face with grease and keeping my clothes baggy. No one seems to be the wiser, not even the captain, who only catches my gaze on the rarest occasions, usually from the ship's opposite side.

It's for the best. Despite his questionable pirate captain morality, there's no denying how attractive he is, and he knows it. If he gets too close, I can't promise myself not to let my gaze linger for one beat too long. And fortunately, he's never been on deck sans shirt like most of the crew. I already know about the dark scattering of hair on his chest and would be lying if I didn't daydream about what it looks like over his stomach. Does he have that thin trail leading to his—

"Anne," Mary whispers nearby, making me jerk with the scrubber in hand, slip, and slam my elbow on the wooden floorboards. She's crouching beside me, her hands dangling between her legs. "What were *you* thinking about?"

I sit back on my haunches and rub my arm. "Being anywhere but this bleedin' ship."

"Who are you fooling?"

My gaze snaps to hers.

"I've seen the way your eyes linger on the sea any chance you get. Know what it looks like?" Her slender fingers bounce, still hanging there, the sun catching the light of a gold ring and bangle bracelet. "Like the longing for a lover you've been forced apart from."

If Mary is this intuitive, how has no one else caught sight of this? Or, if they have, are they simply not saying anything?

"I'd imagine any of these people, given their choice to be a pirate, would look at it the same way, no?" I busy myself with more scrubbing.

"Ah, but you, darling—" Mary taps my nose with a single finger. "—have already made it clear you've no interest in piracy."

Plucking my fingernail against splintering wood on the scrubber, I contemplate my following words carefully. "I do love the sea. But I prefer to be *in* it. Sharks, jellyfish, and the like are keen to make that difficult, though, aren't they?" A warm smile graces my lips.

I've swam with sharks more times than I can count, and I've

been stung so many times accidentally by jellyfish that my skin has become immune to the pain.

"I knew it. Anyway, stopped by to give you this." Mary looks around and holds out a bottle with two swigs left in it.

"What's this for?" I don't take the bottle right away.

She wiggles it, making the liquid slosh. "Take it. It's left over from my ration yesterday, and I see how measured you are with yours. Figured you might need it."

"I—"

I'm beside myself. She's only known me for days, and risking this?

"—I don't know what to say," I finish.

"Will you bloody take it and pour it into your bottle before someone sees it?" Mary shoves the bottle into my limp hand.

As I remove today's bottle from my pocket, Mary shields me with her body while I pour the contents from hers into mine and hand her the empty one.

"There you are. Back to work." Grinning, Mary pats my head and turns away.

"All hands on deck," a man yells.

The deck becomes a fury of scrambles and shoves as everyone races for spots on deck as commanded. I dust my hands and rise, moving away from everyone else in the background but close enough to be a part of the crew and not draw attention to myself.

"Crew, I'm afraid we have a situation we need to address," Jack announces, holding the railing at the helm. "Vane has been on our trail since we left port in Nassau."

Vane. Why did that name sound familiar?

Whispers and carousing flood the crew.

"We've been able to keep ahead—until today. The winds have died down considerably, and I'll be the first to admit Vane's ship, albeit weak in battle, makes up for it at speed." Jack drums his fingers on the railing before descending the stairs. "I'm proposing we use the element of surprise and approach *him* before he can try anything stupid. No need to risk damage to the ship."

"Approach him? With what?" One man asks.

Jack slips his hands behind his back and walks the length of the deck with the crew flanking him. His steps are slow and methodical, his cutlass jingling at his side with each stride. "We'll make him an offer to get him off our backs. Even for a spell."

He's getting closer and closer.

"And what do we have to offer? We ain't got anything but rations," another man says.

My heart thunders against my chest, and whatever I do, I refuse to lift my chin, keeping my gaze focused on the deck.

"We offer him—" Jack's boots appear on the floor I've been staring at, standing in front of me. "—*her*."

SIX

JACK

HER HEAD SHOOTS up like a canon. "What?"

"Yeah, what?" Several of the men echo.

Pure rage and confusion dance in those emerald eyes.

Leaning in, I press a forearm above her head, the same way Mary had, but she reacts much differently to *me*. "You think I don't know what's happening on my own ship, lovely?"

"Then why didn't you say something *sooner*?" She asks through gritted teeth, neck flushing pink and bottom lip quivering.

I blanch. "What? And spoil the surprise? You being a woman was fairly obvious. Thank your mother for those curves."

She says nothing, her throat bobbing and her body tilting away the best she can with a wooden barrel pressed to her lower back behind her.

"You see, gents," I bark over my shoulder before flicking the woman's hat off, revealing luscious long red tendrils. My throat tightens, my limbs going heavy, but I quickly recover.

"We have another woman on board."

This is the woman from the tavern—the one Vane had been speaking with when we first arrived. This is working out far better than I had previously planned.

Gasps, maniacal laughter, and catcalls float across the deck from the crew behind us.

The rage in the woman's eyes morphs into an inferno, and she lifts a defiant chin. "You can't just hand me over."

"Can't I?" I reposition, making my face dip closer to hers. "Out of the two of us—" Using my thumb, I point it to her and then myself. "—who's stealing a free ride on the other's ship?"

Her jaw tightens, and she forces her eyes away from me, saying nothing because she *can't*.

"Precisely. So, Miss—" Using a finger on her cheek, I coax her attention back to me. "I'm sure you know my name by now, but if I may, what's yours?"

She sucks a sharp breath through her petite nose. "Anne Bonny."

A chill settles over my skin. Not quite so "someone walked over my grave" but more along the lines of "a sensual fingernail grazing my spine" type of sensation. I wince but shake it off, focusing on the task at hand.

"Well, Anne, my dear, if you don't wish to be marooned on the next island we come across, and that would be merciful versus tossing you overboard—" I pause to watch the tick in her cheek before continuing. "—then you'll do what I say."

Her hand edges toward the dagger hugging her hip, and I slap it, not losing eye contact with her.

"You're a vile human being," she seethes, those mouse-like

nostrils flaring.

I've been called *far* worse.

Smirking, I rub some of her hair between two fingers, surprised by how soft it is considering it's been shoved under a hat for lord knows how long. "A sentiment you share regarding pirates with most of the world."

"You thought I was referring to you being a pirate, did you?" Her eyes are unfaltering, challenging me with a heated stare.

It lights my veins on *fire*. Anne Bonny is a powder keg.

I let only a deep chuckle rumble from my chest before turning away from her. "Let's give the crew the good news."

The sound of her fingers brushing her shirt, reaching for that goddamned dagger, resonates in my ear, and I slap her knuckles again.

"Try that again, and I may just have to lop your pretty little hand off." I drag a hand over her wrist, threatening where I'd make the cut.

She snaps it away with a grimace, rolls her shoulders, and lets them slump.

"Crew, we have a vote to make," I make my voice boom loud enough for the whole ship to hear. "I propose we give Vane Anne here as a peace offering. Now, before you vote no, hear this—" Raising a finger, I prepare to bring it home. "Vane already has an interest in this woman. Propositioned her at the tavern in Nassau, and the saucy redhead turned him *down*."

I inferred *all* of this from the haughty way Vane had left Anne's table and the extra cork up his ass when he saw me. Given Anne's light growl behind me, I hit the target on the nose.

"This be an easy one," one man says, raising his hand.

The rest of the crew echoes his movement.

"One to save the few, eh?" A man jokes.

When Mary raises her hand, I feel Anne's body tense behind me. Mary's expression remains emotionless, but I have the faintest inkling she's doing it for a reason I don't bother to decipher. She always has her reasons for damn near everything. And with everyone's hands held sky-high, the results are clear.

"That settles that, Anne." I turn to face her, and she's glaring burning splinters into my eye sockets. "We're still a couple of days' sail before we can come about and intercept. Until then, business as usual." Pointing to the back of the ship, I can't help the victorious grin pulling at my lips. "I do believe the shit bucket needs to be emptied this time of day."

"Wait," Anne calls out as I step away and pause. "After this, we're to continue as if nothing happened?"

Unabashedly, I drop my eyes to her booted feet and lazily drag them up her body until reaching her face again. How I wish I could *see* those curves. "You're an uninvited guest aboard my ship. You're to continue with your assigned duties as if, yes, nothing has changed until we reach Vane. Now, you don't have to go about the deck with your head held low like a scolded pup."

She shoves past me, colliding into my side and heading for the back as I'd instructed.

"And Anne," I beckon, smiling at her when she stops to look at me. "Feel free to show a little more *skin* now, too—if you wish."

Her hands clench at her sides, and she storms away.

I let out a breath and drum my fingers on my sword's hilt,

watching her until she disappears into the latrine. It's not always the easiest business, being a leader and making the hard decisions. But it would have only been a matter of time before she would've fucked up—someone would've caught her with her trousers down, squatting to piss, or glimpsed one of her tits when the wind blew just right or through a rain-soaked shirt. And what then? They would've questioned my obliviousness. I can't have that.

"You sure about this, Captain?" Ragnar asks, dragging a hand over his beard and blowing out a breath.

"Vane won't stop for nothing. You know that as well as I do. This plan is foolproof. Trust me." I pat my old friend's arm before making my way to Mary.

Mary's braiding rope with extra pep, glaring at it as if she wishes it would catch flame.

"Piece of eight for your thoughts?" I lean on the ship's side, crossing my legs at the ankles.

"This bloody stinks. That's what. I give Anne this whole speech about us lady folk sticking together, and then I do what? Vote for her to be handed off to that godforsaken sod." Mary pulls the next bit of rope so tightly it unravels.

Reaching for the rope before she destroys it all, I gently take it from her. "I assume this was a lesson of sorts for her?"

"Trust." Mary folds her arms and watches Anne angrily scrubbing the deck. "She *can* trust me, but she needs to learn there's such a thing as far too quickly."

I do nothing but nod.

"You're not going to hand her off, are you?" Mary snaps her gaze to me when I don't answer immediately, and her arms fall slack at her sides. "Captain?"

"I always have a plan, Read." After jostling her, I leave a slack-jawed Mary standing there as I head for my cabin.

Once inside my quarters, I leave my door open a crack and sulk into my chair. Truffles emerges from his hiding spot beneath the desk and hops to my lap, curling up on it with a contented purr. I snatch the small dagger resting in an open drawer, smirking as I remember Anne not only going for the one at her hip once but *twice*—such a little spitfire that one. I stroke Truffles' fur, its softness finally making my body relax. With my free hand, I carve the shape of the jewel that's been consuming my mind for months, ensuring I never forget where this long, arduous journey will take us.

There's a knock at my door, and I slide one of the numerous books across my desk over the drawing before answering, "Come in."

Glog pokes his head in with a curt smile, deepening the groove in his chin. "Am I interrupting anything, Captain?"

"Just self-wallowing. What do you need?" Smiling at my cat, I scratch his head, making his eyes close and his bushy tail sway.

Glog enters with a pewter bowl in hand. He's in his usual attire of a gray tunic shirt, cut-off trousers, bare feet, and an apron that was once white and is now littered with various colorful stains. "Wanted you to try the new bone broth I've been experimenting with. Added new spices and sea biscuits to give it something to chew on and taste different." He holds the bowl out to me, still grinning.

Once I take the bowl, Glog adjusts the red bandana tied tightly over his dark hair with both hands and presses his palms together, waiting for me to taste it.

Eyeing him over the rim, I take a sip. It's good. Really good. As simple as bone broth is, you'd think you were consuming something far more complex. "This is amazing, Glog. I've said it before, and I'll say it again, but this crew is damn lucky to have you."

Glog sighs in relief and slaps his hands together before taking the bowl and turning for the door. "I'll whip up a big enough batch for lunchtime then, yeah?"

"Oh, Glog, before you go." I snap my fingers and motion him back to the desk. "Since you're down there with storage, do you remember that ornate chest we pilfered some months ago? The one with all the lady garments in it that we've never known what to do with?"

Glog puckers his lips and then nods.

"Rummage through it, will you? See if there's something—green."

"Right away, Captain. I've never pegged you for the type who fancies wearing women's clothing behind closed doors." Glog gazes at me with sudden focus.

"You're hilarious. It's not for me." Chuckling, I flick my wrist at the door. "Carry on."

I settle back into carving the jewel and wait for Glog to return with a dress. Ocean waves beat against the hull outside, the whooshing sounds gratifying. The crew croons a shanty on deck, faint melodies of *Fish in the Sea*. They cock up every other verse, but it's still strangely calming to hear it.

Glog returns several moments later with a satin and lace dress in the precise shade of green I'd been hoping for. Resting

Truffles on the desk, I head to the deck, looking for Anne. She's still scrubbing and mumbling all forms of obscenities under her breath with every other stroke. Her long, fiery hair hangs in delicate shambles over her face. She sits back on her haunches, dragging a shirt sleeve over the sweat on her forehead. I eye the opening of the shirt, longing with every fiber of my being to know what those tits look like. Are they rounded, or do they take on more of that tear-drop shape? Are her nipples pink? I grind my teeth together and mentally slap myself.

"Bonny," I yell, waiting for her head to shoot up. "I need to see you in my cabin."

Whoops and catcalls resonate with crew members nearby. I only grin at them because entertainment is severely lacking while on a ship for months. Let them think what they wish.

Anne wipes her hands on her trousers, and with harsh steps that rival a pair of hooves, she breezes into my quarters.

I follow, shut the door behind us, and shove the dress at her. "Try this on."

"No." She's seething at me with her arms crossed so tightly over her chest that it makes her knuckles turn white.

A growl bubbles in the back of my throat. "The threat of marooning you still weighs heavily in the air, Anne. Now put it *on*." I shake the dress at her for emphasis.

Truffles, who typically flees from anyone but Duke and me, waltzes across the desk and rubs himself against Anne's hip, making her tense. Damn cat.

"And if I refuse?" A tightness forms in her neck and jaw.

The growl is full-blown now, and I close the distance between us, lowering my face to hers. "You keep arguing with me, and I'll make you change on deck versus in the privacy I'm so graciously offering you."

Anne's moss green eyes flare wide, her bottom lip quivering before she snaps the dress from my grasp. "Fine. But *why?*"

"As charming as you are in a shit-covered shirt and trousers, we're trying to barter you as irrefutable living cargo to Vane." I point at the dress. "So put it on and make your smiling Irish eyes pop, eh?"

Anne wrings her hands in the green frilly satin, fists shaking, and her lips forming a thin line, but *finally*, she doesn't fight me.

"And you may want to use that water basin in the corner there to wipe whatever in God's name you smeared on your cheeks." Grimacing, I circle the air in front of her face.

She peels back, returning to her rebellious mode, posture erect.

And I'm enjoying every bloody second of it. The only other woman to ever deliver with as much as she can take with me has been Mary. And dear 'ol Jack is all for a good tongue-lashing now and again. I'm a fan of all *sorts* of tongue-ish-related activities.

I turn for the door, resting a hand on my flintlock's hilt. "And don't mind Truffles. He only bites people he doesn't like a *little*."

Anne's eyes shoot to my cat, still rubbing himself along her back and sticking his tail straight into the air. Grinning to myself, I close the door but stand by it in case she attempts any funny business. My gaze, of its own accord, shifts to the crack in the door, catching a glimpse of Anne's gloriously naked body—ivory skin with patches of light freckles, a brief preview of the side of her breast, but she turns her back to me before I can make out the nipple. As she slides the dress over her ass, I note the single beauty mark on her right cheek. Once she's slipping her arms into the sleeves, her eyes cast behind her, landing on me. If she's shy or angry over me watching, she doesn't show it. It's as if she half-expected it and doesn't care. And it has my blood on *fire*—again. I grin at her and wave.

It's been far too long since I've made Vane's life a living Hell. And he'll never see us coming.

SEVEN
RHODE/ANNE

I'M GOING TO *kill* Jack. Maybe some of the crew that voted to hand me off as well. But with the Seas as my witness, I will *kill* Jack Rackham. I tried on the dress Jack forced on me, noting how his eyes roamed my body and stored this in my mind for safekeeping. I changed into filthy clothes to continue my duties for the next couple of days until Jack gave me the "head nod," a universal ship code for "it's time."

I'm now in a dinghy with rope binding my wrists, dressed in the frilly kelly-green dress. Jack's in front of me, grinning and rowing us toward Vane's ship. I keep my face expressionless, save for my eyes, which are mentally carving holes into Jack's skull. I hope that the silence and glower will somehow intimidate this pirate captain.

"Come now, Anne. You're still going to be on a ship, just not—*mine*." Jack lays back as he rows with both oars, still grinning at me and so damn proud of himself.

I rub my palms together and focus on our boat cutting

through the water. "I have nothing to say to you."

"Oh, thank Christ. Thought I'd have to listen to your twaddle the entire ride," Jack mumbles.

And I can't help myself. Grunting, I lodge my foot into one oar, jostling it from Jack's grasp and splashing it into the water.

Jack blinks before reaching for the oar, which is already floating too far to grab. "What in the flying hell are you doing? You do realize two oars make this little jolt far easier?"

I zip my spine straight. "I'll swim if I have to."

"Yeah? With your wrists bound?" Jack scoffs and continues rowing with one oar.

"You'd be surprised how strong these legs are."

Jack hangs his head before raising his eyes to the skies as if in a silent plea. "In normal circumstances, I would've made some quip about accepting the challenge of being between your thighs, but for some bizarre reason—" He slams the oar into the water with extra vigor. "—I'm not in the *mood*."

A victorious smile begs at my lips, but I hold it back.

"Aw. You poor little pirate." I point at his rowing skills. "You'd get more distance if you flipped the oar to the same side every time."

Jack pauses and tosses me a scowl capable of scaring off surrounding fish. "Would *you* like to row, Miss Bonny?" He holds the oar out to me with one fist, droplets landing on my skirt-covered legs and making me rigid.

I pretend to think about it before rapidly shaking my head. "No. I refuse to row myself to my demise."

"Who says you're meeting your demise?"

Men gather at the railing of Vane's ship, pointing at us.

"Some things are worse than death," I answer, my voice distant and whispered.

A man with a tri-cornered hat props his knee on the ship's edge. An unsettling knot forms in my stomach when I recognize him from the tavern. Jack hadn't been exaggerating to his crew; he *did* see him talking to me. But how did he know I shot him down? This *is* Vane. Charles Vane.

"Rackham, you're lucky I didn't blow several holes in your ship in the time it took you to mosey your way over here in that little dinghy." Vane rests a forearm on his raised knee, the crew behind him snickering and barking.

Jack winks at me and touches his finger to the side of his nose. He rotates the boat sideways. "You didn't because you know my crew would've unleashed hellfire on you in return. Wouldn't want your pretty ship with as many holes as your britches now, would you?"

Vane flicks the cutlass's hilt at his hip, making a metallic *pang*. "What the hell are you doing, Jack? And who—" He points a stern finger at me, his dark eyes narrowing, trying to make out my face, but I'm not looking in his direction. "—is this?"

"You don't recognize her? Here, let me get a bit closer." Jack reaches for the oar.

I lift my foot, ready to launch it into the water even if I'll have to swim like my life depended on it, and it *would*. But despite Jack's arrogance and disregard for other beings, I know I'd fare better on his ship than Vane's.

Jack moves the oar before my limb can connect with it and wags a finger at me. "Nuh-uh, lovely. Fool me once; that's on me. Fool me twice—" He inches forward and rows us closer to the ship's hull with an awaiting rope ladder. "—you don't."

I can drown him where he sits—call on an orca to leap from the water and devour him. But I don't.

"Recognize her now, Vane?" Jack calls out but keeps his gaze fixed on me.

Vane is slung over the railing, a devilish grin snaking his lips. "Well, well, we meet again, my dear."

Bile works its way up my throat, and I press my hands to my stomach, fighting back the nausea, and remain silent as the grave.

"And why exactly are you doing this?" Vane's attention turns to Jack.

Jack remains seated, securing the oar out of my reach. "I'm tired of you scaring off merchants because you have nothing better to do with your time than chase me around the Caribbean. I offer you Anne here as a 'Fuck off' gift."

"Anne, hm?" Vane's eyes are on me again, his tongue skirting the corner of his mouth. "And why are you so willing to give up such a treasure? What's wrong with her?"

"Not a thing. I've—" Jack pulls me across the boat, not harshly enough to hurt me, but so suddenly it pulls a gasp from my throat. "—have had my fill of her." Those mahogany eyes drop to my lips, giving me a singular second to process what he's about to do, and his lips are on mine.

A hand presses to the back of my skull, keeping me put long enough for several brushes of our mouths and a final swoosh of his tongue that he easily darts between my lips. He tastes like rum, bananas, and faint tobacco. The moment my stomach twists, I shove him away, using more force than intended. It's enough to make him jerk his head, surprised. He drags a finger over his mouth. Did it feel as tingly as mine does? Static mixed with trickling grains of sand?

"Alright, Jack. She's good for a month of reprieve. No more and no less." Vane pounds his fist against the ship.

"A month?" I seethe at Jack, tugging his shirt. "This isn't getting you a permanent reprieve, but just *one* bloody month? That's what you're giving me away for?"

Jack's nostrils flare near my neck as if smelling me. "That good of a kiss, love? Suddenly don't want to be rid of me?"

I clench my teeth so tight I fear one cracking.

I have never met a mortal or other *being* who enraged me as much as intrigued me all in one breath.

Harnessing my sliver of dignity, I push to my feet with my head held high and move toward the ladder. A hand bunches the back of my dress, and Jack slowly pulls me to the bench seat next to him.

"Vane, I've had a change of heart. I think—" Jack announces. "—we shall take most of your supplies instead."

With precise timing, the sounds of numerous flintlocks cocking behind Vane and his crew echo against the wooden floorboards.

"What—" I blurt out, my stomach growing heavy.

Jack flings hair from my shoulder and grins. "I always have a plan, Anne. And I'm eternally grateful for you being such a *pivotal* part of it."

"You *used* me. Made me think you were—" Heat flushes my chest, my fists rising still within the confines of the rope.

Jack presses a hand over both of mine and lowers them

to my lap. "You make it sound so volatile. It would've never worked if you knew the plan. Think about it."

"You're done, Rackham. Fucking. *Done.* After this, I'll make your life a living hell on the seas." Vane stands at the ship's edge with no sword or pistol at his waist now, his palms held up like the rest of his crew, surrendering.

Meanwhile, Jack's crew rummages the deck, grabbing crates and bags to haul onto the approaching Revenge.

"Perhaps you will, Chuck. Perhaps you will. But it won't be today, and it won't be tomorrow. I'm leaving you with enough supplies to get back to Nassau. But it's *not* enough to follow me and find another place to resupply." Jack rests his chin in his palm. "Think that gives me a decent head start, wouldn't you say? Especially since you have no clue where I'm headed."

"I'll be the last thing you see before you leave this world, Rackham. Mark my words," Vane hisses, balling his hands into fists.

Jack puts a hand on the small of my back, ushering me to the bench across from him before plunging the oar into the water and turning us around. "If I had a ruby for every time I've heard that one, I'd not need to be a pirate." He pauses, catching my gaze. "Still would, though."

Vane roars into the wind, the sound so ear-splitting we can still hear it from the other side of the Revenge. Jack holds the dinghy steady near the rope ladder and yanks a dagger from his boot, pointing the tip of it at my wrists. "You going to try something foolish if I let you out of those?"

The universe knows I want to more than anything.

"I won't. You have my word." I lift my hands to shield

myself as Jack lurches forward. "But, Jack. Since you've made it clear you have no intention of hurting me, I won't hesitate to protect myself should that decision change."

That kiss still burns against my lips, and I fight the urge to touch them. I force my focus on his eyes even though I *want* to look at his mouth.

"The same can go both ways, sweetheart. Do not take my generosity as a sign of weakness. And it's why we'll need to chat when everyone's back on board." With one quick tug of the dagger, Jack frees me from the binds.

"Everyone?" I rub my wrists and grab the ladder.

"It's not only my decision whether you join our crew." Jack holds out his hand. "Need a lift?"

His crew.

"I don't need you—" I start, but his palm cups my ass and hoists me. When I toss him a glare, he grins at me like a damned fool—far too handsome for his own good *fool.*

The deck is a flurry of activity, with everyone carting supplies to store away. I rub my sweating palms down the skirts of my dress, unsure what to do with myself. Mary appears within the sea of bodies, hurling burlap sacks, and I make a beeline for her.

"You," I yell, pointing at Mary.

Mary drops the bag, her blue wide with remorse. "Anne," she shouts, pushing past the grunting crew to get to me.

"What was all that talk about having each other's backs?" Haughtily, I fold my arms.

Mary rests her hands on my shoulders and winces when I brush them away. "You *can* trust me, Anne. But the world of piracy is an entirely different world. You need to adapt. Wasn't sure you could."

Confusion and remorse settle over my brain like a dozen meddling gnats.

"You were testing me? How did you know Jack wouldn't go through with it?"

Mary pulls on her hat's brim. "Because it's Jack. I was ninety percent certain he had something else in mind."

"Ninety—" I flick my hands and turn away from her.

I have no place speaking of trust when I've deceived them once and am already doing it again, hiding my immortality.

"Trust is a fragile thing, Mary." I spin to face her again. "And say I learn to trust you. I can't see myself ever trusting Jack."

"And you shouldn't," she says bluntly.

"What? He's your captain, and you don't trust him?"

Mary's gaze shifts to Jack ascending the helm, garnering the attention of every crew member without an announcement. "I trust him with my life, yes. But do I trust him not to swindle me out of coin during a card game? Fuck no. Persuasion and deception skills are as important in this lifestyle as swordplay and a good sense of direction. And Jack Rackham? He's one of the sneakiest and smartest bastards I've ever met."

She trusts him with her *life*.

"Everyone, excellent work. We brought in more haul than an average merchant ship at half the effort." Jack's voice resonates with command. He paces back and forth and rakes a hand through his long, dark hair.

"I do like it when someone else does the dirty work," one man says, followed by a laugh.

"I'd say the distraction was rather bountiful, too, eh, lads?"

Another man stammers, standing on a crate so everyone can see him holding two melons in front of his chest.

The distraction. Me.

"Yes, but we also must consider how kind fate has been to put Anne in our path. If it weren't for her, we wouldn't have had such an enticing hand to work with." Jack still spots me despite dozens of people cramming the space between us. "She's already been on board for a week and officially committed her first act of piracy. I ask you all, should she swear by our code, will you see her on our crew?"

Committed her first act of piracy.

There's no end to the games, and I doubt there will ever be one. And none of them know the most cunning game of all plays right under their noses—a sea nymph in their midst. I'm as bad as they are.

"Why the bloody hell not?" A man says, throwing his hand up.

Mary smiles at my side and throws her arm into the air.

The deck becomes an endless ocean of raised limbs, the waves of cheering and hollering foreign to my ears. A numbness starts at the tips of my fingers and works into my chest because despite this crew voting for me to become one of them, I remain transfixed on the captain. He's strolling toward me, the men parting ways like a seam unraveling.

His hand is outstretched, beckoning mine. "We have a few things to discuss, Anne. My cabin?"

The kiss was pure fire but a performance nonetheless. Jack did it because he knew it'd only enrage Vane further with his want for me. And I'll still only trust him as far as I can throw him, but welcoming me into their crew has to count for something.

I look to Mary for reassurance, and once she gives me a confident nod, I slip my palm against Jack's and follow him into his quarters.

"Even if you're thinking of swearing to the code and joining this crew, there are a few things to set straight before you do." Jack closes the door behind me and moves to his desk, sitting on the corner.

"Then why put it to a vote now?" I try to hide my smile when Truffles leaps behind Jack and begins to rub himself up and down his arm.

Jack tries to ignore him but quickly succumbs to the cat's will and pets him. "No point in wasting my time or breath on you. If they would've voted no, why would we need to talk?"

"I'll give you this, Jack," I scoff. "You certainly don't sugarcoat anything."

"Life is too short to piss in the rain and pretend it's not happening." Jack scratches behind the cat's ears.

Pressing my back to the door, putting distance between us, I throw my hands at my sides. "You said there are matters to discuss?"

"First and foremost. Is there anything I should know about you that may jeopardize the lives of myself or anyone aboard this ship?" Jack grabs a ball of twine from the corner of his desk and rolls it to Truffles, distracting him as he pushes to his feet and crosses the room.

The proximity gives me nowhere to retreat and no choice but to stare up at him.

And here I am about to lie to the face of a renowned pirate captain. If I wish to make it to the Mediterranean Sea—to *home*—there's no way out of it.

"Me? The daughter of a dead grape farmer trying to seek passage to Greece to lay claim to the land?" I inhale deeply, the scents of brine and something citrus-like lacing his skin, making my head fuzzy.

He presses that damn tanned forearm above my head on the door again. "Lying doesn't become you, Anne. But I applaud you for thinking so quickly on your feet. We may make a pirate out of you yet."

"I thought no one was concerned with the other's background here?" My traitorous hips tilt forward, and I shove my backside against the door.

"All I need to know is if there's something—anything—that we're taking on by signing you to our crew that could come back to bite us in the ass." Jack shakes his head, wavy tendrils of chestnut hair falling over his gaze. "That's all."

The Charybdis can do a lot more than bite an ass. It consumes you. But what are the odds of it coming to that aboard a ship? It *never* attacks ships.

"No, Jack. I'm just trying to get to my family, and I didn't have the money to buy a ticket."

Jack nods, his face closing in on mine, his lips a breath from my brow before he pushes off the wall and turns away. "Family, eh? Husband?"

"Does it matter?" Dropping my gaze to my feet, I adjust the dress's sleeves.

Jack chuckles, swipes a wooden pick from his desk, and uses

it to clean his teeth. "Only curious whose heart I'll eventually break by stealing you away."

My stomach dips, and my chest tightens. I've known enough powerful, arrogant people to last me multiple lifetimes. But they *have* immense power, some with enough to alter the cosmos. And Jack is just—Jack. It's either insanity or abundant confidence—probably both.

"Was that all you had to ask me?"

Jack tosses the pick and yanks the cutlass from his belt, the blade resonating with a satisfying *schling* sound. "Do you know how to use one of these? Because I'd hate to have our lives banking on a dagger." He bounces his brow where I've hidden my knife, attached with leather to my thigh. How does he *know* these things?

Changing my stance, I clear my throat. "I can hold my own."

"Good. Get some rest, then. Because tomorrow, you're going to prove it." Jack sheathes the sword and waltzes for the door. "On deck. So, you can prove it to the crew as well."

My insides become one massive jumble of nerves. It's not because I doubt my skills with a blade; he has no idea what I can do, but how far should I go before I'm unable to explain myself?

"Fine. Where are my clothes?" I follow Jack after giving a fluttery wave to Truffles.

"Your shit clothes?" Jack scrunches his nose. "Tossed 'em overboard. You'll have to make do with that dress. Get Mary to do her magical cuts or tears or whatever the hell she does." He moves about the deck, business as usual, with me following behind him like a rebellious shadow.

"Tossed them—but you had no right." My chest bumps

against his stomach as he suddenly turns to face me, and my skin instantly heats.

"I had no right? Because those clothes were yours? Not stolen?"

I bat stray hair from my eyes. "Not *all* of them."

"It's a new era for you, Anne—time for something new. Talk to Mary and figure it out before tomorrow morning. Because—" Jack lowers his lips near my ear. "—you'll need to move *freely*." The hair of his beard brushes my earlobe as he smiles against it and steps away.

I'll devise *any* excuse because there's no chance I'll let Calico Jack outmatch me in a swordfight. Fighting with a blade—is in my *blood*.

EIGHT

JACK

I'M A WHIRLPOOL of confusion, lust, and weariness. The universe has thrown many obstacles my way, but none as dangerous as Anne Bonny. And I've had my fair share of women—broken enough hearts while in port and felt no qualms about it, but *Anne*? From the first moment I saw her in that tavern, I knew there was something different about her. The fire? The angst? Her willingness and confidence to go toe-to-toe with me physically? Verbally? Fuck. My mind should be focused on *one* thing: the jewel.

I drag a hand over my face, busying myself with the ship's wheel while absentmindedly half-assing the melody of a sea shanty under my breath.

"You know you don't need to steer the ship with every tiny shift, right, son?" Duke asks, appearing at my side with his arms crossed.

Moving the wheel harder than necessary to the right and then back left, I flash him an unenthused grin. "Maybe I just want to feel the power beneath my fingertips."

"Or—" Duke moves in front of me. "—you came up here to do some deep thinking. What's on your mind?"

"There are far too many things to bother you with them, Duke," I grumble, spying Anne emerging from below deck.

Finally.

She and Mary went down there an hour ago to readjust her attire.

When Anne comes into full view, an odd flutter bursts in my chest, floating down to settle in my stomach. I knew Mary would have enough spare clothes to outfit Anne without her having to roam around in shitty-smelling ones. But the outcome? This—I wasn't expecting.

She's not showing an ounce of skin save for her face, neck, and hands, but she has grown more attractive. The green dress has been mostly torn away, leaving bits draping around her waist hanging over a pair of tight brown trousers. A loose-fitting black leather corset hugs her ribs, sprouting from a billowing white tunic shirt. A dark green sash catches the wind breezing over the deck, sending it flying behind her like a ship's colors on the mast.

I can't be sure if I've bothered to blink for the past several minutes. Clearing my throat, I gaze at the water, squinting and forcing my concentration elsewhere.

"Ah, now I see," Duke says with a traitorous chuckle.

"See what, old man?"

Red approaches Anne, bowing to her and displaying his hand over her attire with a shit-eating grin I want to slap straight off his face. What can he possibly have to say to her?

"Taken a liking to our stowaway, have you?" Duke's broad, bushy face appears in front of mine, blocking my view of Anne.

My grip tightens on the wheel. "I'm weighing our options as I always do, Duke. If she can wield a sword as she claims, she'll be far more useful to us than a cabin boy."

"Mm, yes." Duke interlaces his fingers and rests them on his stomach. "And she needs the proper pirate attire to prove this, right?"

Take this for what it is, Jack: Be. More. Careful.

"One must look the part to feel the part, no?" It takes everything in me not to leer at Anne waltzing about the deck as the crew dotes on her.

As if I have a say in the matter. I've spoken no claim to her. Nor does she have a fig of interest in me beyond my ability to get her to her family. She's using me as much as I am her, and I'm almost—*enthralled* by it.

Duke chuckles and nonchalantly shoos me away from the wheel. "Whatever you say, Jack. Now, let me get back at this thing. I'm getting antsy. Never make an old man impatient."

My neck stiffens, but I relent after giving Duke a pinched expression. Anne speaks with Glog now, both laughing. Glog's hands flitter as usual when he's explaining recipes or probing for ideas. I stay out of sight as best I can, snatching Anne's hat from a barrel of grain I'd stored it in. I've gotten close enough to hear their conversation, and they're not talking about Anne at all but Glog's plans for a new drink.

"I've been experimenting with different mushrooms that aren't deadly to consume, but they seem to have a sort of—effect?" Glog teeters his hand back and forth, his eyes widening excitedly.

Anne folds her arms, accentuating her breasts beneath the loose tunic, and I pluck furiously at the hat's brim in my hands. "What kind of effect? And would you put it in addition to the alcohol?"

"Yes. The alcohol makes your head fuzzy, but the mushrooms would make you feel like you damn well never left the ship when on land." Glog slaps his hands together.

"Well, you two sound like you're hitting it off rather quickly," I chime in, sidling beside them and hiding the hat behind my back.

Anne whips around to face me, her gaze briefly dropping to my lips, but it's long enough for me to assume she remembers the kiss. I had wanted to see how long it would take before she shoved me away. To my delight, she lasted several more seconds than I'd predicted. "When everyone sleeps in hammocks below deck except for the *captain*, you tend to get to know one another."

"Anne, my sweet—" Sliding forward, I bump my knuckle under her chin. "I can certainly make room for you in my cabin, in *my* hammock, if you'd be more comfortable."

"I'd be far too tempted to smother you with a pillow, Jack," Anne snarls, snappy as a whip. She smiles, showing most of her teeth, and her chest swells.

"I'd love to see you try." I chew on my bottom lip and let my eyes roam her exposed cleavage.

She pulls her blouse up, denying my view, and huffs. "I wouldn't be caught dead in your hammock."

"What an *odd* thing to say to a pirate."

Anne's cheeks flush, and her eyes become two thin shards of emerald. She opens her mouth to retort, but no words follow.

"I think I'll try a cup of what we discussed, Anne. You two, uh—carry on," Glog says while backing away as if we were a lit cannon on a short fuse.

Anne's hair now has several braids, and she rubs one between two fingers. Her focus turns to the rope coiled tightly around the mast. "I've been making an effort to become acquainted with the crew. Except for the healer. He always seems busy with this, that, and the other."

"Aranck is his name. And you should be relieved if you never have to meet him. That means you didn't need his services."

Anne sticks her bottom lip out as if to say, "Good point."

"Here. It was the only thing that didn't stink to high heaven. I figured you'd want it." Revealing the hat hidden behind me, I hold it out to her.

Anne eyes it and snaps her gaze to me, still not taking it. "Did you piss on it or something?"

I blink. "Do you think me that juvenile?"

Silence. Pure irritating silence.

"No, Anne." I slip the hat on my head and slap it for good measure. "I did not soil a perfectly good hat. Happy?"

Anne snatches the hat and flops it over her hair. "Hardly."

Squid is walking on deck, which is an unusual sight, considering he only ever comes down from the crow's nest during a storm. He typically even sleeps up there during the night. But what shocks me to the core is the sight of him— emptying the latrine bucket.

"Anne, dearest." I trace my fingers through my beard, focusing on Squid gleefully performing one of Anne's chores and *smiling* as he does it.

Anne's neck turns rosy.

"Did you somehow swindle Squid into doing your chores?" I flick my finger in his direction.

She waves across the deck at Squid, and he waves back. They grin at each other. "Yes. I told him I'd give him a portion of my daily food rations if he did it."

Won Squid's heart through his stomach. It doesn't surprise me in the least.

"You know you can't share rations? It's to ensure everyone doesn't die of thirst or starve." This is partially a load of shit, but I want to see how far I can take this.

"If I faint on deck, you can be the first to stand over my unconscious body and tell me you told me so, but I assure you I don't need as much food as he does. Do you know how much energy he uses swinging around up there?" Anne squints at the crow's nest. "And, *Captain*, we're not consuming any more rations than given. We haven't broken any rules."

Fuck. Either this woman is after my heart or leading me into a trap to run her dagger through it. Whichever the case, I'm—intrigued.

"Point taken. Now then—" moving to a barrel with several swords sticking out of it, I snatch one and point to her hat "—since you no longer have the excuse of the sun being in your eyes it's time to prove your worth, Bonny." I toss the sword to her, and the test begins with how she catches it—or doesn't.

She not *only* catches it, but with a flourish. She twirls the blade as if to check its balance and grace.

And here I thought I'd have to pull most of my swings. This is so much better.

I beat the hilt of my cutlass against the mast, signaling to the crew that a duel is about to commence. They gather around us in droves, creating a cage of bodies and leaving us enough room on deck to maneuver but no chance of retreating. Not that I'd ever back out on a fight, friendly or otherwise. It's still to be determined whether Anne truly is friend or foe.

"Are there rules I should know?" Anne asks, already starting to circle me, crossing one booted foot over the other.

I follow her, pace for pace, tossing the handle in my palm. "Are there rules of engagement when you're fighting an enemy?"

"No?" Anne gives a slight head shake.

"You have your answer." I strike without giving her a chance to stew on it any longer.

Her blade swings skyward, blocking me, but her mouth falls open. And in the next moment, the stunned expression melts into determination, and that *sass* I've already begun to like about her blossoms. She dodges to the left and right and slashes downward. I slide backward with my hands at my sides to avoid the tip of her blade slicing my chest.

"Is that how you got that scar, Jack?" Anne spins the sword, her words as daunting as her foot placement. "Poor timing?"

I flash her a grin. "Noticed my scar, did you?" Reaching one hand to my back, I keep my sword pointed in her direction and yank my shirt off, tossing it aside.

No rules.

"Seriously?" Anne pauses and points at my naked torso with her cutlass. Fighting her urge to ogle me is a losing battle with each passing second.

"Feel free to teach me a lesson and follow suit, lovely." I take two strides forward and launch at her right side.

Anne's jaw clenches, and she swings her blade to catch mine in a hold before landing her foot into my stomach, pushing me away, and leaving a boot print on my skin.

Chuckling, I wipe the mud from my belly. "You're full of surprises, Anne. I'd ask you how you learned to fight like that, but you'd undoubtedly lie and claim your dad fought in the Nine Years' War or something equally asinine."

"You have me *all* figured out. So, why ask?" A new kind of fury blares in Anne's eyes, and like oil to a fire, she's at me, slashing, slicing, punching, and elbowing.

Our blades circle the other, and I lunge forward at her arm. Anne deflects, turning her body away from it and using her palm to push the blunt side of the weapon away from her.

These are expert moves that only come from years of practice.

Who *are* you, Anne?

We become a whirlpool of parries, thrusts, and slashes, circling each other and occasionally hopping on barrels or gaining extra momentum from dangling ropes. She's matching me swing for swing, and dare I say, I'm beginning to lose my breath. She's across from me now, her chest heaving, and the next swing she throws, she uses her blade to launch spent gunpowder scattered on a nearby railing into my face.

How. Dirty.

Coughing and sputtering, I grin despite being temporarily blinded. I've been listening to her footsteps as she sneaks behind me. I swipe my arm over my eyes and predict her next move, a thrust at my side that I avoid by sliding. Grabbing her sword-carrying elbow, I yank her forward, turn her around, and push her back against the mast.

She's fighting me, but I tower over her, and her petite wrists are within my much larger grasp. I shove her hands above her, but she refuses to drop the sword. Instead, she seethes at me, but it only encourages me, and I press into her, scraping my chest against hers.

"No hard feelings, dearest," I whisper, still smiling.

Her eyes are unblinking, and I know she's about to try something. But whereas most women would try to knee me in the balls when in a similar situation, she surprises me by slamming her boot into the top of mine. When I grunt, my grip loosening on her hands, she knees me in the *ribs*. I let out a growling wince, and she drops to her knees, sliding across the deck on them only to swivel on her heel and face me again with her blade pointing in my face.

More lust. More fury. More fucking confusion over this woman.

We started as a man and a woman cast together on the same path. We're now two carnal beings out to prove something to each other. The crew cheers and whoops around us, but the noise becomes a distant hum in my ears. My only focus is on those jade eyes glaring at me between crossing blades. My colors, the white skull and crossed swords on black, flaps in the breeze above us, our blades mimicking the very symbol I sail beneath.

I misjudge a step I think she'll take and pay for it, her sword grazing my arm. Hissing, I snap my gaze to the wound, satisfied to see only a minor scratch and a thin line of crimson. "Don't get cocky now, Anne."

"Believe me—" Anne snarls and swings her sword once, twice, and the third time wielding it with more effort and stronger impact "—you have enough cock for the both of us."

"Why, thank you." I spin behind her, and her sword blocks mine with lightning speed. Sliding my blade with hers, I make the tips of our noses almost touch. "And you haven't had the pleasure of its company yet."

"Yet?" Anne growls, pushing away from me. She's at me again, but the swings are more labored now.

And mine aren't much better. Every muscle from my right shoulder into my back is on fire, and my bicep is twitching. She takes an overhead swing, and I smack it once with my blade, stopping her forearm from coming down any further with my other hand. And with one swift kick behind her calves, she's on her back on the wood with a loud *thud* that echoes across the deck, her cutlass clattering several paces away.

I'm straddling her a breath later, putting enough weight on her to keep her from squirming but not enough to keep her from breathing. I shove the blade at her throat, and when our gazes lock, it's not a reaction I could've predicted. Not from her or me. One of us should be furious, or disappointed, or Christ, even concerned perhaps? But she's peering up at me as if she sees me for the first time. And in her, I sense a journey to be explored—a *challenge*.

"I'm about to *kill* you, Anne. I'm the enemy." I press the blade closer to her neck, just enough to not pierce her skin. "And after I'm done with you? I'm going to kill Mary next.

And then Squid and Glog. *What* are you going to do about it?" I'm roaring now, hoping Anne will do what she needs to because I don't know if I can turn her away after this.

Anne's body is shivering, her teeth chattering. But it's not from the cold. It's from *fury*. A small blade pushes against my throat, and a thin bead of warm liquid rolls over my chest—the dagger. I hadn't felt her move for it, hadn't *heard* her reaching for it.

If I didn't think she'd stop me, I'd say to hell with the crew and have her right here on this fucking deck.

Lightly wrapping a hand over hers clutching the dagger to my throat, I pull it away, and she lets me. "You ready to swear yourself to this crew, Anne? To this ship?"

"Aye, Captain," she whispers, bewilderment still in her eyes.

I grind my hips against her stomach, watching her bite her lip, before crawling off and holding my hand out to her. She ignores it, not surprisingly, and pushes to her feet.

Mary tackles Anne's side, pulling on her hat's brim. "Who the *fuck* are you, darling? Really? That was bloody amazing."

"I'm just Anne," she replies.

We stare at one another as I backpedal through cheering men, making my way to the helm and beckoning her with a "come-hither" finger. She soon follows as if in a trance, offering warm smiles to those congratulating her, but her gaze never falters from me.

I hold up my palm and instruct her to do the same. Anne Bonny swears to The Revenge and its crew on this day, blessed by blue skies and sun. She swears to the right to vote in affairs, not steal from her fellow crewmates, always be battle-ready, never desert the captain or crew, and that all disputes will be handled on land and never on the ship. She swears her undying loyalty to her captain and to a life of piracy for as long as she sees fit to remain in our crew.

And on this day, I can swear the sun shines brighter because of it.

NINE

RHODE/ANNE

I'M A PIRATE. I've taken the oath, sworn my loyalty, and I'm lying straight to their faces. What would my father say if he knew? He'd probably be disappointed but not surprised. I smile at this because I miss Dad and my older brother. But a woman can do far worse for a found family.

I've climbed the stairs leading to the deck just as the sun sets after a nap in preparation for keeping watch on the night shift. Squid's legs dangle from the crow's nest, his feet bouncing to the beat of a man playing the flute below him. Mary is hanging new rope from the riggings, her hat resting on a barrel, a rare sight only when the sun's no longer a burden. Ragnar stands near Jack at the helm, and the sight of him makes my stomach clench.

Jack Rackham. What am I to do with you?

It's been days since we sparred, and we've barely exchanged a few words—pleasantries, really. When Jack's hot, he's raging lava, but when he's cold, he's as frigid as they come. Is he toying with me? Trying to get into my head? Or he's afraid. By the Seas,

I know *I* am. What happens when they find out? It's not a matter of *if*, it's when because I can only keep my true self hidden for so long. But every time I think I'm ready to tell someone, fear grips me like a whirlpool. I can't even bring myself to tell Mary, who I've increasingly grown to trust above all others.

Forcing my attention away from Jack, I grab a bucket and brush and drop to my knees. I may have talked Squid into emptying the shit bucket, but there's no getting out of the tedious task of continuously scrubbing the damn deck.

"Hey, Captain," a man says to Jack, tugging on the only thing covering his upper half, a burgundy vest. "What say you to a bit of festivities tonight, hm? It's been *days* since we've seen a bloody boat, and we're all getting restless."

The man is right. Over the past few days, the crew's growing impatience has created a choking tension in the air.

"And if I agree, what did you have in mind?" Jack asks, casually propping against the railing.

I watch his forearms flex beneath the rolled sleeves of his red tunic shirt, and a lump forms in my throat. The sight of his bare torso is permanently etched into my memory. He knew what he was doing, taking his shirt off while sparring and trying to distract me. And I can't say it didn't partially work. I come from a line of supernatural beings who can make their physique appear any way they wish, but Jack? He looks like that *naturally*—toned arms, carved abdominals, the dark scattering of hair, and confirmation that, yes, he has a trail leading into his trousers.

"Maybe some music, a bit of carousing, and, I don't know, an extra ration each of grog?" The man elbows another crew member. "Seeing as Vane was so gracious and gave us extra."

Ragnar rolls his eyes, and Jack chuckles, tapping his rings on the railing before raising a finger. "Know what? I'm feeling gracious myself, and the skies are clear. Why not? Ragnar, divvy up some extra rum to the crew."

The man whoops and claps his hands together. I run the back of my sleeve over my forehead before continuing, but Mary soon looms. Her perfume, unlike any other smell on board, given it's not brine, tar, or questionable body odor, always gives her away.

"Did you not hear the Captain, Anne?" Mary asks.

I sit back on my haunches. "I did. But the deck isn't going to scrub itself."

Mary snatches the scrub brush from my grasp, tosses it in the bucket, and holds out her hand. "It can wait until tomorrow. Tonight, you kick back like the rest of us. Trust me when I say you take advantage of these moments. They're needed and fleeting."

"If there's anything I've learned, you don't argue with Mary Read," I respond, smiling as I take her hand and let her hoist me.

Red is tuning a lute while taking a seat near the flute player. Another man I don't recognize throws the strap of a hurdy-gurdy over his head and plays a quick bar across the keys. Ragnar arrives several moments later, carrying a crate, the bottles clinking together when he tosses it to the deck. Several crew members eagerly move toward it, and Ragnar points his flintlock at them with a furrowed bulldog brow.

Glog appears from below decks, loaves of bread and cheese cradled in his arms. I fold my arms and smile, watching everyone bubbling with excitement. The band begins to play the familiar tune of *Drunken Sailor*, everyone joining in once the song reaches verses they know. Only slivers of yellow, orange, and a thin strip of crimson remain on the horizon, the sun fully setting and allowing the night sky to take over. Aranck, still quiet as always, takes a route around the ship's perimeter, lighting the lanterns.

Ragnar holds a bottle out to me. "Your festivities liquid for the evening."

"Thanks, Ragnar." I grin at him and cheer with the bottle before popping the cork. It takes more than mortal alcohol for an ancient being to feel anything resembling a buzz, so this watered-down rum will do nothing but taste good.

Jack clanks his bottle with a group of men, all taking swigs and laughing. Jack's smile is so radiant the moonlight seems to glint off it. When he glances at me with those caramel eyes, for the briefest of moments, the way it makes my thighs pinch together, it's probably more than a good thing the alcohol won't affect me.

Glog holds out a piece of bread and cheese. "Here you are."

"Appreciate it, Glog." I run my thumbs over the dents left where moldy bits have been removed. "You don't play an instrument?"

"Lord, no. Get me drunk enough, though, and I may belt a bar or two." Glog winks and tears some bread with his teeth before moving on to the next crewmember.

With food in my lap, I hop onto a barrel, letting my feet dangle and tapping my heels against the wood to the song's beat. The minutes tick by, and I'm content perched on my makeshift seat while watching everyone. Squid climbs down from the crow's nest long enough to receive a bread loaf from Aranck. Aranck makes several gestures with his hands, signs I'm unfamiliar with, but Squid laughs, gesturing back to him. The two quietest members of the crew communicate in silence, and for the first time, I witness Aranck smiling. Just like in the tavern, Jack only takes the occasional sip from his drink, not caring that most of his crew are halfway through their bottles.

"What ya looking at?" Mary hugs my side, her breath reeking of rum and cheese.

I eye her sidelong and stifle a cough. "Just people watching. Enjoying yourself?"

"Mm. Definitely. But if I didn't know any better—" Mary squints one eye and pokes my nose with her forefinger. "—and I don't—" She burps. "—you were staring at the dear 'ol Captain."

I am. Guilty as charged.

"I think you've had a lot to drink, friend." Snickering, I flick the bottle with my fingernail.

"No one would blame you, Anne. He's a stunner—even *I* can admit that." Mary guzzles more rum. "You should ask him to grease your fire, if you know what I mean." She nudges me, blinking her eyes awkwardly like she's trying to wink.

"Grease my fire, huh?" I bite the inside of my cheek, trying not to laugh.

"Think about it, darling." Mary shoves off me, stumbling and laughing, before she raises her fists and walks to the band.

I chew the inside of my cheek, but when curiosity gets the better of me, I hop from the barrel and head for the helm. The navigation maps are sprawled on a table near the wheel, with a stone in every corner to keep the wind from blowing it away. I tap my finger on the location we currently sail and slowly drag it toward the Mediterranean.

"Look at you being antisocial over here by yourself," Jack says, swinging a bottle at his side between two fingers.

"Nope. I'm content waiting for everyone else to come to *me*." I hold my hand out to him, displaying that he's done just that, and take a sip.

Jack looks at his chest and smirks. "Well, shit. It works. Here I am—" He bends forward and flashes a sinfully charming grin. "—falling for it."

"Don't be too hard on yourself. This hair is like a smoke signal."

Jack's gaze wavers over my hair. "I've noticed." He deliberately climbs the stairs, one at a time.

My free hand grips the table's edge, and Jack instantly notices this action. His eyes snap straight to my whitening knuckles.

"What's your story, Bonny?" Jack tilts his head to one side and moves in closer, his voice dropping to a rumbly whisper I can feel in my toes.

This is such treacherous territory—both my disguise and my supernatural existence.

"My story? Typical. Boring. It'd put you to sleep." I guzzle some more of my drink, making my best effort not to linger on Jack's exposed chest and that *scar*.

Jack stands next to me now, leaning against the table. His finger brushes my trousers near my hip, and sea angels flutter in my stomach. "I may not be the smartest man in the world, but I *know* you're far from boring. And I suspect there's a bigger story to you than you'd ever share." Jack's hand grows bolder and skirts my thigh.

I draw in a breath through my nose and level a glare at him. "Do you want to lose that hand?"

He flashes me a wicked grin. "Threatening me, Miss Bonny? You won't do it because you know you've yet to experience what these hands can do to you. Afterward, though? Once you've had your fill? I wouldn't be as confident."

There's no stopping the laugh that pushes from my lungs, and I cover my mouth with the bottle. However, the chuckles abruptly stop when Jack's fingers rest on my arm and he slowly lowers it. His nose brushes mine, and his expression turns pensive.

"I think, Anne—" Jack moves his hand to the back of my neck. "—I might be falling in love with you."

He is so full of absolute shit.

I play along briefly, letting my gaze fall to his lips like I'm about to kiss him before lifting the bottle between us. "Are you quite done?"

Jack rubs his forehead and presses two fingers against his breastbone. "You wound me. Here I am confessing my feelings, and you—" When he catches me staring at him deadpan, he cuts himself off. "—that normally works on a woman."

"Pity for them." I edge a half smile and down more of my drink.

He shrugs, still edging close enough we share the same air. "I've yet to receive a complaint."

"Complaints are usually bad for business when *paying* for

the company." I thin my lips, biting back a smile.

Jack's eyes light up, and he pushes off the table to stand straight, laughing. "Level with me, Anne. Give me something. Anything about you."

By the Seas, he's gorgeous.

"And if I don't?" I prop on one elbow, using my other hand to take occasional sips from my bottle.

He's taking up my space again, arms pressed to the table on each side of my hips, and he's grinning like a wolf on the prowl. "I'll only try harder to pry it out of you."

There's no hiding the gulp making my throat bounce.

"I noticed you scanning the map. Do you know how to read one?" Jack turns me to face the table, his hips brushing my ass. One of his callused hands slips over the top of mine, and he guides my finger to several spots on the map, dragging it from one place to the other.

I've never imagined hand-holding to feel so intimate. "What makes you think I don't?"

Because I do, but he doesn't know this.

"Each captain keeps a different style of mapping. It depends on how they label travel routes versus known trade routes." Jack continues to trace my finger along a red line.

My body naturally settles against him behind me.

"And considering you're not pulling away—" his nose brushes my nape and his lips feather my skin "—you either don't know how to read it or want an excuse to have my hands on you."

And here I am, thinking about it. I'm imagining kissing him—*truly* kissing him. I fantasize about how my hands would feel bunched in those long chocolate locks as his callused fingers scrape sensually across my skin.

"Anne," Mary bellows from the front of the ship.

I snap to attention, accidentally striking Jack in the head with my bottle.

"Ow," Jack mumbles, wincing at me but smiling.

"Sorry, I—"

"Anne fucking Bonny," Mary yells with one hand cupped around her mouth. "And you too, Captain. Get your arses over here."

Jack rolls his bottom lip between his teeth. "Something to know about Mary? It isn't wise to keep her waiting."

"Noted." Turning around, I pause when Jack fans his palms and steps back.

"I don't need you threatening any more of my *appendages*."

After scooting past him, I tug his shirt sleeve with a gleaming smile. "You're learning."

"I am always studious regarding women." Jack bows with a flourish.

Rolling my eyes, I brush past, fighting the urge to steal another glance at him.

When we reach the group, most have finished both bottles of rum and are singing and swaying to the music. Aranck watches from afar, not participating but standing guard with his arms folded. Squid still resides barefoot in the crow's nest, bouncing to the music.

Mary punches Jack's arm. "You fuck her yet?"

I choke on my spit and wipe the back of my hand over my mouth.

"Such a delicate flower you are, Mary." Jack pinches Mary's cheek. "And no, because someone yelled at us to come over here. Didn't they?"

Mary snorts and laughs. "Oh, shit. I cock-blocked ya, didn't I?"

Jack says nothing and only offers her a sardonic grin.

"No, you didn't. Any amount of extra time would've made no difference whatsoever." I flick my hand in the air.

There's no convincing, not even myself, of this statement.

Jack closes the gap between us, intrigue and mirth dancing in his gaze. "Do you have any idea what challenge you've started?"

I move an inch closer and crane my neck back to look him in the eye. "If it's anything like your swordplay, it should be over quick."

Jack's lips form a slow, broad smile.

Mary and several of the men hoot with laughter. Jack and I are still staring each other down as Red pats Jack on the chest while Mary jostles me. If ever I can be thankful mortal alcohol does nothing to my inhibitions, it's right now, in this moment. But I also can't blame Jack's leering gazes or words on inebriation either, because he's only had maybe two or three sips of grog. The realization makes a flutter form in my chest.

"Where in Ireland are you from, Anne?" Glog asks, still munching on cheese. "That's the accent, right? Irish?"

Jack crosses his arms and fiddles with his rings, waiting for me to answer.

Without looking away from Jack, I answer, "Near Cork."

"Cork." Glog snaps his fingers. "I should've known that."

Red suddenly passes out, slumping onto the deck with his

ass in the air. Aranck pushes past everyone and helps him up, pouring something from a small bottle into Red's mouth before aiding him below deck.

"What did he give him?" I ask Glog.

Glog shrugs and tosses a piece of bread, catching it in his mouth. "Not sure. Aranck seems to have cures for anything that ails you. The man could've been a surgeon without all the screwy schooling, I swear it."

"Anne," Mary whines, holding her hand out to me. "Dance with me."

"You sure you're in a good enough state for that?" I ask, chuckling at her swaying on her heels.

"Unlike most of these oafs, I can hold my liquor." Mary snaps her hand back and eyes me warily. "Peculiar, why you're not more sloshed." She snatches my bottle before I can resist and shakes it. "The whole bloody thing is almost gone, and you're not so much as glassy-eyed."

I can *feel* Jack's curious gaze from nearby heating my cheeks.

"High tolerance, I guess." Yanking the bottle back, I shove it in a pocket and open my arms. "You mentioned dancing?"

Mary and I dance a drunken waltz, and surprisingly, I only have to hold her upright three times. She attempts to dip me, and I have to press my hand to the deck to keep from landing on my back when she fumbles with my arms. And after several moments have passed, she stalks off without warning, mumbling something about needing sleep. Jack has been watching me the entire time, walking a circle around us from afar. He switches from running his fingers through his beard to clasping his hands behind his back, but the determination in his eyes is plain: he's bent on figuring me out.

Yawning, I stretch my arms above my head. "I should probably head to bed, too. Seems like the party is dying anyway."

Several men have fallen asleep on deck, propped against each other or on crates, the empty bottles held limply in their hands.

"I'll remind you," Jack starts, standing in front of me with hooded lids. "My hammock is far more comfortable, especially with me in it."

I pinch my lips together to rein in my smile and pat his chest. "Goodnight, Jack."

He grabs my hand and presses a chaste kiss to my knuckles. "Goodnight—*Annie*."

The nickname sends my heart racing, and I reluctantly slip my hand from his, backing away until I feel the railing touch my fingertips. I'm clutching my blouse as I sprint for the stairs, pressing my back against the wall when I'm secluded below decks.

This is going too far. I have to tell them. And soon. But—how?

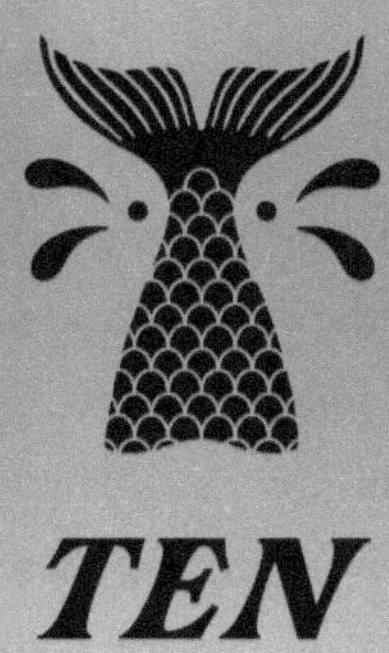

TEN

RHODE/ANNE

A **MONSTROUSLY LOUD** crackle jolts me awake, my hammock swinging so erratically I almost topple out. I hop to my feet, pressing a hand near the porthole window to brace myself. A flash of lightning streaks the midnight sky, the sea pulsing with white-capped waves. Panicking, I race to the stairs, slipping on my boots as I hop and climb to the deck. A wind gust slams into the ship's side, throwing my body against the far railing. Water splashes onto my knuckles, and I gasp, pulling my sleeves over my hands.

"Get those fucking sails secured before they're torn to shreds," Ragnar shouts.

The crew scurries, tying up the sails. Mary helps with the ropes, but they keep flying from her grasp with every other gust. Without hesitation, I move to her side, grabbing one of the rogue ropes and pulling it taut, waiting for the other men to roll up the mainsail. Squid has his legs wrapped around the mast, using one hand to steady himself while the other works the ropes around the sails.

"We all sobered up real bloody quick, huh?" Mary grins at me, winding rope around her arm to hold it firm.

I muster a weak smirk, far too concerned by the looming torrential downpour, the clouds darkening with each passing second. Only hours prior, drunken crewmates littered the deck sleeping, and now every soul is doing their part to ready the ship for a battle with Mother Nature.

"Seems we've pissed off the sea gods somehow, eh lads?" Duke barks, laughing and helping with the rigging despite his age.

My stomach twists into knots.

"Anne," Jack shouts from the wheel before stalking in my direction. "What the hell are you doing up here?"

"I'm helping," I yell back. "What does it look like I'm doing?"

Jack yanks the rope from my hands with a snarl. "You don't have the experience to handle a storm like this. Get below deck. *Now.*"

I need an excuse to get out of the rain and avoid revealing my true self, but not like *this.*

"And hide like a coward?" Pulling the rope from Jack's grip is like tugging on a planet-sized boulder.

"It's not hiding, Bonny. It's surviving. And we need people down there to secure the cannons and anything else heavy that might launch into the side of the ship and make a damned hole." Jack grunts, the rope pulling him forward, his feet sliding until he regains his hold. "You swore an oath. I'm your captain. Now, get below *deck.*"

My sinuses sting with held-back tears of rage, but I know it's the best thing to do.

Balling my hands into fists at my sides, I puff my chest. "Fine."

"Good girl," Jack *has* to say, adding fuel to the already building fire in my breast. He nudges his head toward the stairs.

I sprint below deck so I won't strangle Jack within an inch of his life before realizing what I'm doing. Glog, working ropes around one of the cannons, notices me, and relief washes over him.

"Help me secure these cannons, will you? There's extra rope there." Glog points at a pile of coiled rope, and I spring into action.

Below deck is far more abusive to one's equilibrium, and I widen my stance to give me more purchase as I help Glog. "How many cannons are there?"

"Twelve," Glog says, grunting and tying a knot far more intricate than mine.

Pausing to watch him, I mimic the loops and ties he's doing, applying them to my rope. "And how many have you done?"

"Two." Glog's gaze snaps to mine, realization settling over us.

The thunder roaring outside, rain splashing against the windows, sends a chill through my bones. Snapping to attention, I run to the next cannon. "Let's each take one at a time. We'll not secure them all in time if we don't."

Glog nods, and we're a whirlwind of tying knots and losing our balance with every ship sway. One wave sends me hurtling toward a barrel, and I hold onto it to keep from lurching backward. A crate slides into another, slamming into it with such force that it cracks, and several cannon balls break free, rolling across the floor. Glog clumsily chases after one, using both hands, squatting, and returning it to the crate. I manage to wrangle two, and after checking if Glog is looking, I pick them up, one in each hand, and place them.

A crackle of lightning and a thunderous boom make me wince and hold my head. The next wave that hits the boat turns us almost entirely sideways, and I fly onto my back, my elbows slamming into the wood. The sound of something splashing into the water makes my arm hair stand on end, and when a cacophony of voices screaming the name "Jack" shadows it, my blood freezes.

I scramble to the porthole window, panic shaking me to my core. There's too much wind, rain, and chaos to see if Jack's head appears at the surface. And despite how good of a swimmer I assume this pirate captain is, no mortal could survive this storm, let alone make it back to the ship in one piece before drowning—or worse.

Either I out myself to Jack and the entire crew right now, or Jack is dead. Setting my jaw, I make for the stairs, stripping off clothing and leaving it in a haphazard trail. Glog yells at me, begging me to stop, but his words are static in my ears.

I'm naked from head to toe when I reach the deck, the rain slapping my body and immediately soaking it. It doesn't take long for the scales to shimmer across my skin, the ridges and grooves protruding down my spine, between my breasts, and forehead. There's so much wind and rain that none of the crew can make it out—yet. But their warning shouts fade into the background as I climb to the railing. A hand latches onto mine just as I'm diving forward, and I turn in time to see Mary's terrified face and our fingertips sliding away. I do a backbend, making my fins appear, and collide against the sea with my arms outstretched.

To the mortal eye, beneath the surface becomes a dark, desolate, and eerie existence, particularly during a rainstorm, but not to me. The depths are as crystal clear as a cloudless day. My heart races and my eyes frantically search for air bubbles, searching for *Jack*. The Charybdis is also an issue. As soon as my fingertips touch sea waters, it sends an ethereal ripple that lets *it* know I'm in its domain.

A slow, steady rhythm growing increasingly sluggish pounds in my ears, and a breath catches in my throat. In the distance, Jack sinks further into the depths, his body limp but not yet lifeless. I flick my tail and launch through the water, my nerves sizzling against my skin once he's in my arms. Sea nymphs can speak underwater to understand others with the same gift, but mortals hear nothing but muffled stammering.

I shake his chin, waiting for a response. Nothing. Cradling the back of his head, I press my mouth to his, pushing air from my lungs into him, praying it's enough to make it to the surface. There's nothing romantic or intimate about this gesture, but it still sends a sizzle down my spine into the tip of my tail. With one arm wrapped around his chest and the other reaching above me, I cut through the water, snapping my tail furiously.

And this is when I see them—threatening me through the haze of bubbles and mist—two enormous glowing red eyes. Terror grips me, and I only allow it to paralyze me for a single breath before I'm swimming to the surface, pushing, grunting, and not caring that my tail and arms burn and ache from the strain.

The coarse rope ladder brushes my skin, and I hoist myself from the water, carrying Jack with me. I shove him to the deck and will my fins back into human legs, the nip of the Charybdis grazing my tail before I scrambled aboard the ship. Crawling, I collapse over Jack, breathless and terrified when he isn't breathing. Despite the sound of rain punching the deck and booming thunder fading away as the storm passes, the silence from the crew staring at me is painful to my ears. Ignoring it for now, disregarding my nudity, I tilt Jack's chin and pinch his nose shut. I press my mouth to his and give him the air from my lungs.

Holding back a sob, I pound my fist against Jack's chest. "You stubborn jackass, come back," I yell, pressing my mouth to his again. The rain coating my eyelashes blurs my vision.

After a few seconds, salt water sputters against my lips, and Jack is coughing, gasping for air. A tear streaks my cheek, masked by the wetness already coating my face, and I turn Jack on his side. The crew surrounds us in a circle, still not speaking but staring at me slack-jawed. My ears, now pointed and webbed like tiny fins droop, because I'm ashamed of my appearance, of my *betrayal*. I sit back on my haunches, my ears twitching, and I drag my hands down Jack's legs, not ready to let go of him.

"Anne?" Jack croaks, a hand pressed over his ribs. He squints at me through blurs of falling water, gratitude in his stare, which soon freezes into confusion tinged with fear.

The look alone carves a hole in my stomach, and I rasp, "Are you alright?"

"Am I—" Jack sits up too quickly, his palm flying to his lolling head, but he doesn't lose sight of me, anger suffusing his words. "What the *hell* are you?"

I hold my palms up, splaying the webbing between each finger, the shiny, pointy claws catching the moonlight emerging from behind dark clouds. "I can explain everything."

Jack's jaw ticks, strands of soaked hair falling over his eyes. I wish I could sweep them over his ear and out of the way. "You'll do it from the brig."

I've been metaphorically kicked in the gut, and I push out a breathy, "What?"

"Take her to the brig," Jack shouts over his shoulder.

"But Captain, she—" Red starts, but abruptly shuts his mouth when Jack's hand rises.

"Shouldn't we vote on it?" One man asks.

Like a fool, I look at Jack, hoping he'll agree, but all I get is a steely glare. Behind those eyes, there's disappointment, a melancholy sadness laced with uncertainty. And I can't blame him for it—I just can't.

"Not the time, lad," Duke answers him.

Mary shoves through the crowd, peeling off her jacket. "I'll bloody well take her. At least give the woman some clothes."

"Woman," Jack mutters accusingly.

Aranck is pushing his way through next, and I rise once Mary covers me with the coat. I say "sorry" to Jack as Mary leads me away, meaning it with every fiber of my being, but he only continues to peer at me, his glare softening like he can't decide how to view me.

ELEVEN

JACK

ARANCK FUSSES OVER me, checking me over, astonished by what Anne has done to bring me back to life. It's one of many questions in an ever-growing list consuming my mind. It's enough to make the world spin, and I push Aranck away along with anyone else who tries to stop the trek to my cabin. It didn't feel right to send her to the brig, but what else could I have done?

She's a fish. Or something, or fuck me, I don't know. And she saved my *life*.

I cross the threshold of my quarters and slam the door behind me. Instead of the satisfying sound of wood pounding against wood, something muffles it and keeps it from closing. Sighing, I spin on my heel and flop in the desk chair. Truffles is on my lap and kneading within three seconds, and his soft fur against my palm barely calms my nerves this time.

Duke breezes into my space, closing the door behind him and holding his hands up like he's about to get chastised. "I'm only here to talk some sense into ya."

Groaning, I slump into my seat and rest my head on the chair's back. "You're wasting your time, Duke. She lied. She deceived us. And I can't risk her harming anyone on the crew with those death claws she calls nails."

Duke combs his beard with his fingers and begins pacing a square in front of my desk. "She lied. She deceived. She's a *pirate*."

"Correction." I lift my head long enough to say, "She's a *fish* pretending to be a pirate."

Duke stops and glares at me. "You know she's not a damn fish. And yes, this is a blow, but have you stopped to think of the advantages of having a creature like her on our side?"

No. I haven't. I've barely had the time to process her hiding it, let alone what she is and how I can use it.

"It started as a plan to manipulate a *human* woman. I *know* human women. Know the way they think. But her? Whatever *she* is makes her unpredictable at best and a liability to the crew." I poke my finger into the desk with every point made. "She also never mentioned it. Not once."

"Why the hell would she?" Duke splays his arms to his sides. "She's a being that's not supposed to exist. If you ask me? She put a lot of faith in you and this crew to not turn her in to the first interested party we may come across."

My lip twitches.

No doubt she's worth a lot of money. And no doubt they'd strap her to a table and do ungodly, despicable experiments on her.

"Answer me this—" I lift a finger and scratch Truffles' head before moving him to my desk and rising. "—I've always believed in magic, myth, and the paranormal. So, why now, am I the one being cautious and skeptical?"

Duke grimaces in pain before limping to my desk and sitting on the corner. "Because honorably, you're concerned about your crew. But me? I'm not getting any younger, and I'm only glad I've gotten to witness magic, which is *real*." He chuckles and slaps his knee. "Believe me, everyone out there is feeling a mix of fear, excitement, and disbelief."

A knock sounds at the door.

"Come in," I call out.

Ragnar enters and looks between us. "Are we tossing her overboard or marooning her?"

"Ragnar," Duke scolds, flashing a warning glare at him. "Don't give him any ideas."

Ragnar jerks his head back. "I don't understand. *Bror*, you know it's dangerous keeping her on the ship. Not only has she been hiding it, but we don't know her capabilities."

Nausea bubbles in my stomach, and I turn to stare out the porthole window. The storm has moved on, the dark clouds streaking to reveal patches of glowing white starlight. And the rain has finally stopped. "I hear what you're saying, Ragnar. But I'm contemplating all possible uses for her. Because given what we've witnessed, she could've *also* killed us and commandeered the ship—" I catch Ragnar's gaze. "—but she hasn't."

Ragnar scrapes the pads of his fingers over his beard. "A single person cannot sail this vessel. She'd need, at minimum, six to operate it."

"Semantics, friend. You know where I was going with that."

Truffles bumps his head under Duke's arm, waiting for him to lift it so he can stroll onto his lap.

"Considering she's been on this ship for some time now and has posed about as much of a threat as Jack's damn cat, I'd say she's worth more to us not held up below deck." Duke sputters as Truffles flicks him in the mouth with his tail to tell him precisely what he thinks of that remark.

"And I say, there's no stopping her from using her powers, and only God knows what those are. Now that we all know she's not human—" Ragnar tugs on his hair. "—she has no reason to hide them, so what's to stop her from murdering us in our sleep?"

A pain begins to throb in my right temple, and I slam my fist onto the desk. "Enough. Both of you. You're giving me a bloody headache."

"Go *talk* to her, Jack," Duke encourages, welcoming my cat into his arms in a silent apology.

Ragnar thumbs his ear. "I'm going to come right out and say it. This is a bad idea."

"Opinion noted," I say, more gravel in my tone than usual. Checking my flintlock is adequately armed, I slip it back into my belt and crack my neck. "If you hear screaming, make sure to check on me. Otherwise, I'm not to be disturbed. Understood?"

Ragnar's mouth draws into a rigid line, and his grip tightens on his cutlass, but he nods in affirmation.

Sucking in a breath I intend to hold until I reach the brig, I make my way on deck. Murmurs, accusations, and outlandish remarks from the crew flood my ears.

"Think Cap will let us keep her?" One man asks Red.

Red rolls his eyes and shoves the man. "She's not a bloody dog."

"Did you see those scales? And those *bumps*? Disgusting," another man spats.

Irritation courses through my veins. Over what? The crew turning Anne into a scandal? Why did I *care*? Or do I *like* the way she looks? Scales and all. I awoke from unconsciousness only to find a sea goddess peering down at me. She could've left me for dead—could've let the water in my lungs drown me on the deck and claimed she did all she could to save me and steal my crew. Or she could've not bothered to pull me from the ocean altogether.

But. She. Did.

Growling, I storm below deck, pausing only when I hear Mary's voice. She's saying the crew is willing to bleed for each other because of my captaincy. And it edges into Anne earning my trust again.

Trust. Such a damn concept. And one I've never been much good at.

Anne and I need to hash this out *now*.

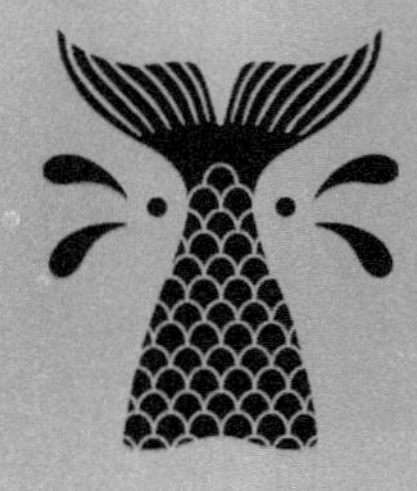

TWELVE

ANNE

I'M QUIET AS Mary leads me below decks, partially astonished she hasn't shunned me too. She put trust in me that I defiled by hiding who and what I am. Not to mention, my very existence will jar these mortals' beliefs. Had they believed in magic before? In myths and legends? I'm living proof it all exists. Would some of them not be able to handle the epiphany?

"I don't want to have to do this, darling, but Captain's orders and—" Mary whispers, opening one of the iron cell doors.

"It's alright, Mary. I understand. I'm not who I said I was. How can you all possibly trust me now?" My throat numbs. I gulp it away and walk into the cell. "Will you please grab my clothes? They're by the stairs."

"Of course," Mary says, leaving the door ajar as she fetches them.

She's still so trusting. But why?

After she returns, I clothe myself and hand her jacket back

116

before sitting on the cold stone floor, knees pressed to my chest, arms wrapped around them. "You can lock the door, you know?"

"I'll lock it when I'm good and ready. Why do it now? You gonna jump into the sea again if I don't?" Mary crosses her arms and presses to the cell entrance.

There is no way in the Seven Seas that I will return to the water soon. Now that it knows where I am, the Charybdis will undoubtedly follow us.

"No," I say hoarsely.

"Good. Glad we got that cleared up." Mary squats in front of me, nudging my knee with a finger. "I think you owe me an explanation, Anne."

I do, and then some. But where to begin? It's been centuries since I've had to explain this to a mortal.

"I'm a sea nymph," I start, wiggling my webbed toes that have begun to disappear the drier I become.

Mary pans her gaze from my feet to the ridges on my forehead. "Not a mermaid?"

"No. Mermaids can't conjure legs at will and have many more pointy teeth."

Mary's expression becomes grave, and she nods. "I get why you didn't say anything. You hid it to protect yourself. Many of us would have done the same, but—why are you here? And why can't you swim to where you need to go? Or *poof* there— or, I mean, do you poof?"

An ethereal headache forms in my temple, and I let my knees flop to the ground, plopping my hands in my lap. "Mary, I wouldn't know where to begin. But I can tell you I stole away on Jack's ship because, though I have powers, there's not much I can do to get back home with the Charybdis after me. It's a vast ocean out there."

"And where's home?" Mary, eyes blazing wide, hangs on to my every word now.

Atlantis. But I can't say this—one step at a time.

"The Mediterranean Sea," I whisper. And for once, this isn't a lie.

Mary's bushy brows furrow, and she taps a finger on her thigh. "This can't be a coincidence. Jack has never proposed going outside of the Caribbean. And when he does, it so happens to be to the Mediterranean, and *that* is where *you* need to go?"

My chest swells with something more than heartache—hope.

I sit up straight. "And I was in the tavern…"

"And you were in the fucking tavern." Mary drags her hands down her face. "Am I part of some divine happenstance here or something? Because I'm not sure this is what I signed up for." She cracks a gooey smile.

I want to hug her, cry on her shoulder, and wish to go back in time to try it a different way.

"How are you so calm? How are you not furious with me?" I dig my nails into my thigh to keep from crying.

"Oh, I'm mad. You lied to me. Hid this from me. But strangely, I'm also proud. I thought you were naïve and too quick to trust, but here you are, outwitting the entire crew. Even—Jack."

I hug my knees again and rest my chin on them. "I feel like I was just starting to earn his trust, and now—I'll probably never get it back after this."

"Bullshit," Mary quips, making my gaze snap to hers. "He has to be wary of you right now because he's got an entire crew to protect. There's something you gotta understand about a crew. We're closer than family. It goes deeper than blood." She presses her fingertips together. "We're loyal. We sail together. Kill together. Shit together. And with a captain like Jack? We *bleed* for each other."

Not knowing if I'll ever see my family again has me yearning to be a part of *this* one more than anything. But I wonder if I'm worthy of their trust because there's still so much about me they don't know and that I can't share.

"You've sworn to the code but now need to commit to it, darling, if it's what you want. Because if you do, it won't matter to us what you are." Mary rubs my arm. "But now comes the hard part. Convincing Jack of it. And for that, I don't envy you."

"Read, will you give us some privacy?" Jack's gruff voice says from the shadows as if he's been waiting for the right moment to announce his presence. "And lock the door."

My stomach flutters, my heart thunders, and my throat goes coarse. Mary sighs and backs away, closing the metal door with an ominous clang before locking it with a rusted key from a ring with several more.

The lantern illuminates only Jack's hand as it reaches out to take the keys, and Mary disappears. "Start *talking*."

THIRTEEN

JACK

I PEER AT Anne through the bars, struggling between disappointment and admiration for what she's done. Her scales and ridges have disappeared, that fiery red hair falling in damp tendrils over her shoulders and face. She's still so goddamned beautiful.

"Jack, I'm so sor—" Anne starts, leaping to her feet from the floor and moving to the bars, grabbing them.

I hold up a hand, forcing my expression to remain stony. "No. No apologies. No lies. All I want to hear is the *truth*."

Anne wrings her hands together after dropping them from the cell door. "Where do I begin?"

Great question.

"Why did you need my ship when you possess—" I make flapping gestures with my hands because I can't bring myself to say *fins* despite my fascination with them.

Anne sighs and backpedals until her ass hits the far wall. "I got lost and ended up here somehow—" Defensively, she fans her palm at me. "—honestly. I don't know how I got here, but my home is in the Mediterranean, and when I heard in the tavern that you were headed there, I thought it was as good of an opportunity as any to get out of Nassau."

I can't say I would've done much differently. But having the tables turned on you is still just as irritating as being the table-turner.

I let my eyes roam her forehead where blue luminescent ridges and scales had been only moments before. Her eyes have returned to their emerald hue, and her hair has regained its vibrant fire. It's a conundrum trying to decide which version of her is more gorgeous.

"And what exactly *are* you?" I pick at the worn leather on my belt with a thumb.

Anne's slender hands wrap around the bars, fingers idly caressing the rusting metal. "A sea nymph."

The skin beneath my right eye spasms.

"Most confuse us for mermaids, but we're different. I can conjure my tail or legs and control the seas. A mermaid is more categorized *as* a sea creature, whereas I'm more of a—" Anne pauses, waiting for me to lift my gaze to hers. "—deity."

The floor becomes wading waters, and I stumble back on my heels. How did I let this slip through my fingers? How could I have let something like this around my crew? And yet, as much a threat as she poses, she can also be the best asset any pirate captain could hope for.

"Jack," Anne whispers, reaching a hand through the bars but withdrawing it before I can decide if I want to touch her. "Another truth? I expected a ruthless captain and a vile crew that I wouldn't care if I used or not. The plan was to keep my head down, get where I needed to go, and take advantage when possible."

She sounds more like me with each passing second, which agitates me. But I don't want her to *stop*.

"I assume these plans changed at some point?" I dip my face near hers, grabbing the bar closest to her head.

She nods, her eyes panning to the floor, and I get lost for a few breaths, counting the freckles scattering her cheeks. "I didn't expect a crew to feel more like a—" Anne's eyes pinch shut, a pained wrinkle creasing above her nose. "—a family."

I suspect this single word weighs more on her than she'll ever admit. She's skillful at hiding her intentions, but some expressions are more complex to mask.

"And this *ruthless* captain?" Slipping a hand between the bars, I lift her chin with my knuckle.

When her eyes land on mine, a tightening coils in my gut. "Ruthless when he *needs* to be, not simply because he *can* be."

Agitation laced with optimism and intrigue sizzles in my chest. Growling, I turn away from her for fear of her gaze entrancing me somehow. "Anne, you have no idea what complications this causes. I don't know if I can trust you not to jeopardize us all."

Frantically, Anne uses the bars to pull herself closer to me, to the furthest corner of the cell. "I'm not asking you to trust me immediately. But I'm asking for the *chance*."

Keeping my back to her, I run the orange sash hanging from my waist between two fingers, the fabric snagging on my callused skin. "This would've been so much different if you'd have just come forward from the beginning."

"And what? Risk you all turning me in for profit? I didn't know you. And *more* truth? If it weren't for you falling into the sea, I probably still wouldn't have told you yet." Anne sighs and presses her forehead to the bars. "Call it cowardice or whatever you wish, but my kind has remained in the shadows for centuries since mortals stopped believing. How was I to know the reaction? The dangers?"

Damn it all to hell. There's no winning this round for either of us.

But then, something she's said perks my ear, and I swivel on my heel. "Your *kind*? How many of you are there?"

"I'm not sure. I couldn't give you an exact number. Hundreds? Thousands?"

The air is torn from my lungs, and I press a hand to my ribs. *Thousands*? "How do you all keep so hidden? If there's this many of you, surely, we would've seen one by now before— before you."

Anne traces a fingertip over her chapped lips. "We've become experts with blending in. Well, I suppose for me, until recently, that is." A weak smile tugs at her mouth.

Grinding my teeth, I yank the small bottle of rum water from my pouch and slip it between the bars for her. "Is Anne your real name?"

"Thank you," she whispers hoarsely, popping the cork and taking several small sips before answering. "No. Do you want to know what it is?"

This question creates a battle in my mind. On the one hand, I want to know out of sheer curiosity, but on the other, learning this will only make things too real. And with a name like Anne, it makes her so—human.

"Not today. Perhaps another time." Sniffing once, I scratch my chin and backpedal from the cell, trying to ignore the subtle disappointment edging her eyes. "At any rate, you will remain in the brig for now."

"What?" Anne exclaims, her eyes going wide as sand dollars. "Jack, you—"

"You are safer down here, and the crew is safer—" I clench my fists at my sides. "—from you."

"Jack," she whispers again, and the pain surrounding my name floating from her lips is almost enough to undo me.

Not daring to look at her, I move for the door. "I'll be sure Ragnar delivers daily rations to you."

"You *need* me," Anne declares, a new form of venom sparking in her voice.

I pause with my hand splayed at the door knob. After counting to three so as not to react impulsively, I storm back for the cell, glaring at her through the bars. "I don't *need* anyone, lovely."

"In this case, Rackham—" Anne rises to the balls of her feet, bringing her eyes to my chin level. "—you do."

She knows something I don't, the little minx.

A tick forms in my cheek, and I look to the heavens, reining in the bubbling irritation, before leveling my stare back on her. "Enlighten me."

"The jewel you're after? The one you incorrectly called the Sailor's Jewel?" Anne taps a fingernail against the metal, making rhythmic panging sounds.

I hadn't mislabeled it per se, but any accounts I've found through the years never named it, and I required something punchy to spark awe in my crew. "Continue," I encourage through gritted teeth.

"That jewel—" Blue luminescent scales seem to shimmer over Anne's cheeks. "—is the beacon for Atlantis."

Atlantis. It can't possibly—and she can't be—or, is she?

I furiously rub my chin to maintain composure. "I still fail to hear why I need *you?*"

Anne looks me square in the eye. If all of this hadn't happened, I may have torn the cell door from its hinges and had my way with her on the damp floor.

"Because even if you have a precise location, which I know you don't, you'd swim beneath the surface and see nothing but open water."

My brows squish together. "I'm not following."

"Atlantis could be right in front of you, and because you're a mortal, you not only wouldn't be able to access it, but you won't know it's *there.*" Anne gives a taunting glare to rival Blackbeard himself.

Twirling the brass ring on my right middle finger, I slowly nod. "And I'm going to guess you, being what you are, can access it?"

"And there's those smarts again."

A chuckle vibrates from my belly, and I reach between the bars, stroking my fingertips over those scarlet tresses. I know how soft they can be, but strangely I enjoy how taut the salt has made them. "Let me make something clear. If you're toying with me and whatever you claim puts me or my crew in danger, I will not hesitate to leave you at the next port. There are plenty of other ships you can steal away on."

Anne presses her face between the bars so nothing is blocking her razor-sharp expression. "And if you become my worst fear by telling anyone about what I am after I saved your life, putting it *all* at risk? I won't hesitate to kill you or any of the crew who threaten me."

I never knew my cock could grow hard from a woman's poisonous words, but here we are. Grinning, I lower my nose to hers, ever so lightly brushing it. "You sure you're not a pirate?"

She gingerly chews at the corner of her lip. "I don't know what I am anymore, Jack."

Nodding, I force myself to pull away with every molecule of my willpower, the memory of her hair tantalizing my skin. "I appreciate this information. But you'll still stay in the brig until I know I *do* need you."

And because I possess very little strength at this point in the conversation, I turn away before those jade eyes lure me in like an unforgiving Siren's call.

"You *cannot* be serious, Jack," she calls out, but I don't look back. "Captain," she yells, trying again, but I'm already exiting and pushing my back to the door once it's closed.

I'm fully aware the crew will vote for her freedom within days, but I'll leave her to her thoughts for now. Mythical being or not, Anne needs to realize who she's *meddling* with.

FOURTEEN

RHODE/ANNE

IT'S BEEN A week since Mary released me from the brig after announcing the crew unanimously voted on my freedom. It irked me to the core when Jack ordered, not once but twice, for me to stay imprisoned despite everything I'd told him. But after days alone with my thoughts and with nothing else to do but my ship duties, I realized I couldn't blame him much either. I pose as much liability to these mortals as the protection I can offer. And still, despite knowing I could escape my cell at any point, I stayed there to build trust with Jack. Little good it's done me.

Seas, it's been so long since I've felt this vulnerable and out of place. Most of my family have taken up lives amongst mortals, blending in and making the most of their eternities. But I've been content under the sea, protecting Atlantis and surfacing long enough to visit my family. It worked for me—until Atlantis had other plans. I've never imagined being this close to humans and *myself* with them. And piracy? As on-theme as it is, I've always been meant for life in the water, not sailing *on* it. But this, all of it, it feels—*right.*

Mary and Red are the only two crewmates who have tried to converse with me. Others pass by, uneasy or shaken, and most ignore my presence and *allow* me to exist among them. But the one person I want more than anything in the known universe to acknowledge me has given little more than nods and mumbles of greetings.

Calico Jack Rackham.

What in the Seven Seas is it about him that makes me unable to look away? To *yearn* for his trust and approval?

Tsking at the thought, I press my forearms to the ship's railing during my first much-needed breaks from swabbing the decks. The wind tousles my hair, and for once, the chilled sea mist coating my cheeks doesn't have me frantically drying my face. I close my eyes, relishing the bliss for the first time since Atlantis swept me away. The scales come and go, but by this point, they're familiar to the crew and they pay no mind. Their reservations toward me are warranted because they don't know the power I possess.

It's too much to explain to them, and I plan to keep as secretive about the details as I can unless situations force me into it—like Jack almost drowning. A man clears his throat beside me, gruff and hoarse, scents of tar, gunpowder, and tangy rust wafting from him. Not Jack.

"Basking in the sun, nymph?" Ragnar's voice asks.

I flutter open my eyes and crane my neck to look at his imposing form. "On a scheduled break, quartermaster. I assure you, I'm not idle." Turning my gaze to the water, I sip my liquid rations.

"That's not what I came to talk to you about." Ragnar's tanned, leathery fingers drum on the railing near my forearm.

When I turn to look at him full-on, he's staring at me steely-gazed. His eyes are glacial blue, but one is paler than the other, foggy even, as if he's partially blind in his left eye. "And just what do we have to talk about? The weather? Proper flint-lock loading techniques?"

The latter wouldn't be such a bad idea, considering I've only ever handled a blade in battle.

"Do not take the captain's warnings lightly, *rødtop*," Ragnar continues to beat his finger against the wood, his gaze unwavering.

I lift my hat enough to scratch my forehead. "Which one? He's created quite the list against me. It's become increasingly difficult to keep track."

Ragnar lowers his face toward mine, his jaw clenching and accentuating the thin, gnarled scar at the corner of his chin. "If we feel the crew is in danger from you at any point, we will take action. The captain gives the orders, but the QM is the one to carry them *out*." He points to his eyes with two fingers and then to my face. "Do we understand one another?"

My skin crawls. Mary always talks so highly of Ragnar, like they're two peas in a pod and the best of friends, but this version of him is one I don't wish to be on the wrong side of. Jack can be ruthless, cunning, and deceitful, but Ragnar is anarchy waiting to be unleashed. And now I know why Jack made him his right-hand man.

Sliding closer, I rise to the balls of my feet, bringing me another inch or two closer to the mountain that is Ragnar. "If

I try to harm any of these people, I'll *leave*. But like I told Jack, I'll also not hesitate to defend myself."

It's gone instantly, but there's a hint of an upper lip twitch. "I'd expect nothing less. Glad to hear we're on the same page." After he gives a curt nod, he beats his fist once against the railing and is off to intimidate another unknowing poor soul.

Instinctively, I rub my throat.

"What the hell did Ragnar have to talk to you about? Looked intense." Mary sidles beside me, hanging both arms over the ship's side.

"Promises. Threats." I shrug, sighing as more sea mist soothes my drying skin. "Nothing I've not gotten peculiarly used to since setting foot on this ship."

Mary bumps into me. "It'll get better. I promise. You've made the first step, and we haven't brought in a haul yet."

Chewing on my lip, I glance at Jack standing stoically at the helm. "Not so sure everyone is as quick to accept me, Mary."

Mary grabs my face with one hand and turns it to look at her. "He'll come around, too. Trust me. How can you be *this* impatient when you've been alive for hundreds of years?"

"Decades-old or centuries old, I'm still a living creature with emotions and feelings." I bat her hand away and shove the rum bottle in my pocket. "Better get back to work."

"Anne, I didn't mean any offense, I—" Mary says with a frown, cutting herself short when she spots my warm smile.

"Yes, you did. And it's alright. I'll keep scrubbing this deck so clean I can see my reflection until something else warrants my attention." I kick the bucket in front of me and drop to my knees.

Mary squats behind me, her arms wrapping around my torso, and she gives me a quick peck on the cheek. "Your passive aggressiveness is legendary, darling."

I bite back a grin as I scrub the deck and watch Mary shout orders at several men who are holding the ropes limp instead of adjusting the sails as they should be.

An hour passes before I catch Jack staring at me from the opposite side of the ship. I expect him to quickly avert his gaze, to pretend he'd been leering at something else—anything but me, the traitorous sea nymph. But he doesn't. Instead, he holds me captive in his eyes, the wind tousling his dark locks in wavy tendrils. I've been hunched over on my hands and knees, but I sit up straight, resting on my haunches and limply holding the scrubbing brush in my palm.

Then I hear it, distant at first but too recognizable to ignore. The melody is enough to tear me away from Jack's lingering gaze because nothing else could've coaxed me. I leap to my feet, terror wrenching my spine, and sprint to the ship's side, closing my eyes to focus on the overlapping voices catching in the wind. The haunting and eerie refrain has a breath hitching in my throat. And when I open my eyes, catching sight of the fog building from the sea's depths, I sprint for the hull, pushing crewmates aside. The wind launches my hat from my head, and I don't stop to retrieve it.

Sirens. Fucking Sirens.

"Jack," I shout, breathless and frantic.

Jack pauses with his hands on the wheel, his jaw tightening. "What is it?"

"Everyone. Every single crew member except for me and

Mary, you're—" Pausing only long enough to catch my breath, I stare at Jack pleadingly. "—you're in danger."

Jack drums his fingers on the wheel's pegs. "Why not you and Mary?"

"It won't affect us because the call only persuades—" Gulping, I climb the stairs to stand in front of the pirate captain. "—mortal men."

Jack's squint deepens, his hands clenching the pegs now. "What's happening, Anne?"

"Sirens," I whisper. "Have you heard of them?"

A tick forms in Jack's cheek, and he turns his gaze to the fog, which is nearing closer and closer to the ship. "Of course, I have, but—"

I press a hand to Jack's face and turn him toward me to *focus* on me. "*I'm* real, Jack. So are they. And we only have moments before their song falls on your ears."

The gleam in his eyes tells me I have him at first, but skepticism and mistrust soon take over, and he brushes my fingers away. "So, we *ignore* them. Shove cloth in our ears if we have to. They can't possibly affect every man on board."

"No, Jack." Grabbing his face again, I hold his gaze using *both* hands. "There's nothing you can do to stop it. We must secure all of you; it's the only way."

"Secure us?" Jack nuzzles against my touch for a fraction of a second but grimaces soon after. "What do you mean? Like with bloody rope?"

"Yes," I breathe, tightening my grip against his cheeks. "Please. Now isn't the time to let your stubborn-ass attitude overshadow what's happening. I don't want you to *die*, Jack."

He lifts a hand and lightly trails a fingertip down my forearm, still looking at me. "And I suppose you can't reason with them? Being maidens of the sea and all that?"

It's the first time he's openly discussed it since we spoke in the brig, and my heart is soaring at the most inconvenient time.

"No. I'm afraid it doesn't work like that." Goosebumps litter my skin, and he's still tantalizing it with his touch.

Jack searches my face before he surveys the clueless crew going about their business behind me. "Alright. There's extra rope in the back corner below deck. Get Glog to show you where it is and bring it up. Meanwhile, I'll tell the crew why we're asking them to be tied to heavy, immovable objects." Jack pinches the bridge of his nose.

After nodding vigorously, I give Jack's cheeks a final squeeze before I slip across the deck toward the stairs. The Siren song has grown so loud that several men are already lured toward it, eyes wide and entranced, feet dragging across the wood.

When I get below deck, Glog stares up bewildered, a metal spoon dripping liquid within his grasp. "Was that you singing up there, Anne?"

It's not as loud down here, and I pat his face, snapping his attention away from the sound. "No. And I don't have time to explain, Glog. But you're all in danger, and I need you to help me lug some rope on deck. Can you do that, please?"

Glog's eyes keep rising skyward, and I have to snap my fingers at him. "Yeah. Yes. I can do that."

With coils of rope wrapped around each arm, we cart them upstairs. Mary is already tying several men to barrels filled with cannonballs, shoving them back whenever they try to stand and move toward the melody.

Jack is still at the helm, focused on something in front of him, head twitching every other second. I point at a spot for Glog to sit and quickly get to work, tying him while Mary secures Duke despite his barking protests.

I'm heading for Jack next when he turns toward me, his nostrils flaring and teeth bared. "If this is a trick to steal the ship or run us into the ground for your own—"

I slap a hand over his mouth before he can finish, my stomach tingling at the feel of his beard tickling my palm. "It's not a trick, Jack. And if it is, Mary will see that you all are safe. Right, Mary?" I shout to her but keep my eyes fixed on Jack.

"It won't come to that, Captain, but you know I'll keep your balls intact," Mary yells back, tugging on the final knot she's tied around Red.

"Come on, Jack," I whisper, holding my hand toward the anchor pull and lifting the rope into view.

He runs a knuckle under his bottom lip before relinquishing his hold on the wheel and taking a seat, encircling his arms around the device. I kneel beside him and start winding the rope several times, making the appropriate knots to keep him still.

"You've done this before. My, my, aren't you always full of surprises?" Jack's voice is like a caress—silky, smooth, and the faintest hint of gravel near the shell of my ear.

I pull the last knot extra tight, making him grunt, and flash him a crooked smile. "Shut up, Jack."

Our noses are a breath apart. I can count the golden flecks in his eyes amidst the mahogany, and he tilts his head to one side. "You certainly like to say my name a lot lately," he says.

"It's a simple, strong name. I like saying it." I pan his face, noting the line of hair missing in his right brow from a small scar.

"Anne is simple and strong too, you know." Jack sighs and beats the back of his head against the anchor hold, his knees bouncing. The Sirens' song is now affecting him. "What's your real name?"

My throat tightens, and I fight an internal battle between desiring nothing more than for him to know *me* and adoring that he knows *this* version of me, the pirate version. "Rhode," I whisper into his ear.

Jack waves his hand, dismissing the name. He bumps his head against mine like a lion with his lioness. "You'll forever be Anne to me."

My heart plummets, soars, and blazes into the sky.

"And you're going to—" Jack winces and pulls at the ropes, the Sirens' call booming across the deck now. "—you're going to want to add another rope. Because I'm not sure how long this will hold me." He flexes his arms, loosening one knot, and I quickly scramble for another rope, winding it around him. "Don't let any of the crew get loose. Promise me."

Mary struggles with Ragnar at the mast, shoving him back as he digs his heels against the deck to push closer to the sound. All the male crew members writhe beneath their bindings, wailing over not being able to answer the Sirens beckoning them.

Drawing a breath, I give the captain a firm nod. "I promise."

It's the last thing I get to say to him before the Sirens' melody consumes him.

Feet dangle from the crow's nest, and I gasp. How could we

have forgotten about Squid? "Mary, Squid is still up there," I shout.

Mary shoves her foot to Ragnar's chest, pinning him to the mast. "He'll be fine. He can't hear a thing," she says, pointing to her ear.

It explains so much. He prefers being alone because he can't hear conversations and prefers the ability to *see* in all directions from up high.

Jack growls and loosens the ropes again, his nostrils flaring, cheeks puffing as he stretches his arms. I grab on one end, pulling it taut, but he shrugs out of it before I have a chance to retie the knot. He's free and storming for the railing, shoving me aside like a discarded flour sack before I can stand.

The fog lifts one Siren to Jack's eye level. Her true form, with blazing red eyes, onyx snake hair, sunken cheeks, and curved claws, is obvious to me. But to Jack, she'll appear as what he finds most beautiful in a mortal.

I'm at his side, using my divine strength to wedge myself between the Siren and Jack. The Siren is hissing at my back and speaking obscenities in ancient Greek.

"Jack," I shout, bunching his shirt and shaking him. "You've got to resist. They aren't what you think."

"It's so beautiful," Jack mumbles, his gaze glassy and in another realm. "The music. Can't you hear it?" He pushes me aside, but I'm back in front of him, shoving and punching his chest.

"Don't do it. You can't," I plead, slapping him in the face, but it does nothing. My slap is a minor inconvenience in his grand plan to leap from the ship to the jagged rocks hidden by the fog below.

"Watch me," Jack declares, climbing onto the railing.

I'm unsure what motivates me to do what I think of next or why it'll work, but I do it anyway. Grasping his face, I pull it to mine and kiss him. It's like kissing someone unconscious at first, but soon, his lips brush mine, and his arm snakes around my lower back.

Jack's eyelashes brush my cheek, and I pull away, staring at him gazing at *me* and no longer focused on the Siren. "That's the third time our mouths have been fused for all the wrong reasons," his voice croaks, that arm still firmly wrapped around me, almost possessively. "We're going to have to rectify that."

I press my palms over his chest. "Right now, we need to save the crew. And you need to steer this ship away from those rocks." The same rocks we brush against the moment the words leave my lips, making the ship lurch to a grinding stop.

"Shit," Jack shouts, turning away.

Testing a hypothesis, I run to Red and plant my lips to his, befuddled when he doesn't kiss me back and still pulls at his ropes.

"What the hell are you doing?" Jack shouts. "Are you *trying* to make me jealous, woman?"

My mouth falls agape. "It worked on you. I thought maybe I—" I throw my hands to my hips and glare at Jack. "*Are* you jealous?"

"No," Jack answers defensively, lacing it with a snarl, and leaps to the wheel, skipping the stairs.

"Is Jack alright?" Mary asks, a wrinkle forming in her brow. She's still fighting with Ragnar to keep him put.

"Yes, he—" I trace my middle finger over my bottom lip.

"—he fought through it somehow."

"Anne, fend off those bloody Sirens while I get us heading in the opposite direction," Jack grunts as he furiously turns the wheel. The ship groans and cracks, slowly dislodging from the rocks.

I yank my cutlass from its sheath and stand posed at the railing. That same Siren floats in front of me, her tail whipping through the fog like water, her long fingers wrapping over the ship's side. There's no hesitation from me before I bring the blade down at her knuckles, but she moves away in time, cackling.

"Curious as to why a nymph carouses with the likes of humans," she's speaking in scattered whispers. "You've cost us a meal. And we are *starving*."

"Tough. Shit. These mortals—" I raise the sword. "Are mine." Jabbing it forward, I catch the Siren by surprise, slicing her shoulder.

She hisses with her black forked tongue, her hair spiking. The ship whirls in the other direction, and the Sirens' song morphs into shrieks of agony and despair, gradually snapping the crew back to reality. The wind favors us, kicking up and filling the sails, giving us the speed to distance ourselves from the Sirens' forsaken island quickly. I release a shaky breath, sheathe my cutlass, and undo everyone's bindings.

Everyone is still alive. Everyone is safe.

As I undo the final knot on the last remaining crew member, I catch Jack's gaze at the helm for what has to be the umpteenth time since I snuck onboard The Revenge. But unlike any other time, *this* time, his eyes blaze with intensity, understanding, and ravenous intrigue.

FIFTEEN

JACK

IT'S THE SECOND time the red-headed fiery sea nymph has saved my hide since joining our merry band of miscreants. My ego should be far more bruised, but it's also gotten her mouth on me multiple times, and I have *zero* complaints. The Sirens' song had muddled my brain like the fog disguised the perilous rocks they lured us toward. A part of me, internally screaming from the back of my brain, remained completely aware of *everything*. As soon as Anne's lips met mine, I felt them but couldn't react until suddenly, the haze lifted, the Siren's influence disappeared, and I held her in my arms.

It's been several hours since we sailed from the rocky island, and the crew still showers Anne and Mary with unending gratitude. Those two won't have to do chores for the unforeseeable future.

"I've seen everyone thanking our mythical visitor except for one mule-headed individual who rhymes with *smack*," Duke says gruffly.

I rub the pad of my thumb against one of the wheel's wooden pegs. "In due time, Duke. Can you blame me for being a smidge jittery that some random rocks will appear to impale my ship after those escapades?"

"I *can* blame you, and I will because that sounds like an excuse for not pulling your head out of your ass." Duke coughs into his fist, grimacing and scratching his beard after it subsides.

Anne's coral hair stands out amidst the crew like the brightest star in a clear night sky. She laughs with them, slaps their backs, and talks about lord only knows what, but she makes it look effortless. This crew, these people, have already become her friends and family.

"I *will* thank her. But I can't grovel at one of my crew member's feet in front of the rest of them." I wet my lips, that goddamned twitch sparking in my cheek again.

Duke clears his throat, swigging some grog to keep from coughing before wiping his sleeve over his mouth. "She's not just a crew member. We both know that. I'm not saying to declare your undying gratitude aloud in the middle of the deck, Jack. Take her somewhere private and ensure she knows you appreciate her risking her life for you—twice."

Somewhere private. Heaven help me, as if I can trust myself anywhere in private with this woman now. But then again, maybe I don't *want* to trust myself.

"I'll talk with her," I clip, turning the wheel to make the sails catch the wind.

Duke steps closer, his stare burning the side of my head. "I meant *now*."

Rolling my eyes, I step away from the helm with my palms lifted. "You are as stubborn as I am. We've been spending entirely too much time together in close quarters."

Duke chuckles—gravelly and hoarse. "On *that,* we agree."

Cutting through the busied crew hauling rope and repairing the small holes the ship received from the rocks, I motion to Anne with a finger, keeping my face neutral. "Anne, a word?"

Anne gives sidelong glances to Glog and Mary, who tease her, playfully shoving her as if she's about to be chastised by the captain. I open the door to my cabin and hold it, ushering her inside before following and closing it behind us. It takes three seconds for Truffles to emerge from his cat slumber and immediately begin curling figure eights through Anne's calves.

"Aw, hey, little one. It's been so long since I've seen you, yes it has," Anne coos, crouching to pet my cat's back and head.

Making a clicking sound with my teeth, I produce a dried fish. Truffles happily saunters to my desk to receive the small treat.

No sooner is the cat content and Anne stands; I cross the room, making her backpedal until her ass presses to the door, and I hover my chest near hers. "It's come to my attention that I've yet to thank you properly."

"And you chose to do that by cornering me?" Her slender fingers explore the sash tied around my hips.

I inhale her scent, the memory of those satin lips moving against mine, torturing my very being. "Mm, does it make you—uncomfortable?"

"Not in the slightest," she breathes out, her back arching, pushing her hips against me, and those emerald eyes grow sultry and heavy-lidded.

Slipping her hat from her head, I toss it behind me, ignoring the sound of skittering claws as it almost lands on Truffles. "What kind of a name is Rhode, anyway?"

She smiles, sweet and bright. "One not of this world. But I'm not so sure how much it suits me nowadays." Her finger traces the scar on my brow, the touch trailing down my cheek, neck, and collarbone.

"Thank you, Annie," I whisper, catching her curious hand and kissing her knuckles.

Her eyes brighten, her body shivering, *shuddering* from my touch. "You don't have to thank me, Jack. Because I'd do it repeatedly, and a thousand times over if it means—" Anne rises on her toes, bringing her mouth a breath from mine. "—having you in my life."

I cup her chin with both hands, ready to devour her, to make her mine. Our mouths are so close now her breath moistens my chapped lips, and as I draw closer, my thumbs swirling her cheeks, her eyes closing to receive me, the clanging godforsaken bell goes off on deck.

"Christ," I curse, sucking in a breath and steadying myself against the door with one hand.

Anne flops back to her heels, concern wrinkling her forehead. "What does that sound mean? An alarm of some kind?"

"They've spotted a ship. Either it's a shipment vessel or the Royal fucking Navy here to ruin our day. I sincerely hope it's the former," I mumble before giving a peck to her forehead.

We both freeze. How easily the action came to me.

"You're welcome," *Saint* Anne says, blissfully breaking our silence. "Captain," she finishes, chewing on her bottom lip as she says it.

This woman is bound to be the death of me, and I can die the happiest, luckiest son of a bitch on the planet.

"Ready for your first sea battle that doesn't involve melodious wenches trying to skewer us with jagged rocks?" I open the door and hold my hand to the exit.

Truffles stares at me indignantly before he plops his butt on the center of the map resting on my desk, his tail swishing, waiting for me to call him.

I sigh because I rarely allow my cat on deck, and he scarcely has an issue with it except for now, which is the worst possible moment for a feline to scurry the floorboards. "Sorry, Truff. Maybe next time."

And as I close the door, he lets me know what he thinks of my answer by hacking up a furball that he'll undoubtedly plant dead center on my desk—little bastard.

Anne rushes on deck but steals a glance at me—a sensual quirk of her brow, which I can only hope means something akin to "we'll continue what was about to happen in your cabin later."

I flash her a wink and a knowing smile before rolling my shirt sleeves to my elbows. "What do we have, gents?"

"Squid spotted a merchant due east. The first one we've seen since leaving Nassau," Red announces, eagerly rubbing his palms together.

Thank Christ. The last thing we need is the Navy pricking our asses after dealing with the Sirens. What we *do* need is a win in a big, big way.

"Right then. You all know the drill. Hoist the colors, ready the sails, and for fuck's sake, ensure your flintlocks are loaded and cocked," I command, making my voice thunder across the deck.

Anne scurries to Mary's side, shoving the pistol handle at her. Anne cinches her brow and shakes her head, pushing the flintlock away. Mary glares at her before shoving the weapon into her hand and pointing at Anne's belt.

Better to have it and not need it, is what I'd be saying to her.

I storm for the helm, Ragnar tossing my hat as I pass him. He's already barking orders to the men in charge of the rigging.

When I reach the wheel, Duke is peering into a looking glass, and he holds it out to me with an affirming nod. "Should be some nice haul on that one. Judging from the route, they seem to be crossing from the British colonies to Africa. They're probably carting rum and gunpowder, if not other goods."

"Now that's what I like to hear." Grinning, I lift the glass to my eye, squinting at the blurred image of the ship in the distance. They only have four cannons.

This was one of the advantages of stealing from merchant ships. Though they were armed to protect from pirates, it was never something we couldn't handle. And that's *if* several men became brave enough to take a stand. This is rarely the case. With any luck, it'll be a quick job with new plunder below deck in time for supper.

With the black and white Jolly Roger skull and crossed swords flapping defiantly in the breeze atop the mast, I patiently wait as we edge closer to the vessel. The cargo ship doesn't try to outrun us, nor does it attack, but it simply sails to a crawl so subtle it's as if they've stopped altogether.

Once we're resting side by side in calm waters close enough for the men on the other ship to hear me, I cup my hands around my mouth. "Which one of you do they call Captain?"

"I'm Captain," one man says, holding a hand skyward as he steps forward from the crowd.

Like a proper jackass, I grin and wave. "Good afternoon. I'm Captain Rackham. By now, I'm sure you've noticed we're not, in fact, a fellow merchant vessel."

The other captain rolls his eyes before folding his arms in a huff. "We took note of your flag, yes. But you lot are shit out of luck. Another pirate crew already looted us."

Big fat liar.

"Huh. Funny." I tap a finger on my lips. "Because you'd think, if that were the case, you'd be headed east back to the Americas. And here you are heading straight on the trade route to Africa."

A man beside the captain elbows him in the side as if to silently say he'd told him it'd never work.

The captain sighs and drags a frustrated hand over his silver beard. "Fine. Alright. Can you blame me for trying?"

"Not one bit." Hopping from the helm, I move to the railing, looking at him dead in the eye. "I *can* be a fair captain. That choice is yours. Let us peacefully board and allow us to relieve you of most of your cargo. Or resist, and things will get ugly quickly. But know this—" I hang onto one of the rope riggings and hover over the ship's edge. "—we *will* board either way."

Grumbling, the captain tears off his hat. "Just get what you want and get the hell out of our way, pirates."

Music to my sinful ears.

"Smart lad." Flashing the fellow captain a wink, I turn to my crew. "Boys, would you be so kind as to drop anchor and lay out the planks?"

The crew is a flurry of activity, and Anne sidles beside me with her hands on her hips. "And you say I'm the one full of surprises."

"Come again?" I check that my flintlock is ready while pretending to only half pay attention to her despite the urge to undress her with my eyes.

"Wouldn't it have been just as easy to catch them off guard and raid the ship?"

I swear this woman is after my heart, balls, and anything else she can get her gorgeous hands on.

"Sure. But why risk injury or the lives of my crew when ninety-five percent of these merchants value their lives and families over something as trivial as material possessions that don't belong to them?" I'm watching the crew lay out the first plank from our ship to theirs, and anxious jitters have me flicking my belt.

She moves closer, brushing our jacket sleeves. "You *do* run a different outfit here, don't you?"

"Someone said to me once—" Without hesitation, nor shame, I wrap a hand over her hip and lower my lips to ear. "—ruthless when I have to be, never simply because I *can* be."

The sound of her swallowing air, *gulping* it down, pulls a wicked grin to my lips. And when the last plank falls with a gratifying *thwack*, the smile turns villainous.

I pat Anne's waist and step back. "Shall we plunder

graciously?"

A certain glint I haven't seen in her gaze sparks before she bites her lip. At Mary's side, the two pirate women are among the first to walk across the planks to the awaiting merchant ship. I follow behind them with an extra swagger in my gait.

Once my boots thud against the deck, I tip my hat to the disgruntled captain. "We greatly appreciate your hospitality on this fine day, Captain."

The captain refuses to make eye contact with me and snarls when he sees my crew hurrying past him with crates and sacks cradled in their arms. "There's no need to talk, scallywag. Just get the fuck off my ship."

Wagging my finger at him like scolding a dog, I meander through the crowd of nervous merchants. "Now, now. There's no need for such hostility. I used to be one of you, you know? Such a lonely existence it becomes—and a poor one at that."

"You? A merchant?" The captain scoffs and spits tobacco. "You're a disgrace to the profession."

My jaw tightens, heat flushing my neck, and I'm ten seconds from retorting when Anne pauses near me, a crate of rum bottles in her grasp. Her ears perk, and she slowly pivots on her heel. "Jack, something isn't right."

A knot carves into my gut, and I hear it the moment she speaks—the hammer of a flintlock pulling back. In unison, Anne and I turn toward the sound, our pistols removed from their holsters and aimed. The crate of liquor falls to the deck, the bottles clanging together but, fortunately, not breaking.

"It *isn't* right," a younger blonde man shouts, the arm holding the pistol shaking uncontrollably.

With our weapons raised, I sidestep to one side while Anne covers the other.

"What the shit are you doing, boy? I ordered you all to stand down," the captain shouts, keeping his hands poised in the air.

"What—what happened to us all voting?" the blonde man asks, switching his aim between me and Anne. And I sure as hell wish he'd keep it on *me* because every moment it turns on her, I want to tear his eyeballs from their sockets.

"What do you think this is? A fucking democracy?" The captain stomps his foot. "Stand. Down."

The boy's gaze flares with rage. He's not going to listen. "No. It isn't fair. We go back without delivering the supplies, and we don't get paid while these—these fucking pirates get to take it all by force. It isn't—" He points the pistol at Anne, his finger moving for the trigger, and I blow a hole in the side of his head before he even entertains the *thought*.

This had to be the day of the *other* five percent. And now—we do things the hard way.

If a man's blood sprayed on her cheek and shirt bothers Anne, she doesn't show it. The deck quickly becomes a tidal wave of clashing cutlasses and pistol fire. Anne drops to her knees, avoiding a slashing sword aimed for her neck, and still crouching, circles to the other side of her attacker, plunging the blade into his back. Anne doesn't pause or react. She pulls her sword free, swings it, and lunges toward the next enemy.

I'm the one standing dumbfounded, and I may have blocked a blade or two, may have even stabbed several men trying to catch me off guard, but my focus remains on *her*—Anne. Just as she had made socializing with my crew look effortless, so too is her prowess with a sword. It's dawning on me—she's a mythical being. These moves and these instincts can very well be ancient. The thought makes my pulse race. Anyone can run me through where I stand, and I won't care because I can't tear my gaze away.

Mary's voice shouting my name snaps me back to reality—but only partially. I'm cutting through merchants to get them out of my way. Their foolishness keeps me from the majestic sea nymph currently defending me *and* my crew with every thrust and sway of her cutlass.

I break long enough to snatch my leather gunpowder pouch from my belt and reload my pistol, snapping the cartridge back once finished. Mary removes both daggers from their hilts at her hips and stabs them into the neck of a man who dared to tackle her. She shoves the now-dead man off and leaps to her feet, collecting the daggers from the corpse. With Mary's back turned, another man storms behind her. I aim my pistol and fire at his chest, sending him flying to the deck on his back before he gets within paces of her. Mary nods in appreciation.

Anne continues to handle anything the petty merchants, unaware they're fighting a deity, bring her way. We're fighting for our lives, the cargo, and our way of life. Gradually, the merchants' numbers dwindle. The battle continues around the perimeter of the ship, but I take the opportunity, trotting behind Anne, my chest heaving at the sight of her torn shirt stained with blood, dirt, and oil.

"Anne," I call out, my voice thunderous.

She's nearly breathless when she turns to face me, the sword held firmly in her grasp, but her expression softens when her gaze lands on me. I grab her free hand and yank her toward me, our chests colliding, and my mouth is on hers before she has a chance to rationalize any of it. Keeping my sword ready at my side, I use my free hand to curl around the back of her neck, pulling her tighter against me and deepening the kiss.

Anne kisses me back, a sweet taste laced with the rust and dirt coating her lips. She whimpers against my mouth, her hand bunching my shirt between my shoulder blades. The metallic clangs of the crew fighting the remaining merchants around us fade, replaced by only her breathing and the sensual murmur in her throat.

The wind catches her hair when we pull away, making a fiery tendril blaze between us. I secure it behind her ear, and an uneasy yet calming sensation settles around us like a dull shockwave. It's enough to make us stumble, and I press a hand to her back, squinting at her to gauge if she felt it, too.

"Did you—" I start, searching those mossy eyes for an answer.

"Feel that?" She finishes for me. "Yes," she whispers.

"Please, we relent, we relent," the merchant captain shouts, falling to his knees in a defeated heap with his hands clasped behind his head.

Ragnar stands over the captain, the point of his blade a hair from the man's nose. "When only you and three of your men remain, *now* is when you surrender?"

"We—we can still get back home with this many. Please, the boy is dead. I never wanted any of this to happen," the captain pleads, tears staining his dirt-ridden cheeks.

Ragnar shoves the point of his sword into the man's sternum, making him cry out.

After squeezing Anne's hand, I turn to the scene unfolding

before us, dragging the point of my cutlass dramatically across the deck as I walk. "I don't recall you sounding as apologetic when you were telling us *pirates* to get the fuck off your ship." Moving in front of the captain, I poise on the blade. "Nor when you called me a disgrace of an ex-merchant."

The captain clasps his hands together in prayer. "Please. Please, I beg you. I have a family."

Ragnar growls beside me, still thirsty for blood.

Grasping Ragnar's shoulder, I coax him back and bend forward to make the captain look at me. "You should be eternally grateful I'm feeling merciful today. But remember this: you'll be hard-pressed to encounter another pirate captain with the same scruples. You might want to re-think your life's choices, *family* man." Standing straight, I shove my boot into his chest. "Round up the rest of the cargo, and let's get the hell out of here."

Anne sheathes her sword and rejoins me at my side, exhaling a haggard breath. "Ninety-five percent, huh?"

Smirking, I ignore her jab and wipe my sleeve over a patch of dirt on her cheek, swiping it away. "You're quite the sight with a sword in your hand."

"Oh, yeah?" Grinning like a vixen, she strolls past me, brushing her hip against mine. "You should see me underwater." And she leaves me with that gem, making her way to Mary, Red, and the rest, checking on them.

I've believed in magic since my late mother told me bedtime stories about hydras, epic heroes, and flying horses. And while I can't place or make sense of what settled around us after that kiss, something in my gut tells me that it was some form of acceptance—by the *universe* itself.

SIXTEEN
RHODE/ANNE

THE CREW MOVES around me, hauling loot or limping toward Aranck for assistance with the few injuries we took from the merchants. I'm carrying a sack on board, but I focus on Jack. Something happened during that kiss. And not just a spark between us, but something far beyond even what I, an ancient being, could comprehend. It's made me all the more curious about him—ravenous for him. I've rarely befriended mortals during my time and have never been with one romantically. But Jack Rackham is more worthy of godhood as a human being than half the actual deities I know.

Jack busies himself with barking orders at the crew, directing which items to store below deck. I'm listless and unmoving, when Mary elbows me, arching her thick brows once I finally look at her.

"Where in the flying hell is your mind?" Mary squints an eye and darts her gaze in the direction I'd been staring before I can look elsewhere.

The burlap sack in my grasp falls to my feet in a heap, and I'm tracing my middle finger over my lips a breath later. "He kissed me, Mary."

"You're saying that like it was the first time." Mary lifts my abandoned bag to the top of the crate she's carrying and ushers me to walk in front of her.

"No. I mean, *really* kissed. It was—" I'm at a loss for words and walk across the planks to The Revenge in a daze, instinctually ducking below riggings and avoiding barrels sticking out in the walkways.

Mary rests the crate on a barrel and grabs the crook of my arm, halting me. "You're actually put off over this—like head in the clouds, kitten with a ball of yarn type level."

She's right. This *has* distracted me. His absence has made me jittery, and I feel like I'm endlessly swimming circles around the ship.

"It's fine. I'm *fine*." I yank the sack from the crate. "Everything is just delightful."

Mary snorts and chuckles, following me below deck to store our crates. "You can lie to yourself all you want, but not me. Only cure for what's eating at you, Miss Bonny, is a good fucking from our resident pirate captain." Mary pats my cheek and barks with laughter as she walks away.

Using my boot, I kick a barrel with a disgruntled sigh. I'm almost a thousand years old and perfectly capable of controlling *urges*. She's speaking to me like I'm an adolescent girl. Jack isn't the first handsome, charismatic, intelligent warrior—my thighs pinch together, heat pooling in my belly.

Seas. I *am* gone for him.

"I heard you were quite the spectacle on that merchant ship," Glog says, jotting in a journal as he takes inventory of the loot. "That your skills with a sword saved most of the crew?"

The heat moves from my stomach to my cheeks, and I smile humbly. "It wasn't just me. *Everyone* contributed to that victory."

"Modest, too. You really are a gem, aren't you?" Glog pauses with a quill pressed to the page, eyeing me for some form of response. When I can't muster one, he licks the quill's tip, grins, and continues writing.

Jack's voice rolls over the deck like a wave—an authority demanding respect. It sends a current of static fluttering beneath my skin. He waves an arm to get Squid's attention. "Squid, look lively up there."

Slowly, taking one step at a time, I ascend the stairs.

"The first spit of land you spy, we're going to make camp and celebrate our first haul by consuming *this* crate," Jack adds.

I've reached the top when Jack hoists a crate of clanking bottles to the ship's railing, grinning as the crew cheers. Squid smiles from the crow's nest, hurrying to the highest point and balancing with one hand.

Ragnar yanks the box from Jack's hands, hiding it from the crew until the right time. Jack laughs and pats his quartermaster's back before wrapping his hands around the wheel's pegs. The impatience to be near him, within the same breath as him, is almost too much to stand, and I'm working through the crowd, my legs moving at their own will despite my brain's protests.

It's taking far too long to reach him between crew members

thanking me or pulling me to their side in quick flashes of celebration. But once I'm there, his scent—citrus, and brine—calms me in a way I never thought possible.

Jack casually props a hip on the wheel, the smug grin plastered to his lips all too telling. It's as if he knows what plagues my mind from my body language. "Hello, Annie."

His voice is liquid velvet when he says my name—birth-given or not. I slide closer to him, purposely brushing our elbows. "Hey, Jack."

He brushes his thumbs against the worn wood, a devious glint in his gaze as he eyes me side-long. "Can I—help you with something?"

"Is this how we're going to keep playing it? Fleeting moments we pretend to ignore? Back and forth like a fox and hound?" I flick something from my fingernail.

Jack clucks his tongue against his teeth before his hand snatches my hip and pulls me in front of him. His chest is at my back, and every inch of me relaxes and tenses simultaneously as he presses against my ass. "All you had to do was ask, Bonny. And I'd hardly call that last moment *fleeting*."

My arms stay glued to my sides at first before I trace my fingers up the ship's wheel. "You *know* what I mean."

A carnal chuckle—deep, rough, and glorious—rumbles from his chest. He presses his nose at the corner of my jaw and whispers, "This is probably a stupid question, but have you ever sailed a ship?"

If the crew knows what transpires at the helm between the stowaway sea nymph and their Captain, they don't give it away. They're performing their duties, keeping the sails taut and still celebrating the victory, oblivious to Jack's advances.

"No. I'm born of the sea. In it, seldom *on* it." I turn to peer at his lips, noting the dark hair surrounding them and continuing over his chin to form a luscious beard.

"Well, then." Jack picks up my hands, scraping my knuckles with calluses formed from years of pulling rope, wielding swords, and making a life for himself as this daring pirate captain. "Today is your lucky day."

No. It started as an *unlucky* day, but steadily blossomed into one of the more fortunate *years* of my life.

He wraps my fingers around two pegs and slips his hands away, resting them on my waist. "It's less about the need to steer it in any given direction, but more about feeling her at your fingertips."

Not only can I *feel* the ship as he describes, but the ocean itself.

"How did you learn to fight like that, Anne?" Jack keeps his tone low, and our bodies sway with each lull of the waves beneath the ship.

"Do you mean aside from the hundreds of years of practice?" I grin, knowing it's a smartass response Jack himself would've given.

Jack chuckles, and his grip tightens on my hips. "I've never seen anything like it, is all."

"My father, brother, uncles, and cousins. I've had a lot of teachers and experiences along the way. Surrounded by warriors, heroes, and war goddesses alike." I crane my neck, resting it briefly on his shoulder. "What about you?"

His gaze lazily trails down my neck, pausing where my linen

blouse parts at my chest. His eyes then lift to the setting sun in the distance, squinting at it. "Life. Life taught me most of what I know."

And this will be the moment I remember where I fell, *plummeted*, for Jack Rackham.

The bell clangs furiously from the crow's nest, and we jolt to attention. Squid waves his arms before pointing north, several palm trees sprouting from an island blurring into view.

Jack pats my thigh before moving to the railing. "You know the drill, boys. Ready the sails. The faster we drop anchor at that island, the faster you'll be halfway into the night celebrating."

The crew moves with extra intensity, and I make for the stairs, ready to help.

Jack catches my hand and squeezes it, offering a warm smile before letting go. He doesn't try to tell me that no assistance is needed, nor does he give me another duty, because he knows I want to be with the crew as much as at his side—and we *both* need to share.

When we reach the island, settle the anchor, and cart supplies, the sun is a sliver of red and orange in the dark amethyst sky. The land isn't much bigger than our ship, but its intimacy will suit us. Several of the crew are assigned to search for firewood, and Mary is "helping" Ragnar carry the rum crate, each holding onto one end.

"Anne, would you like to try my new concoction tonight?" Glog shakes a bottle of liquid in front of me.

"That depends." I take the bottle and pop the cork, sniffing it. Though slightly bitter, the coloring is three shades darker than average rum water, and the odor doesn't smell foul.

"What's in it?"

Glog covers his mouth with a hand and taps his finger against his cheek. "I'd rather not say my secret ingredient quite yet. Rest assured, however, there is nothing that will poison you, make you sick, or spew liquid from both ends."

I'm a deity. Considering how difficult it is to kill us or make us sick, what harm can come from me helping a friend?

Taking a sip for good measure, I sigh at the tinge of lightheadedness tantalizing my brain. I already desire to continue feeling this way, but my curiosity over the drink's ingredients will soon become a distant memory.

"Then I'll be certain to report to you my findings by night's end." I grin, hiding the bottle from view in my pocket so I don't chug half its contents before the bonfire roars.

Glog elbows my side. "With any luck, it won't be until the *morning*." His grin is mischievous, and he leaves little time for me to contemplate his meaning before running off to join the others.

Several men have staked claim to places in the sand, sitting and holding their rum bottles to the sky after Ragnar hands them one. Wood is piled high in a triangular pattern in a cleared patch of sand. Red uses a small amount of gunpowder, and a spark from a flint rock flickers a blazing fire, illuminating the island.

Mary drags a large piece of driftwood near the fire, sitting on it and patting the spot next to her, beckoning me to join her. I oblige, but my eyes roam the shadows outside the fire's glow, searching for Jack, who's nowhere in sight.

"You going to cut loose a bit tonight, Bonny?" Mary smiles

and takes a swig from her bottle.

"I'm certainly going to try."

"Cheers to that, mate." Mary raises her drink, and we cheer.

The night dwindles with drinking, roughhousing, conversation, and music from the fiddle and hurdy-gurdy. Whatever Glog has put in this drink has me swaying on the log next to Mary, our arms curled over the other's shoulder, belting *Whisky Johnny O'* to the top of our lungs. Only two mouthfuls are left of my drink, and the world has turned blissfully serene, even as my head buzzes and my lips tingle.

Glog heckles Mary and me until we're on our feet, bottles raised to the stars, and dancing circles around one another. My feet sinking in the sand does nothing for my foggy brain or my balancing, and I trip more than actually dance but laugh my head off. My heel catches on a rock, and I fall backward. Mary reaches for me, cackling, but I land in a pair of strong arms.

"Having fun, Annie?" Jack asks. He's upside down as I look up at him, and his glorious grin turns me into a jellyfish within his grasp.

Letting him support me, I sip from my bottle. "I'm even better now." The fire casts shadows over his face in the most perfect places, accentuating his already strong jawline and high cheekbones. "Dance with me." I don't ask, I *command*.

Jack tips his head to one side. "Yes, ma'am."

He helps me stand upright and takes my hand in his. I'm uncertain why I thought Jack wouldn't be able to dance, but he still surprises me by leading us in a pattern of skips, turns, and side steps. His hand presses to my lower back, spinning us in circles, and I'm at his mercy, letting the world spiral out of control around me. The lively music fades into a somber tone, the fiddle player edging a knowing smile.

Jack slows us to a sway, his fingertips brushing the top of my trousers. "I think, perhaps, the crew is mocking us."

"Can you blame them?" I throw my arms around his neck, and Jack snatches my bottle before I accidentally smack him on the head with it again. "How you look at me is like you're starving for unobtainable food."

Jack's eyes seem to darken from the bonfire shadows, and an irresistible grin edges his lips. He trails the bottle up my spine, lifting my shirt enough to expose my lower back, and presses his other hand there. "Don't think I haven't caught you staring at my ass when I walk away—*lingering* even."

I shrug like his posterior is the last thing on my mind. "It's a nice ass."

"Then tell me—" Jack lowers his mouth to my ear and whispers, "—how badly do you wish to see it without these pesky trousers?"

I choke on air and bunch my hands in his long, chocolate locks, pulling him closer. My lips part, ready to take him in.

"Alright, boy," Duke interrupts, grabbing Jack's tunic shirt and prying us apart. "Don't be hogging *all* the ladies. Let the old man have a dance."

A chuckle flutters from my chest when I spot Jack pouting with an exaggerated protruding bottom lip.

Jack rakes a hand through his hair and points a stern finger in Duke's face. "You're lucky you *are* an old man, Duke."

Duke slaps Jack on the back, hurrying him away before scooping me up. I'm still laughing when Duke begins to waltz us around the fire, but I catch Jack's gaze when he burns me with a lustful glint. He spins on his heel and, keeping eye contact with me, removes his shirt before sitting on one of several wooden chairs procured from the ship by Aranck.

Jack slumps in his seat, half-naked and bronzed, with a rum bottle propped on his knee. Time marches on, and he's been watching me for the past few minutes—or maybe the past hour? I've lost track. And I've milked every smirk he's given me, every cheek twitch, and *every* time his lids grow hooded.

I'm fearless at this point in the evening, so I let out a shrill whistle, gaining everyone's attention. Mary zips her spine straight, a curious grin playing on her lips, watching me. Climbing atop a barrel near the fire, almost falling twice, I stand tall and raise my bottle to the stars. "I have something to say."

The music dies off, and the drunken murmurs soon follow as all eyes play on me.

Mary laughs and belches. "This should be good."

Jack rests his forearms on his thighs and digs the bottle into the stand between his ankles. He grins at me. Given this distance and the haze of the fire, it's subtle, but I catch it, and it only motivates me further.

"I want to personally thank the Captain for not only not giving a shit about what's between a person's legs to join his crew but also accepting me—scales and all." I'm speaking to the crew, but I dare not take my eyes away from Jack. "Because here I've found liberation. Here, I've found *family*. And here, me and Mary are the She-Wolves of the damned seas." With each passing word, my voice grows louder, and my fist rises as high as it'll go.

Mary trots to my side, holding up her bottle. "Fuck that. We're pirate fucking *Queens*," she bellows, the rest of the crew bursting into cheers and laughter.

The music picks up livelier than before, and the crew goes into exuberant jigs and turns wobbly circles around each other. The tune resonates with the typical tavern fare—quick, frantic, and upbeat. I spot Jack through the bouncing bodies, holding up his bottle to me, and that devilishly handsome grin has my nymph powers in a frenzy with an entirely different tune playing in my mind.

Mary is tackling Ragnar, begging him for a piggyback ride he will give her if she promises not to yell in his ear again. Red and Glog are practicing some convoluted friendship handshake, and Aranck enjoys the fire in silence, his gaze captivated by the flickering orange flames. Even Squid, still perched in the crow's nest, watches us from up high.

My hips start to sway, and I curl my arms above my head, my wrists turning and my fingers gracefully extending with each motion. We sea nymphs are driven to do this when our interest is piqued when we sense that matching attraction from a potential lover or partner—*mate*. My late mother had found my father in much the same manner, and centuries later, I'm luring my *own* catch.

Jack perks to attention, draping one arm over the chair's back and sliding his brawny legs wide. The alcohol isn't numbing my intentions but rather unburdening me, and it's the most relaxed I've felt in eons. I drag my hands up my body, purposely catching my fingers on the blouse, revealing hints of skin—my stomach, ribs, and the underside of my breasts.

Mary and I had tossed our half corsets and hats aside when the fire first blazed. It's just me in a white linen shirt and trousers and my crimson hair falling in shambles around my face.

With every swerve of my waist, I'm stepping closer to Jack. My back is to him now, hands trailing the length of my neck until they're playing in my hair, ass sweeping from left to right. I keep this part of my body facing him until his scent overtakes my senses, and I know I'm close enough to touch him. When I turn, the sand throws me off balance, and I wobble, laughing. Jack's arm snaps like a whip to catch me.

"*Almost* had it," Jack whispers, smiling and helping me stand upright.

Sucking in a slow breath, I bend forward and run my hands down his thighs, resting them there for a beat. "Oh, I still have it, *Jack*."

The dips and grooves of his abdominal muscles capture my attention, and the chiseled wonders of his chest and arms have me wetting my lips. I trace my fingertips over the tattoo, circling his left wrist and forearm and traveling the rest of his arm and chest. But another tattoo, hidden on the underside of his right forearm, has my heart racing—a simple black-lined silhouette of a woman with long hair, peering over her shoulder, and a *fishtail*.

Jack doesn't pull away from my touch and scoots closer. "I see you've discovered the irony."

I brush our noses together, breathing him in, the sound of his steady but gradually quickening heartbeat like thunder in my ears. Crawling onto his lap, I straddle my legs on each side of his hips and wrap my arms around his neck. Jack's hands find their way to my waist, fingers exploring under my shirt and grazing the skin that dips between my hips and ribs.

"Do you know how often I've been *this* close to calling the entire jewel hunt off?" Jack's eyes roam my chest, the roaring fire's light behind me making the fabric transparent.

"What?" I cup his chin in one hand, lifting his eyes to mine. "Why would you do that?"

Jack keeps one hand curled over my ribs and, with the other, grabs my ass and pulls me against him until our hips meet. "Because you *are* a jewel."

His words are like electric raindrops over my skin, and I press my lips to his, swirling my tongue inside his mouth and rubbing myself against his stomach. Jack grunts but takes everything I'm giving him.

Pulling away, I press my forehead to his, trying to catch my breath. "Jack, let's sneak off somewhere in the darkness, we could—"

Jack groans, rolls his head back, and peers skyward. "You're *killing* me, Annie."

The fog in my mind grows denser, and I shake my head. "I don't understand. You don't—want me?"

"Christ, no." Jack's head lifts, and he slides both hands over my lower back, holding me as if I'll fall from his lap. "It physically *pains* me how much I want you so damned badly, but love, you're *insanely* inebriated."

In one instance, Captain Rackham outsmarts his foes, deceives them, and robs them blind, killing them if necessary. In another, he's cordial and considerate.

I chew on my bottom lip, grinning at him. "Is Calico Jack—

gentlemanly?"

"I wouldn't go that far." Jack moves one hand to my breast, cupping and kneading it, his thumb flicking the nipple. "I'll still take advantage." He presses a feathered kiss to the corner of my mouth. "I'm not without *any* morals, I'm just more of what you'd call—a gray area. Besides, I'm not certain how much bruising my ego could take if you couldn't remember how skillful I was at *ravishing* you."

I'm completely and *utterly* gone for this man. This human. This mortal warrior.

Swaying my hips on his lap, moaning at the feel of his rough hand on me, I slide my blouse down one shoulder, then the other. "Kiss me then."

"That—" Jack tears the rest of the shirt away, dropping it on the sand at his feet. "—I can do."

He lifts the bottle and uses his teeth to pull the cork. With one hand pressed to my back for support, he dips me backward, my chest on full display. He pours rum between my breasts, letting it trickle down my stomach, some of it collecting in my belly button. My scales shimmer to life, some of the ridges protruding from my breastbone. Jack's tongue laps the delicate skin beneath one breast, then the other, and drags it over the ridges, a growl bubbling in the back of his throat.

"Beautiful," he whispers to my scales before pulling me to him, claiming my mouth with his and encircling me with his arms.

We're a storm of snarls, whispers, kisses, and short breaths beneath the canopy of stars and blanket of warming firelight. I'm topless and bare for all the crew to see if they care to look, but it doesn't matter to me. Because here I feel safe. Here, I feel unbridled. Here, I feel *home*.

I *am* Anne Bonny.

SEVENTEEN

ANNE

THE RISING SUN blazing through my eyelids awakes me the following day. Jack's salty, citrusy scent hits me immediately—strong and potent. I'm curled in his lap, my head resting on his chest. I'm still topless, but Jack has his frock coat on, minus one sleeve, so I'm snuggled within it—warm and safe. The crew is stirring in patches, groaning and stumbling to the water's edge to relieve themselves before dousing the fire that's dwindled to nothing but glowing embers. I remain still, smiling at Jack's steady mortal heartbeat thrumming against my ear.

Jack is slumped in his chair, his head propped on the seat's back. He jolts awake, smacking his lips together. "How long was I out?"

Murmuring against his skin, I flutter my eyes open. "All night, I'd imagine," I answer, chuckling.

Jack rests his chin on my head so easily that it makes my heart burst. "And how are *you* feeling this morning?"

The buzz from the alcohol has disappeared entirely, and I

feel more rested than I have in a long time. "Fine. What *should* I feel like?"

"Considering how drunk you were, I'd say a splitting headache, nausea, and a penchant for repeating the words, 'I'm never drinking again'?" Jack sits up, taking me with him.

"Can't say I feel any of that." I bite the inside of my cheek to suppress a smile.

Jack's squint morphs into a glare. "None of it? How much do you remember from last night?"

"Mm." Sitting straight, I press a quick kiss to Jack's lips. "Don't think I forgot about your claims to ravish me skillfully."

Jack clears his throat and drums his fingers on my hip. "You remember everything, don't you?"

I can't answer without bursting into laughter, so I nod emphatically.

"Fucking hell," Jack growls and bunches his hair, pulling it. "You know, there's still time, and I saw a thicket of bushes back there that'd hide just enough to—"

My stomach dips, and I press a finger to his mouth before I do something rash and take him up on his offer. "But *you're* the captain, Jack. And it's *you* that'll get us underway and sailing again. And trust me, they'll need all the instructions they can get." I nudge my chin at the hungover crew shuffling around us, holding their hands above their heads to block the bright sun.

Jack moans in protest before his lips trail kisses over my neck, the tip of his tongue teasing my skin. "Why don't you stage a mutiny? Let someone else take over?"

I chew my bottom lip, his caress lighting my skin on fire,

and I close my eyes, moaning and tilting my breasts toward him. "As enticing as that is—" Snapping out of it, I cup his chin in my hand. "—you're born to lead, Jack. Besides, you'd hate me for it later."

Jack peels back, frowning, and a deep groove forms on his forehead. "I could never hate you. Perhaps greatly dislike you in a given situation, but *never* hate."

"Oh? What if I cut off one of your toes?"

Jack stands, lifting me from his lap and resting me on the ground. He slips the jacket from his arm and slings it over me. "That's strangely specific, but I'd throw the bloody stump at you, and we'd be square."

Scrunching my nose, I playfully swat him in the chest. "I should get situated on the ship." After scooping my shirt into my palm, I turn away.

Jack pulls me back to him. "Have you entranced me somehow, Anne?" His eyes roam my hair, and the back of his hand trails down my cheek.

"Maybe," I whisper, nuzzling against his touch. "But I wouldn't need to. A nymph's magic serves to get your attention."

"You have it." Jack's words are clipped and stern. "You've had it since the damn tavern."

A breath hitches in my throat because I can rationalize this in every way imaginable, denying my immediate attraction toward him when his boots crossed the bar's threshold. But I'd be lying to myself. We've spoken no words, but actions have always been far louder, and ours have declared it to the world: he and I, Jack and Anne, are *together*.

Tears sting my sinuses, and I hold them back. Pressing a

hand to his cheek, I rise to my tip-toes and give Jack a tender kiss before flopping back to my heels. "I'll meet you at the helm later, yes?"

Flashing a debonair grin, Jack bows, bending from the waist and extending one arm to his side. "M'lady."

Chuckling, I clutch Jack's coat around me, lifting the collar to inhale. Mary, hair unkempt and dark circles under her eyes, hobbles toward the ship and groans.

"Is this the Afterlife?" Mary asks, opening one eye and squinting with the other.

Frowning, I smooth back Mary's hair from her face. "The Afterlife?"

"Yes. Because I surely must be dead." She moans, holding her stomach, and her cheeks puff.

"How *do* you all have celebrations like this and still function so well the next day?"

Mary waves me off and lifts her shirt to scratch her ribs. "Little bit of water, a few vomits over the side once we haul away, and we'll be right as rain. It just stinks first thing in the morning." She snorts and elbows my side. "And you, darling, are a little vixen, aren't you?"

"Pardon me?" I feign innocence, my boots thudding against the wooden ramp as we clamber on board.

"Don't even try it. I saw you all over Jack, swaying your hips, tits in the wind whilst on his *lap*." Mary prods me. "I like you more and more with each passing day, friend."

"It was a fun night," I say, flashing a cheeky grin.

Glog scurries past us, and I trot to catch up with him, quickly switching the frock coat wrapped around me for my linen shirt. "Glog," I call after him, folding the jacket over my arm.

Glog is in his own world, distracted, but his face brightens when he notices me. "Anne. Good morning. How are you feeling?"

"Fine, but I need to ask what you put in that drink. I've never felt that kind of buzzing in my head before."

Glog stands proudly with his fists on his waist. "Sea snail mucin."

Queasiness forms in my gut, and I stick my pinky in my ear as if I've suddenly become hard of hearing. "Mucin? As in *secretion?*"

"Precisely." Glog snaps his fingers. "This particular species of snail's mucin is poisonous to small predators, and as a toxin, I thought to myself, it may act as a sort of psychedelic in correct doses with humans."

My eyes grow wider with each passing word. "Your skills are wasted on food and drink alone, Glog."

"Nah. It's my passion. But I do get ravenous for outside exploration, and it's not like I expected everyone to go around licking snails to test their effects." Glog barks a laugh and scratches the back of his head, gaze glossing over in lost thought again.

"Well, it worked. I felt uninhibited but still somehow acutely aware." Absently, I trail my fingertips down my throat, remembering Jack's hands on my back and breasts as he poured the rum on my chest to make my scales appear.

"Splendid. I'll whip you up a batch whenever you like, just let me know." Glog gives me a tender smile before continuing.

We've hauled anchor and set sail within the hour, and by mid-day, most of the crew are back to normal, some puking their guts out several times to get there. I've kept myself useful by swabbing the decks and touring the ship, asking where others needed help. Every time I near the helm, I can feel his gaze on me, which bursts butterflies in my stomach. I'm constantly battling between keeping my distance from Jack so as not to arouse the crew and planting a million kisses on him when I pass. And proudly, I've only snuck several kisses and a few careless whispers by the time the sun sets.

When the first blast hits, it's minor enough for me to feel only the slightest vibration through my feet, and I think nothing about it. But moments later, when the second one goes off, it sends a chill down my spine, and an ominous pang clutches my gut.

"No," I whisper, rushing to the ship's side to watch the rolling dark waters. "It's not possible."

The first ripple is the faint call of Atlantis—a summoning I cannot heed. But the second wave, the much more intense one, belongs to a creature answering it—the Charybdis. It never breaches the surface. It waits for its prey to be underwater, where it has the advantage. And why would it try to attack me on a ship this large?

The creature calls my bluff when a colossal wave hurls against the ship's side, turning the hull cock-eyed before leveling. I grip the railing and snap my attention to Jack and

Duke at the wheel. The crew panics, looking to the captain to give them direction. But he has no idea what we're up against. How can he?

"What the hell was that?" Duke asks, his gaze lifting to the blue skies void of ominous dark clouds suggesting a storm.

Jack peers over the ship's side and sprints to the opposite end when he doesn't spot anything. "Ready the cannons," he yells, and the crew scrambles below deck while others keep their eyes peeled on the water.

I remain still, perking my ears for further signs of the Charybdis. Is it so much to ask that the monster got courageous at first and quickly realized it wasn't worth the effort?

The ship violently lurches, only this time, there's no wave accompanying it, only the alarming sound of wood cracking and creaking. Sucking in a breath, I run to the helm, grabbing the stair railing when the ship jerks to the right, my knees buckling.

"Jack, it's the Charybdis," I shout.

Jack fiddles with his rings, an exasperated stare wrinkling his forehead. "Can you please get to the part where you tell us how to get rid of it?"

We can't. We can only hope to attack it enough to will it away—for now.

"Don't bother with the cannons," I yell, a loud *thump* resonating as the creature launches against the bottom of the ship.

"What?" Jack asks, rage coating the word.

"It won't be able to penetrate its skin. We'll waste ammunition."

A wave crashes over the ship, drenching Jack, Duke, and me. My nymph form slowly appears, reacting to the wetness, but Jack isn't enthralled by it this time.

"Then what the hell are we supposed to do?" Duke barks, circling his mouth with a hand to remove water.

Jack stomps his boot three times, an unspoken order to the men downstairs to stand down on the cannons.

I'm already freeing the belt and cutlass from my hips and heading for the ship's side when I reply, "Let me fend it off. Catch the wind and *get* out of here." Standing on the railing in only my linen shirt, I hold onto the rigging and stare at the water.

It's the least I can do, considering I've led this thing straight to them.

"Like hell you're doing this by yourself." Jack removes his belt and sash, yanking a rope with a grappling hook on one end and winding it around his shoulder.

A tightness seizes my chest, and the fear of losing him soon consumes me—*devastates* me. "Jack, are you insane?"

Jack kisses the tip of my nose and smiles. "Why do you think I'm so good at my job?"

Before I can protest further, he dives into the water with perfect form. My knuckles turn white from gripping the railing. I watch, waiting for him to surface before I jump into the depths. The Charybdis' mouth protrudes from the water, hundreds of overlapping spiky teeth in a circle surrounded by thick, scaly skin and its throat sucking in water and anything else unfortunate enough to be in its path. And latched onto one of its dozen broad tentacles—is Jack. He sputters water once breaching the surface, tossing his hair behind him in a mist of sea spray. His feet press against the monster's body, the hook lodged in its flesh keeping him secured.

Ragnar runs to the railing right as I'm readying to jump in, his pistol raised. I grab his forearm and shake my head. "Don't bother. It'll only feel like a tickle to that thing, and you might hit Jack."

Ragnar clenches his jaw, winces, and lowers the weapon. "*Pokker.* Then what am I supposed to do?"

"Keep the ship moving and the crew from panicking. We need our wits about us." After squeezing Ragnar's arm, I launch into the water, morphing my legs into my tail before hitting it.

Underwater is a flurry of bubbles, and my heart races, being this close to the monster who's haunted my life and dreams for as long as I can remember. The Charybdis is so massive its bottom half disappears into the darkness below. Three giant tentacles with barbs on the ends shoot from its mouth, aimed at Jack, still riding its back. I throw my hands forward, sending an immense pulse through the water and catapulting it into the creature's side. It dives, taking Jack along with it. Jack crouches, still keeping his arm wrapped with the rope.

Flicking my tail, I'm a harpoon with my sights set on one of the Charybdis' barbed tentacles. Materializing my Atlantean sword, I hold the hilt in one hand, using my other arm to plunge through the water like liquid lightning. The monster makes a sharp turn, hurling Jack off its back. The grappling hook tears into the creature's flesh, carving out a chunk that floats away. The Charybdis' focus now lies on Jack, and it bares its teeth, sucking the water through its lungs and creating a whirlpool that pulls Jack towards it.

No.

Gritting my teeth, I push my fins faster, straining through the effort. Lifting the blade, I swing it down on one tentacle, cutting it in half, sending crimson tendrils through the surrounding waters. The monster screeches and halts, spinning to face me, the remaining barbed tentacles in its mouth splaying and vibrating. Its black tail rises from the depths and plunges into my side before I can maneuver away. My back slams against the ship's side, the wind knocking from my lungs. The Charybdis darts a barb at my midsection, and I push off the boat to twirl away, but it still manages to flick my stomach, cutting it. I wince and hiss but push through the pain. It's only temporary and will heal before night's end.

Jack is yelling and on top of the creature again, beating his fists against it, luring its attention away from me. His lungs must be burning for air by now, and if the brave idiot doesn't surface for air soon, he'll pass out. Swimming to the creature's opposite side, I dodge the slashes of its tentacles and dart from the snapping pointy teeth. When I reach Jack, his cheeks are puffed, and he stares at me wide-eyed. I grab his shirt and pull him toward me, clamping my mouth over his to give him enough air to get back on deck. After pulling away, I push his chest and send a blast of energy through the water that'll forcibly move him to the ladder. And I can only pray he'll be smart enough to *use* it—to get to safety.

Turning to face the Charybdis, I know there's no way I can defeat it, especially not alone. Only one being in the cosmos stands a chance against it—my father. But he isn't here, and it's only me. I can't kill it, but I sure as the Seven Seas can send a message that I won't be easy to destroy.

With my hands poised at my sides, I dig into ancient power I've rarely summoned. It's like recalling muscle memory, and the power isn't full force, but maybe it's just enough to scare the terrorizing monster. As the magic courses through my veins, my scales glow brighter, shimmering until my eyes blast open, and I hurl the power from my chest, using my arms as weapons, throttling the energy at the Charybdis. It sends the creature flipping, toppling, and spinning into the abyss below. The monster roars as it plunges into darkness, and soon, silence blesses the sea.

I float motionless for what seems an eternity, my chest heaving, waiting and praying the monster doesn't return. Not so soon. I can only hope the blast is enough to make the creature take time to regroup before it attempts to attack us again. And when there are no signs of it returning, for tonight at least, I lazily swim to the ladder, dreading what will undoubtedly wait for me on board.

I've returned to the ship with human legs, while the rest of me remains in nymph from being soaked to the bone. The linen shirt clings to my skin, and my finned ears flick water from them when I scan the shocked faces of the crew.

"It's not supposed to surface," I whisper as if they can hear me.

Jack, his hair and clothes still wet, storms to me, glaring daggers into my gut. "You knew about this damn thing, didn't you?" His words are loud and cut me to the core. The moment we shared last night was a striking contrast to the venom seething in his gaze now.

Opening my mouth to answer him produces nothing but a gurgle in the back of my throat. Water beads on my eyelashes blur my vision. Or is it tears?

Jack scrapes a hand over his beard, his nostrils flaring, and he paces before pointing at his cabin. "My quarters. *Now.*"

I flick the ridges and grooves over my knuckles as I fold my hands in front of me and make the walk of shame to the captain's quarters. My ears droop at the sight of Red frowning at me. From the back of the ship, Mary frowns, too, but her expression is far more sympathetic.

Keeping my head held low, I step into Jack's cabin, wincing when Truffles' claws scratch against the wooden floor and he retreats to his hiding spot in a darkened corner. Sucking in a quick breath, mustering my courage, I turn on my heel. "Jack, let me—"

My words are cut short by the door slamming with such force it rattles the frame. Jack holds up a finger between us and invades my space, towering over me like a Titan. "I'm going to speak my theories, and I need you to tell me if *any* are wrong. Understand?"

I stare at my hands, the scales starting to fade, and nod.

"You knew this thing was after you from the beginning. Not only did you fail to mention it when I caught you on my ship, but also when I blatantly asked if there was anything else I should know that'd put the crew in danger. Am I right so far?" Jack moves closer, gaze ignited when those brown eyes catch the hanging sconce firelight.

I nod again and blink at him.

"And I'm going to guess you did *not* say anything either time out of fear that I'd say to hell with the jewel or maroon you to keep the crew safe because the creature is after *you*."

There's no point in saying anything. He's right about all of it. The man is far too intelligent for his own damn good.

"And you still kept mum about it for your own gain because you needed me, this crew, and the ship to get to Greece." Jack dips his chin, forcing me to look at him. "Am I wrong about *any* of it, Anne?"

Lifting my chin, I widen my stance. "No."

Jack's pupils dilate, his breaths quickening, and his mouth crashes against mine. He bunches my hair in a hand, his head tilting from side to side, and his tongue plunging in my mouth, lapping at mine. I whimper against his lips, my fingers greedily roaming the muscular arms beneath his wet shirt.

Without pulling away from the kiss, Jack wraps one arm around my lower back and guides me backward until the coolness of wood presses to the backs of my thighs. He lifts me with that one arm, resting me on the edge of his desk. His other hand has been undoing the clasps of his trousers, lowering them far enough the top of his bronzed ass pokes out. Gripping his wet shirt, I chew on my lip and grunt in protest as it keeps sticking to his skin. Jack takes hold of my wrists, and with me grasping the tunic, he pries them away from each other—*hard,* and the shirt tears in half.

He cups my ass and pulls me as close to the desk's edge, balancing me on it, his eyes growing feral when my nails scrape his bare chest. But this first time together isn't about ogling the other but coming undone. It's about *claiming*. As if he can read my thoughts, his hand pushes my blouse up my hips and bunches it at my stomach.

His cock is in his hand now, thick, hard, and *ready*. Jack presses the tip to my entrance, barely giving me time to prepare myself before plunging into me, filling me to the hilt. My head throws back, and I cry out, not caring if the crew can hear me. Seas, I don't give a damn if the *stars* can hear me. He's thrusting with such passion that it's smacking the desk's side against the cabin wall with repeated *thuds*.

Jack keeps a palm pressed to my ass, pulling me harder onto him each time our hips meet. I tangle my fingers in his hair, my nails digging into his neck, almost enough to draw blood. Not only does the pain not faze him, it drives him further over the edge. Jack presses his forehead to mine, our skin a mix of sweat and saltwater. I circle my legs around his waist, locking them together at the ankle. He pushes a hand to my chest, coaxing me to my back, and once my skin meets the wood, he's over top me, his arms caging my head.

His hips grind against me, pumping faster and faster. And the sight of him above me, those dark strands framing his face, and the carnal yet tranquil expression playing in his gaze, is enough to carry me to a blissful, exhilarating release. I cry out and *scream* through the climax, my back arching from the desk, and I cling to his arms to not fall off the fucking planet.

Jack's teeth nip my neck, a guttural snarl following as he gives two final harsh thrusts and pulls out of me to shudder through his own release, expelling it on the floor. One of my legs rests on his shoulder, and he trails kisses down my calf, playfully biting the skin on the inside of my knee.

"Jack," I whisper, sitting up on my elbows. "I'm sorry."

Jack sighs, tracing absent circles over my thighs and stomach. "I wanted to be angry with you. But then I'd be a damn hypocrite."

I move to sit up, but Jack strong-arms me to stay put with a palm pressed to my belly. He dips his fingers in the water basin he uses to wash his face, cupping some of it in his palm and trickling it down my chest. His gaze brightens as the scales and ridges appear, mesmerized by them. "You say the word, and I'll abandon ship. I don't want to see you or anyone on the crew hurt."

"Annie," Jack starts, settling between my thighs and resting one arm on the desk beside me. "Things are different now. You *are* a part of the crew. And if there's an incredibly terrifying sea creature after you, we do what we need to protect our own. And that isn't abandoning you when things get tough."

Between the satiation and his words, I could burst into tears.

"Thank you," I say, hushed and strained.

"For the ravishing?" Jack grins.

I laugh and swat him.

Jack catches my hand. "Just promise me one thing, Anne. From here on out, we're partners—you and me. No more secrets that endanger us. No more lies."

Partners.

"I promise, Jack. You and me." I comb his hair with my fingers, a heaviness swelling my chest.

You and me.

"Good." Jack stands, patting my thigh, and rips what remains of his shirt from his chest. "We should get some rest, yeah?" He drops the shirt, using it as a makeshift rag to scrub the floor with his foot. "But I seem to remember you saying something about *never* being caught dead in my hammock?"

Sitting up, I hug one knee to my chest and let the other foot fall from the desk. "That's before I laid eyes on *that.*"

Jack's cock pokes from his trousers, still so damn inviting and thick. He looks down, the muscles in his stomach flexing, and he drags a hand through his hair with an arrogant smile. "Oh, yeah? I should've paraded it in front of you when you were pretending to be a cabin boy, then. Would have outed you sooner." He yanks the trousers down fully with zero shame and folds them over the desk chair.

It's all I can do not to grab both of his ass cheeks and squeeze until my fingers go numb. Instead, I bite my knuckle, my face blazing with heat.

"Have you ever been in a hammock with another person?" Jack asks, crossing in front of me, that glorious butt flexing and somehow becoming perkier with each step.

I turn on the desk to face him, shaking my head.

"This'll be easier if I get in first. Just try not to flip me out of the damn thing, hm?" Jack pulls his hair into an unruly knot at the base of his skull before expertly crawling into the hammock. Once it stops swaying, he beckons me with a curl of his finger.

I slip the shirt over my head, discarding it with Jack's trousers, and saunter to him. His hand is behind his head, and his gaze devours me. Once at the hammock, I grip the side, lift a leg, and stumble—a laugh, bordering on a giggle, bubbles from my chest.

"Almost had it," Jack says, smiling, the hammock swinging from my failed attempt. "You're going to have to just go for it."

Taking his words to heart, I try again but jump onto it this time, shrieking as I fall on top of Jack and he grunts. My elbow lands in his gut, and after he helps me adjust, keeping me from falling out, I'm secured and curled into his side, our legs entwined.

Jack kisses the top of my head, wrapping one burly arm around me. "Comfortable?"

"Very," I coo, already feeling the lull of sleep tugging at my bones.

He reaches for a blanket hanging on the wall and pulls it over us. Truffles harrumphs from his hiding spot, flicking his tail at us as if to say, "Finally," before he makes a mad dash across the room. He's airborne over a maroon pillow and lets out a tiny meow when he contentedly plops onto it on his stomach.

I settle against him and drag a finger over his sternum. "Why piracy, Jack?"

"Long story short, I got tired of waiting for my country to take care of me. I had been a merchant for years, already knew the workings of a ship, and decided to start taking care of *myself* for a change." Jack folds his arm behind his head and gazes at the wooden ceiling.

I'm exhausted but still feel this urge to know more about him.

"I'm curious what your mother thought of your chosen career path." I grin against his chest because the answer here makes no difference.

A buttery chuckle escapes his throat. "My mother passed long before she had a chance to question my life choices. And my father and I have been estranged for the past decade when I refused to follow in his footsteps and join the Navy."

I've always felt a bit cheated not having a mother for most of my life, but I often forget how much worse it could've been if Dad and I didn't have as close of a relationship as we do.

"I lost my mother as a child, too, but my dad and I became a lot closer because of it."

The ship sways, making our hammock swing.

Jack's chin rests on my head. "Is your father like you?"

"He's a sea deity, if that's what you mean."

Jack taps my arm with his middle finger, not speaking again straight away. "And he can sprout a tail and all of that?"

Craning my neck to look up at him, I smile. "Yes."

"Huh," Jack replies, his gaze going glassy and distant.

The jagged scar slashing his chest captivates me, and I trail my touch over it, starting at his right collarbone and dragging it diagonally until I reach his left pec. "Did a sword do this?"

"That's a parting gift from our dear Charles. It'll be the first and last time someone bests me with a blade." Jack takes my hand and presses my palm to the center of his chest. "It taught me to always to be the one they underestimate and never the other way around."

He's learned so much in his mortal life it almost makes me envious.

"I like it. It gives you extra character. And besides—" I prop on one elbow and run my thumb over his hairy jawline "—you can't be too perfect, or your head might pop."

Jack's gaze is drawn to my lips before he leans in to kiss me. It's brief but still has my toes curling beneath the blanket. "You're not wrong, Annie."

We grow silent, staring, captivated with each other and grinning.

"I'm glad the universe saw fit to place you in my path," Jack mumbles against my forehead.

I run strands of Jack's hair through my fingers and steadily let my eyes shut, relaxing into his arms.

For whatever reason, his words don't ring true in my mind. My godly intuition says to me that this wasn't happenstance. What *is* the more accurate statement?

We finally *found* each other.

EIGHTEEN

JACK

WHO WOULD'VE GUESSED the only woman ever to steal my heart would make me equally angry and entirely captivated by her? It's someone's idea of a cruel joke or the most profound gift. Whatever the case, I'm eternally grateful this someone or *something* saw fit to introduce us. And that she fancies me to boot. I've plundered goods, gold, and gems, but nothing is more valuable than the sea nymph sleeping contentedly in my arms.

Truffles remains splayed on his pillow, all four limbs stretched like a star, his tail lazily swaying in his slumber. I don't dare move, let alone breathe, from fear of disturbing her, but when she stirs awake, moaning and rubbing her head against my chest, I pull her to me tighter.

"Morning," I mumble into her hair, my voice gravelly as it usually is first thing when I wake up.

Anne's fingertips trail my bare chest, tantalizing the bit of hair at my sternum. "Mm, what happened last night?"

An iceberg can't compare to how frozen I've become. I rhythmically tap my forefinger on her shoulder, treading lightly on my following words. "You—don't remember?"

She yawns and turns until she's almost entirely on top of me, resting her elbow on my chest. "I remember the Charybdis and us fighting it underwater. But after it hit me, things started to get fuzzy."

I'm still a rock-solid statue save for my eyes blinking and fingers relentlessly tapping. "You've got to be shitting me."

The corners of her lips twitch before she breaks into a fit of laughter, making the hammock sway and nearly toppling us out of it. "I am. I *am* shitting with you."

Blowing out a breath and holding the hammock taut to keep it from making a full spin, I drag a hand down my face. "I knew that."

"Yeah? You looked a little worried—possibly mortified." Smiling brightly, Anne tugs my beard.

Snaking my hand down her smooth back until I reach her ass, I grab it. "You're right. You should probably recount last night in grand detail to reassure me."

"Or—" Anne starts, trailing her hand up my thigh until she reaches my cock, fisting it. "We can repeat it this morning, step by step." She enunciates the last "p," and I move my lips to hers, my length twitching in her grasp, eager to feel her again.

Meow.

My eyes fly open, and I peel away with my lips still parted.

"My cat has other plans," I say through gritted, grinding teeth, flashing Truffles a seething glare.

Truffles blinks once and flicks his tail, moseying to the door where he plops onto his butt and waits, facing it.

"Does he usually relieve himself inside of your cabin?" Anne asks, biting back a smile.

Groaning, I shift a leg from the hammock and slowly crawl out, holding it for Anne. "Christ, no. My cabin already smells questionable without adding cat piss to it."

Anne climbs down, those fiery tresses hanging over her porcelain back like a waterfall ablaze. "Well, you can't deprive him of shitting simply because you want your piece wet again." Her hand grips my cock—*hard,* and I groan, kissing her before Truffles' whining meows plague my eardrums.

"I know, I know," I mumble, swiping my trousers from the floor and hopping into them. "Lest I neglect *either* of my pussies."

Anne rolls her eyes but still grins and slaps my ass. "Go, Jack. I need to get dressed and wash up."

After giving her a final peck on the lips, I open the door and waltz on deck, shirtless and bootless. Truffles screeches and sprints to the back corner of the ship, where the crew's wooden crate is filled with sand for him to do his business.

Duke approaches first, his thumbs looped in his belt, and he whistles some random sea shanty. "G'morning," he says as if his body language alone doesn't spell it out.

"Yes, we fucked. Am I to be ashamed of such a feat?" I arch my back toward the sun's warming rays, stretching and scratching my head.

"'Course not. It's only a bit unconventional the way it happened. You were furious with her over failing to mention that a giant mythical beast has been chasing her." Duke drums his fingers at his hips.

"Your point?" Combing my beard with my fingers, I move past him, my bare feet slapping against the moist deck wood.

Duke chuckles, following several paces behind me. "You're a strange bird, Jack."

"I wouldn't say that. My anger stemmed from her ability to pull the wool over my eyes, which, ironically, was the exact reason she also impressed the hell out of me." I yank a bottle of grog from Ragnar's crate as he passes, ignoring his grumblings. Popping the cork, I take several swigs and wipe the back of my hand over my mouth. "We're both passionate people, Duke. What do you want me to say?"

Duke folds his arms, shaking his head as if he doesn't know what to do with me. "I stand by my statement. Strange. Bird."

Flashing a devious grin and lifting the bottle, I whisper, "We've seen stranger."

"At least you're happy, son."

The word takes a moment to process—happiness. After England went to shit, few things have given me glee over the past few years—rum, the oceans, piracy, sailing, gold, the smell of gunpowder, and the rare warmth of a woman's touch. But if I boil it down, these trivial things keep me satisfied or content. The connection I have with Anne, however, *this* is pure pleasure—pure *merriment*. We're two drops of water, she and I, despite my mortality and her ethereal background. In her, I've met my equal, someone who can go toe-to-toe with me and fancy sex afterward—a woman skilled with a sword in more ways than one. And I've seen the loyalty dancing in her gaze. It wasn't there when she first boarded, but it glinted from her teary eyes when she rescued me, fearing my death. And it *poured* out when I questioned my trust in her. Her expression in response to that still stings my heart.

Anne clears her throat behind me, fully dressed in a tri-corner hat, tunic shirt, and cutlass slung on her hip. "Captain." She fights desperately not to let her eyes linger on my exposed chest, clearly trying to hide the smile from memories of last night dancing through her mind. She clasps her hands in front of her as if resisting the urge to touch me.

How long can she keep this up?

"Bonny," I answer, bowing my head and not trying to disguise my smile.

Anne folds a piece of hair over her ear, only glancing at Duke long enough to acknowledge his presence. "Duke. I should get to my duties."

She rushes past me, and I sidestep so my ribs brush her chest. The gasp that escapes her throat and her brief pause to regain her composure has me immediately ravenous for her. And if it wasn't for Mary calling her over, I may have escorted her *right* back to my cabin.

"Are you going to tell her the crew doesn't give a shit if the two of you are together?" Duke asks, tapping his sword's hilt.

After taking another long swig from my bottle, I shove the cork in it. "Soon enough."

Anne won't be able to last long if she's anything like me, and I know she is. She'll eventually find any excuse to sneak a kiss around a hidden corner or nonchalantly fondle my ass, my cock beneath my trousers. The only question is: how long will it take to drive her mad? Knowing she may think the same things about me makes my attraction to her swell.

"Captain," Red shouts, sprinting with a fishing rod in one hand, his other closed into a fist. "Captain, a word?"

Duke eyes Red suspiciously as he circles his beard with his hand.

"Talk to me, Red." I press my shoulder to the mast, crossing my bare feet at the ankles.

Red stands straight, fighting the compulsion to salute his superior, as he had countless times in the Navy. "We was fishing as we do. And when the boys hauled the net in from last night, they found *this*." He opens his hand, revealing a gold piece. The bits left untarnished or chipped catch the sun's glint.

"Is that what I think it is?" I whisper, as if speaking too loudly would make it vanish. But there's no mistaking the crossed symbol on the side facing me.

Red grins and nods, dropping the coin in my open palm. "Spanish gold."

"And where there's one—" Trailing off, I lick my thumb and rub some dirt away. The sight of such a coveted beauty makes my mouth water.

"There's bound to be more," Red finishes for me, rubbing his hands together.

The possibilities race through my mind, and I clutch the coin in my fist. "Get Squid's attention and have him watch for an island. Whoever found this was bound to be on their way to Nassau to *spend* such coin."

"Aye, Captain. I'll do you one better and alert the whole damn crew to be on the lookout." Red barks a laugh before hurrying away.

"Suppose I should get dressed," I tell Duke, keeping the coin within my vice-like grip.

"Suppose you should. This could be a hell of a score before a hopefully, much bigger one." Duke continues to stroke his beard, and holds back a cough.

Grinning, I clap a hand on Duke's shoulder and turn for my cabin. A slender arm encircles my waist and pulls me to the side. Anne has my face in her hands, her lips pressing to mine before I can take a breath.

After pulling away from the kiss, a guttural chuckle escapes my throat. "Miss me already?"

"Be quiet. You know what you do to me, Jack." Anne chews on her bottom lip, her petite fingers playing at the top of my trousers.

"Mm, I seem to have forgotten. Perhaps you should remind me." I slip a hand to her ass, pulling her tighter against me.

Anne gasps, frantically looking around and pushing my chest. "We can't."

And here I thought Anne would be the first to break. But if I'm being honest, I want to touch and kiss her whenever I damn well please, and *this* simply will not do.

"You realize there's no fraternization rules between crewmates, right?"

Anne pauses, her hands still resting on my skin, and blinks. "I guess I assumed—I mean, you're the *captain*."

"The only rules—" I trail my hand up her back, pressing it between her shoulder blades and groaning at the sound of her sensual whimpers. "—are the ones you swore by. And not claiming what's yours in public wasn't one of them."

"Don't worry, we heard you staking your claim all of last night," Glog says in passing, carrying a basket of bread and snort-laughing.

Anne's cheeks turn a light shade of pink, but otherwise, she doesn't seem embarrassed. "I *can* be a tad loud, can't I?"

"I *did* promise you a ravishing." I point a stern finger.

Anne runs one of the thin braids in her hair between two fingers. "I have a confession."

"Oh? How scandalous." Playing along, I lower my ear to her mouth.

"You—" After licking her lips, she lowers her voice. "—you were my first."

Unintentionally, my spine zips straight. "I—hold on." Catching her by the elbow, I lead her into my cabin, checking for snooping ears before closing the door. "I'm your first? Don't tell me you're a virgin. Your age. How is that—"

Anne laughs and grabs my biceps. "No, no. I'm not. You were my first—" Her gaze pans to my chest, and she hesitates. "—human."

"Hold on. Wait. Then what the bloody hell have you been with? Dolphins?"

The idea sounds absurd, but I cannot think of any other explanation, and I pray I'm wrong.

Anne's nose scrunches like Truffles left a heaping pile of shit on my desk. "By the Seas, *no.*"

"You're going to have to level with me here, Annie. Though I believed in all of this—" I circle my finger in front of her. "—long before we met, I only recently found out I was *right.*"

Anne wraps her arms around herself and taps her foot, her

gaze darting from one side of my cabin to the other. "Mostly—mermen."

Heat prickles the back of my neck, and a peculiar mix of confusion and jealousy fills my mind. "Mermen?" I repeat, in case she said something other than grown men with fishtails served as her previous lovers.

"Yes," she answers, wincing.

I nod questioningly. "And so does that entail doing *something,* or do you release eggs into the water that they're intended to fertilize or—?" The thoughts plaguing me are enough to turn my stomach into the world's most complicated sailor's knot.

"Oh, my—no. Fertilize, Jack? Really?" Anne's face reddens, and she rubs her forehead before continuing. "It's like how dolphins or sharks—" she pauses, scratching her head as if mulling over the proper word "—mate."

"And it's—" I point at my pecker. "—different?"

Anne bites the inside of her cheek to avoid showing she's amused by my discomfort. "Yes."

"How different?" The frown that distorts my features is unavoidable now.

Anne saunters toward me, her fingernails walking the length of my stomach. "Let's just say I now know why other nymphs would go on and on about their mortal escapades."

My cock is superior to ethereal men fish—a stroke to my ego if there ever was one.

I clear my throat and flex my arms. "And you were never curious to indulge?"

Anne stays silent and shakes her head.

"Why's that?" I inch closer, trailing the back of my knuckles over her cheekbone.

"I've never met one who could keep up with me." Those jade eyes fall to my mouth, her tongue skirting her bottom lip.

"And how, pray tell—" Sliding a hand over her hip, I massage her there. "—do I compare to these *mermen*?"

Anne laughs and tugs my beard. "One step at a time here, Jack. We wouldn't want your head to explode."

"It is far too late for that, lovely." I close the remaining distance between us, pressing the hardened bulge building in my trousers against her stomach.

Her hands snake around my neck, and she grins wildly before planting her mouth to mine. I pick her up from the waist, carrying her until we reach the desk.

Knock. Fucking knock.

"Captain? Sorry to interrupt. But we've spotted an island," Red announces from the other side of the door.

Groaning, I hold my head low. "I swear to God they do this on purpose."

"You *did* ask them to look for an island. You should be excited." Anne is still smiling, and she bumps a knuckle under my chin.

I slide my lips against hers, soft and fleeting, with a tenderness reserved solely for her. "You're right."

I splash water on my face and pause at the mirror. The reflection is of a man freed of all bindings. A rebellious, adventurous, and untamed man. How far I've come since my days as a merchant.

"Think you can keep your hands to yourself long enough for me to take the wheel?" I let my lips melt into a cheeky grin at Anne.

She picks up my sash from the desk and throws it at me. "A *good* captain wouldn't let such a petty thing distract him."

I catch the sash with one hand, work it around my waist, and tie it in a knot on my right hip. "And how would you know that? Have you been with that many captains?" Hovering over her, I bump the inside of her thigh with my knee, teasing her. "Or am I a first there, too?"

A shaky breath brushes past her lips, and she parts stray strands of hair from my forehead. "You're a lot of firsts, Jack."

The words have my heart racing, and I give her cheek a quick peck, slide away, and adjust my trousers. If I'd done anything else, the crew would've beaten down the door in the middle of Anne bent over my desk with me behind her. And I don't need them seeing *everything*.

"Ready?" I offer her my arm, which she accepts with a sparkling smile.

Heavens above, let this island have more of this coveted coin. We still have a long voyage ahead of us before reaching Greece. And nothing will boost the crew's morale more than a bit of gold jingling in their pockets.

NINETEEN

ANNE

I'M ACUTELY AND painstakingly aware of Jack's absence whenever he's not around me, and a long-forgotten impatience prods and pinches at my skin until we're close again. Is this type of connection typical? Is it a nymph trait? Human? I never had the chance to have this conversation with my mother, and my father wouldn't have known where to begin. Whatever the reason, *I* like being with Jack—enjoy who he is and what he represents, and I can't recall ever smiling this much. And it's because of *him*.

"It's uncanny to me this big island still exists out here uninhabited," Mary says beside me, jarring my daydreaming.

We carry shovels, meandering with the rest of the crew into the thicket of palm trees and bushes. Jack leads the charge but continuously looks behind him, concern cinching his brow every time until he spots me within the crowd. Ragnar barrels behind us, serving as a lookout while the rest of us search the island for buried treasure. Aranck splits from the group in search of any medicinal herbs the island can provide, and Squid stays behind with the ship to keep a weathered eye on the horizon.

"Who'd want to live here this far away from civilization?" I rest the shovel's handle across both shoulders, propping my forearms on top.

Mary pauses, throwing the shovel in the sand, and quickly braids her hair. "Sounds like a dream to me. Tell you what? I'll live here, and you can swim supplies for me every few weeks or so, yeah?"

"*Swim* supplies to you?" I laugh and wipe sweat from my forehead. "Just because I can materialize fins doesn't mean they don't get tired."

Mary thins her lips. "That's no fun."

"My deepest apologies." Tipping my hat at her, I poke her ribs with my shovel's handle.

"Captain," a crew member shouts. "May have found something over here."

What starts as a group of exhausted people dragging their feet through the sand and whining about the infernal sun turns into a lively bunch practically skipping to the location. The blind promise of gold turns the tide and mood.

Glog trots past us with his hands raised, fingers crossed, and manages not to run into anyone with his eyes closed. "Please let there be gold. Please. Please."

"How many false alarms have there been?" I ask Mary, keeping my voice low.

Mary bats a rogue branch from swatting her face. "I wouldn't say so much false alarms as dead ends. Jack won't take us on a wild goose chase unless he has decent evidence it exists."

"What about the Sailor's Jewel? He based that on myth and legend."

Two crabs scuttle sideways past our feet with their claws open, and I lift my boot to keep from accidentally squashing one.

"Pretty sure he's got all the proof he needs." Mary squeezes my hand, and I lift my gaze to hers. "I'm lookin' at her."

My face warms, and I can't help the sheepish smile edging my lips.

"There she is." Mary cackles and pinches my cheek. "Captain cock looks good on ya."

Laughing, I shove her forward. "You're salaciously filthy, you know that?"

Mary shimmies, and we join the crew surrounding a tree. Jack has his hands on his hips. He winks at me but keeps his expression neutral.

"Someone marked the tree, pointing at the lake, and when we searched the water's edge—" The crewman opens his palm, the sun peeking through the canopy, making what's in his hand shimmer.

"More Spanish gold," Jack says, his voice trailing as if distracted by the gold's glitter. He picks one up and holds it to the sky, inspecting each side.

Bubbles swarm my stomach as I watch him stare at the treasure covetously, mainly because I've only seen him gaze at one other thing in the same manner—me.

"Is it possible the treasure is hidden somewhere at the bottom of the lake?" I ask, resting a hand on my sword's hilt.

Jack offers a warm grin and nods. "It's possible, but it isn't a small body of water to search." He closes his hand around the coin.

When he looks back, I'm already undoing my belt and yanking off my hat. "Good thing you have me, then."

Jack cups my elbow, halting me. "Anne, wait. It could be dangerous. That thing is after you, for one."

It's a strange mix of appreciation and irritation that someone worries about my well-being besides my family.

"The Charybdis?" I snicker. "Jack, it's bigger than this *island*. It'd beach itself trying to attack me through a *lake*."

Frowning, Jack rubs my arm before letting go. "Fair point. But I refuse to let you go in by yourself."

"Why am I not surprised?" With a sly grin, I slip off the rest of my gear, leaving only the shirt.

Jack grasps my chin with two fingers and wiggles it. "You're incorrigible, Bonny." He kisses me, ignoring the surrounding crew's snickering.

"Red, you're our best swimmer next to Jack. Go with them," Ragnar orders, gesturing toward the lake.

"Why, *thank* you, Raggie." Red balls his fist at his mouth, feigning tears.

Ragnar sneers at the nickname but turns to the remaining crew. "As for the rest of you, keep searching. There's a lot of ground to cover."

Mary scoffs, shoving a reed she'd found in the sand in her mouth and chewing it. "You get to splash around in a lake while I traipse in the heat searching for a tick on a horse's ass."

"When you can sporadically grow fins and gills, we'll switch roles," I reply.

"Now *you're* the ass." Mary points at me, her narrow eyes forming slits.

"Read," Ragnar barks, whistling at her. "*Lad os flytte.*"

Mary waves, smiling and mumbling through her teeth, "As if I understand Danish. Coming!"

Moving to the lake's edge, I dip my toes into the water, wincing at its coolness, shocking and comforting given the stagnant heat. Jack and Red flank me as I wade into it, cursing once the water reaches their hips.

"This goes pretty deep. I can cover more ground, but don't want to startle you." My toes no longer touch the sand below, and I tread water.

Jack sputters and slicks his long hair back. "What would startle me?"

Sucking on my bottom lip, I will my legs into a tail, the blue and green iridescent scales catching the fractals of sunlight piercing the water.

Jack's eyes widen at first before his face softens. "Ah, yes. Your other half." He's far calmer than I expected and even reaches for my tail. As his fingers explore the textured scales where my thighs would be, I tremble against his touch. He quirks a brow but doesn't stop. "Sensitive?"

I'm aware of each individual scale as they spark to life, reacting to Jack's skin. "Yes," I whisper.

"As happy as I am for the two of you, I really am; *I'm* averse to voyeurism and *not* finding any gold." Red swims past us, using only his feet, his hands resting interlaced on his stomach.

"Apologies, Red." I'm speaking to Red, but my gaze remains glued to Jack's. Curling an arm around his neck, I use the leverage to pull myself from the water, raising my lips to his ear. "There'll be plenty of time for tail-play later."

Jack squints confusedly until his expression melts into lust and greed—the *same* look he gave the gold coin in his hand.

"I can stay underwater indefinitely, so let me do a little searching, and I'll let you both know of any promising spots. Save your lungs." As Jack's lips part to disagree, I dive underwater before he can.

I forgot how tranquil lakes are. In the oceans, I can hear the whales calling to one another from fathoms away and other chirps, warbles, and aquatic life chatter from thousands of animals, fish, and crustaceans. There's no shortage of life in lakes, but it's quieter and easy to forget all of what lurks below. Yet if I concentrate hard enough, I can hear their heartbeats no matter how faint.

The sunlight hits at the right angle, bouncing from something shimmering below. It's enough piercing brightness to make me squint, blurring whatever it is. But once I recognize it, I flick my tail, pushing myself to the surface with feverish strokes. When I breach the surface, I toss my hair skyward, flicking it from becoming a scattered mess over my face.

"Christ," I hear Jack whisper.

I'm already grinning, but the smile spreads wider when I spot Jack. His eyes are wide, his hand rubs the back of his neck, and he covertly chews the inside of his bottom lip.

"I think I found something directly below us."

That same fiery vitality ignites in Jack's gaze, and he swims closer. "Show me."

I take his hand under the water and tug him, using my tail

to take us to the lake's bottom far more quickly than two pairs of human legs could achieve. His grip tightens on my fingers once he sees the glittering metal buried in the sand. After giving a reassuring squeeze, he lets go and sinks to the bottom, feverishly shoveling the dirt away until a dozen coins reveal.

If I let him, Jack will stay down there until his lungs ache and burn. He'd wait until the last moment to resurface, carrying as much coin as possible, using only his feet to guide him upward. And he shouldn't have to do this—feel *compelled* to do this because he has *me*.

Once he's cradling enough coin to settle in the crook of his arm, I tap him and point up. As predicted, he waves a finger and turns for more coins, but I yank him back. More sternly, I point again and signal that I'll carry more by curling both arms over my stomach. Thankfully, he nods and swims above me.

When I return, plopping the treasure onto the bank, Red and Jack talk excitedly, sifting through the coins. Smiling to myself, I leave them to celebrate. I dive back in but stop halfway when an underwater current pushes me backward, making me flip out of control. Shooting my arms out at my sides to slow the spinning, I flick my tail and regain composure, but there's nothing but quiet, empty water.

A distant growl, bordering on a masculine moan, echoes from nearby. I turn enough circles to look for the source, but it makes me dizzy. Something is baiting me, trying to lure me like a siren without words or melody. My heart seizes in my chest. I zoom to the surface, wiping water from my eyes as soon as I breach.

"Ah, there she is," a man with wavy golden locks to his hip

bones says, keeping his back to me but holding a hand up at Jack and Red, blocking them with a water wall.

Fury curls in my belly like a sea serpent, and I materialize my Atlantean sword, lunging for the mystery figure. Once I reach the shoreline, my tail morphs into a pair of legs.

The man keeps one hand splayed at the boys while holding his other at me. He snaps his chin in my direction, a pair of glacial eyes glaring at me. "If you wish to see these two still breathing, I wouldn't do that."

My instincts scream to kill him where he stands. That I'll be quick enough, but something holds me back. I stand poised with the blade above my head.

"Anne, run him through," Jack barks, snarling at the invisible shield blocking him from getting to me. And yet, he still tries. Over and over, he throws his shoulder into it, punches it, kicks it. He is *relentless*.

It should be so easy. I've plunged my blade into countless creatures and people, when necessary, through the centuries. But this man isn't human; he isn't a shifter or kelpie either, and I can't grasp what he is. But it's enough to make me stand down. Jack and Red's lives are at stake, and if I'm unsure if a sword can kill him, then it's too risky. Of everything my father taught me, one was to be ruthless when needed and cunning at any other moment. And so, I lower my weapon.

Jack is roaring behind the water shield, beating his fists against it. Spit flies from his mouth as he tries to gain the man's attention. I can only ignore him despite the sound of his wails eating at my insides.

"And she is intelligent as well." The man lowers his hand

from me but keeps the other one raised. His angular jawline sharpens as his lips curve into a grin, revealing starkly white teeth. "You are quite the *catch*, are you not?"

Balling my free hand into a fist, water from my soaked hair trickling in a droplet down my cheek, I stare the man down, not bothering to ask who he is but getting straight to the point. "What do you want?" My gaze shoots to Jack for a fraction of a second, but the mysterious man quickly catches it.

"A conversation I would rather not have here. Especially not in front of another—" he man glances at Jack, who's glaring the life from his bones "—well, let's just say I would rather talk in private."

"No," Jack bellows. "Red, run back to the crew *now*." Red hesitates at first but nods. Jack shimmies to the part of the wall I'm near and beats his hand against it. "Annie, listen to me. Kill him. I know you're only doing this because you think he'll kill me in kind. But I'll be *fine*. Don't let this piece of shit take you *anywhere*."

I want so badly to look at him, to tell him he's right about all of it, and to admit to him that I could never live with myself if his ending became *my* fault. But I won't be able to save him if I see his anguished expression, the hurt and fear gleaming in his eyes.

The man makes an impatient *tsking* sound, his angular nose drooping further as he frowns. "You come with me now, and I assure you that your—counterpart—will remain unscathed. But it has to be *now*."

It can't end like this. The Fates wouldn't have united Jack and me, only to see us torn apart so quickly. They never spin threads so haphazardly, only to see them wither and break. And it gives me the strength to nod at the stranger, agreeing.

"No," Jack roars against the wall.

Before the man can whisk me away, I leap at the wall, pressing my palm to it. When Jack's hand touches mine, I still feel his warmth despite the impenetrable water shield standing defiantly between us. "Find me, Jack."

"I'm not one to beg, but I will drop to my knees now if it keeps you from doing this." Jack's words are frantic, angry, and pained.

Shaking my head, I back away before my willpower fails me. "*Find* me, Jack."

Jack beats his fist against the wall, the realization that this *is* happening regardless of his words, cinching his features into a furious scowl. "I won't leave this island until I do. And you—" Jack points to the man behind me. "Are a fucking dead man."

"Empty words falling from powerless human lips," the man says, his tone chilling me to the marrow.

As the man's arm wraps around me from behind, Jack locks his gaze with mine, and I mouth to him a final time, "Find me." This connection we share, despite our not having named it, will give him insight no one else on the crew will have, I'm sure of it. The man's arm morphs into water, followed by the rest of his body and my own.

We appear in a cavern, stalagmites hanging from the ceiling, dripping into a small wading pool. In one corner, a living space resides with a makeshift cot, hearth, lit torches, and other paraphernalia. The man backs away slowly, letting his hands slip away before clasping them beneath his chin, his gaze roaming my body like he's surveying a livestock purchase.

None of this makes sense.

"Who are you?" I bark the words, impatient and furious.

The man grabs one of the torches and brings it between us, using it to light my face and body as he circles me. "For eons, I could only ever dream I'd meet someone like you. I was told by every witch and hag that some existed. But how could I believe a supernatural creature *and* an aquatic one would cross my island? And yet here you stand—" he draws a breath through his nose, pausing in front of me and letting his eyes roam my hair "—living proof they were right."

He makes no move to touch me, so I stay put to avoid further antagonizing him. "About what?"

"My name is Nøkk. And you, my dear sea nymph—" he touches me now, but only to graze his fingertips over my cheek "—are my *mate*."

TWENTY

JACK

THE FEROCIOUS HOWL that thunders from my lungs is unlike any sound I've ever made. My fists slam against the invisible wall a final time after this insufferable asshole steals my Anne from me, and I stumble forward when it disappears. Its purpose is pointless now. It was meant to keep me away— to keep me from *her*, and now he's *taken* her. Seeing blood red, I kick the trunk of a palm tree and crack it in my rage.

"Jack, I brought—" Red starts, breathless from sprinting back. "—where the hell is she?"

The question infuriates me even more, and I slam my boot into the tree, splitting it in half and narrowly avoiding several coconuts collapsing into the sand. "He. Took. Her."

Ragnar sidles beside me, side-eyeing me cautiously as if he's the next tree I intend to use as an outlet. "Who took her?"

"I don't know," I answer through a snarl, picking one of the coconuts up and squeezing it between my palms.

Mary's eyes blaze with confusion, and she shoves between

us. "Someone took Anne, and you don't know who they *are*?"

Ragnar pulls her away. "Now's not the time, Read."

"He came out of nowhere from the lake and conjured an impenetrable wall of water." Red rubs the back of his neck. "We tried everything to get through it, and it wouldn't budge."

Grunting, I hurl the coconut at the lake, my chest heaving as I watch the ripples from the splash. "He threatened to kill me if Anne didn't go with him. Whoever he is, he was interested in her because of her *fins*."

"Do you think he wishes to use her somehow?" Mary's arms go slack at her sides.

The memory of us rowing toward Vane's ship plagues my mind, and I shove a thumb between my eyes. "Undoubtedly. What other reason would someone have to kidnap besides their own gain?"

"Ransom, perhaps?" Ragnar offers, flicking his middle finger and thumb together.

The look on the water man's face—desire, longing, surprise. I'll slit his throat as soon as I'm within arm's reach of him.

Anger swells in my chest, but I do my best to shove it away this time. It'll only cloud rational thought, and right now, I need to do everything I can to figure out a way to rescue her.

Find me, Jack.

She said it with such clarity and confidence, like she *knew* I would, and it was the only reason she could fearlessly disappear with him.

Glog hunches forward with his hands on his knees, catching his breath. "Where do we start looking? If this thing that took her is mythical, he might be able to cloak."

"Why are we bothering going after some wench we barely know? We *should* be concerned about finding the rest of that gold," a crew member, whose name escapes me, bursts out brazenly.

The man's back is against the nearest tree, my blade at his throat before anyone can blink. I snarl in his face and shove my forearm against his collarbone. "You call Anne a wench again, and I'll have your fucking head."

The man's eyes blink once, and he holds his palms up. "Captain, all I'm sayin' is we should be voting on this. Because it's a matter that affects *all* of us."

"Yeah? You want to vote?" I slam my elbow into the man's gut as I turn to the rest of the crew. "Is that how you all feel? You want to vote on whether or not we abandon one of our own?"

Mary, Red, and Glog stand firm, but the remaining crew glance at each other. Even Ragnar doesn't look entirely convinced.

After grinding my teeth, I pace between them. "Before you answer, however, let me remind you this—you all took the same oath as Bonny. And one such part is never to desert your captain or crew." I stare them down one by one. "Make of that what you will."

Going silent, I let them mull it over and weigh the pros and cons of what is about to transpire. Most crew members lower their gazes, rubbing their heads and necks uncomfortably. Mary has her arms folded, scowling at anyone who so much as looks unfazed by my words. Red sighs, Glog kicks the man beside him in the leg, and Ragnar—doesn't move his eyes from me. His decision in this weighs heaviest because he's my right hand. He still has as much of an individual say as any other crew member.

"And now I ask you again, are we to put the matter of searching for the gold over Anne Bonny to a vote?"

More uneasy glances and unspoken words are exchanged, but ultimately, the island falls pin-dropping silent.

"Alright then. We split into four groups. Each takes a different direction and searches every inch of this island." Pointing a stern finger, I pass it through the air before them. "And if I catch any of you looking for the treasure before we find Anne, you will *not* be re-boarding *my* ship."

"Let's move, people," Ragnar barks, snapping his fingers.

The crew jumps and hurriedly creates four groups.

"Ragnar, Mary, you're with me." Despite Ragnar's apparent indifference toward Anne, I need my best fighters. Something in my gut tells me that finding her will be easier than prying her from the water man's fingers.

The man who entertained the idea of ditching Anne for the gold in the first place tries to sneak past. I grab his shirt and pull him toward me, his collar choking him on his way. He gurgles and claws at his neck.

"And you," I seethe. "I'm tempted to leave you here regardless of your actions for betraying your oath."

"Didn't mean no disrespect by it, Captain. I know you're sweet on her and all, but—"

My nostril twitches, and I tighten my grip on the shirt, choking him now. "Don't pretend you know anything about my personal life or that it's any of your business, worm."

"Captain," Mary beckons, raising both brows at me as a cue

that I'm taking things too far.

Reluctantly, I let the man go but shove him. "Get your ass moving. But I swear to the heavens, if I get even a whiff that you're doing anything but what I commanded, I'll stake you to this spit of land by your feet and leave you for the birds. Understood?"

The man is shaking now but nods before fleeing off with one of the groups.

"Captain, any idea where we should start this goose chase?" Mary asks, hanging her thumb from the cutlass on her hip.

No damn idea and it's infuriating.

"South is the only direction no one has gone. But I'll go wherever the wind takes me." I grab a piece of twine from the satchel on my belt and tie my hair back.

Anne trusts me to find her—she sacrificed herself for us. And like hell I'll let her down.

"I don't understand how she got taken in the first place," Ragnar grumbles.

We form a triangle and trek forward, my head constantly swiveling for any signs of movement in the sand, trees, or branches. I even keep my nose tilted to the surrounding air to pick up her scent—salt mixed with something floral and sweet.

Mary nudges Ragnar's side. "Does it bloody well matter?"

"The man is something—folkloric. Made an impenetrable wall of fucking water between us and——" the next bit gets my blood fuming, and I gulp it down to the pit of my stomach "—he threatened to kill me if Anne didn't go with him."

Ragnar mumbles incoherently in Danish. Mary stalks closer to him, hops, and flicks him in the ear. He seethes at her.

"What the hell was that for, Read?"

"If you're going to talk shit, at least make sure we can understand you." Mary's lips press into a white slash.

I've always admired Mary's loyalty, but not knowing what Ragnar said is preferable with my current volatile state.

Ragnar circles his mouth with a hand. "I said, this is why you don't let strangers know who you care about or, in other words, who and *what* your weaknesses are."

And I'm right. I was far better off *not* knowing.

Turning on my heel, I get into Ragnar's face. "The water man has some sort of magical intuition because I can assure you, we both were fucking statues."

A long, deep sigh pushes from Ragnar's chest. "With all respect, Jack, you two have this way about you that I don't think either of you realize. *Kærlighedssyg.*"

If he thinks this is a passing infatuation, so help me, God.

Various colorful words and retorts flutter at the forefront of my brain, but instead, I poke a stern finger against Ragnar's sternum. "I'm not doing this with you right now, mate. But rest assured, I won't be forgetting it."

Ragnar's right eyelid has always drooped more than his left, and when a frown deepens his features, it gives the illusion he's been punched there. And I can't say the thought hasn't crossed my mind. But Ragnar is never one to talk out of his ass. It pisses me off to know he'll undoubtedly get to hear the words "you're right" from me—the asshole.

"Hey, Jack," Mary beckons, standing on a riverbank and tilting her head from side to side.

After Ragnar and I share a look of silent understanding, I

move to Mary's side and stare at the entrancing waters.

"Anything look strange to you?" She nudges her head at the river, encouraging me to look closer.

When I don't see anything, I eye her sidelong and she points to the water. After a few more beats, it dawns on me.

"We're walking *up*hill," I start, combing the bit of hair below my lip with a single finger.

Mary folds her arms, waiting for me to draw a conclusion. "Uh-huh."

"And the stream—it too flows *up*ward." I wave my hand through the air, my cheek twitching at the revelation. "That's not right."

Mary squats near the river. "No, it isn't. It's almost as if—"

"It's hiding something," Ragnar finishes, his gaze traveling the water's length where the mouth opening appears to disappear into *nothing*.

There could be acid, man-eating piranhas, or the river might turn my hand to stone, and yet I still feel the compulsion to stick my finger in it. Aside from the pleasant coolness given the dank island heat, nothing happens.

A putrid brown glob plops onto my boot, and I frown at it. "Read, I thought you stopped chewing tobacco?" Grimacing, I stand and shake my foot. When the spit doesn't come off, I dunk my boot in the river.

"I did," Mary responds, her expression blank.

Something scurries through the trees behind us, a brief high-pitched cackle follows it, and fades away. Scents of shit and sulfur waft, and I glue my heels to the ground.

"Don't anyone—" I begin, but Mary steps forward. A roped

trap catches her ankle, pulling her skyward toward the tree's canopy. Unsheathing my sword, I slash the rope, cutting it clean and sending her flying to the dirt on her back. "Move," I finish, glaring at our surroundings.

More laughter echoes—dozens of voices, if not more. Numerous pebbles launch from the bushes, pelting Ragnar's face and bouncing off my back. Given the weak force they were thrown, it's mostly minorly uncomfortable.

Ragnar runs a hand over his cheek. "What the hell is this?"

Mary coughs, still lying on the ground, holding her stomach and groaning. "Whoever it is—" he sits up on her elbows, glowering at the surrounding brush "—I'm going to strangle them to their last breath," she shouts.

A tiny creature, no taller than my knees, scampers from a bush, moving so quickly I can scarcely make it out before it's hiding in another plant. My eyes may deceive me, but I saw a forked tail. Maybe even—horns?

"That looked like—" Mary hurries to her feet and points where the creature fled. "—was that a—" She inches forward but stops, tossing a wide-eyed expression. "Are we dead, Jack? Are we in Hell? I mean, it wouldn't surprise me, but you'd think I'd remember—"

I raise a hand to silence her rambling. "We're very much alive."

"It can't be the only one. I heard more." Ragnar unsheathes his sword and sidesteps near the bush.

We all edge forward with weapons held firmly in our grasp. I kick the bush, jolting back when the creature yelps. Mary slashes her sword through the branches. The being screams, the tip of a severed tail flopping to the ground, oozing black blood. The creature runs past us, holding its bleeding tail. Seven more emerge from the shadows, letting the injured one hide behind them.

"Christ. What are they?" Ragnar asks, readying his blade.

With my pistol in one hand, I twirl the hilt of my sword in the other. "No idea."

Certainly not of our world. More like Anne's world.

Anne. I need to get to *Anne*.

With Mary's sword pointed at the tiny creatures, her face kept forward, she says, "Are they going to do something? Attack us? Or will they stand there gurgling and drooling with their knuckles dragging on the ground?"

They vary in height, with only one tall enough to reach my mid-thigh. Some are a deep red, while others are muddy brown or taupe. Each has long, slender, pointy ears. One has a chunk from its left ear missing, another's ears droop toward their cheeks, and all have small brass hoop earrings adorning their ears. Their eyes blaze yellow and orange like a raging fire, and their noses are gangly and pointed. They're naked save for random bits of burlap slung around their waists or chests.

One slides forward, the tallest of the bunch, and clacks its long, jagged black nails together. Its mouth opens, revealing rows of yellowed razor-sharp teeth, and a series of garbles, clicks, and snarls follow. The rest of the creatures throw their fists in the air and charge us. We hold steady with our weapons raised, preparing for them to attack with their claws, tails, or teeth, perhaps? But they do none of this. Instead, they circle us, darting between our legs and hanging from tree limbs to swat our heads, cackling maniacally.

One wraps around Ragnar's ankle and holds fast even when he attempts to shake it off. Grunting, Ragnar kicks forward, causing the creature to let go in a shriek and fly into a palm tree.

"These things aren't trying to kill us. They're just being a *nuisance*," Ragnar spats, his nose wrinkling.

"They're distracting us." I swing my sword at several nearing my knees, warning them to stay back. "Which means we're heading in the right direction. Push through them."

A command easier said than followed.

Whenever one of us gets more than two steps ahead, the creatures swarm our feet, forcing us to step and trip over them. I kick at some, bash others in the head with my pommel, and avoid all-out murdering them because I've never been one to kill while not being threatened. Except for the being who stole Anne from me—a threat on her life is a threat on mine.

Mary glares at one creature and slams her boot on its tail, halting it from running away. It makes a squeaky noise of surprise and blinks up at her, feigning innocence with those dewy, devilish eyes. Several of them have snuck behind her and are climbing her body until they're at her head, pulling her hair and covering her eyes. Mary grabs each one and tosses them.

With every passing moment, these hellions wreak havoc, increasing the chances that something is happening to Anne. And to add oil to the fire, I have no idea why the asshole wanted her in the first place, which could make things worse.

"Enough of this," I yell, my voice thundering. Picking one of the creatures randomly, I shove my blade's point at its throat. "Either you let us pass, or I start lopping off heads."

The creatures freeze but look at one another bewildered. One clacks its nails together; another pulls on its ears, and one squints a single eye at me.

"Can't even make a proper threat because they don't understand you. Of course," Mary says with a groan.

I don't lower my weapon and pan from one creature to the next, waiting for them to break. Because I don't believe them as far as I can throw them—and that's pretty damn far. Grinding my teeth when none of them make a peep, I shove the blade closer to the creature's neck, drawing black blood. "Fine." I start to slice.

"Wait," one shrieks. A tiny creature, the smallest of them, standing only to my mid-shin, shuffles from the group. "We let you be." This being is dark red, bordering on burgundy, and both horns are broken, leaving only nubs.

The other creatures swat the outspoken one, hissing and snarling. The swats become more violent, evolving into shoves and pushes. The talking creature covers its severed horns and dashes behind us, disappearing into the forest.

Ragnar moves to go after the creature, but I raise a hand to halt him. "Don't bother. They're retreating." I lower my sword from the trembling creature's neck, and it takes off, leaving a liquid trail of piss in its wake.

And I point at a trail leading *up*river.

TWENTY-ONE

ANNE

"YOUR MATE?" I reel backward, defensively curling my arms to my chest. "I'd say you're delusional, but that much is abundantly clear."

Nøkk grins, with a serpentine twist of lip and flash of pointy incisors. "Your willing participation would've been far preferred, but something tells me I'm going to *enjoy* your oppression."

This man is a few pearls short of an oyster.

Taking another step back, I stiffen when my butt meets one of the cold, wet cave walls. "And if I never accept this?"

"Eventually, you will." Nøkk clicks his nails together, crossing one foot in front of the other as he strides to a curved rock, collecting water dripping from the ceiling. He dips his hand in, holding some in his palm, and walks toward me.

I hiss and call to my powers, willing the oceans to drown him from the inside out. Saltwater bubbles from his mouth, dribbling down his chin, but he doesn't gurgle or choke. His eyes remain focused on me, and with little regard for my attempts to kill him, he reaches out and lets the water trickle over my skin. The blue scales appear down the length of my arm, and his gaze turns feral and ravenous.

"Because that will be the last water I give you until you agree to be my mate." Nøkk slips his hands behind his back. "And if you're anything like me, which, being aquatic, I assume you are, it becomes increasingly uncomfortable without water and *inconveniently* never kills you."

Unease pulls my throat tight, and I press my fingertips against the moisture behind me, grazing on it as long as I can before he'll undoubtedly force me away.

Find me, Jack.

I repeat these three words as if, by some universal miracle, Jack will hear them and use them to find me.

Nøkk cants his head to the side like he's studying me before his hand lifts. Droplets of water float past my head, and soon, the cave wall behind me is bone dry. "Clever. But I meant it. I'll cause you pain as long as it takes for you to agree."

"How romantic. I'm succumbing to your charm already," I say without emotion or inflection.

Seeing as Nøkk has no intentions of threatening my life, this has become a matter of distracting him, keeping him busy long enough for Jack to find me. Despite Jack being human, he ironically has more of an advantage over him than I do, given our aquatic powers cancel each other.

"Curious about why a powerful sea nymph has joined with *pirates*." Nøkk sits at the table, crossing his legs and resting his forearm on one knee.

By the Seas. This is going to be a long night.

"Why? Does being a sea nymph somehow put me above them?"

He stares at me blankly. "Of course it does. We are immortal. We control an element humans have yet to discover barely half of."

Irritation pricks my skin, and I can already feel my throat drying, the process accelerated by heavy emotion. "We are *not* the same. Just because we both call a body of water home doesn't make us alike. I'm one with the Seven Seas." I take a step toward him, pointing at myself. "*I'm* a protector of Atlantis. And you?" I scan his body and sneer. "Are nothing more than a lake troll who lures creatures to your banks for sport."

No sooner have the words left my lips than Nøkk's in front of me with his hand wrapped around my throat. He's tightening his grip on my neck, but not enough to hinder my breathing. "I could choke you without the need for water, Nymph."

Despite fear rearing its ugly head, I suppress it and square my jaw. "You're doing a wonderful job selling yourself to me, Nøkk. It's a wonder you haven't been scooped up by now."

A snarl vibrates from Nøkk's chest, and he releases me only to snatch my chin between two fingers. "I can play like this all day. But how long will you last, *Protector of Atlantis*, until you succumb to me?"

Yanking from his touch, I dig my nails into my palms. "I'd have thought you, too, would be used to people underestimating you."

"Such fire you have," he says, walking toward a small body

of water surrounded by jagged rocks. "I wonder where you get it from. Your—late mother, perhaps?"

Shock hits my system like a rip current, and I stagger backward. Hardly anyone remembers my mother, not even me. I'd been so young when the universe took her from us, but for *him* to somehow know she's dead? "How could you possibly—"

"It took me a moment to recognize you, that much, I'll admit." Dozens of piranha leap from the pool's surface, snapping their jaws at the diced meat Nøkk plops into the water. "But I'm older than your father." His icy eyes cut me a glare, gauging my reaction.

He could be prying me for more information to build on what little he already knows. So, I play dumb and stay dead of winter silent.

"Considering my age, if you know anything about custom, *Rhode*," he pauses after lacing my real name with venom to rival that of a lionfish.

I've given up trying to rationalize how he knows anything about me.

"Then you know," he continues. "That an offer of mating from someone of my ancient caliber is a privilege."

The man's ego knows no bounds.

"If you know so much about *me*, you should also know you'd require my father's blessing." I press my hands at the outside of my thighs to keep them from shaking.

It's a lie—partially. There are a few situations in which I'd require his approval, but this certainly isn't one of them.

"And you think he'd object? Two powerful creatures of the

waters joining forces? Creating offspring to rival that of a sea serpent or Kraken?" One piranha briefly latches to the tip of Nøkk's finger, and he doesn't so much as wince.

Nausea coils in my stomach at the thought of sex with this thing. I can't recall his true form, but I remember the stories told to me as a child. And this grimly beautiful man standing by me? It's a *mirage*.

"It's funny how piranhas have developed such a bad reputation with mortals. They depict them in stories as bloodthirsty man-eaters and vile creatures." Nøkk tosses the remaining meat in his palm to the water, brushes his hands of excess crumbs, and stands.

The air within the cave suddenly becomes chillier and danker, and I wrap my arms around myself. "It's not like they're exactly the prettiest of fish."

Nøkk smirks and slips his hands behind his back. "Not everything needs to be beautiful to have worth." He dips his head to look me dead in the eye. "—except you, of course."

I know what he means but refuse to take a compliment from this sea snail.

"I'm only worthy because of my beauty?" I press against the cave wall behind me, rubbing my lips together. They've grown increasingly drier.

"I—" Nøkk blinks, taken off guard. I doubt he does this often, considering he kidnapped the first aquatic female to strut on this island and claimed her his mate. "—I only meant to refer to you as attractive."

I roll my eyes and shift to the other foot. "You're saying beauty holds only so much worth because this isn't your true form." Displaying a hand down his body, I squint at him. "What is your true form, anyway? How far off base was I—calling you a troll?"

Nøkk shakes his head and moves to the hearth ablaze with orange flames. A ladle sticks out from an iron pot, and he stirs whatever is inside. "Why should it matter? I can take any form I wish."

"Any? And this is what you went with?"

His appearance isn't *unattractive*—quite the opposite—but I won't let him have the satisfaction. As handsome as he managed to make himself appear, it's a *lie*.

Nøkk freezes and aggressively shoves the spoon back into the pot with an echoing *clang*, spilling boiling contents over the sides. He spins on his heel and shoots me a glare that could melt the marrow in my bones. "Not what you prefer, my dear?" His form gets lost in darkness, a shadow swallowing him before appearing in front of me. But it's no longer Nøkk's face—it's *Jack's*. "Perhaps this is more to your liking."

A jellyfish's sting shoots through my veins, and I seethe at the monster stealing my pirate captain's face. But Nøkk can't even do *this* right. He's got Jack's face and eyes, but he doesn't sound like him. He doesn't walk or carry himself like him. And the bit of chest I can see poking from the shirt—he sure as hell didn't get Jack's *physique* right.

Despite the consequences, I spit right in the son of bitch's face. Because it's worth it. Jack's worth it. They're *all* worth it. "You couldn't dream of being half the man Calico Jack is as a deity, let alone a *mortal*, Nøkk."

Nøkk is physically shaking, and he slaps a hand over his

eye, wiping my saliva away. The previous face he'd chosen returns. He lets out enough of a monstrous growl to rattle pebbles from the cave ceiling, several bouncing off my head, but I ignore them. "Of all the insufferable females to grace my island, it had to be you."

And now he's singing an entirely different tune.

"Mm, spoiled *goods*, Nøkk?" I'm a breath from his face, fighting the compulsion to gag from the damp stench he's exuding. The sun doesn't settle in this being's skin; the salt from the water and air don't cling to it. He's a bog creature. And I'll live an eternity suffering from thirst before giving myself to him.

Nøkk snarls before turning his back on me. "I will *not* spend another thousand years alone." His right hand is trembling, and he stretches his fingers wide before curling them into a fist and waiting for the tremor to pass.

My bottom lip has begun to crack, and I lick it, but my tongue is like coarse sand against it. "I'd rather be alone than forced into eternal companionship with someone I don't wish to be with."

"It's because you've never had to endure seclusion." Keeping his back to me, Nøkk grabs a small wooden bowl from the table and moves to the hearth, scooping the steaming contents into it. "It can drive you mad. Force you into such an abysmal place of desperation you'll do just about anything to numb the pain, even if it's temporary." Nøkk takes exaggerated sips from the bowl, occasionally tossing me a challenging stare from the corner of his eyes.

My mouth no longer maintains moisture, and the sound

of water sloshing in the bowl causes pain in my temple. "This sounds like excuses from a *weak* mind."

Nøkk tilts his head back, draining the rest of the broth, letting some of it roll down his chin and not bothering to wipe it away. "Your cousin was weak then?" He rests the bowl on the table and snaps his fingers. "Wait, no. Your *uncle*."

I still refuse to acknowledge how he knows so much about my family.

"You and he are *nothing* alike." I had intended to lace my words with a growl, but my voice cracks, and I seethe at him instead.

"Are we not?" Nøkk sits on the table's edge and folds his hands in his lap. "Was he too not desperate for a companion? Forced her to be with him?"

My shoulders start to slump, but I force them back and fight the urge to wince from the strain. "He made her his entire *world*."

Nøkk's hands move to the table, gripping it so tightly his fingers shake. "You think I can't do the same?"

In quite the literal sense, I'm withering away in a freezing corner of a cave, and he dares to ask this? I give him the middle finger as my answer.

"Those two have lived a very long and fulfilling relationship after they surpassed the rockiness." Nøkk drums his fingers against the wood. "I dare say she grew to love him. You can do the same, Rhode. End your suffering. Agree to be mine. And we, too, can eventually be as your uncle and his beloved are."

She grew to love him because she had no one else to love. The Underworld tied her to him with no hope of escape. I *do* have that hope. And the possibility of something true with Jack. Something I've *chosen*. I close my eyes and hang my head, calling to my powers by only a fraction, barely a sliver, only using enough to mist my skin. An ounce of relief settles over me before being lifted away.

I flare my eyes open, and Nøkk stands there with a hand outstretched, pulling the water from me. Hundreds of tiny droplets suspend in the air before he lowers his hand, and they fall to the cave floor as forgotten fog. My knees find the ground in a slump. I need to preserve my strength, and pretending I still possess the ability to stand after he takes my last effort to cure myself would be futile.

"It's pointless to try, Rhode. You cannot beat me. Suffer or succumb. Those are your only choices." Nøkk slides the chair in front of the hearth and reclines, settling.

No. I have many choices. And they're out there looking for me. I can't beat him alone but with my crew? We can make him pay. I need to hold out—force my mind anywhere else from the pain ratcheting through my body, begging for water.

I'd fallen asleep, lulled by the flickering flame of the hearth and the consistent rhythm of a single drop of water landing in a puddle on the cave floor from a jagged ceiling rock. Sometime later, I snap awake with a gasp. A knot has formed in my neck from my chin hanging toward my chest at an awkward angle. A violin sounds from the darkness—a macabre melody with soothing undertones. It's almost hypnotic and makes my head fuzzy despite how weak my body has become.

Nøkk slithers into the light, a dark wooden violin at his shoulder. He grins at me, a flash of dagger teeth catching the still blazing fire. "Look who's awake. I think it was due to my particular aptness with a good set of strings."

The music swirls through my mind like liquid metal, waiting to harden, to *imprint* itself there. I pinch my eyes together so tightly that I see stars in the blackness behind my lids. "You mean—" I pause, swallowing what little saliva I have left to coat my gravelly throat "—that tune that sounds like a cat's tail being run over by a chariot?"

Nøkk chuckles, but his tone is noncommittal and distant at best. "Soon, you won't have the strength to speak above a whisper, and that's what you chose to say?" He edges closer, his hands moving with more flourish, his playing elbow propped skyward.

It's a bizarre feeling to be lured by music when Sirens do little to affect me. But as he changes the tune to something far more ancient and primal, my limbs relax, and my chin lifts in his direction.

"Do you enjoy my playing, Nymph?" Nøkk's voice echoes in my skull like we're both ensconced in a glass bottle.

No. And I could care less if his fiddle-playing rivals muses, bards, and demons.

But no matter how often I replay these thoughts to convince myself it's how I feel, my eyes lazily open and my cracked lips part to say, "Yes."

Nøkk's smile widens, and he stands above me now, his body swaying with the melody. "There's nothing quite like a perfectly tuned instrument. And I've made it a permanent staple of mine." He slowly sinks until he's squatting in front of me, still playing and grinning like a fox who finally cornered the rabbit they've been chasing.

I say nothing, partly because my throat cannot handle it, and I can't tear my eyes away from his fingers nimbly working the strings.

Find. Me. Jack.

"Now, Rhode, my dear, all you have to do is say one little word. Your suffering will end, and you can listen to this music for the rest of eternity," Nøkk whispers and lowers his face to mine, his serpent-like eyes fixed on me. "Will you be my *mate*?"

My throat bobs, but nothing happens save for a burning pain and a strained breath. I chew on some of the dead skin falling from my bottom lip before opening my mouth to speak. Nøkk's face has blurred, the violin now in sharp focus, sea mist floating from the strings as he plays.

"Like fucking hell, she will," a voice roars from the cave entrance.

No, not just a voice. *His* voice. Jack Rackham. *My* Jack.

TWENTY-TWO

JACK

MY RAGGED BREATHS strangle me at the sight of Anne on her knees, paler than usual, with dark circles under her eyes and lips so dry they're cracking. All I want to do is pull her toward me, drown her with affection, and douse her with water, but this vile creature needs to *pay*.

Anne falls to her hands, my name barely escaping her throat and coming out as a scratched wheeze, which only adds oil to the fire raging in my chest.

"Back the hell away from her," I threaten, storming forward to run my blade through his throat despite not knowing if it'd kill him.

He raises the violin and bow he's playing in surrender. But the wry smile contorting his lips tells me he has no intention of making any of this easy. With a flick of his wrist, that same damn impenetrable water wall keeps me from nearing him and separates me and Anne.

"Goddammit," I roar, punching the wall with my sword's hilt.

Ragnar and Mary flank me with their weapons drawn and stare dumbfoundedly at the suspended water they'd yet to witness.

Anne lifts her chin, her forehead wrinkling, once she spots Mary. It's as if she wants to cry but can't find the tears. Nøkk slides in front of her, blocking her view of us, and I slam my fist into the wall, making it splash against my knuckles.

"It's going to be alright, Annie," I reassure her but keep my focus on the walking dead man.

The man waves a finger at me, *still* fucking smiling. "I understand pirates are known for deceptions and lies, but why lie to *her?*"

Moving to the wall, I stand close enough that the tip of my nose almost touches it. "We're partners, she and I. No lies between us. And considering Anne and I have just found one another, I know neither of us will let a shriveling shrimp come between us simply because you don't know your way around women."

He chuckles, crouching near Anne now and stroking strands of her red hair away from her forehead. The way his fingertips lightly graze her skin has me pounding my fists against the watery prison this wall has become. "You'll never get past my power, mortals. I can be just and let you walk away with your lives, but you cannot win this one."

"Why," Mary grunts between repeated kicks against the water. "Does this feel like concrete?"

Ragnar remains unusually quiet, the skin beneath one eye twitching as he studies Anne's captor. He folds his arms and edges closer to the water. "Who are you?"

Despite barely having the strength to lift her chin, Anne tears away from the water man's touch. It's agonizing seeing her in such pain. And worse that I can't do a damn thing about it but watch her suffer from the other side of an impenetrable barrier. I chew a hole in the inside of my cheek.

"What use is my name to you?" The man stares curiously at Ragnar.

Why *did* he ask his name?

"I normally prefer to know the name of the people or creatures I kill," Ragnar responds, motionless like a gargoyle statue.

No, he doesn't. He's not known the faces of half the people he's killed, let alone their names.

The water man scoffs, air puffing from his nostrils. "Then there's little reason for you to know it."

"Nøkk," Anne croaks, her fingernails digging into the stone floor, cracking one of them.

Ragnar's eyes blaze, and he drops his hands at his sides. "Nøkk," he repeats, pronouncing it like Scandinavian languages intend.

Suddenly, Nøkk is nervous, and his smile fades away. "Do I know you? Who—are you?" He directs the question at Ragnar, his confidence faltering.

"*Ingen*," Ragnar shakes his head, his jaw tightening. "But I know plenty about *you* from the stories told to me as a child."

Nøkk shoots to his feet, palms up. His unease now borders on fear. "Wait."

"*Nyk. Nyk. Nål i vann,*" Ragnar begins to chant.

I have zero idea what Ragnar is saying, but it has Nøkk covering his ears and wailing, so I stand back to enjoy it.

"*Jomfru Maria kastet stål i vann.*"

"Stop," Nøkk roars. "I'll let her go. Just stop."

But Ragnar doesn't stop. He speaks the last line louder, emphasizing each word. "*Du sinker, jeg flyter.*"

"No," Nøkk bellows and the water wall falls to the ground, splashing around us.

We charge with swords raised, and I stand between him and Anne. I'm seconds away from impaling him with my blade, but he's—changing. His human form turns rail thin, gangly, gray, and scaled inhumanly. Multiple red fins sprout from his elbows, hips, shoulders, and head, with two much larger ones extending like ears. His blonde hair falls away, replaced by straggly, greasy black strands. The nose has become two nostrils, his face short and broad with deep ridges and grooves above a pair of pupil-less glowing yellow eyes.

"You're—" I scrunch my nose at him "—disgusting."

The thought of this thing's hands on Anne in a human form had me raging, but this? It sends me over the edge.

"*Du sinker, jeg flyter,*" Ragnar repeats, a command this time.

Nøkk bares rows of pointy teeth before squatting to the floor, his head and back turned at odd angles. And then—he's gone in a splash of muddied water, leaving patches of green algae behind.

"The chant is meant to ward him away. I don't know how long it'll last." Ragnar tosses me a stern brow.

"Get her to water, Jack," Mary cries out.

I'm already sheathing my sword and scooping Anne into my arms before barreling out of the cave, grunting as I slip once, catching myself on the wall with a shoulder. She doesn't have enough strength to wrap her arms around my neck, and they hang limply at her sides, her head resting against my chest.

"Jack," Anne whispers.

"I have you, love." After kissing the top of her head, I sprint through the woods, not caring when branches snag on my clothes, leaves slap my face, or stray barbs cut my forehead.

Anne's groaning, her cheek pressing against my collarbone. I hold her tighter, running as fast as I can without hurting her, and finally, the sea appears on the horizon. I've always held a special place in my heart for it, but now, holding a *piece* of it in my arms, the ocean has become something far more than a mere sanctuary. It's become—*everything*.

Night has overtaken the sky since I left Nøkk's cave. White light spills over the sand from the full moon and makes jagged shapes on the choppy water of the sea's surface. I slow only a little once I reach the sand, my boots sinking into it. Anne's nose twitches, and her eyes flutter open, her gaze flicking to the beckoning water before us.

"Jack," she croaks.

"Yes?" I cradle her like she's soaked parchment, careful not to let it wither and tear in my arms.

"My trousers."

Pausing where the tide laps at the shoreline, I do as she asks, crouching to one knee and quickly removing her trousers and boots. Not bothering to remove my clothes or shoes, I scoop her back into my arms and wade into the sea. It's freezing, and the temperature resembles a thousand tiny pin pricks piercing my skin, but I grit my teeth and bear it. The water welcomes her while still supported in my arms.

It takes only seconds before her legs morph into a tail, the teal fins at the tip of it brushing the backs of my thighs. Blue scales appear over nearly every inch of her body, her hair darkens to a sapphire color, and her ears shift to webbing. She's motionless for far too long for comfort, and I find myself holding my breath. Her eyes burst open, the nymph glacial blue replacing her emerald gaze, and she gasps.

I stare at her with acute stillness because this is the first time I see her like this—the sea nymph. Both sides are equally beautiful, and I'm thanking whatever higher power is willing to take the credit that today wasn't the last day I'd witness both parts of her.

Her head lifts from the water, lips lightly sputtering, her gaze fixed on me. She presses a hand to my cheek, the webbing between each finger somehow softer than the rest of her, which already feels like liquid silk against my skin. Her eyes roam my face as if searching for signs that what I see displeases me somehow. It's not possible. She's perfection.

"Thank you," she whispers, her voice more vital and more like herself.

The words take me aback. "For rescuing you? Don't you dare thank me for that. I told you we're partners. And you're a part of this crew, this family, and—" a shiver catapults through me from the frigid waters settling into my bones "—you mean a great deal to *me*."

Anne frowns at my body trembling from the cold, her ears drooping toward her chin. She slips a hand in mine and coaxes me to the shore. "Let's get out of the water."

"Are you feeling better?" It's my turn to frown because I'll not forgive myself if she's not fully healing herself because my body betrayed me and decided to *shiver* at the most inconvenient moment.

She tugs me, easing me through the water and toward the wet sand. "Much better."

Flopping my ass to the ground, I rub my arms, working heat back into them. Anne still dons her tail and sits behind me before wrapping the tail around my lap. It's surprisingly warm, given my experience with the usual fish scales, but she's not a fish.

Her arms envelop me next, chin resting on my shoulder. "Is that better?"

"Much better," I mimic her words.

The moonlight gives her scales a celestial glow, and the tip of her tail lazily sways, making arched patterns in the sand. "You could've frozen, Jack."

The chills have passed, and I allow myself to sink against her. "You would've never let that happen."

"You're right." I feel her lips smiling against my cheek.

I trail a finger over her tail where a human knee would be, making the scales glow brighter. "Was what Nøkk said true?"

"Is what true?" She tilts her head.

"That you're his—" I pause, finding it difficult to say out loud, and add another finger to her tail "—*mate*?"

Anne's arms tighten around my ribs. "No. I'm not."

Shifting so we can look at each other, I drag a hand through my wet locks. "Are you sure? I don't understand how this works, but how would you know otherwise? I'd like to know if I'm stealing another man's destined betrothed."

A half smile tugs at Anne's lips, and she lightly tugs my beard, the pointed translucent fingernail scraping my chin. "It's hard to explain how I know, but trust me, Jack. He's *not* my mate."

Blowing out an exaggerated sigh, I hang my head. "Damn."

This makes her laugh, vibrant and lively. "Excuse me?" She playfully jabs me.

"It would've been far more my niche if I were to have stolen you away. You would've been the most valuable haul in my pirating career." I lift my eyes to hers in time to see them widening and softening, slowly materializing to Anne's emerald gaze.

"What if—if you and I—" she's turning into Anne bit by bit, the red hair swirling her face and neck, scales melting away "—were mates?"

Contemplating this, I let my face fall. "Well, that'd be no fun. I can't rightly steal you for myself *from* myself."

"Jack," she shrieks, tackling me with the human legs that have returned, and I'm painfully aware she's now naked from the waist down.

I'm sitting with Anne in my lap, knees straddling me. I trace a thumb across her cheekbone and grin at how she nuzzles my hand. "I'm not sure what I would've done if Nøkk took you away from me. Probably scoured the Earth looking for you and taking out my rage on poor bastard merchants."

"You don't have to wonder." Anne presses her forehead to mine, and we close our eyes, listening to each other breathe. "I'm right here. With *you*."

Sitting back, I take her face in my hands, waiting for her to look at me. "Are you alright? The son of a bitch denied you water for days. I still wish I could've harpooned him to Davy Jones' Locker. Still do."

"I'm fine, my Captain," she reassures me, pressing a chaste kiss to my lips. "I've been through worse."

"Worse than dying a painfully slow death in the equivalent of immortal drowning?" I blink at her.

"Funny thing about being immortal. A sword through your stomach won't kill you, but you can feel it all the same." Her eyes turn glassy like she's remembering the moment it happened.

"Anne." Waiting for her to return to reality, I edge my thumb under her bottom lip. "We should get back to the ship. Nøkk could reappear at any moment."

It's peculiar to feel protective of another life above your own. But I dare say I'd be swallowed whole by the Kraken if it meant saving her life in the process. Is this what love is? Devotion? Commitments of the heart?

Anne chews her lip, her mossy eyes suddenly heavy, and unbuttons her shirt. "The sea is *my* domain. He has no power here."

Her domain. Anne can *command* the seas and oceans. The realization should make me feel inferior as a mere mortal, but surprisingly, it only draws me to her more. Because I know she'd be willing to share it all with me. And even if I never ask, this knowledge puts her on a pedestal far above me.

I slide the unbuttoned garment from one of her shoulders, then the next. "I do suppose the crew can wait a few moments longer."

She grins at me, propping on her elbows and spreading her milky thighs with a beckoning finger. As I remove the wet clothes, still clinging to me like a second skin, the tide has grown closer and splashes over us, making Anne's blue scales on one side of her body shimmer in the moonlight. And as I crawl across the wet sand, hovering over her still smiling face, half sea nymph, half pirate queen, I admit what a lucky scoundrel of a pirate Calico Jack truly is.

TWENTY-THREE

ANNE

HE DID IT. He *found* me—a mortal man without powers and only his mind, intuition, and strength to aid him. It's remarkable, and not only can I not explain it, but I also had no doubts he'd succeed. There's no way to rationalize *that* either. Then he took care of me, rushing me to the sea despite the frigid temperatures he *knew* could harm him. And when I opened my eyes, in complete sea nymph form, he gazed down at me like a prized, glittering jewel. No semblance of shock. No hints of distaste in his expression for my aquatic persona. Despite the cold seeping into his bones, he didn't even appear in pain.

And now we sit on the sandy shoreline naked and devour one another with our gazes. There are so many destined unions among ethereal beings—soulmates, fated bonds, clandestine love that can withstand time and circumstance. But Jack is right. How would I know one way or the other if I have no idea how it's supposed to feel? I don't. But Nøkk? I can say with absolute clarity that he's *not* my mate.

Jack hovers over me, trailing the back of his hand down my cheek. "Give me your tail."

The command gives me pause, and I blink at him.

The confusion must be evident in my expression because Jack smirks and kisses the tip of my nose. "I believe there were promises of tail play?"

A knot coils in my stomach, and I play a heated stare. I don't know how much more perfect this man can be for me. Anything more, and I'd call him a liar for claiming to be merely human. Shifting my leg from his other side, I join my knees together and will the tail to return. My limbs fuse with a seam of shimmering blue light. The feet are the last to change, morphing into dark blue fins that I flap against the sand. "I can't move much, beached like this."

"Sounds like you'll be at my mercy," Jack whispers, coating his words with filth and silk.

A wave from the sea laps against my arm, the cerulean scales gleaming back to life. I curl my tail toward my chest, but Jack places his palm where my human knees would be and slowly shakes his head—left to right. My heart is racing like we haven't done what's about to transpire once before. As if we haven't shared countless kisses and intimate moments. But this—this is different in so many ways. This is us going farther than lust and attraction alone.

"Lay on your stomach, love," he says, coaxing me to turn and drumming his fingers against my tail's scales.

I do as he asks, my breasts pressing to the wet sand. Turning my head to one side, I rest it on my hands, my tail's fins involuntarily swaying in anticipation. An excited surge of nerves bubbles in my core, and I gasp when his callused fingertips trace down my spine. He reaches the spot where my hips meet the apex of my tail and spends extra time stroking me there. The central fin at the tail's tip flicks skyward, a sensual coil tightening in my stomach.

No one has ever touched me like this—exploratory, appreciative, and seductive.

Jack gently drums his fingers across my scales, skirting to one of two smaller fins protruding from where the tops of my thighs would be. His hand flutters over it, sending shivers and trembles through my lower half. My fingers dig into the sand now, my face lifting, eyes pinched shut. He's trailing his touch down the tail's center, paying particular attention to the seam where he saw my legs joining.

Pleasure builds and builds, the two smaller fins near my ankles flapping frantically. When Jack reaches my main fin, tracing through the primary vein, I blank out and cry through a climax I never knew possible. My body quakes through the aftershock. Jack's beard brushes the skin at my nape.

"Am I a first for that too?" Jack smiles against my skin after giving it a playful nip.

Seas below. Even his arrogance has netted me.

I answer him by hoisting my hips in the air, thumping into his gut, and arousing a satisfying grunt and chuckle.

"Now give me your legs, Anne." Jack's hands curl around my waist, and he leans back on his haunches, watching my legs materialize with sapphire shimmers and ribbons of suspended bubbles.

I'm on my hands and knees in front of him, my ass propped

in the air, presenting myself to him. A masculine groan pulls from his throat, and he grasps each cheek, squeezing them. The tip of him pushes at my entrance, but unlike before, he takes his time sliding inside—the slowness of it blissfully excruciating. When he's filled me completely, he stills, bending forward to trail kisses down the length of my spine. He scoops water into his palm and trickles it over my back. As each scale appears, my skin sends jolts of pleasuring stings around their edges, making me acutely aware of each.

He's thrusting now—rhythmic and claiming. I reach behind me for his hand to latch onto something real because, despite my chimerical existence, I've somehow been thrown off my axis. He interlocks his fingers with mine, keeping the other palm at my hip, pulling me on and off him, and kneading the dimple at my lower back.

The sea's waves become choppier and unruly, matching my erratic heartbeat. I can hear the waves rolling toward the shoreline before it reaches us, and as if Jack somehow senses it too, he hoists me up, slamming my back to his chest. The water splashes against our sides—frothy, salty, and majestic. I keep the chill from settling into Jack's skin, not daring to let it ruin a moment like this. With me writhing against him behind me, he tilts my chin up to meet his lips, kissing me so deeply I can feel the sensation in my toes. He presses our foreheads together as we work in tandem. His thumb dips into my mouth, his other fingers gripping my chin.

After nibbling on his fingertip, I let out a shattered gasp, the euphoria sneaking up on me, and I reach for the back of his head, fisting his hair. One of his burly bronzed arms wraps around me, his hand splayed at my stomach right above my sex, and he pushes me against him, keeping me deliciously captive in his grasp.

"Incredible," Jack moans against my neck, still pumping in and out of me in languid motions. "I can feel the ocean *through* you."

His words make my scales hum and blaze with vibrance. I turn to face him, smiling at the sight of him soaking wet, his hair falling in tendrils of wavy onyx over his eyes. "You haven't even *begun* to feel it, pirate." Placing one hand on his chest, I give him a light push, coaxing him to lie on his back.

Jack doesn't fight me, willingly settling on his elbows, his muscular, tanned legs spread wide, waiting for me. He bites his bottom lip, caramel eyes roaming my face, breasts, and hair. I straddle him, positioning myself over him, and slowly sink, whimpering at the feeling of fullness the lower I get until finally, our hips meet. Jack growls, his head dips back, his toes digging into the sand. He grabs my hips, and I sway on top of him, pulling the thrumming heartbeat of the seas into my veins. Jack's lips spasm, and he flares his eyes open, staring up at me as if to ask if what he's feeling has to do with me.

Grinning, I press our chests together and kiss a trail over the hair on his jawline until I reach his ear. "You're as much a part of the seas as I am, Jack. Only now can I formally introduce you."

Jack grasps the back of my neck and kisses me, unleashing a masculine moan against my mouth. Another wave stirs, and we don't pull away once it plows into us, soaking us to the bone. Jack finishes the kiss as the tide ebbs, water droplets still hanging on his lashes. His gaze drops to my mouth, tongue licking salt from his bottom lip, and then he's flipped us in one swift motion. I'm beneath him, his body above mine, forearms caging my head. The seas drip onto my cheeks from his hair, and he drives into me—deep and all-consuming.

"You say you can talk to the ocean?" Jack rolls his hips, hitting against that sensitive spot, rubbing it just the right way. "You tell her—" he lowers his face, brushing his nose to the tip of mine and over my cheeks "—she has to *share* you now."

The declaration makes me clench around him, and I can't help but dig my fingernails into his back. There's a path that neither of us would have to share with the seas—a version where we could live in and out of the waters as we please. But it's a fever dream. He's not of my world, and the only person who could make it possible, even *if* Jack chose to become a part of it, is eons away.

He's thrusting faster now, our eyes locked and never faltering, even when my back arches from the sand as blissful release overtakes me yet again. Jack still pumps into me through my climax, using his knee to hitch my thigh, going deeper. A tic forms in his cheek, his cock throbbing several times inside me. He goes to pull away, to expel himself anywhere but here, and I grab his ass, keeping him put.

Jack's gaze searches my face, his lips parting to question my actions, but I press a finger to his mouth. "Trust me. Come undone inside me, *Captain*."

Like many deities' fates with others are spun by the universe, so are children. And I've yet to seek blessing for our union, let alone offspring from it.

This makes Jack's gaze grow feral, and he crashes his lips

against mine, pounding into me several more times before he finds his release. I pinch my knees at his ribs, grinning once he comes up for air.

Supporting his weight on one arm, he lets most of his lower half rest on top of me, and I love the heavy feel of it—safe and comforting. "And now, that was a first for *me*."

It takes a moment for me to realize what he means. "You've never—ins—"

Jack slips a gentle palm over my mouth. "I have *not*. The last thing I need is a bunch of random little Jacks running around that I didn't know about."

For whatever reason, the idea of Jack having children with other women makes me sad, but hearing it isn't possible raises jubilance in the same instant.

Smiling, I part his hair from his eyes, securing it behind an ear. "But they'd be so cute."

"Well, that's a given." Jack lifts his chin, the moonlight creating shadows over his features, making the sharpness more handsome. "Have you seen this jawline? The well-angled nose?" He keeps a straight face for several seconds but cracks a smile.

"I'm certain I have sand in places I never deemed possible." A laugh bursts from my chest—fluttery and *alive*.

Jack grins and takes a handful of said sand, trickling it over my shoulder before lightly rubbing it against my skin. "You get used to it. It ironically makes your skin smoother. Besides, can't you—" He snaps his fingers, wincing as some sand flies at his face.

Skirting my knee up his thigh, I take his hand in mine and

trace the lines and patterns on his palm, laughing. "I have aquatic powers. That doesn't include making sand disappear from crevices."

"Noted. But in my defense, I'm quite new to all of this." A warm smile edges Jack's lips, and he lazily traces one of my nipples.

The thrum of the sea thunders in my ears, and despite how happy I've been since the catastrophe in Atlantis, I still can't stomach the thought of my family searching for me with no idea where to look. Or worse, they don't know if I'm alive. This sends a chilly current washing over me.

"Jack," I beckon softly.

He must hear the change of tone in my voice because his gaze snaps to mine, a cinch forming in the skin between his eyes. "Yes?"

"I have another favor to ask of you." Lifting his hand to my lips, I kiss each knuckle and trail the dark scattering of hair.

"The way you say that sounds like you think there are to be no more favors after this one." Jack trails a finger down the length of my nose. "Ask away, Annie. Anything."

"I wish—" I sit up, grasping Jack's hand, but my eyes turn to the sea. "I wish to send a message to my family."

Jack delicately touches my jaw and returns my gaze to him. "But how do you intend to do that? Parchment in a bottle? Tossing it into the waves and hoping it makes it where it needs to go?"

"Yes. But a *charmed* bottle."

Jack scratches the back of his head. "I don't quite follow. Spell it out for me as if I'm a child."

Sighing, I sit up straight and take both of his hands. "There's a sea witch. I can sense her grotto, which is not far away. She'd possess the power to enchant the bottle and guide it home."

Jack's head bobs like he's mulling over my words. "A sea witch?"

"Yes."

Jack points to the sea. "Underwater?"

"Also, yes."

"And it's—" Jack walks his fingers along where the sky meets the water "—on the way, so to speak?"

"Mostly." A crab bumps my ankle, and I hold out my palm, letting it crawl onto it. "It's a little off our path, so I hesitated to ask."

Jack cups my cheek and kisses my head. "My sails are yours, Anne. And the crew will understand."

Warmth pools in my chest, and I grin at Jack swinging his finger above the crab, which opens and closes its claws but never tries to clamp onto him. We simultaneously glance skyward at the moon's position.

"Sunrise will be soon. I suppose we should sleep somewhere other than a sandy beach?" I lower my hand and encourage the crab home.

Jack lets out an overly dramatic sigh. "If we must." He stands and helps me to my feet.

We dust the sand away from our bodies, dress in still very wet and cold clothes, and follow the sea's shoreline back to The Revenge. When we board, I expect the ship to be quiet, with everyone except those taking the first watch asleep below deck. But it isn't silent at all. Most of the crew crowd in a circle near the main mast, pointing down at something.

"What in the hell—" Jack squeezes my shoulder before shoving through the crowd. "Make way, make way. Captain on deck and all that."

When Jack freezes and goes silent, I'm next to push through.

"Oh, Cap, you're back," Red says. "Where's Anne?"

No sooner does he ask my whereabouts than I arrive and pause, much like Jack, at the sight of Truffles and an imp with broken-off horns *playing* together. It doesn't pay the pirate crew much mind, enjoying its frivolous tackling with Jack's cat, but it stops when Jack bends forward, the imp's eyes as wide as scallops.

"Will someone please explain why this imp is on my ship?" Jack says in his imposing captain voice, and he doesn't look away from the tiny creature. The imp backs up with its forked tail wrapping its body, claws twirling around its fingers.

"I caught him rummaging through a barrel of rice," Glog answers, shaking his head and smiling.

"And *why* is he still on board?" Jack asks.

Mary tackles my side, hugging me and feeling every inch of my face. "Fuck, Anne. Don't scare me like that."

"Scare *you*?" I elbow her ribs. "I'm not that easy to get rid of, immortality or not."

Mary grins and bounces in place. "Cap, we decided to keep the little ugly cute thing around because he doesn't pose a threat and could come in handy."

"Handy?" Jack displays a hand toward it. "For what? Shimmying through our legs and tripping us? You all realize this creature belongs to the very same lunatic that kidnapped Anne?"

"This is Nøkk's imp?" I point at the fantastical creature.

And Jack points at me. "See?" He asks the crew. "Yes, it *is*."

Truffles ignores the drama unfolding and licks the imp's face, proceeding to clean him.

"If I—" The imp's hooved feet turn inward, and it curls its tail over its hands repeatedly. "If I may speak?" His voice is meager and higher-pitched.

Jack sighs but gives a curt nod.

"I've wished to run from my master for a long time." The imp frowns, pausing and dragging a hand over one of the horn stumps on its head. "Treated badly. They said a pirate crew is where one goes to escape. To be—free?" The imp's eyes brighten with hope toward his would-be captain.

Jack beats a fist against his thigh. "And I suppose you have all voted on this already?"

"We have," Duke chimes in, several crew members stepping out of the way to let him join us. "And it's unanimous."

"Of course, it bloody well is." Jack snaps his gaze to Ragnar. "Even you?"

Ragnar shoots a glare at Mary. "I've been *persuaded*."

"For the love of—" Jack pinches the bridge of his nose. "Anne? Are you alright with this?"

The imp gazes up at me with eyes to put a puppy to shame, his ears drooping toward his chin.

"He *is* pretty adorable, Jack." I tilt my head.

Jack huffs a breath through his nose. "Fine. But he's not staying in *my* quarters, and you lot are in charge of feeding, watering, or doing whatever the hell else an imp needs." He turns away but swivels back to face them with a lifted finger.

"And for God's sake, give him a name. I'm not calling it *imp*."

"Aye, aye, Cap," Red says, at the cheery imp creature as he settles contentedly into Truffles' fur behind him.

Jack holds his hand out to me. "Anne, my dear, shall we retire?"

I take it and let him lead me to his cabin, exhaustion weighing heavy on my body. We settle into his hammock, and I drift to sleep thinking about our newly recruited imp crewmate and mentally preparing myself to make a deal with a sea witch.

TWENTY-FOUR

ANNE

THE SUN HAS barely risen, and I've gotten no more than an hour of sleep, but I'm restless. The run-ins with the Charybdis, the encounter with Nøkk, and the impending meeting with Morgana, the sea witch, have my stomach in ever-tightening knots. This unintended journey started with me fending for *myself,* and now, it has blossomed into harboring an entire crew under my fins. I've never been responsible for this many mortal lives at once. It puts my uncle's job, the immense pressure on his shoulders, in perspective.

Jack lies motionless beside me in a deep slumber, the low rumble of his snores vibrating the top of my head. He looks too peaceful to interrupt, and genuine rest comes so infrequently for him that I don't dare. Slipping from under his arm, astonishingly not flipping myself to the floor, I tip-toe out of his quarters, frowning as his body's warmth fades from my skin.

Like his cat dad, Truffles is curled up on his back with his front paws in the air, snoring away. Despite the creaking floorboard, he doesn't stir when I sneak past him, and I successfully arrive on deck. Squid's feet hang from the crow's nest, and Aranck sits on a barrel, organizing herbs. Everyone else still sleeps, and I rest my elbows on the ship's side, letting the cool breeze and sea mist calm my nerves.

My eyes are closed but fly open when I hear a tiny voice humming a shanty and crunching—*loud* crunching. The imp is walking past, having not noticed me despite my being triple his size. I clear my throat, and the imp freezes, cradling several biscuits in his arms. When he turns to look up at me, crumbs surround his mouth, and more fall out when he grins.

"Hungry?" I pinch back a smile.

The imp swallows the chunk of biscuit with a loud gulp. "Been long since real food. Master only ever fed us oats."

Damn. Poor thing.

"I can understand that." Squatting to be more at his level, I hold my hand out. "But we have portion rations for a reason. Can't have any crew starving to death, can we?"

The imp frowns and hesitates. But eventually, three biscuits rest in my palm. He's busy licking every crumb from his fingers, and I offer him one. "I suppose one extra won't hurt. But it'll be our little secret, yeah?"

The imp's eyes brighten, and he receives the food with both hands. He takes the tiniest bites I've ever seen in hopes of savoring it. "Thankful."

"Did you already have a name?"

The imp feverishly shakes his head. "No. Master only use numbers. But have new name now."

"You do?" My head jerks back. "What is it?"

"Laust," the imp answers, grinning with cheeks full of biscuit.

Tapping my knee, I squint against the sun. "Oh, yeah? And who named you that?"

With a chunk of biscuit still in his grasp, Laust raises his arms skyward. "The big, grumpy one with the foggy eye."

"Ragnar?" A light laugh bursts from my throat because I'm delightfully surprised by this.

Laust blinks a few times and nods. "Yes."

Now I realize Laust and I have something in common. We stowed away on Jack's ship, hoping it would lead us to better places. Given his reasons were to escape servitude to a cruel master, and mine were far more selfish by comparison, a brief flash of guilt prickles the base of my neck.

"You know, Laust," I conjure sea bubbles to my palms, flashing the scales through my skin and holding them to his eye level. "I, too, am born of myth."

Laust's orbed eyes widen, the sunlight above us casting a brightened glint. He's lost interest in the biscuit, a chunk falling from his gaping mouth and landing on the deck. He reaches a clawed hand toward the bubbles, wincing before finding the courage to touch them. His ears fold backward, pressing to his head, and a delighted smile follows. "What are you?"

"A sea nymph." Grinning, I clap my hands together, sending a water spray at Laust's chest.

Laust lets out a joyous yelp and rubs his hands over the tattered burlap that serves as his clothes, his tail bristling at the watery sensation. He suddenly halts, ears drooping, and he frowns. "Master hurt you?"

The genuine concern in his expression, the way his tail

curls around his leg as if he had anything to do with Nøkk's behavior, has my heart strangling.

Offering a reassuring smile, I rub one of his horn stubs. "Only a little. He's been taught a lesson, and I don't think he'll try it again soon. Besides—" I bump a knuckle under his chin, encouraging him to hold his head high now that he *can*. "You're one of us now, Laust. You need not be concerned about him anymore."

A jolt of confidence zips Laust's spine straight, a gleam in his eye, and he snatches the biscuit from the floor. "Right. I go find fluffy horse."

Laust scurries away before I fully register that the "fluffy horse" is Truffles. Chuckling, I rise in time to catch Duke yawning and stretching his arms above his head. He's made his way to the helm, lifting his shirt to scratch his round belly, and spits over the ship's side, settling at the wheel. He spots me and motions me over.

"Morning," I say, shielding my eyes from the sun blazing yellow and pale orange behind Duke.

Duke coughs into his fist before grinning and curling his fingers around the wheel's pegs. "Good morning. I see you've taken a liking to our newest miniature recruit?"

Sitting on a crate near the railing, I cross my ankle to the opposing knee and stretch my arms wide. "Laust."

Duke arches a brow. "Bless you."

I laugh and let my head fall back, closing my eyes and feeling the sun warm my skin. "No, the imp. That's his name. Given by Ragnar, no less."

"Bah. Now you're a pirate *and* a liar." Duke lets out a raspy huff.

"It's true," Mary's voice adds, and I let my eyes flutter open. She's cleaning her teeth with a wooden pick and hops to the helm, joining us. "I bore witness to Ragnar, with no influence from me, name our little cute and ugly."

"And now it's a conspiracy," Duke scoffs.

Mary combs her dark hair before putting on her tri-cornered hat. She flops on the seat next to me, still chewing on the wood pick, and slaps my knee. "Are we making friends with imps now?"

I've had acquaintances of all species and sorts, not to exclude satyrs, pixies, and gnomes. But an imp? This is a first.

"Yeah. I'd say we're threaded from the same cloth. I offered companionship as the only other *fantastical* being on board."

Mary makes a *tsking* sound and goes from slouching to sitting with perfect posture. "I'm *enchanting*. Isn't that the same damn thing?"

"If by that you mean possessing the ability to disarm a man with a look and three words or less, then I wholeheartedly agree with you, Read," Jack says, propping a foot on one step. He's wearing his captain's jacket, shirt open and billowing in the breeze. My insides are already flipping at the sight of him, but when his eyes meet mine, I'm sugar in the sea.

Snorting, Mary flicks the wood pick overboard. "I'll take it."

Jack doesn't look away from me as he hoists himself to the wheel. "Duke, we're taking a slight detour. Reroute us in—" Pausing, he holds his hand out to me. "What direction, love?"

Though more of a pet name versus a declaration, the way the word "love" rolls from Jack's tongue sends my nerves into sizzling static. "Straight east."

"Due east?" Duke mumbles something under his breath. "That's more than a detour, Jack. We still need to get further north if we're going to—"

Jack shifts his attention to Duke. "Due. East."

Rolling his shoulders, Duke takes the wheel. "Aye, aye."

Jack spins on his heel, returning to me with his fingers interlaced behind his back. "You sure about this? All the legends I'm familiar with never make any witch, be it land or sea, something to trifle with."

The truth? I'm *not* sure about it. And he's right. I'm certain righteous witches exist somewhere in the vast universe, but I've yet to meet one. Morgana, infamous for her high stakes, is no exception. I hope she'll have mercy on me.

I urge him to hug me by sliding my arms around Jack's waist. When he obliges, wrapping those burly limbs to my shoulders and back, I rest my head on his chest, listening to his steady mortal heartbeat. "I'm not sure, no. But I don't have a choice. She's the only one I know who can do this spell without us traveling much further off course."

"Then we know what to do, Annie. But are you sure I can't come with you? I have to say, the idea of you dealing with another magical sea creep by yourself makes me a tad nauseous." Jack's body tenses, and his grip tightens on my back.

"Jack," I start, peeling back and twisting his shirt within my grasp. "I told you. She lives und—"

"Underwater," he finishes for me, averting his gaze elsewhere. "Yes, you said. But we don't know how *far* underwater."

It brightens my spirits and simultaneously tears me up

inside. Jack is trying to find any way possible to be at my side during this exchange.

"Dealing with her is going to be a sensitive matter. I know you're the best swimmer on this ship, but we can't risk you being unable to make it back if the grotto is submerged." Lifting my palms to his face, I turn it toward me. "This won't be like Nøkk. I *promise*."

Jack sniffs and sucks spit through his teeth before letting out a defeated sigh. "I swear to the heavens, Anne, if something happens to you, I can't say I won't wish to watch the world burn."

In a deep cavern in my gut, I believe him. Passionate people love hard, but they also *fight* hard.

"It won't come to that."

Jack nods and lightly takes my hands in his, kissing my fingertips and palm. "I'm holding you to it, but I need you to know that whereas I'm one of the more honorable pirates sailing the seas, my soul is fully capable of wickedness. Because as much as I live for myself, I also *live* for my people."

Ruthless when needed.

"I hear you, Jack."

We both nod in unspoken agreement.

The wait for the spot where I'll dive into the water, praying to the Seas the Charybdis hasn't been following us, feels like an eternity. I sit on a barrel between Jack's legs, with his arms cradling me for the duration of the trip. He whispers sweet and filthy words in my ear, which keeps me distracted. Laust has finally coerced Truffles into letting him ride on his back like a great steed. The sight of a red imp holding onto bunches of cat fur while Truffles runs from one side of the deck to the other,

Laust holding on for dear life, is *also* quite the distraction. Glog plays his hurdy-gurdy, the tone growing somber as I tell Jack to drop the anchor because—we're here.

I'm perched at the plank, undoing my belt, resting my flintlock in my pile of clothes, and securing the cutlass at my back.

Jack grabs my elbow. "Listen to me. I'm no idiot, and I know this witch will ask you to bargain in exchange for the parchment. Don't agree right away. You hear me? *Listen* to her words. There's always a catch. You might as well be making a deal with the Devil."

He's right again. There is always a catch. The trick is to weigh out how detrimental that particular catch will be.

Not answering him straight away, I rise to the balls of my feet and kiss him deeply. "I have no words for how concerned you always are for me, an immortal, Captain."

He traces his thumb under my bottom lip. "It doesn't matter what you are. I'll act the same. Haven't you learned that by now?" Jack grins against my cheek and, resting a hand on my hip, lightly pushes me toward the plank. "Go before I do something stupid."

After blowing him a kiss, I flip from the plank, morphing my legs into the tail before hitting the water. Following the familiar thrum only other sea creatures can hear, I reach Morgana's grotto without a run-in with the Charybdis. She's situated her lair in an air bubble, floating and held still with rows of seaweed attached to the sea bed. The entrance is a glittering waterfall that only reveals itself to me once my scales shimmer.

"Who in the fu—" Morgana begins to say but stops short,

her black eyes wide and staring at me.

"Morgana. Been a while, hm?" I flick my wet hair behind me, crossing the threshold without invitation because she never denies anyone entrance. No one.

"Awhile?" She clacks her long black fingernails, a cauldron unironically boiling in the corner with green smoke. "The last time I saw you, you were fourteen." Her long raven hair falls in animated waves down to her hips.

A rebellious adolescent who made a deal with a sea witch to get back at Leiana, another young nymph, for kissing the boy she liked on the cheek. I had to bring her various fish for use in her concoctions for an entire month. It killed me watching so much aquatic life die for nothing and knowing it was *my* petty fault.

"I've come to ask another favor." Even saying it aloud has my throat clamping.

"Oh?" Morgana's lips slither into a serpentine grin, and she whisks to her pot, her charcoal robes swaying with her webbed feet, allowing her to stay afloat on the shallow water beneath us. "Do tell." She grabs a jar of grubs from a rickety wooden shelf and tosses them into the mix, their short, high-pitched wails making me second-guess my decision.

No. I must do this. My family deserves to at least know I'm alive.

"I need an enchanted parchment sent to—" Pausing, I lick my lips and take a deep, staggering breath. "—my father."

Morgana dusts her hands and tilts her head inhumanly to the side. "Could you not simply send a carrier pigeon?"

"I don't know where he is. The parchment would find him

no matter where or *when*, correct?" I hate how desperate I sound, but I can't help myself.

Morgana materializes a seahorse and tosses the poor thing into the cauldron next, causing bile to climb up my throat. "Curious how you've been separated?"

"Why does that matter? Do you want to make the deal or not?" I'm anxious and furious and only wish to get this *over* with.

She cackles until she gasps, her broad smile pulling the high sunken cheekbones tighter. "Such fire to match your hair, which I'll need a lock of to connect you to dear old dad." Morgana holds out her palm and makes a hurry-up gesture.

Using my sword, I cut a piece and slap it into her hand, glaring at her and waiting to hear what I'll need to bargain this time.

Morgana throws the hair into the pot, blue vapors spiraling from it. She chants something in a language that resembles a mix between Latin and something far more ancient than I am. A parchment sheening with a rainbow prism rises from the pot's magical waters, and she snatches it, her villainous gaze zeroing in on me. "Now. For what *I* want."

Someone's gasping for air and splashing through the waterfall entrance. Jack hunches forward, his hands on his knees. He takes several deep breaths and sputters. "Thank Christ, it's an air bubble."

Terror overcomes me. No. What if she tries to bargain with him? She can't know he's mine.

"Jack, what the hell are you doing? Your Captain told you to stay on board. Are you disobeying orders?" I fold my arms and lift my chin. "I should make you walk the plank for such insubordination."

Jack's glaring at me, and he looks between Morgana and me before dragging a hand through his soaked hair. "Apologies, *Captain*. But me and the crew were worried. Seeing as I can hold my breath the longest, we voted for me to come check on you."

"I don't believe you." Morgana floats in front of Jack, and how close she is has my skin on fire. "Because no mortal could break past my shielding spell unless—" Her eyes cut to me, and her lips slowly curl upward. "I know what I want from you, sea nymph."

"No," I shout without reason or composure. Sliding in front of Jack, I shake my head at Morgana. "No. Please, anything else—"

"Shh." Morgana taps a pointed nail on my cheek. "You haven't heard my proposal."

Jack's hand wraps my hip, pulling me against him.

"Then *speak*, witch." My voice isn't my own. It's venomous and cold.

Morgana twirls once before speaking. "For the rest of eternity, you may not harm my daughters. In *any* capacity."

Her daughters. The Sirens. I've never harmed them, to begin with. What difference will this make?

I open my mouth to answer, but Jack clamps a hand over it. "Remember what I said. What could she *gain* from this?"

Hours can go by, and I'd still come up empty on ways a trickster like Morgana can twist this to her advantage. There's no doubt this will come back to bite me straight in the ass, but I know we can handle *anything*.

Peeling Jack's fingers away, I nod at Morgana. "Agreed."

Morgana appears in front of me in a swirl of black smoke, grinning and holding out her hand. "We have a deal then."

I stare at her fingers, taking one final moment to think of the worst scenario that could come of this. But the more time I spend hesitating, the more time passes with my family fearing for my safety, and the more time passes before we reach Atlantis. And so, I shake her hand. There's a blinding flash of light, and she's holding the parchment out to me and dropping it in my limp hands.

"Write on it what you wish, put it in a corked bottle, and throw it to sea. The scroll will know its way from there." Morgana says this to me but winks at Jack.

With the parchment crinkling in my grip, I lurch forward, but Jack grabs me, coaxing me toward the exit.

"It's not worth it, love," he whispers.

Morgana waves at me, one finger at a time. "I'll be seeing you *real* soon, Rhode."

The name is like a hundred jellyfish stings striking my body. And before I realize it, I'm back in the water, swimming with Jack to the surface and on board the ship. Jack lets me use his cabin to write my message in privacy, and I now sit in silence, staring at the blank parchment, not knowing what to say. There's the possibility of saying both too much and not enough.

I grab the quill resting at the corner of Jack's desk, lick the tip, and start writing from the heart.

Dear Dad,
If you're reading this, that means the crazy sea witch was right,
and this enchantment actually worked. I hope it does because I

want to let you know I'm alive and safe. I'm in the Caribbean and have made the most of my life that I can here. Don't worry. No one knows who or what I am.

Wincing, I pause, questioning whether I should say this because it's a partial lie. But I *need* him not to worry, so I continue.

If I know you, you're doing everything in your power to find me, find a way to me, and probably running yourself ragged over it. Thank you. But just know, if, for whatever reason, we aren't able to see each other ever again, I'm your daughter, and I'm a survivor. I love you to the stars and back.

Your little seahorse,
Rhode

TWENTY-FIVE

JACK

I *KNOW* I'M an idiot for diving into unknown waters to ensure Anne's safety. But I've not gotten very far in life by doing everything smartly. Some of the best decisions have been those where I acted on impulse versus mulling it over. This mentality has saved my life and crew members' lives, leading me to my captaincy. Is she alright? Yes. Do I regret the risk? Never. Because if something had happened down there, I wouldn't have been able to live with myself. I'd rather die trying than lie down and wait for things to occur one way or the other. Or worse, wait for someone *else* to do it.

No sooner had we arrived back on deck than I knew Anne would immediately wish to write the letter to her father. I whisked her to my quarters, saying nothing, and shut the door behind me with her nestled inside. We're now back on course for Greece, and I'm at the helm, letting out my fifth deep sigh until finally, Duke pushes his glasses down his nose with raised bushy brows.

"Something on your *mind*, son?" Duke's holding back a smile. I can tell from the deep grooves forming in his cheeks.

"How kind of you to ask." I turn to lean my elbows on the railing and sigh for the *sixth* time. "The deal Anne made with the sea witch keeps playing in my head. There has to be more to it."

Duke's shoulders pull back, insinuating I've piqued his interest. "What was it?"

The way the witch's fingers constantly curled, her wrists rotating, still plagues my thoughts. I won't go so far as to call her "beautiful," but she was far from what I imagined witches would appear to be. They're supposed to look so old they could be on the brink of death, littered with hairy warts and missing teeth or something. "That Anne can't harm her daughters, whoever the hell they are, for the rest of eternity. Under *any* circumstances."

Nodding, Duke strokes the hair surrounding his mouth. "And your first hunch?"

His question elicits a smile from me because this is Duke's way. He's human like any other man and doesn't possess all the answers, but he knows how to guide you to answer them for yourself.

"Not sure what gives this witch her jollies, but something tells me it's watching others suffer, knowing she's to blame." Truffles is on deck in rare form, and he rubs against my calves, flicking his tail at my knee.

Duke removes his glasses and uses his shirt to clean dried water spots. "And how would this deal, in particular, make Anne suffer?"

A twitch forms in my jaw, and I gaze at the crew. Mary

barks orders to those pulling ropes for the sails; Ragnar stands motionless with his arms folded in a shadowed corner, and Squid leans forward in the crow's nest, holding onto the mast with one hand and shading his eyes with the other. "Mary, you, Glog—" Pausing, I avert my eyes back to Duke. "—*me*."

"Ah, yes." Duke slips the glasses back to his nose and takes hold of the wheel. "Making one suffer by inflicting pain on those closest to them over them alone."

I punch my knuckles against the wood. "And what's worse? She'd feel helpless not being able to *do* anything about it."

"Who are her daughters, I wonder?" This time, it's a genuine question from Duke, not one to provoke thought.

Retrieving my sash from a pile of effects I'd left on deck before diving into the sea, I tie it around my waist. "I haven't the foggiest, but I'll ask Anne when she's ready."

The door to my quarters swings open, and Anne steps out with the parchment clung to her chest. Her eyes are wide and verging on petrified.

Speak of the Angel.

"Anne, love," I reach out a hand, placing it at the small of her back. "Are you alright?"

She sucks her lips into her mouth and rapidly shakes her head. "No. I'm terrified this isn't going to work. It *has* to work."

I rub up and down her arms. "It will work. And look, I already found a bottle." Plucking the empty one I procured, I prop it between us. "Still reeks of rum, but it's dry, and it'll—" Before I can finish, her arms wrap around my neck, her nose nuzzling my jaw. I smile into her scarlet hair. "It's only a bottle."

"No, it's—" Anne pulls back, sniffling, her eyes brimmed with red as if she's about to cry. The mere thought of her in tears makes me anxious. "—will you do it? I can't watch."

"Of course." Gently, I take the parchment from her, rolling it tighter until it's small enough to fit through the bottle's opening. Once secured inside, I shove the cork into it, using my palm to wedge it further.

With the bottled scroll in hand, I turn to the sea, wind up, and toss it into the depths. The bottle floats on the surface, deep blue waves crashing against the glass. After several seconds, it disappears in a shimmering flash of blue. My grip creaks against the wood, and I snap my gaze from left to right, looking for any signs of it, but it's just—gone.

"Um," I blurt, clearing my throat.

Anne's eyes are closed, her hands clutched under her chin. "Um? Why, um, Jack?"

"Is it—" This news can go one of two ways, and I'm praying it's what she wants to hear. "—is it supposed to disappear into nothingness?"

Anne joins me at the railing, a wide grin plastered to her gorgeous face, eyes glossy with tears. "Yes. It worked." She slaps her hand on the wood. "It *worked*. They'll know I'm safe." She grabs my face, pulls me to her lips, and kisses me, sweet and salty, with a tear rolling down her cheek.

"Glad someone's safe," Duke barks. "Because we're sure not."

Despite clear blue skies, an unexplainable fog appears, surrounding the ship.

"Anne, who exactly are the sea witch's daughters?" I draw my cutlass and ready my pistol in the opposite hand.

Anne reacts in kind but freezes with her cutlass halfway from its sheath as if stuck. She pulls and pulls until her emerald eyes flare at me. "The Sirens."

It's both an answer to my question and the cause for the fog, their eerie singing tones piercing the air. That same buzz I'd experienced before rattles my brain, but I shake it away. I'd overcome the Sirens' pull with Anne's aid and can do it again. Or, if I'm *really* lucky, perhaps I'm immune? I'm not banking on this because I never did believe much in dumb luck.

"Didn't the sea witch threaten you only some thirty seconds ago?"

"Plug your ears," Anne shouts, still struggling to wield her sword. She curses against the wind and relents, spinning on her heel to face me. "When she said I couldn't harm them, I didn't think it meant I wouldn't even be able to have a weapon in *hand*."

Always a fucking loophole.

I hear her, but she sounds distant and echoing, the buzz growing louder in my head, *pounding* in it. "Annie, I—"

Snap the hell out of it, Rackham. If you let this witch win, Anne won't be able to defend herself, let alone any of the crew.

"Jack," Anne yells, patting her hands on my cheeks repeatedly. "Stay with me."

Her words pull me back. But when her lips fall on mine, the kiss doesn't cure me. Anne realizes this, too, when my mouth stills against hers. She slowly steps away, her eyes frantically searching my face, her bottom lip trembling.

"No harm can come to them. My kiss won't work now because it'd allow *you* to harm them because of me." Anne pushes against my chest, using her elbows, legs, back, and anything she can to force me away from the ship's edges.

My brain disconnects from my body. No matter how hard I try to tell my legs to stop walking or yell at my arm to raise the cutlass, it's all ignored for this damnable, unrelenting melody. Every man aboard is meandering in the same direction as I am, their feet shuffling the deck like it's covered in sticky sludge.

Anne wraps a rope around my ribs, pinning my arms at my sides. As she ties a knot, it refuses to stay tight, repeatedly loosening with each attempt. She roars the word "fuck." Considering I've only heard her curse a handful of times, and most of those times are when I've been pounding the daylights out of her—this can't be good. And I swear I can hear the sea witch's cackles floating along with the wind. The pistol and cutlass fall from my grasp, rattling and bouncing to the deck.

Anne slides in front of me, pushing my chest, punching it, and slaps me in the face. It smarts like a son of a bitch, but I can't so much as joke with her about hitting like a girl. She suddenly gasps and snaps her fingers. "She said *I* can't harm them and had no idea we have another woman in our crew."

Mary. My intelligent, beautiful Anne is going to get Mary to *slaughter* them.

"Jack, try to hold out a little longer for me. *Please.*" Anne kisses my cheek and squeezes my hand.

Her pleading makes me grimace, and I'm able to stop walking for a few seconds, the guilt of me willingly dragging myself to the grave to *leave* her punching at my gut. How can I be so selfish?

Anne sprints across the deck, shoving Red, Glog, and Aranck

away from the railing. For fuck's sake, it's entrancing Truffles and the imp as well. What kind of maniac lures a defenseless cat to their death? Honestly. This realization should make me far more furious than I can feel. No. The only thought as I edge closer and closer is to step into their warm embrace. To let the soothing song make it painless as they consume me.

Several human hands grip the railing, snow-like skin and knuckles turning red as if trying to pull themselves from the water. As if—they're drowning. My steps quicken, and my fingers reach for the first hand I see gripping over the railing. A woman's head appears from the fog, hair as dark as midnight, eyes a muted red. Her crimson lips part, the melody fluttering from her throat, lulling me toward her. I've never been this close to them before. I want to think they're beautiful but can't seem to *say* it.

The Siren's hand curls around the back of my neck. Given how warm the song makes me feel, it's far colder than I imagined, but I'm still letting her pull me toward the water. A sword slashes the air in front of me, narrowly missing the tip of my nose, and slices through the woman's arms. She lets out such a bone-chilling shriek, so at odds with the song she'd been singing, it makes me blink, temporarily jolting me back to reality.

"Not today, Captain," Mary says, patting my cheek and shoving me backward. She barrels across the deck, slicing, slashing, and leaving a bloody Siren massacre in her wake.

Anne rushes back, the world diving into slow motion as she pierces me with that frantic jade gaze. She's worried and panicked, and somehow, the Siren music starts fading to a dull buzz. My heart concentrates instead on the sound of the waves crashing against the hull, the fish leaping from the water, and seagulls squawking above as they circle, looking for food. The alarm in Anne's expression when she spots me peering straight at her softens, and it coils a tightness in my chest.

Mary continues to fend them off, dark blue blood spattering her clothes and cheeks, but she doesn't relent. Each man begins to gradually come to their senses as the Sirens retreat into the depths, cradling their wounds and leaving inky trails behind them. Anne's lips mouth my name, but I still can't hear her. Only the sea echoes in my ears. And like the backdraft from an explosion, everything comes bursting in at once—the Sirens' fading screams, the chatter from the confused crew, and Anne repeatedly shouting my name from only a few paces away.

Wincing from her loudness, I close my eyes and slip a hand over her mouth. "Yes, Annie?"

"Thank the Seas," she breathes and leaps against my chest.

I catch her and peck kisses across her cheeks and nose to reassure her I'm back to my old self.

"You were right," Anne whispers, her slender fingers twirling my hair.

My hands are cupping her ass, and I tap a finger against one cheek. "You'll need to be more specific, as I'm right on quite a few things."

I receive a well-deserved swat on my collarbone, and she rests her head there. "I should've bargained with her more. Instead, I put you and every man on board in danger."

Nodding, I carry her with her legs wrapped around my waist and sit on a barrel. "Are any of us dead?"

Anne quickly surveys the crew, letting out a breath when all are accounted for, and then relaxes on my lap. "No."

"And did you think on your feet? Took care of it?" Brushing her hair away from her neck, gazing at the bare skin, I kiss her there.

"Yes. I mean, Mary did."

"No, *you* did. Because Mary wouldn't have started dicing up sea folk out of respect for you." I poke a finger between her breasts. "She did it because you asked."

"Damn right I did." Mary saunters to our sides, wiping her cutlass blade on her sleeve, ridding it of Siren blood. "And Anne, darling, anytime you want me to take on a horde of evil sea creatures, just say the word." A flash of white blazes between her lips, brightened more by the dark speckles on her cheeks.

"What in the ever-loving hell? Who can say they've been attacked by Sirens not only once but twice and not remember a fucking thing?" Red is nearby talking to Glog, and both men drag hands over their faces, taking turns to snap a quick look at the water and ensuring they're gone.

The fog has lifted, and blue skies return, the wind picking up precisely where we need it to continue northeast. I pat Anne's thigh, setting her back to the deck, and take her hand, leading us to the helm. But I pause, spotting a scared imp clinging to an equally terrified Truffles, shaking like leaves in a stern breeze. Squatting, I pick up Truffles, and the imp comes with him because he won't let go of his fur.

"You're strangely calm about all of this, Jack." Anne curls her arm with mine.

I take the steps to the wheel, resting Truffles and the imp in his cat bed in the corner. "Don't see much of a point dwelling on it. We've quite a bigger fish to deal with, and I mean that metaphorically as much as I do in the literal sense. We're all alive, and I've no scratch on me."

"They can return, but I still can't do anything." Anne strokes one of the wheel's pegs, and the sight turns my dick into granite.

Chewing on my bottom lip, I force my eyes away and squint at the horizon. "If they're stupid enough to return and succumb to Mary Read's wrath again, then they *deserve* to die."

"How do you always know the right thing to say?" Anne's smile rivals any fire guiding sailors home.

"Life, Annie. Life." I turn the wheel enough to make the sails catch the wind and let it take over.

"Considering all we've dealt with already, there's no way it can get any worse," Glog says, chuckling and receiving death glares from the surrounding crew.

My grip tightens on the wheel. "Glog, I know I'm not superstitious, but what did I say shan't ever be spoken on my ship?"

Glog's gulp is so profound you can see his throat bob. "Never say never?"

"That's right. Don't repeat it, or I'll dangle you from the plank as shark bait." It's a hollow threat, as I'd never demand such a punishment for a simple word, but it'd certainly make me feel better.

I do not believe in jinxes. I don't. But to sail to Greece, we'll need to pass through the place that hunts pirates, which I left behind without looking back. We'll need to sail waters crawling with Navy ships—England.

TWENTY-SIX

ANNE

AFTER THE SEEMINGLY unending string of incidents, it's been days of blissful quiet on the seas. As much as I love adventure, the rare moments you can breathe and simply *be* are most appreciated. There have been times, much like now, when I sit on a barrel, watching Jack in his element. He rests his hands on the wheel, running his thumbs over the wood, and lifts his chin when a stronger breeze graces the deck. He'll tilt his head toward the sun when the clouds part and never fails to gaze at the water when dolphin pods breach the surface. Jack Rackham is one of the most fascinating mortals I've ever met. And I get to call him *mine*.

Truffles has been spending more time on deck lately, and we have Laust to thank for this. The two of them have become nearly inseparable except when they wish to nap and fight over the prime spot, also known as my *lap*. Laust won today and curled himself into a ball atop my thighs. His tail wraps around his torso, and his hands are tucked into his chest to keep his claws from accidentally scratching me.

As usual, Aranck keeps to himself in a corner, mixing and organizing his herbs. It dawns on me that I've never had the chance to introduce myself to him formally, let alone have an entire conversation. Carefully cradling Laust in the crook of my arm, I approach Aranck and nudge my chin at his stone bowl. "May I ask what you're making?"

Aranck lifts his dark eyes to mine, a familiarity settling there like we've talked numerous times before this. "A mix of ashwagandha and turmeric. I am using what I have left from my supplies to make a healing salve. I get the feeling we will need it."

One of Laust's legs falls, his hoof dangling from my arm. "That's a bit ominous."

"Perhaps, but the odds are against us. We have no choice but to enter English waters, and there is a great chance we will fight for our lives." Aranck's squared jaw tightens as he grinds the herbs with extra force.

It astonishes me that Aranck hasn't even glanced at the imp snoring in my arms. His intense fixation on tasks impresses me.

"Not that I'm not thankful for your talents aboard the ship, but I've been curious why you chose a pirate crew?" I continue to watch him working with the herbs, dusting his hands on his trousers before grabbing something different. The way he moves so meticulously is mesmerizing.

A smile cracks his usual stoic face, and Aranck nudges his head behind me. "Jack is the biggest reason, honestly."

"Jack?" My brows launch skyward, and I point at the ship's wheel. "Jack Rackham?"

The grin continues, and Aranck pauses what he's doing, resting his palms on the barrel he's been using as a table. "Yes. Before he earned the title of captain, he spent some time with my people, the Cayuga. He had been sailing for months searching for a crew and docked at the first land he came across—our land."

As much as I know about Jack, this extra information makes me feel even more for him. I steal glances at the pirate captain during Aranck's story.

"We became quick friends, and I told him I desired to see more than the same lands. I wished to see oceans, seas, and beyond, and that is when he offered to take me on as part of his crew. I gave him the ink markings on his left arm in gratitude."

"You were one of the first?"

He nods. "Yes. Me, Duke, and then Ragnar. We were also a part of the mutiny that replaced Jack as captain over Vane." Aranck shakes his head and returns to his herbs, his jaw setting. "That man was far too cruel for no reason. And I knew Jack would not be such a tyrannous leader."

Now, the feud between Charles and Jack makes more sense.

"I—" I start, ready to ask more questions, but I'm interrupted by the furious clanging bell alarm from the crow's nest.

Squid points to the north, and in the hazy distance, a ship appears with radiant white sails—an enormous ship. Even from this distance, its sheer size has my heart thundering in my chest.

Aranck hastily gathers his supplies. "Prepare yourself, Anne. This will get worse before it gets better."

The deck becomes a sea of chaotic activity, Jack and Ragnar

barking orders to the crew. I'm sprinting with a bouncing Laust in the crook of my arm, and in just that short amount of time, the ship has gotten close enough that I can make out the red flag flapping from the mast—the Royal Navy.

Jack lifts a spyglass to his eye and curses under his breath. "It's The Ambition."

Duke jerks his head. "We're never going to be able to outrun them, Rackham. We barely out-gun them."

"We're going to damn well try." Jack collapses the spyglass and hangs it from his belt. "This girl has a few tricks up her sleeve." He trails his fingers over the ship's wheel.

"Jack, if we turn back now, we may be able to lose them when the wind picks up at our backs." Duke lowers his voice to say this, his mouth near Jack's ear.

"Since when do I retreat with my tail between my legs?" Jack does *not* lower his voice. "I'd much rather go down fighting versus rolling over and taking it in the ass. But we *won't* go down." He harshly yanks the wheel, banking the ship from going head-on with the other. "Pull in the sweeps," Jack shouts over the roaring waves. "Red, handle the guns below deck. Read, be on those lines. I'm going to be maneuvering the fuck out of her."

Laust has woken up and is now trembling in my arms. "Jack, where do you normally keep Truffles?"

"Take them to my quarters, then get your ass back here, Bonny. Going to need you on those upper deck cannons." Jack's face flashes a troubled expression. One that displays so much with so little—he's frightened for my safety but knows this is part of being a crew.

I catapult to Jack's cabin after scooping Truffles into my other arm. Securing them inside, fluffing pillows around them to hopefully block out some noise, I secure the door behind me and bolt to the deck. The British vessel has gotten seven ship lengths from us now and turns to give us its broadside.

"They're getting in attack formation. Everyone, prepare to duck," Jack barks, grunting and gritting his teeth as he keeps our side from paralleling theirs.

Duke and another crewmate are ready at one cannon. Ragnar waves me over to one several down from theirs.

"I'll load. You fire. Got it?" Ragnar points at a pile of cannonballs.

Nodding and forcing away a nervous lump forming in my throat because I've never participated in warfare like this, I duck my head and grip the railing for dear life.

"When I say fire, you give it all you got," Jack orders. "Aim for the stern and the rigging. I want that ship stuck in the middle of the fucking ocean. Everyone understand?"

Mary shoves one crewmember away from the ropes and grabs it herself. "You keep being one step behind like that, you arse, and you're going to hang yourself accidentally."

Squid shimmies down the mast to the upper deck before the naval ship fires. With Jack's maneuvering, he's kept us at a distance, and the shot lands in the water, sending a spraying geyser near the bow.

"Ready yourselves." Jack furiously works his hands over the pegs, turning our broadside to the massive British frigate. "Fire!"

The sky becomes a barrage of smoke as cannons from

both decks fire at the naval ship. Most miss because it's nearly impossible to aim with these damn things, but one successfully slams into the rigging, taking several ropes with it. Several more could take out the mast if we time it right. Jack narrows his eyes, waiting for the smoke to clear, and his face falls, quickly turning our ship in the other direction.

As two cannonballs launch into the lower decks, the ship lurches and rocks. There's a loud splash as one of our cannons falls into the water. Hundreds of pieces of wood float in the ocean now, and the sight ignites something in Jack. He moves us into an attack position instead of turning our broadside away from them.

"Forget the rigging. Aim for the goddamned stern. That's where most of the officers will be." A steeliness settles over Jack, a sneer bouncing in his lip when the naval ship's flag comes into prime view. "Fire! Fire!"

Both ships are launching cannons at the other now. Each blast from The Revenge sends sprays of splintering wood cascading around the English ship. Most are somehow missing us or barely grazing the hull. One slams into the railing near me, and I squint at the wooden projectiles the splinters become, blocking my face with an arm. We fire over a dozen rounds at the stern before the rudder becomes unusable. A grin as wide as the Baltic Sea spreads Jack's lips, and he hurls the wheel back in the direction we'd been heading before the Navy's interruption. Relief washes over me because I half expected him to command us to board the ship. But no, Jack had intended to incapacitate them so we could continue our journey in peace. I adore him for that.

Cheers echo along the deck, and Mary slams into me, hugging me and Ragnar to her sides. "Good shooting, you two." Cloth curls Mary's palms, light blood stains on them from rope burn.

I pry away long enough from the brief victorious moment to scan the crew. Aranck was right. We'd gotten away from them—for now. But it didn't come without a price. Several crew members suffered scrapes and bruises, or were impaled by shrapnel. One lies motionless in an ever-growing pool of blood beneath him, which lurks closer to my boot.

"Duke," Jack bellows.

The anguish in his voice makes my throat squeeze. No.

Turning, I run to a kneeling Jack with Duke propped in his arms. Blood spurts from his mouth, and he has so many splinters sticking from his chest and stomach that it's a wonder he's still breathing at all. Tears prick my eyes, and I slowly sink to my knees, helpless and hollow.

"Duke, you hold on until Aranck can take a look at you. You stubborn old bastard, can you hear me?" Jack shakes Duke, panic flaring as he looks for Aranck.

Duke chuckles and coughs, spraying more blood over his shirt and beard. "Jackie boy, if the cannon fire wouldn't have gotten me, my body was close to doing it its damn self."

"What?" Jack barks.

Duke winces in pain, and I stroke his sweat-stained forehead, hoping it'll comfort him.

"Consumption. I've known by days were numbered for some time now." Duke smiles at me and places a shaking hand on my thigh. "You take care of him, Anne. He'll need you far more than he'll be ready to admit."

Jack sniffs once and holds Duke closer. "You knew, and you didn't think to tell me? To prep—"

"Jack," Duke interrupts him. "I didn't tell you because I wanted to die a pirate and not some old man having a coughing fit on his deathbed. If you knew, you would've ordered me below deck instead of letting me fight. Don't try and deny it, son."

Son. The word strangles my heart.

"Have I ever told you I hate how you're always right?" Jack cracks a small smile and wraps his jacket around Duke when he starts to shiver.

Aranck arrives but frowns, bowing his head, knowing he can do nothing for him. Mary, Ragnar, and most of the crew have gathered in a circle around us. No one wears a hat, and everyone is stone-cold and silent.

"You remember which direction is north?" Duke asks, his voice cracking.

Jack sniffs again, and his jaw tightens before he points to the sky.

A final chuckle floats from Duke's throat. "Don't get lost without me," are his final words before his body stills and the light flickers from his eyes.

"Not possible," Jack whispers, his head held low, Duke still cradled in his arms.

Tears roll down my cheeks. I've been around so much death, but never like this. Mortal demise, though a natural part of life, is depressingly poetic.

Mary kneels beside me, her eyes glistening with tears, but none fall. She reaches for Duke's glasses, delicately slipping them from his nose. She folds the stems and slips them in her pocket. With a still hand, she closes Duke's lids.

"I'm so sorry, Jack," I whisper, not knowing what else to say.

Jack's sadness turns into irritation in a blink, and he clings to Duke. "You didn't do this. What do you have to be sorry about?"

"I know he was like a father to you. I'm just sorr—"I rest my palm on Jack's cheek and stop myself from apologizing again.

Jack softens against my touch but goes rigid moments later. "No. He *was* a father to me. Just one more fucking thing England has taken from me."

I know that look in his eye. He's going to want revenge. He'll crave it at any cost.

"Jack, let yourself grieve before you think what you're thinking."

Jack rests Duke on the deck and slowly rises. "Prep him for a water burial. Come get me when you're done."

Jack takes one final look at Duke before he turns from us and heads toward his cabin. I chase after him, wishing nothing more than to comfort him, to offer an ear or a shoulder. But when I follow him into his quarters, he doesn't so much as glance at me before slamming the door behind him.

TWENTY-SEVEN

JACK

THEY ALL WILL die. Maybe all at once and it may also take years, but each person aboard that ship is responsible for the death of a man I considered a second father. He. Is. Gone. And they'll *pay* for it. We all knew the risks of agreeing to be part of a pirate crew. Most days, we can avoid the inevitable, and then there are days like today when we become part of pirate jargon. And if I'm being honest, longer stretches of time without incident trick you into believing you're unsinkable. But it wasn't me they took. It's far worse.

I've been standing in my quarters with my forehead against my arm, pressed to the door, for too many minutes to count. It's not until soft fur brushes the insides of my calves that I even bother to open my eyes.

"Truffs," I grumble, turning my back on the door and letting my body slide until I sit in a defeated slump on the floor. "I feel like shit."

My cat purrs and saunters onto my lap, kneading the tops

of my thighs much like he'd done to Duke's stomach. The memory initially angers me, but watching Truffles curl into a secure ball on my legs melts some of it away. Sighing, I beat my skull against the wood behind me, my sinuses burning and stinging. Maybe this is why the likes of Low, Roberts, and Blackbeard became merciless. When you don't give a shit about anyone or anything, it's harder to *feel* it.

Not Calico Jack. I had to go and decide to be a *righteous* pirate.

Hooves slide across the dirt-covered floor, one at a time, with methodical slowness. The imp steps from the shadows, its fingers threaded behind his back. "Something happen? Heard lots of booms."

My chest aches, knowing Duke had wanted this creature in our crew. Considering he hasn't lit the ship on fire or drank half the rum while we slept, I gather he won't be an issue. "Have they named you yet, imp?"

His chin lifts, his ears flicking tight, and his gaze brightens. "Yes. Laust."

The name manages to pull a laugh from me despite my grief, and I motion for him to come closer. "Come here, Laust, and hold up your hand like this."

Laust does as instructed, his black claws scraping together, hooves turned inward.

"Do you swear your undying loyalty to The Revenge and its crew? To never steal from your crewmates, never desert me as your captain or any of the crew?" I lift my brows, waiting for him to answer.

Laust's orbed eyes blink, silent.

Bending forward, I lower my voice. "This is where you say *yes*, Laust."

"Yes," Laust shouts, immediately crouching in fear. When I make no move to chastise him for being loud, he regains his confidence and stands tall. "Yes. I swear."

"Welcome officially to the crew of The Revenge, Laust." I stick out two of my fingers for his tiny hand to shake. He does this so brazenly that it makes my entire arm wiggle.

A light knock sounds against the door, followed by a silky sweet voice saying, "Jack? I understand if you want to be alone, but I—"

Anne. I slammed the door in her face, like an idiot.

Reaching above me for the doorknob, I twist it and let my back fall to the deck at her feet. Truffles, still sleeping on my lap, grumbles in protest. Anne's head snaps downward once she realizes I'm not standing in front of her.

"I'm angry, Anne. Furious." My jaw hardens.

A sympathetic wrinkle forms between her eyes, and I avert my gaze from it because the last thing I want is for Anne to feel sorry for me. There's been enough bullshit happening to her without me adding to it.

"And I don't blame you. But can we talk?" Anne presses a hand to the doorframe.

"No."

She kicks me with her boot. "Get up, Jack."

Groaning, I sit up and remove Truffles from my lap, plucking two clinging claws from my shirt. The cat flicks his tail when I re-enter my cabin without him, and Laust scampers past us, slipping through the door before Anne closes it.

"The crew needs their captain now more than ever," Anne states, not missing a beat.

I sit on the edge of my desk, propping one leg up. "And they have me. I told you I'm angry, not incompetent."

"They have you?" Anne folds her arms and crosses the room, taking calculated steps. Heel, toe. Heel, toe. "You're telling me that you're not consumed by thoughts of murdering the entirety of a certain Royal Navy crew?"

My top lip quivers, and raking a hand through my hair, I push from the desk to pace. "Of course I am. They killed five members of my crew. Five. And one of them happened to be a dear friend." I whirl to face her, curling one hand over her hip. "So, you tell me, Anne, how do you expect me to be? I've already told you I'm a jaded man and a pirate scoundrel."

"I expect you to be exactly the way you are." Anne's fingers press to the back of my neck. "But what I expect, my Captain, is for you to *prioritize*."

I know what she means, but I don't want to think about it. Putting Duke's revenge as an afterthought feels like a betrayal.

"Bury him. Say goodbye." Despite my fighting her, she pulls my forehead to hers. "And then you need to figure out how we repair our ship in the middle of English waters. After The Revenge is whole again, after we have the jewel to boost morale, *then* we seek vengeance."

Anne sounds like a captain herself, and I struggle between admiration and irritation.

"As long as you look me in the eye and tell me you understand that I *will* kill every last one of them." I lock gazes with her gleaming emerald eyes, steadfast and strong.

"I'll be there with cutlass keen beside you, Jack."

Securing an arm around her waist, I breathe her in, salty and sweet. I'm increasingly grateful this woman chose me. I let my lips brush hers, soft and fleeting. "I still don't know what I've ever done to deserve you."

"Maybe it's not because of what you have or haven't done. But what we'll do *together*." Anne cups my face and presses a kiss to my temple.

Another knock sounds at the door, this one harsher and with purpose. "We're ready for you, Captain," Red says without stepping inside.

Reality comes crashing against my chest like a ruptured dam. Anne takes my hand, securing our fingers tightly together, and curls my arm to her ribs, guiding me to the broadside of my ship, where five bodies wrapped in cream sailcloth rest on the deck. Ragnar and Mary hover near one in particular, and I know it's Duke, but I can't bring myself to stand by them.

Anne rubs my arm and delicately tugs me along. One crewman recites the funeral prayer we've always done, but it echoes in my ears, the words drifting in the wind. Other crew members lift one body at a time, letting it slide down a wood plank into the water.

Thy kingdom come…daily bread…forgive us our trespasses.

One after the other meets their sea burial, and my throat hardens more with each passing body. I'm choking, not breathing, by the time they reach Duke.

Lead us not into temptation.

Snapping out of it, I pat Anne's hand and hurry to help lift Duke's body onto the plank, resting it on the railing with

Mary, Ragnar, and Aranck.

"Goodbye, old friend. May wherever you're going be filled with mermaids and endless rum."

"Amen."

And with a final nod to each other, we tilt Duke, and I watch his shrouded body plunge into the sea, the waves enveloping him like an embrace, welcoming him. And I don't look away until he's so deep I can scarcely make out his outline. My palms squeak against the railing, knuckles cracking as I twist and grip, reining in the fury I know I need to swallow—for now.

"Everyone," I shout, slapping my hand against the wood and turning around. "Pay attention. We need to repair the ship but don't have the proper supply on board."

Glog's mouth gapes. "How the hell do we get supplies with the Navy at every turn?"

"We go to the only place we can." Brushing past those standing near me, I make for the ship's wheel, the wind picking up enough to fill the sails. "London."

The gasps and stunned expressions are well warranted. I'd be lying through my teeth if I said the idea didn't terrify me to my marrow, but we have little choice.

"Jack, with all due respect," Red slides his hat from his head and holds it to his chest. "That's suicidal."

Locking my eyes with Mary, I don't need to give a command because she sees me at the wheel. In a breath, she's ordering crew members to ready the rigging and drop the sails. "No. So long as we're not caught."

"Not caught?" Red barks a laugh. "Cap, The Revenge isn't the biggest ship in these waters, but it's certainly not the smallest."

I frown at this.

"And it's known by the community at this point. We can't simply lower our colors and pull up to the dock," Red finishes, holding his arms at his sides as several mumbling crew members agree.

Anne steps to my side, arousing the urge to feel her skin against mine. I pull her to my side and kiss her cheek. Her smile in response is glorious and heart-shattering.

"We're not making port at the London dock," I announce.

Anne raises a quizzical brow, and I wink.

"There's an island not far that I've used in the past. We dock the ship without colors and split up disguised as fishermen within what dinghies we have." Reluctantly, I let go of Anne to use both hands on the wheel, turning us in the opposite direction. "As long as we're not recognized as pirates and caught with no King's permission papers, we'll be *fine*."

The crew goes silent, and my neck tenses. I've never worked this hard for their trust and approval.

Anne steps forward when several beats go on with still nothing but shaking heads and murmurs of disapproval. "I agree. We *will* be fine. This'll work so long as we do precisely as the captain says." She tosses me a sidelong glance. "This *will* work, right?"

"It has to. We've no other choice." Though my confidence wavers, I flash her a cocky grin as reassurance. "But it's under control. I *am* Calico Jack, after all."

Ragnar raises his fist into the air. "*For fanden*. We need supplies. And unless you all want to float around waiting for our asses to be handed to us by the next Navy ship we pass, you'll agree on this too."

Red and Glog hang their heads but start the sea of "Ayes" from the crew. And now that I have them all on board with the only plan I can muster, it's time to prove why they trust me as their captain.

TWENTY-EIGHT

JACK

DARK, OMINOUS CLOUDS litter the sky as we row in three dinghies, growing closer and closer to the London Bridge. Anne and Glog sit behind me, and we've removed anything on our persons that might give us away as pirates. My shirt sleeve covers down to my wrist to disguise my tattoo, my hair's tied back, and I left my captain's jacket in my quarters. We will appear as fishermen and wouldn't have a "captain" on a tiny boat. The sight of the buildings in the distance makes me uneasy, and the hanging scents of oil, perfume, and horse shit agitate me. Thinking I'd never have reason to be back here was foolish.

"Remember. Our mission is to find repair supplies. We don't stop for any other reason, keep your heads down, and do *not* run." I lean back with each stroke, rubbing my palms against the oar's wood.

"Want me to talk to the shop clerks? Figure you're the most recognizable of us," Glog asks.

"Fair point and a grand idea, mate."

Anne's chin appears on my shoulder. "I hope you realize how backward this is pretending to be a *fisherman's* wife. Cannibalistic, really."

Smirking, I turn just enough to give her lips a quick peck. "In and out, love. Why don't you focus more on the wife portion of it, hm?"

Anne has yet to remove her head from my shoulder, and I can feel her smile through the thin fabric of my shirt. "Was that a proposal?"

It's impossible to hide how my upper body tenses at this. Not that the idea of it disgusts me. I only never thought I'd find a woman I could see spending the rest of my life with, let alone making one my *wife*.

"Did you—want it to be?" I say the words slowly, keeping my tone neutral.

She laughs and pokes me in the ribs. "I'm not sure I'll ever grow tired of making you sweat, Jack."

Chuckling, half-heartedly, I narrow my eyes at her. "I'm going to hold you to that when we're back on board, Miss Bonny." I jut my chin at her oars. "Now, back to rowing."

Anne lets out a final laugh before the butt of said oar is jammed into my side, making me grunt. The London port is characteristically bustling with activity. Dozens of dinghies matching ours float between larger fishing boats. There are two tall ships within the massive mix, undoubtedly belonging to privateers—bloody traitors. A forlorn sigh pushes from my lungs because this is the last place I wish to be.

"Captain, if we're supposed to be fishermen, shouldn't we have, I don't know, *fish* on our boats?" Glog asks while we're paces away from the dock.

"Shit." I look at Anne pleadingly. "Would you be a dear? I promise we'll toss them back." Pressing my hands together in prayer, I offer her my best fluttering puppy eyes.

Anne glares at me while she does it, but soon, our dinghies have flapping fish and enough water for them to survive, but not so much to sink our boats. I pick one up and smear its scales over my face, neck, and hands.

"What in the name of the Seas are you doing?" Anne asks, sneering at me.

After I feel sufficiently scented, I toss the fish back into the water. "You think fishermen smell like lilacs?"

"No." Anne slaps her hands atop her thighs, and rises. "But I'm sure you're thankful I *do* smell like lilacs versus the alternative." She eyes one of the fish in the boat.

"And I have been ever the gentleman not insinuating nor asking such a question of a lady." I bow my head just as the boat bumps against the dock.

Much like every other time, Anne's laughter gives me renewed life and purpose. She kisses me as she passes, and I offer a hand to help hoist her onto the wooden planks. She takes it, and I swat her ass on the way up.

Glog steps forward and daintily holds out his hand. "Going to help me too, Cap?"

I smack his fingers. "Get up there yourself, you knob."

We've made it to port, our dinghies docked, and no one the wiser. London may be risky due to how active the Navy is here, but it's also prime for blending in with its constantly expanding population. Horses' hooves clop along cobblestone roads, and so many pairs of feet are walking the streets that it creates a constant dust plume. The gray clouds have muted the setting sun, and they've begun to light the torches bordering the walkways.

Ragnar and Mary are behind us, and I point at the gunpowder shop that they're to visit. We used most of ours, continuously firing the cannons, and no longer have reserves. They nod and disappear into the store.

We continue to walk, and I keep my chin lowered. My body freezes whenever we pass anyone resembling a Navy sailor or officer. We near every manner of shop selling poultry, linens, and jewelry but have yet to find one for carpentry. I pause long enough to get my bearings before Anne's hand curls around the back of my neck, and she yanks me into an alleyway. Whether she's suddenly grown extremely horny or she's doing this for a reason, I don't give a shit. My hands are instantly groping her back, up to her shoulders, kissing her, nipping at her lips. Breathlessly, I whirl us around until I'm in front of her and press her to the stone wall.

Anne flutters her eyes open, those pale fingers tracing her reddened lips. The way she's looking at me like she'll never get enough of this, has me pressing my hardened cock against her stomach.

"There was a Naval officer lingering on you too long for comfort. I was scared he recognized you," she says.

My precious Anne.

Pressing an arm above her head, I grip her waist and grin. "If you wanted to have your way with me in an alley, all you had to do was ask, Annie. No need to make excuses."

"Jack," Anne laughs and shoves my hip. "I'm being serious."

"Thank you." After kissing the tip of her nose, I tilt my head to one side, peeking at the bustling streets. "Are they gone? Or should we continue our ruse?"

She tugs my beard and slips a hand into mine. "They're gone. Come on. I saw the carpentry shop across the street."

It's probably for the best. The last thing I need is getting caught because I'm distracted by fucking my pirate queen in an alley. There are much better towns for such things—other alleyways.

We are in and out of the store within minutes, our arms stocked with new supplies of tar, oakum, dowels, and a small batch of lumber. The rest of the crew should be halfway back to the docks, and we make our way as briskly and discreetly as possible.

Almost there. I can see the docks in the distance.

"John Rackham, is that you?" A man's voice *roars*.

Anne's eyes go wide, and we halt. I can ignore whoever just yelled my known name through the London streets, but doing this may risk him repeating it. With any luck, no one of note heard him.

Slowly, I turn and force a smile when I notice the voice's owner is none other than Robert Carlisle. A man with far too much money and a frequent buyer of goods I used to ferry for coin. Despite being filthy rich, he never once tipped me.

"My word, it *is* you." Robert looks shocked at my appearance—the long hair and beard I've acquired over the years. "How have you, uh, how've you been, my boy?"

"Out of England. So, I've been right grand." I glare at him, my lip bouncing in a snarky smile, and edge closer. "And you? Still stiffing people out of their money?"

Anne tugs my sleeve. "Jack, we should be going, love."

Robert grimaces, holding a lacey handkerchief from inside his jacket sleeve to his nose. "I have my *own* trading company now. No need to hire outside work."

"Why doesn't that surprise me?" I grind my teeth, Robert's presence making my blood boil.

"Jack," Anne whispers again, *yanking* my arm this time. "We need. To. Go."

Robert gives an incredulous stare. "And taking orders from a woman now. That *does* surprise me."

And the gasket pops.

Anne tightens her hold like she knows I'm about to lose my shit, but I shrug away from her and stand toe-to-toe with Robert. Snatching his frilly handkerchief, I deliberately wipe my hands with it, keeping eye contact with him. When I throw it against his chest, it reeks of tar and fish and has black and brown stains. Robert holds it between two fingers at arm's length.

"Have a nice life, Bobby. And if you ever see me in this shithole again, do me a favor and don't say hello next time, yeah?" I lift my hand like I'm about to slap him, reveling in his wince before lowering my arm and turning away.

Anne threads her arm with mine, and we walk a bit faster now. "Thought for sure you were going to punch him square in the jaw."

"I should have. But we've been through too much lately for me to jeopardize your lives over a meaningless cod like him."

My blood still boils, and the surroundings don't do well to

let it simmer.

When we finally make it to the docks, I blow out a breath, some of the tension in my back releasing. But we have yet to be safe. We still need to return to the ship, repair it, and sail away with England unawares.

Back on board, hammers are flying, sails are being sewn, and wood planks are slapping against holes in the hull. Anne offers to help Mary, and Laust has proven himself useful in helping repair the holes.

I'm in my quarters, staring at navigation charts. Duke has always been better at this than me. And it's not as if I can't get us to where we need to go, I simply hate charting.

"Goddamit, Duke," I seethe, tossing the metal compass to my desk and slumping in my chair. The compass bounces to the floor, narrowly missing Truffles' tail, and he lets out a shrill screech.

I hold my face in my hands, wishing this weren't reality. But if this *is* a dream, Anne would be a figment of my imagination. She's as real as the scales scattering her skin and the hauntingly beautiful teal eyes that appear when she's a nymph.

"I know, I know," I say to the ceiling. "I can hear you now, Duke."

He'd tell me to pull myself together and focus on the tasks at hand. No one has ever gotten anywhere wallowing in self-pity. And he'd be right.

I'm just starting to make myself feel better when the crow's nest bell starts ringing. I lunge from my cabin to the deck only to see in the distance precisely what I'd hoped I wouldn't see. A Naval ship heads straight for us, and we have no means of escape now. Panic chokes me. Not for fear of myself being captured or even the thought of the gallows, but terror for them taking Anne and the crew. How in the hell did they know we were here?

Anne runs to me. "Jack, what do we do?"

"Listen to me." I curl a hand behind her neck and point a stern finger in her face. "I don't care what happens, do *not* use your powers."

Her mouth opens to protest, and I slip my palm over it.

"Promise me. Because when we're captured, and I hate to say that we *will* be, I can't stand the thought of anyone strapping you to a table and experimenting on you or doing other heinous things." Letting my hand fall from her face, I keep her gaze trained on me. "Promise me, Anne."

Her lips form a thin line. "I won't use my powers."

"Good." I turn to the crew all staring in terror at the approaching ship. "Prepare to be boarded."

"Captain?" Red asks, confused.

"This isn't the end, ladies and gents. Look at it as a minor inconvenience because I'll be damned to have come all this way just to be hanged like a dog." Standing on a barrel, I look around at the men and women who've put their faith in me. "If we fight them, we will die. But once we're on land it will be an entirely different story. We *will* get out of this. And we *will* see more treasure."

A man appears at the railing of the Naval ship. "Ahoy there, Rackham. They promised me a pardon if I told them where you were." His arms shoot out, and a shit-eating grin so vast that I can see it from this distance slithers over his lips. "How could I refuse?"

My blood goes beyond boiling—it explodes.

Charles Vane.

TWENTY-NINE

ANNE

IT'S ASTONISHING WHEN you feel like you're drowning, even though water can never conquer you. The pleading look in Jack's eyes as he begs me not to use my powers for fear of my life has me unable to breathe. And now, knowing Vane is to blame for what's about to happen has me sinking to the bottom of the sea. It can't end like this. I won't let it. I made a promise to Jack, but I have used my powers discreetly before and can do it again. But it means waiting for the right moment. It means allowing ourselves—to be captured. Jack hid Truffles and Laust in his cabin, ordering Laust not to let the cat out of sight until he heard no more movement.

When the marines board our ship, the sight of everyone surrendering makes my limbs numb. Mary spits in the officer's face as he slips irons over her wrists. Ragnar glares at his captor, making the man work for it with trembling fingers. Squid refuses to come down from the crow's nest, and several men begin the arduous climb to retrieve him.

When the officers approach me and Jack next, we catch each other's gazes, speaking without words—we *will* get out of this. Jack ignores the man with dangling shackles in his hands and bends to kiss me. It's brief because the officer pulls us apart, but enough to spring eternal hope through my chest. The metal is cool against my skin and just as daunting as the dark overcast sky above us. I fall in line with the rest of the crew, and we're escorted across a plank from The Revenge to an awaiting naval ship.

Vane saunters on deck, chewing on a piece of straw and looking far too happy with himself. "Your good friend Carlisle bumped into me saying he miraculously ran into *you,* and it got me thinking, where oh where could his ship be? Did you forget we both have used that island?"

Jack's cheek quivers. "Didn't forget. Figured you wouldn't *be* here."

"I'll witness your hanging, Rackham. Out of respect." A venomous grin slithers Vane's lips, and he tilts toward Jack's ear. "And I did tell you that I'd be the last thing you see before this world is rid of you."

"You've done many idiotic things since I've known you, Charles. But this? Has to be the worst." Jack widens his stance. "Because we could've been square, you and I, minding our businesses." He gets in Vane's face. "Now you're as good as dead."

Jack's words don't faze Vane, or he does an excellent job of not showing it.

"What are you planning to do, hm? Haunt me from the afterlife?" Vane flicks the straw at Jack's chest.

"I do love it whenever you underestimate me. Makes the

victories that much sweeter." Jack turns away from him before he can get in another word, and I'm quick to follow him.

"You should've stuck with me, sweetheart. This is where Jack's leadership takes you." Vane props against a cabin wall with so much unfounded confidence I want to kick him in the balls.

I pause long enough to shrug at Vane. "Then you don't know Jack."

Given our numbers, there are too many of us to shove into the brig. They corral us like cattle on the main deck, instructing us to sit on our asses with our backs to each other.

I press the back of my head to Jack's, squinting at the sun, attempting to peek through the clouds, and hum *Randy Dandy Oh*, one of my favorite shanties I've heard the crew sing. Soon, more men join me, humming first and then singing it.

The marines let it go for only one verse before a red coat moves in front of us and barks, "Pipe it down."

Jack's head shakes against mine. "You take our dignity and now take our human right to sing, too?"

"You gave up rights the day you decided to participate in piracy." The officer kicks Jack's leg with his boot.

Jack's body jostles from the impact. "That's a bit harsh, don't you think?"

"Pipe. Down," the marine repeats and continues.

Sneaking my hands near my hip, careful not to let the chain make noise, I tug Jack's trousers. His skin grazes my knuckles, and he uses a fingertip to caress the skin between my fingers where the webbing appears in my nymph form. Despite our trek to the gallows, his fleeting touch still elicits a smile.

We're back in the London port in the few moments it takes for a massive naval ship to get there from the island. They remove all weapons from our persons, including my beloved dagger. They're herding us through the town center, where people aren't reacting as I thought they would in our presence. I half expected them to throw food or rocks at us—to curse us for being pirates. But they barely notice us. And if we make eye contact with them, they look away. A wooden sign hangs above an alcove with simple black lettering: Paternoster Row, and they shove us here, forcing us into a line.

The soldiers tear me from Jack's side, and panic suddenly shakes me to my core. I can end this with one tidal wave. London be damned. But I promised him, and we both swore there would be no more lies. Sorrow pulls at Jack's features, but he nods at me to tell me that it'll all be alright. Swallowing my swelling anxiety, I settle beside Mary, where they've separated us from the rest of our male counterparts.

An officer stands before us, chin held high and at attention. "You all are convicted and found guilty for acts of piracy. You are to be hanged until dead come sunrise."

Mary fidgets beside me and blurts, "We're pregnant."

All heads snap in our direction, including a bewildered Jack. Discreetly, I shake my head at him.

I know with utmost certainty I'm not with child, and considering Mary's taste, I'm willing to bet she isn't either.

"That's to say Anne and I, *each* of us is pregnant."

The marine lets out a deep sigh, mumbles something about "bloody pirates" under his breath, and feverishly taps his foot. "Very well. The women will spend the rest of their days in a jail cell until the birth of their babes and thenceforth share the same fate at the gallows." He clicks his heels together. "Take them away."

A soldier takes hold of me and Mary's chains, pulling us in the opposite direction from the rest of the crew. I'm searching for Jack's face, and when I spot him, he's peering directly at me with a single finger pointing at the side of his nose.

Deception. It's how we'll get ourselves out of this mess.

We're placed, more like thrown, into cells across from one another, and Mary grips the bars, shouting all forms of insults colorful enough to make a sailor blush. But the soldier ignores her and only slams the hilt of his rifle against her cell.

Once the marine has disappeared, I get Mary's attention. "How long do you think it'll be before they return to check on us?"

"I'd be surprised if they returned for the rest of the night." Mary guffaws and kicks the pebbles covering the stone floor.

"Good thinking on buying us time with the pregnant plea," I say, but my gaze remains glued on the exit, and I pray a guard doesn't appear.

"What?" Mary gives a snarky grin and pats her thin stomach. "Don't think I could be pregnant?"

My face falls silent, and I cross my arms.

"You're right. Far too much effort." Mary makes an expression like she's gotten a sudden whiff of whale shit.

I'm anxious and tapping my fingernail against one of the metal bars. After several more minutes, I can't take it any longer. Willing my nymph form, I turn enough parts of myself into softening water, the shackles falling from my wrists, and I slip through the bars with ease.

Mary's light eyes fixate on me, and her mouth is agape. "Did I just witness you turning into a jellyfish?"

"Not quite." I'm back to human and reach for Mary's hand between the bars, holding it. "If someone does come back, say you fell asleep and didn't see what happened. They're going to have a hard enough time rationalizing how I escaped shackles and a locked cell."

Mary stares at our joined hands and shakes her head. "Right. Yeah. But Anne—" She folds her other hand over mine, fusing our palms. "Be careful. I don't give a fuck if you're immortal. Just be careful, yeah?"

After giving her one last reassuring squeeze, I take to the hallway, pressing my back to the wall and listening for anyone passing. Once clear, I'm scrambling for the next opportunity to hide while figuring out how the Seas I'll get out of this labyrinth. The light from a flickering flame bounces off an adjacent wall, and I duck into the opposite hallway.

"That one pirate we arrested today? Fucking Calico Jack," one marine says with far too much snark in his tone.

"No bloody shit. Guess he's not as unsinkable as they say he is, eh?"

The sound of the man slapping the other's back reverberates off the stone walls, and the laughter that follows has me seeing red. I dig my nails into the wall, crack one, and stand my ground.

It takes tip-toeing through another four hallways, turning around twice to make a complete circle back to the same stop, and a hair-raising moment with an officer staring down the only walkway I could take to the exit before I'm safely back outside. It's late evening, and so many passersby crowd the streets that shoulders bump into me from every direction.

I'd been worried someone might recognize me from our pirate procession to the row, but they didn't care if they did. Stopping a woman in a gray bonnet carrying a basket of bread loaves, I comb a hand through my hair and smile. "Pardon me, but I hear there's going to be a pirate hanging tomorrow. I love such a spectacle, but I'm new here from Ireland, and I was wondering if you could tell me where it'll take place."

The woman grins with all of the six teeth she has and points. "There's a dock by the Thames. But getting there early is best if you want a good spot. Or you can always go to any of the taverns along the river and watch with a telescope."

With a *telescope*?

"Thank you." I go to shake her hand, but realizing they're full of parcels, I awkwardly wave.

Flicking my jacket collar over my face, I shove my hands in my pockets and head toward the river. A frigid chill has formed in the air, and a putrid smell invades my nostrils the closer I get to the dock. I cover my nose with my sleeve, gagging because it reeks of—death. A lifeless pirate hangs from the dock, their feet drooping in the water.

"Seas below," I whisper, a knot twisting in my throat.

Imagining Jack in this man's place raises a crazed bout of nerves and desperation—to do something. But without using my powers, what do I—

"Anne?" A familiar voice beckons from behind me.

Slowly turning, I spy Omar, the brothel keeper, and smile. "Omar? What are you doing in London?"

He looks far fancier than the last time we met, sporting a burgundy frock coat and pristine powdered white wig. "Business, of course. But I'm quite curious about what *you're* doing here considering the particular ship I saw you boarding." Omar looks around for prying ears.

Closing the remaining gap between us, I usher him further away from town and keep my voice low. "Jack, the crew, they've all been captured. They're sentenced to hang tomorrow, and I—"

Omar cups my chin, turning my face from left to right. "You've gone and fallen for a sea wolf, haven't you?"

There's no point hiding it; honestly, I don't want to keep it a secret. I'd shout it to the depths of the oceans if I could.

"Yes. Me and Jack, we're—"

Omar's eyes close, and he waves a hand between us, fluttering one finger at a time. "Say no more, my dear. I had a feeling you stowing away on that ship would leave you with far more than you bargained for."

And it did. Friends. Family. A lover and confidant. A sister.

"Can you help me?" I curl my hands under my chin. "Sunrise is only hours away."

Omar nods and leads me further down the docks. "There's a group here who positively hate red coats. Given some incentive, I'm sure they'd be delighted to provide a distraction and give the Royal Navy hell."

"Incentive?" Frowning, I feel my heart plummet to my toes. "Omar, I don't have anything. We were on our *way* to the score."

Omar presses one finger between my shoulder blades. "Then you'd owe me. But Anne, I expect compensation as soon as you're able."

If we make it to Atlantis, I can pay him back and then some.

"I'm good for it, Omar." I extend my hand.

A twinkle sparks in Omar's eye, and he shakes in agreement. "Then let me round them up." He snaps a velvet coin purse from his belt and holds it up to his ear, shaking it. "Yes, this should be quite enough."

"You're going to use your own money to hire them?"

Omar chuckles and hangs the pouch on his hip. "We've already shaken on it. You're a pirate now, so how I get what you need should be no concern of yours, should it?"

"Probably not, but I can still be thankful." I offer him a warm smile.

"Make yourself scarce until morning. I'll provide the distraction, but the rest is up to you." Omar slips a small knife from his pocket, much like the dirk I'd found when first arriving in the Caribbean. "Something tells me you'll need this. Good luck, Anne." Omar squeezes my bicep before walking away as if we'd never seen each other.

Holding the knife to the moonlight, I smile at the glittering green stones in the hilt. When I first met Jack, he'd have hated the idea of our lives banking on a dagger. And now, I'm going to *save* him with one.

THIRTY

ANNE

FINDING HIDING PLACES to keep warm from the cold autumn nights in England is a feat. I've not slept a wink when the sun's orange and red rays peek at the horizon. Omar's words were vague when he said he'd provide a distraction, and this makes me antsy.

When will this distraction start? Will it make the crowds rowdier? Should I expect pistol fire or even explosions?

My eyes have acclimated to the darkness, and the piercing brightness overtaking the sky makes me squint. I rub my arms, working the chill from them and coming to my full senses. Using the brick wall behind me as leverage, I push to my feet and secure the abandoned gray shawl I'd procured from a street bench around my head. As early as it is, the streets are already steadily filling with townsfolk.

"I hear they're hanging the captain first," a man in a brown tweed knee-length coat, trousers, and frilly linen shirt says to a young boy bouncing at his side.

The captain. My captain. *Jack.*

The boy's blonde curls bobble as he jumps into a puddle. "But why?"

"The man's made a name for himself. Known as Calico Jack. I figure they mean to make a spectacle of him to discourage others from treating piracy as a popularity contest." The man shoves a leather-bound portfolio under his arm.

As much as I loathe the idea of them trying to humiliate Jack during his walk to the gallows, I know he won't give them the satisfaction. I *know* his charm will win the crowd along the way. And I know the more time they take to finish the deed, the longer it gives me to rescue him and the crew.

Pulling my jacket around me tighter, I keep my chin low and follow the people chitter-chattering and whispering about the soon-to-be hanging pirate. Some gather streetside while others have tied off smaller boats in the river. It's sickening how many wish to witness a man they've never known meet his end. And I'd kill them all for it if I could.

"Here comes the cart," a woman in a white bonnet and apron shouts across the road. She points, and everyone pushes and shoves to get the best view.

I let them elbow past me, a deep frown forming once Jack's face appears. His head isn't lowered, and a cocky grin plays on his lips. Jack's kneeling in a rickety wooden cart with a coffin resting beside him. The chaplain and executioner flank the cart, walking alongside it, and two soldiers lead, with one trailing behind it. Soon, the rest of The Revenge crew, minus Mary, parade behind Jack in shackles.

Now is not the time. Too many people surround him in

close quarters here.

Keeping hidden behind the sea of bodies, all edging their way forward to catch a glimpse of the infamous pirate, I stay in time with the cart, not tearing my eyes from Jack. He's not going to like it, but this may need to wait until the last possible moment because it's when there'll be the fewest people standing in our way.

"Why'd you do it?" A random man standing on a bench asks Jack.

Jack chuckles and lifts his dirtied hands, covered in irons, for the crowd to see. "I was an Englishman like the rest of you. And I told jolly 'ol England to suck my cock."

Gasps and hoots of laughter fill the air. A woman in a corset dress and tavern apron walks alongside the cart and pours him a cup of something amber-colored before handing it to him with a grin.

Jack bows his head to her. "Appreciation." He downs the drink, tossing the mug to the crowd upon finishing it.

They *fight* over it—shoving, punching, and pulling.

The procession continues for nearly an hour, and what they hoped to make into a humiliating, dehumanizing, torturous parade for Jack is the exact opposite. Because he's Calico Jack Rackham for a reason. He says everything they wish to hear, flashing the grin that's had me melting even when I couldn't stand him, and he never lets his confidence falter. They're praising him as a hero by the time he reaches the docks and have given him so many alcoholic beverages he begins fake drinking them so as not to be sloshed for our escape.

They line the remaining crew shoulder to shoulder at the

dock's edge, facing the awaiting noose to watch their captain hang. I swivel on my heel, searching for any sign of Omar's "distraction," but nothing from the cheering boisterous crowd seems out of the ordinary. Propping against a pole so as not to draw attention to my jitters, I flick my thumb over the dagger's hilt nestled safely in my belt.

They're leading Jack off the cart now, and my heart races. He's only paces away from me, and I can't act yet. Must. Wait. And I don't want him to notice me because I don't trust us to maintain neutral faces. One moment lingering on the other too long or one change in demeanor could make this all for nothing.

Keeping my face hidden from the crowd, I wedge between two people on the dock's edge with a prime view of the noose hanging over the water. The rope's length is far shorter than the average noose, which makes a pirate's death longer. There'd be no chance of their necks snapping, and they'd sway and slowly suffocate. Nausea curdles my stomach, and I press a hand there.

The chaplain recites a prayer to bless Jack's soul in the afterlife, and Jack squints at the piercing sunlight inching through the clouds. "You're wasting your time there, mate."

The chaplain ignores him and continues from a small red bible he holds in his withered hands. Jack rocks on his heels, waiting and still smiling at the adoring crowd. Some people beg the executioner to spare Jack's life, while others shame the marines standing by him.

Once finished, the chaplain slaps the book shut and turns to Jack. "Any last words?"

I'm honestly shocked they allow this.

Jack scratches his chin and addresses the townspeople instead of the officers. "They call pirates low-life degenerates, but what's truly *criminal* is that you can fight like a man and still be reduced to dying like a damn dog."

"Amen," a man with a shaved head wails from behind the crowd, laughing and firing a round from his flintlock into the air.

Everyone shrieks and drops to their knees, shielding their heads with their arms. The marines point at the executioner, encouraging them to see their job through before sprinting after the—distraction. What starts as a single man raising turmoil through the on-lookers turns into three, four, and soon a dozen pirates are running through the streets of London, firing pistols that harm no one but still evoke fear.

My eyes snap to the executioner tossing the noose over Jack's neck, and I fight people who are trying to flee in the opposite direction. Panic consumes me, and I'm slamming my shoulders into them with such force that a shooting pain spikes down my arms. The executioner tightens it around Jack's neck, and in a moment that splits time and space, the world slowing, Jack's body drops from the blocks. I kick the man in front of me behind the knee, toppling him to the ground and using him as momentum. Jumping from his back, I grab my dagger and throw it. I hold my breath for the few seconds it takes to slice through the rope, Jack landing in water up to his shins, coughing and gagging.

The executioner leaps down, but Jack already has the knife poised in his grasp, and after a few dodges, he slashes it across the man's throat. I hurry across the dock and climb to where Jack stares bewilderingly at the small blade. He's more attuned to *it* than the man who was about to hang him gurgling and spurting blood behind him.

"Jack," I breathe out.

His caramel eyes lift to meet mine, and a tiny smile cracks the corner of his lips. Jack shakes the dagger at me and laughs. "*Cutting* it a little close there, weren't we, love?"

"Are you dead?"

Yanking the dagger from his grasp, I secure it in my belt.

Jack feels himself, ending with cupping his crotch, and replies, "No."

"Then accept my rescuing," I tease, touching my fingers to his shackles and turning them into water that falls to our feet, blending in with the rest.

Jack glares at me. "Annie—"

I leap and wrap my arms around him, kissing him and shutting him up. "We need to grab the rest of the crew and haul ass back to The Revenge. This distraction will only last so long before the Navy sends reinforcements."

"Where did you find a pirate crew willing to crash a pirate execution in enemy territory?" Jack's nose wrinkles, and he hoists me onto the dock.

"A brothel keeper," I answer.

Jack pauses with his hands on the dock and blinks at me. "My dear, you are beautifully intelligent, but that makes no sense whatsoever."

"I'll tell you all about it in your cabin later." Crouching, I encourage him onto the dock, trying not to laugh at his confused expression.

We race through the streets where most of the crew have

taken advantage of the chaos and used it to escape. Jack lets out a shrill whistle. The crew members snap to attention with jovial smiles upon seeing not only Jack but me, too. And everyone's here except—Mary.

"Jack, we need to get Mary. She's still in that cell. I left her there." I slip a hand over my mouth. "By the Seas."

"This Mary?" Her voice is an epic hymn sung through the clouds.

Grinning, I turn, and there's Mary, twirling her shackles around one finger, a set of keys hanging from her other hand.

"How did you—" I stop myself and flick my hand. "—you can tell me when we're out of this shithole."

An eerie quiver seizes my spine, and it's then I spot him pushing through the crowd, shouting and pointing at us—Charles Vane. We lock gazes, and I set my jaw. There are too many people rushing past Vane, and his voice is drowned out by the cacophony of gunfire, screams, and pirate laughter.

Ignoring Jack's nemesis, despite the seething anger raging in my blood, I turn Mary and Jack away, hoping they've yet to spot him. It's hard enough for me to fight the urge to attack Vane, let alone those who've dealt with him for far longer than I.

We undo everyone's shackles once we're a safe distance away and at the shoreline, staring blissfully at the island in the distance, The Revenge floating there. But the dinghies are all on the ship now.

I'm already whisking primary pieces of clothing off, and Jack is beside me, repeating the same actions. "Jack, what are you doing?"

"I'm going for a swim. What are you doing?"

"It's way too far. You'll never—"

Jack cups my face, and, just as I had with him moments ago, he quiets me with a kiss. "A giant sea monster is after you. I'm not letting you go alone, and we need two people to row and tow the other boats behind if we're going to get the crew back on board in time." He swirls circles on my cheeks with his thumbs. "And you know I'm the strongest swimmer next to you."

It kills me that he's right and positively guts me, but I relent and nod. "If you get tired, you tell me, and I'll pull you along."

He agrees but never says a word, the stubborn bastard. We make it to the ship without any interference, and he flops on deck, gasping for air and swallowing mouthfuls of it with his palms pressed to his knees.

"Tired, Jack?" I hide a smile while undoing one of the rope ties.

Jack shakes his head but still hasn't regained enough breath to answer me.

We row the dinghies back to our awaiting crew and safely return to The Revenge while the other pirates have been practically turning the River Thames into a pirate tavern. The reinforcements arrive, but they give them the runaround and buy us enough time to shove off. I'm exhausted, grateful, and didn't once fear for my life or secret showing my scales. It's unbridling.

Jack smiles at me from across the deck, where he's discussing something with Ragnar. I wave at him but frown when the seas beneath us rumble and turn foamy. I search the water, unable to make anything out until I notice it—a glittering gold three-pronged spear—a trident. My heart plummets to my feet because I'm terrified *and* elated to see this. A giant water horse raises its front hooves from the water, and there's no mistaking who found us—my father.

Poseidon.

THIRTY-ONE

JACK

I'VE BEEN IN harrowing situations numerous times throughout my life. Since becoming a pirate, that number has tripled. But the gallows? This was a new one for me. And I was hanging from the noose for several seconds before Anne cut the rope free. I, Captain Jack Rackham, almost pissed my trousers. I had complete confidence Anne would figure something out, but considering it went so far as the blocks were being kicked out from under my feet, that split second when you think, this is it, can put many things in perspective. Was it enough to convince me to hang up my cutlass and dry off my boots? No way in hell.

The crew is all safely back on board, every head accounted for, and we're on track heading for Greece with England forever in our wake. I'm unsure how Anne convinced the other pirate crew to risk their necks, giving us a distraction long enough to escape, and I can hardly wait to hear her story. All is right again. It's unsettling without Duke at the helm *with* me, but matters could be far worse. The ship lurches, the seas violently crashing against the hull.

And this is what happens when you don't follow your own bloody rules.

As I sprint to the railing to survey what in God's name can make that prominent of a wave without the aid of a thunderstorm, I tense. A gold trident slips through the surface, the sun glinting from its three *very* sharp and *very* pointy prongs. I'm so tense my grip cracks the wood as a giant water horse leaps from the waves, eyes glowing a fiercely vibrant blue. It's galloping toward the ship, and I widen my stance.

"Brace for impact," I shout to the crew because what the hell do you use against *that*? Any firepower we possess will go straight through it.

Anne uses the rigging to hoist herself to a barrel. Flailing her arms, she's fearless against the water steed. "Poseidon," she yells.

Poseidon? He's real. Of course, he is.

The horse still gallops and rears, its front legs batting the air.

"Poseidon, stop. Please!" Anne climbs further up the rigging, still waving her arms and fanning her fingers.

Anne seems to know this fellow.

The first blow happens, the horse sending a tidal wave over the ship, slamming into barrels and soaking the deck. Mary is blown backward, but I catch her coat and pull her toward me. I snap my hair away from my face, running a hand over my eyes to rid them of water droplets. The attack puts several holes in our sails, but it is not so catastrophic that we can't repair them. And then the horse rears, ready to strike again.

Anne stands on the bow. "Daddy, stop!"

Jesus. Christ.

My throat, my chest, my hands, they *all* go numb.

"Did she just call him *daddy*?" I ask no one in particular.

Mary snorts and laughs behind me. "I certainly wouldn't want to be the man who's fucking a sea king's daughter right about now."

I've yet to release my death-like grip on the railing but slowly turn my chin at Mary. "I *will* throw you overboard."

"You'd miss me too much, Cap." Mary grins and bats my nose.

The titanic-sized horse begins to shrink, water dripping away, and in a surge of sea spray, a tall man with wavy ash blonde hair falling to his chest and a full beard appears. He's holding his trident in one hand while his other reaches for Anne's face, his eyes blinking as if holding back tears. The sun reflects off his golden armor, particularly the greaves, and the man is large enough to make me stand taller and flex my arms beneath my shirt.

"Rhode?" Poseidon whispers, his thumb stroking her cheekbone.

Anne smiles at him, pulling her sleeve back to reveal the cowrie bracelet she wears, tears glistening in her eyes. "It's me, Daddy. You finally found me."

Shit. Hours ago, I was being paraded through a London street to be publicly executed, then fearing for my life as a giant seahorse tried to drown me, and now I'm witnessing some bizarre family reunion between Greek deities. This is quickly becoming an average Tuesday for this crew.

Poseidon is oblivious to the rest of us as he pulls a matching bracelet tucked away in his gauntlet to show Anne. Her smile broadens, and she jumps, wrapping her arms around his neck. He catches her with one arm, still wielding the trident, and hugs her to him, breathing a relieved sigh.

Two more bursts of sea spray sprout on deck, and a shorter woman with chocolate brown hair and armor matching Poseidon's steps forward, followed by a tall, slimmer, and younger man with short bright blonde hair wearing—cut-off trousers, I suppose? I've never seen such a garment.

"Triton?" Anne asks the younger man, pushing back from her father, but pauses when her gaze lands on the woman. Her expression is hard to read—confusion? Fear? Joy?

Rhode stands perfectly still in front of the woman, tilting her head from side to side. "Mo—mother?"

The woman cups her hands over her mouth. "Rhode, I wanted to—"

The reunion is cut short by several barbed tentacles plunging from the depths and smacking against the ship's sides.

Poseidon twirls his trident and runs to the railing. "Rhode? In your letter, you said you were safe. And you've had the Charybdis after you all this time?" His voice is an anguished roar.

"I—" Anne pauses and throws her hand out at her side, producing her Atlantean sword instead of her cutlass. "—I didn't want you to worry?"

Poseidon shakes his head and points a stern finger at her. "We'll talk about this later." He hoists himself to the railing and looks at the other three sea beings. "Between the four of us, we should be able to put this thing out of existence for good this time."

Poseidon, the woman, and Triton dive into the sea. Anne rushes to me, pressing a quick palm to my cheek. "I'll explain everything after this is over, Jack. I promise." Her lips brush mine, and she turns, joining her father in the ocean below with a flick of her sea nymph tail.

Nope. That's not happening. I refuse to stay on deck while Anne and her family do my dirty work for me. I *am* still the captain of this ship.

I'm removing my belt and shirt when Mary shoves me. "You cannot be serious. I'm quite certain they have it handled."

"And why should that matter? An extra pair of able hands can't hurt." I twist my cutlass handle in my hand and jump to the railing with bare feet. "Besides, I should probably start winning her old man's favor. Perhaps it'll lessen the lashings for corrupting his daughter in more ways than one, hm?"

"You're insane," Mary says, snickering.

"And thank God for that, Read." After giving Mary a wink, I backflip from the deck and plunge into the frigid water.

The mythic sea beings are already a force to be reckoned with underwater. Three of them wield varying forms of tridents, with Anne being the sole sword wielder, and the sight of it makes my chest tighten. I swim beside Anne, ignoring her shocked expression and shouts of protest, which are muffled to my ears. Poseidon, her mother, and Triton give me equally fearful and bewildered looks, but I silence them by slashing my sword through two tentacles, dodging the barbs as the tips float away in swirling inky ringlets.

Once they see I'm not retreating, we become a fury of slicing and dicing. They've all conjured tails at this point, giving them more maneuverability, and I, in contrast, use the tentacles, latching onto them to get where I need to go faster.

Unlike the rest, my lungs are burning, and I know I'll need air soon, which strangely irritates me. Such a trivial thing is taking me away from the fight. The sea monster nears the surface, and I spin, jamming my sword in its back. And as the Charybdis breaches, I'm riding its back like a damn raging bull. My head emerges, and I take a massive gulp of air before I'm back underwater, gripping both hands to the hilt as the monster does a barrel roll, attempting to launch me off.

Tiny bubbles spiral around me as we spin, and I roar into the water, still holding on until, finally, it stops. Triton zips past me at such speed he's a blur, lunging his bronze trident into the creature's side. Anne comes from below, her sword a sharp twirling nightmare, picking off barbs from the tentacles as she swims past. Anne's mother swims from one side, Poseidon on the other, and, in unison, they launch at the monster with their tridents, stabbing it.

The Charybdis' spiky tooth mouth gapes wide, its tentacles shaking, trembling, and lashing anywhere it can. It wails, and its mouth still hasn't closed. This is when I always live up to my reputation for taking risks. With my sword stretched out in front of me, I launch into the monster's mouth, pinning my elbows at my sides to avoid its dagger-like teeth and curl my knees to my stomach when the creature snaps its jaws closed, narrowly missing my feet. Holding the blade above my head, I use my legs to propel me forward, carving a line through the Charybdis' innards on my way.

I reach the end and slice my way back to the water. My lungs burn, and my vision has begun to blur from the inky, bloody shadowing of the water. Holding my ribs, I feel my sword's hilt go limp in my hand, darkness spilling over my gaze.

And then her mouth is on mine, breathing life into me. My Annie. She makes her sword disappear, carries mine now, her arm wrapped around my waist, and swims us to the surface. Her soft fins brush my feet, and the rest of her family form around us, all pushing skyward until we're bobbing in the water near The Revenge's hull.

"Did we win?" I ask, smiling, my voice croaking.

Anne laughs and pushes me to the rope ladder. "Yes, you handsome idiot."

The crew cheers as Anne and I appear over the railing. I help her despite my mushy and tired arms.

"I cannot believe you did that, Jack." Anne shakes her head, but she's still grinning.

Pulling her to me, I slip a hand to the back of her neck and kiss her. "Can you not, though? Really?"

"No, I suppose you're right." Anne laughs, but her smile suddenly disappears.

Mine does, too. Standing several paces from us is a soaked King of the Seas, his hands wringing around the trident's hilt, his glare capable of boiling the Baltic Sea. And he's staring right at *me*.

THIRTY-TWO

ANNE

I SLIDE IN front of Jack, shielding him with my body against my father. Not that Jack can't hold his own, but there's no telling what the King of the Seas will do to the man he saw kissing and groping his only daughter. Leave it to my dad to throw all heroic deeds Jack had *just* done below water and boil it down to this singular sight alone.

Fanning my palm at Dad, ready to ask him to stop for the second time, I freeze at the sight of my mother appearing from behind him.

Her tan hand, contrasting with my porcelain skin, gently curls around his trident, lowering it. "Let's not start skewering people before we've had a chance to be properly introduced, my love."

Introductions aside, I feel as if I need to be *re*-introduced to my mother because the one *I* knew was taken from me as a small child. Zeus banished her to the cosmos for all eternity because she didn't uphold her duties—a mother I rarely saw and scarcely remember. A cloudy mix of resentment, anger, and joy cyclones in my mind.

"Fry," my older brother, Triton, says, a nickname he's called me since we were kids. "It's her. It's *mom*."

My brother looks so desperate for me to be happy to see her. To throw everything at my feet and run into her waiting arms. But this is how Triton has always been. Positive. Quick to forgive and forget. Naïve. I needed it growing up, but I've become the opposite of his breezy personality. What I need now is for my mother to realize *how* she fucked up.

Jack rests a gentle hand on my lower back, out of view from my family. It's a grounding touch I didn't know I needed.

"What do you want me to say, Amphitrite?" I can't bring myself to call her mother, not this soon.

The Queen's jaw flexes and tenses, her hands dropping at her sides. Her throat's bobbing, and her eyes are glassy, like she's holding back tears. "Rhode," she whispers, taking a cautious step forward.

I hold up a finger, ignoring my father's disappointed frown. Considering he isn't trying to convince me as Triton has, I'm assuming their reunion didn't start as blissfully as it seems now. "That's not my name anymore."

And it's just as well. My mother named me Rhode. It's a sea nymph's name. But I'm more than a sea nymph. I'm a pirate queen and live a new life now. It calls for a new label and identity.

Amphitrite's reaction isn't what I expected. She's shocked at first but then strangely understanding. The crew is all dead quiet, busying themselves with chores they don't necessarily need to do, or looking anywhere else but at our family squabble.

Jack notices it, too, and abruptly clears his throat. "This seems like something we should handle in private. Follow me to my cabin." Jack gestures to his quarters.

Dad quirks a brow, emphasizing his trident, slamming the hilt against the deck with each step. "Cabin? Are you the captain of this vessel?"

Jack stands straighter. "I am." I swear his voice deepens a little. "Sir. Majesty?"

"Sir," my dad says, passing us and brushing arms with Jack. They're the same height, with Dad being only a bit wider in the shoulders but otherwise having a similar build. "Will do fine."

Tension weighs heavy from the unexpected appearance of my father and brother and my late mother. Not to mention, they discovered that I've not only become a pirate but also am with the captain himself. A boulder lands on my chest, and I press my hand there. But as soon as Jack splays his fingers and presses that warm palm against my back, guiding me toward his cabin, most of the anxiety melts.

We're all standing in Jack's quarters, and Jack squeezes past Triton to scoop a prancing Truffles from his desk. He nuzzles his fur before resting him on the floor as Laust appears from a darkened corner, yawning and scratching his sides.

"Laust, take the cat and go find some grub." Jack edges his head toward the door.

Laust's eyes brighten at the mention of food, and with Truffles at his side, they scurry from the room.

Triton looks from the door back to the desk, pointing. "Was that—an imp?"

Jack snatches a fig from a bowl on his desk and sits on the edge. "Yes. We don't tend to turn anyone away here. Mythical or otherwise." His gaze lands on me as he pops the fruit into his mouth.

Dad props his trident against a wall but doesn't move far from it. "And you are alright with this?"

"With what exactly, sir?" Jack looks genuinely perplexed by this question.

My mother stays at my dad's side and delicately touches her throat. "With the magic? The fins and scales?"

"I happen to quite like that side of Anne," Jack answers, not missing a beat and smiling at me—*beaming*.

"Anne?" My mother repeats, a wistfulness in her tone.

I press my fists into Jack's desk, already regretting what I'm about to say. "I'm not sure how it should matter one way or the other to you, Amphitrite. I believe you gave up the right to be a concerned mother the day you decided the sea meant more to you."

"Rhode," Dad warns, stepping forward; simultaneously, Triton says, "Fry."

My mother lifts a hand to halt them and looks square at me. "No. I deserve every last bit of it." She folds her arms and a crease forms on her forehead. "I never forgave myself for not being able to see you grow up. Especially you, you were so young when it happened." She pauses to look at Triton, who gives her a sympathetic frown. "I knew it wouldn't take long for Triton to warm up to the idea that I'm alive and reconnect, but you've always been my little lava rock. So full of fire and grit."

"Then my reaction shouldn't surprise you." A certain

lightness fills my chest, and my fists relax into open palms on the desk instead.

A sad smile plays on her lips. "It doesn't. And I can't blame you in the slightest if you even hate me for what I did—"

I cut her off, standing straight. "I don't hate you."

"I'm saying I wouldn't blame you if you did. I can't erase my past actions and don't expect you to forgive me, but I ask if you can find it in your heart to someday be a family again." My mother holds her hand out behind her, and Dad quickly takes it, threading their fingers.

My resolve grows softer, but I'm still so angry inside. "Did you make this easy on her, Dad?"

"We all have our grievances, Rhode. And I know better than to try and tell you what to do, but she's changed. I've changed. Tartarus—" Dad sucks on his bottom lip and takes a good look at me. "—you've changed."

My mother smiles, a reminiscing glint in her eye. "I don't know if I agree with you there, Seid. She's a woman now, but I still see that little girl who'd steal shells and baubles for her secret stash. The little girl who slapped an eel in the face with her tiny fins because it'd bitten her big brother."

My throat tightens, and I dig my nails into the wood. My right central fin has a small tear because it caught on the eel's tooth. "You remember all of that?"

"I do." My mother smiles again. "I remember all the moments I had with you and still cherish them. And it makes sense to me why you've taken to this lifestyle." She references the ship. "And—to him." Her gaze zips to Jack at my side.

Jack rests his mouth on his fist and pans the room once he

realizes we're all looking at him. "I've been perfectly fine as a living backdrop to this family affair I'm pretending not to hear."

"Don't think I've forgotten about you, boy," Dad says, grabbing his trident and moving toward Jack. Triton follows him.

"Wait, wait." I step between everyone. "Can I introduce you to him before you feather and tar him?"

My mother is still smiling.

Dad grumbles and flicks his wrist at me to continue. "Everyone, this is Captain Jack Rackham. Jack, this is my father, Poseidon, brother, Triton, and my—" I pause, eyeing my mother's hopeful expression. "—mother, Amphitrite."

My mother is pleased by this but reins in her excitement and clasps her hands over her mouth.

"And now that you have a name," Dad continues, moving closer to Jack.

Jack stands confidently, not like a man about to be impaled by a trident. "I understand a pirate wouldn't necessarily be your first choice for your daughter. And I realize I make a *dishonest* living, but it's a living nonetheless, and I'm quite good at it."

Dad stops in front of Jack, sizing him up and hanging his arm between two trident prongs. "Do you care for her?"

"Sir, I'd put her life before mine despite my mortality." Jack presses a hand to his chest and doesn't lose eye contact with my father.

Standing on my tip-toes, I side-bend between them. "It's true. He almost drowned once because of it, the crazy bastard." I give Jack a grin, which he returns.

"And let's not forget he almost got eaten by the Charybdis," my brother adds, making me love him that much more. "That was idiotically heroic, by the way."

Jack bows his head at Triton. "Thank you."

"You understand what it means to be with one of us, Rackham?" Dad's cheek spasms, and he tosses his long hair aside.

He knows something that he isn't letting on yet. I'd recognize that face anywhere because I know my father better than anyone.

"No," Jack answers. "But I know what it's like to be with Anne, and I couldn't dream of being with anyone else."

My heart topples over itself, and I wrap an arm around Jack's waist because I genuinely can't help myself. My mother grins warmly at this interaction while Dad fights everything to not look at it.

"She's immortal. This means she won't age, and *you* will. If your 'heroic' deeds don't get you killed one day beforehand, she'll have to watch you die of old age." Dad's expression turns stony.

Seas. I've been meaning to have this conversation with Jack. We've just been too busy trying to stay alive.

Jack nods slowly, his eyes panning to my arm around him. "I'll take whatever time I can get with her, so long as that's something she can live with." His honeyed eyes meet mine, and there's genuine concern there.

Dad and I share a glance because I know he's fishing for the approval of bringing up the alternative or not. But I can't yet, not like this. I want it to be Jack's choice and his alone, without the possible pressure of my entire family staring at him and waiting for his answer.

"I'll take whatever time I can get." I comb a rogue strand of dark hair from Jack's forehead and secure it behind his ear.

"Good." Dad wrings his hands around the trident's handle like he's about to give bad news. "Because you two have a—" A deep sigh pushes from his lungs, and a hint of an eye roll follows. "—fated bond."

The world around me grinds to a screeching halt.

Jack bends to my ear, still looking at my father. "Am I supposed to know what that is?"

My mother is positively jubilant as she trots over, gasping. "Do you think Atlantis knew of it? Her coming here was by *design?*"

It's all becoming more evident with each passing moment.

"It makes sense," Triton adds, his expression swirling with hesitation and pride.

I turn to face Jack and take his hands. "Those little moments we've had that we couldn't explain? After our first kiss? The way you somehow found me when Nøkk kidnapped me?"

"What?" Dad growls, stepping forward, but stops when my mother gives a quick head shake and slaps his chest.

Jack circles my knuckles with his thumbs and nods his head, listening. "So, this bond gives us a special connection somehow? Jack and Anne were *meant* to be together?" The cockiness melting into his grin at this is charming me all over again.

"And the connection will be stronger once it's accepted," Dad adds.

We turn our gazes to the sea king.

"And Rhode, I'd feel better if you did because I have a sinking feeling you're not coming back with us?" Dad's frown is slightly masked by his beard but still noticeable.

My family stands on one side of the desk, Jack on the other, all silent and looking at me longingly for an answer to the burning question.

I take in a long breath and gulp. "I've found a new life here. This crew has accepted me even after discovering what I am and is like family. I can be both sides of me without care and still have a purpose."

Triton rubs the back of his neck. "You never did like disguising yourself and wandering amidst mortals. A ship, the open seas, it suits you, sis." He smiles, but it's a sad one.

Tears prick my eyes. Sniffling, I curl my arm with Jack's. "And Jack will get himself killed without me here. I'm sure of it."

The melancholy in the room momentarily subsides, with everyone chuckling.

"I don't think you realize how much I will miss you." Dad rounds the desk, and I hug him tightly. "Does it *have* to be a pirate, though, honey?" He whispers against the side of my head.

"Honestly, Dad?" I peel back and playfully poke him. "If you weren't King of the Seas, you might've been a pirate too."

My mother twirls her hair and grins. "I like the sounds of that, Seid."

Dad doesn't retort because he knows I'm right and steps past me, holding his hand out to Jack. When Jack slips his hand into his, Dad pulls him closer. "If you hurt her, I promise you'll find your ass on the wrong side of a trident, Jack. Do you understand me?"

Jack winces from Dad's godly grip, and he nods. "Absolutely, sir. I hurt a lot of people and have lied to even more of them.

But never her now. It's a promise."

"Glad we concur." Dad lets go and moves to my mother.

Jack shakes out his hand and holds it limply at the wrist. "How does this acceptance deal work? A secret handshake?"

It's a question I myself can ask.

Dad hugs my mother to his side. "I needed to be sure, but it would seem you two accepted it without knowing some time ago."

Jack and I look at each other differently now. We'd been fighting a cosmic pull, and neither could win until we succumbed to our bond.

"Where are you heading, anyway?" Triton asks.

I freeze and slowly turn on my heel, tapping my fingernail on the desk. "Greece. Atlantis, specifically. Thought I'd try and find my way home there."

Dad glares from me to Jack. "And *pirates* found it in the grace of their good hearts to barter you?"

Jack folds his arms and leans on one hip, eagerly awaiting my answer.

"I—" Tap. Tap. "—I promised the Tavros jewel."

"What?" My mother shouts, and my family immediately goes on the defense, lurching forward.

"That jewel powers the beacon. If you remove it—" Dad starts, his words frantic.

I raise my voice to get them to hush. "I wasn't going to let them take it. I just needed them to get me there." Pausing, I eye Jack sidelong, and he's *grinning*. "The plan, at first, was to murder Jack in his sleep and threaten the crew they'd meet the same fate if they touched it."

Speechless. I've rendered my family *speechless*.

Jack turns me to him, and he cups my face, his grin widening at my admission. "And who needs a damn jewel when you've got a woman like this?" And much to my father's and brother's chagrin, Jack kisses me, sealing the bond we've accepted.

"Can I expect you back in Atlantis?" Dad asks.

"I'll always come back to Atlantis to ensure it's safe and to see you all. This isn't goodbye." I squeeze Jack's hand before hugging my brother. "Someone needs to remind you how to swim occasionally, right, big bro?"

Triton embraces me and laughs. "Fat chance, you brat." He ruffles my hair.

My mother looks at us with pride, her hands curled under her chin, and I realize it's the first time she's seen her children together as adults.

"Jack," I wait for him to look at me, knowing he'll do what I ask without hesitation. "Why don't you show Dad and Triton your ship? Introduce the crew to the King of the Seas?"

Jack looks surprised but not fazed and stirs into action. "Of course."

"You don't have to leave right this minute, right, Dad?" I steal a glance at my mother.

Dad looks at her, and she's beaming. "No. We've got some time. Atlantis can fare for a few moments longer."

The three most important men in my life exit the cabin, shutting the door behind them and leaving me and my mother alone. We stand there for several heartbeats, staring at one another, each fearful of speaking the first words. But my mother, as brave as I remember her being, is the first to talk.

"The new name you're using, I understand what you mean, my beautiful daughter. Because I've chosen to do the same." My mother presses her palms to the tops of her thighs, not knowing what to do with them.

I pull out the desk chair and motion for her to sit. "And what do you call yourself now?"

"Cordelia," she answers, making her way to the desk.

I smile, beside myself. "Jewel of the sea."

"Ironic, isn't it?" My mother sits, and I prop on the desk near her.

"Well, Cordelia, I'd love to get to know you."

We both smile and spend the next several hours telling each other stories of our lives and how my parents reconciled and made good on their second chance. She tells me that Jack is my other half, as I am his, and despite my father's grumblings about his career choice, she knows Jack is a good man. I cursed the day Atlantis betrayed me and sent me to a place unknown. But now I realize the kingdom I've spent the better half of my ethereal life protecting was returning the favor. Jack and I are stronger *together*. And despite no need for physical protection due to my immorality, Jack defends something far more fragile—my heart.

EPILOGUE

THREE MONTHS LATER

JACK

"I THINK IT'S about time you give up, mate, before you lose your share of everything we just scored." I'm sitting at one end of the barrel, a set of dice resting between me and Red, where I've rolled two doubles for the fourth time in a row.

Red's leg bounces furiously, and he rubs his face. He stares at the dice before slamming down another gold coin. "Double or nothing, Cap. I'm feeling lucky."

Grinning and shaking my head, I gather my winnings into a pouch hanging from my hip. "You're done, Red. Save some of that for ale and pleasurable company once we're in port, yeah?" I point at his wandering eyes, looking for another crew member to challenge. "Don't let me hear about you tricking Laust again, or I'll *leave* you in port."

Red rolls his eyes and stands, stretching and rubbing his stomach. "Could probably use a jogging lap around the deck, anyway."

Flicking my thumb against the emerald ring on my forefinger, I snort. "You? Run? Since when?"

"You're right, Captain. I should stick with the exercise I'm best at—" Red reaches behind him and lifts a mug of grog. "—tankard lifts." Grinning, he bends his arm to his mouth and sips.

"Carry on," I jest, smiling and saluting him.

After smoothing out my coat sleeves, I slip my hand behind my back and parade the deck. The past months have been eerily quiet after the drama of sea monsters, witches, the Royal Navy, and the King of the Seas. At times, it's almost been— boring. But we struck gold from a shipwreck off the coast of a small Jamaican island. Thanks to her sea nymph lungs, my beloved Anne retrieved the remaining treasure the rest of us couldn't. What I wouldn't have given to be able to see the gold in the broken chest still nestled in the same ship it originated.

Sighing and quickly ending this self-pity party I've started, I turn to Ragnar at the ship's wheel. "The wheel suits you, brother."

"It suits you far better, Captain. Why don't you take over?" The skin beneath Ragnar's eye quivers.

I'm still captain and perform all forms of captain-like duties, but more recently, I've handed the reins to Ragnar to spend more time—in my quarters.

Hoisting myself without the stairs, I jostle him. "But I do *so* appreciate you taking on this responsibility, old friend, so that I can concentrate on more *productive* things."

"Despite the cotton I stick in my ears, I've heard your *appreciation* through closed doors." Ragnar gives me an indignant expression, but I've known him long enough to notice the tiniest smile tugging on his lips.

Resting my hands on my hips, I inhale the brine wafting in the air, and sigh. "Tell me this spot doesn't have one hell of a view, though."

"You owe me three pieces of silver, by the way." Ragnar says this so "matter-of-factly" that it takes me off guard.

"Pardon me?"

Ragnar hangs lazily from one of the pegs. "Our bet? Three pieces of silver, you'd settle down within two years?"

Bollocks.

"We're not married. At least in the biblical sense." I drum my fingers on the railing.

Ragnar barks a laugh. "No, you're only eternally bonded to her. You've risked your mortal life for her on more than one occasion, and you can't take your eyes off her whenever she's around. I'd say you're quite settled down, *ven*."

I know this in my gut and have zero issues with it because Annie is my world, but my best friend, a man I consider a brother, pointing it out? It puts such a giddy smile on my face that I swear I'm drunk.

Digging into my satchel, I feel for three pieces of silver and slap them into his awaiting palm. "Don't spend it all in one place. Or do. At the brothel." I chuckle before noticing Mary staring at a map with—spectacles. "Read?"

She lifts her head, eyes largely distorted through the lenses of the wire-framed glasses. "Yeah, Cap?" Mary says this like seeing her with such a thing atop her nose isn't unusual.

Upon closer inspection, I realize they aren't just any spectacles.

"Mary, are those—were they Duke's?"

"Yeah," she says, removing them and turning them in her hands with a remembering grin. "I'm still trying to teach myself to read these bloody maps and thought if I put them on, it might channel him somehow. It's stupid, I know."

I cross my ankles and smile warmly while leaning on a barrel. "Not stupid. I miss him, too. Did it work?"

Mary rolls her big blue eyes with exaggerated mock annoyance. "No. But—" She lifts the map and holds it in front of her with stiff arms. "I've been wondering why I have to hold parchment out like this to make sense of it." After she slips the spectacles on, she rests the map on the barrel. "Turns out I need *glasses*. Can you believe that?"

Imagining Mary slashing her sword and swashbuckling with spectacles pulls a chuckle from my throat. "Are you certain you don't want to find a different pair in Nassau?"

"Why?" Mary frowns and peers at me with those fish-eyed lenses again, perplexed. "What's wrong with these?"

I haven't the heart to say anything further and shake my head. "You know what? Not a thing, Mary." Passing by, I kiss the top of her head. "You're perfect just the way you are."

"Damn straight," Mary mumbles, flashing teeth at me when I toss a glare.

The flag hangs from the crow's nest, displaying our emboldened colors of a black and white skull and cross swords, and flutters in the breeze above me, strong and true. The sails pick up the wind, which hasn't died down for days. Thank God for it, too, because it's getting us to land faster.

"Captain, there you are. I've been looking for you," Glog

rushes toward me with a wooden spoon, his other hand cupped underneath it as if he doesn't wish to get this already filthy deck dirty. "Try this."

I open my mouth to the approaching spoon without fear because if he wishes to poison me at this point, I figure he'd have already done it. It's a surprisingly spicy, warm broth. Beverage? "What is this? Tastes like wine but mixed with something else."

Glog does a quick jig, sloshing some red liquid onto my boots. I arch a brow at him. "Sorry. But yes, the wine in storage was close to going bitter, so I thought I'd try something with it. It's some random spices we had left, fermented fruits, and wine *warmed* by fire."

I lick what remains from my top lip. "It's delicious. What do you call it?"

"I'm thinking of naming it after myself." Glog clicks his heels together, closes his eyes, and proudly stands straighter.

"Someone is certainly full of themselves," I jest, strolling past him.

Glog's eyes frantically blink open, and he stutters. "But I—" He catches my smile and points at me with the ladle, splashing the rest of the contents onto the deck. "—you're taking the piss out of me, aren't you?"

Still grinning, I don't answer and keep moving. Something drips on the top of my head, and I pause, peering at the clear blue skies without a cloud in sight. Huh. As I walk further, two more drops fall, one on my head, another on my shoulder. Wiping some from my shirt and rubbing it between two fingers, I sniff it. Rum?

Looking up again, squinting against the blazing sun, the crow's nest in the foreground, I see Squid's dangling legs swaying with more zeal than usual. I shield my eyes and scoff at the shit-eating grin he's giving, holding up his rum bottle, gesturing at it, and then his head and laughing. He's become quite the little prankster as of late. I point at him and make a walking gesture with my fingers to insinuate that he is walking the plank. Squid laughs again, shakes his head, flicks his wrist at me, and continues drinking.

There's splashing from the rope ladder hanging over the railing, and my heart races. Anne went for a swim hours ago, and I've been impatiently waiting for her to return. I prop against a barrel, sporting my best swagger, and when I see long *black* hair instead of red, I deflate.

"Aranck. Not the long-haired beauty I was expecting." I dust my trousers off for no other reason than to not peer at Aranck half-naked.

Aranck wrings out his dark tresses and uses a rag to dry his face. "You think I'm beautiful, Captain?"

My neck stiffens. "I wouldn't say beautiful per se, but you're certainly not ugly?"

"That woman can swim," Aranck says, graciously changing the subject and catching his breath.

The woman is Anne.

"She *is* part fish," I add, the skin on my fingertips tingling, remembering how her scales felt against them.

Aranck loops the rag over his neck. "She used her legs. Swore not to use her powers."

"Aw, Aranck. And you believed her?"

We agreed not to deceive each other, but this most certainly applied to no one else.

Another splash from the ropes, and there she is, my gorgeous sea nymph emerging from her domain. If Aranck has walked away, I don't notice because I'm fixated on her—the shimmering scales, the fins on her arms morphing away, and the electric smile she gives when she spots me.

"Captain," she coos, sauntering toward me.

Grabbing her hand, I pull her to my chest and run the back of my hand down her cheek. "Nymph. How was your swim?"

Anne lets out a relaxing sigh that rivals the sensation of warm water after being chilled to the bone. "Invigorating. I could've stayed in longer, but—" She curls her arms around my neck. "—I missed you."

Involuntarily, I make a *tsking* sound because I've grown increasingly envious of her ability to swim underwater indefinitely and sprout a tail and fins as she pleases. I've also become jealous of the seas themselves, knowing I can't truly *be* with her there.

"Jack?" Anne peels back, squishing my face in her hands. "What is it?"

There's no getting anything past her—damn bond.

Focusing on her skin, I trail the tip of my finger over the scales still visible. "It must be a euphoric feeling, freeing even, swimming like that without the need to come up for air and with your limbs tiring from the strain so quickly."

Anne licks her lips, hesitating to say something. "There *is* a way you can have that too, Jack."

My heart stops beating, and I've forgotten how to breathe

or think.

Anne grabs my hand and leads me to the cabin, quietly shutting the door behind us. She has to sit me in my chair because I'm useless. "Because of your bond with me, you can become one of us. And—" She lifts my chin, begging me to look at her. "—immortal."

I paw the armrests and stare at her. "One of you? What would I be?"

"A shifter." She says this with such simplicity as if we're talking about the weather. "You'd be able to shift at will for land or sea like my brother Triton. And it's possible because of Poseidon's power."

Shooting to my feet, I pace the room and rub my chin. "And I could have a tail?"

"Yes." Anne's grinning now, patiently seated on my desk.

I stop and snap my fingers. "But I'd keep my legs?"

"Yes, Jack. You can shift as you see fit."

"I'd be an absolute fool to turn this down. It's a seaman's dream. A *pirate's* dream." An uneasy feeling gnaws in my gut. "What's the catch? There's *always* a catch."

Anne sighs and moves in front of me. "Immortality itself is the catch. You and I will live on forever, but the crew? Truffles? They will all meet their mortal ends."

Truffles meows from his pillow, stretching and smacking his tiny cat mouth together. Laust flops on top of him, his mouth wide open and snoring, his ass perched in the air. His hand loses grip on an empty grog bottle, which clatters to the floor.

"Laust, however, will be with us through it all because he, too, is a supernatural." Anne brightens at the sight of the little imp.

It pains me to think of losing Truffles, of losing *any* of them, but I lost my parents long before immortality. I lost Duke. Eventually, I'd lose them all, no matter what, or they'd lose *me*. Choosing to be with Anne would mean an eternity with her. It means adventures with her forever, swimming the seas, and whatever the hell else a sea deity does.

"I want it, Annie." I press my hands to her back and pull her against me. "I want you and everything that comes with it."

Anne's eyes fill with tears. "Are you sure?"

"Wait—" Holding a finger up, I eye her speculatively "—I can still be a pirate? Plunder, pillage, and murder upon necessity?"

Anne laughs, one tear escaping and rolling down her cheek. "I certainly hope so because I still wish for those things too. It's why I chose to stay here."

"Then, love—" I press a chaste kiss to her forehead "—give me a tail."

"It's not me who does it," Anne whispers.

A sea spray goes off behind us, and I clutch Anne as if I don't know who it could be.

"I'm going to take one wild guess as to why I'm here, daughter?" Poseidon asks, scratching his head, his blonde hair now pulled into a knot at the base of his skull. But no trident this time.

Reluctantly, I let her go and she blinks emerald eyes that match her father's. "Daddy, Jack wants to be with me. *Forever.*"

Once Ragnar hears about this, I will *never* hear the end of it.

Poseidon turns his gaze on me and raises a thick eyebrow. "You understand the implications?"

I feel the urge to stand tall, to puff my chest and lift my

chin. "I do, sir."

"Very well. I'm honestly surprised it took this long." Poseidon holds out his palm, and a glowing orange mass appears. He holds it out to me, I reach for it, but he snaps his hand shut. "Just so we're *clear*. Once you both stop aging enough for it to be noticeable, you *must* become a footnote in history and start over elsewhere. Understood?"

We nod in unison.

Poseidon offers me the strange glowing substance again. "This will make you immortal."

"Do I lick it? Say a prayer to it?" I take it, holding it dumbly between two fingers.

Anne laughs, her face bright and full of life. Poseidon smiles at this. "You eat it, Jack. It's ambrosia."

The food of the gods. This *is* happening.

An electric zip surges from my toes to my brain as I consume it. It borders on painful but never fully gets there, settling in my skin like raindrops. My chest tightens, making me breathless, and then—it's over. I feel my head and chest.

"That's it? Why don't I feel much different?" I look between Anne and Poseidon.

Poseidon closes the distance between us. "You will. Give it time." He curls a hand over my shoulder. "Especially after this last part. But remember what I said about my trident, boy. Immortal or not."

"I won't forget for as long as I inhumanly live." My cheek twitches. "Sir."

A flicker of blue light courses down Poseidon's arm and into me.

Rhode hugs her father's side and whispers, "I love you, Daddy."

"And I love you." Poseidon kisses the top of her head. "Now go show him how to use his new tail."

I'm in my cabin one moment, and the next, I'm underwater. My eyes blaze open, and at first, I'm gasping for air, clinging to my throat like I'm drowning.

Anne appears before me and presses a calming palm against my cheek. "Breathe, Jack. You *can* now."

To test this, I take a slow breath through my nose, and it's the same as breathing on land. I can also *hear* Anne in much the same way.

"This is incredible." My voice is crystal clear to me despite being fathoms underwater.

Anne points below my waist. "Look."

A dark green tail swooshes from left to right, sending the oddest tingling sensation up my spine. It's my tail. *I'm* moving it. Gasping, I momentarily panic because I do not see something *else* below my waist.

"Annie? Where is—"

Anne laughs and takes my hand. "Still very much there, Jack. It's just hidden for now. Come on, I want to show you something."

With our hands intertwined, I let her guide me through the water, showing me the proper uses of my tail, barrel rolling over each other, and stealing kisses every other moment. A pod of dolphins swim with us for several moments, and I've never felt more connected to something in my entire life.

Anne leads us to what appears to be more open water, but

she pauses and presses her hand to a particular spot. The sea parts, revealing an expansive city I've only ever imagined in fairy tales—gold and silver shimmering castles and towers. All forms of aquatic life swim within its confines, and at the center is a spire towering over it all.

"Welcome to Atlantis. Your second home." Anne squeezes my hand, assuring me this is my reality now. She points at the spire, the beacon. And there, glowing in vibrant blue glory is the jewel that started it all and brought Anne and me together.

Anne curls her tail with mine, sending a shiver down my spine. With our hair floating in bubbling wisps around us, she kisses me—a deep, claiming kiss that I pour everything into to say to her, yes, I *am* yours. When we peel away, we rest our heads against each other's and stare at the beacon. I've spent most of my pirate life coveting and safeguarding coins and jewels. Now, I understand Atlantis's purpose in choosing me. Not only to protect Atlantis and its jewel but also the treasure in my arms.

THE END
...for now.

Catch the first book in the Contemporary Mythos series:

HADES

The King of the Underworld may have found a woman
truly capable of melting his cold, dark heart.

HADES (Contemporary Mythos, #1)
BUY IT ON AMAZON

Experience more of Rhode's story in the following
Contemporary Mythos series book:

POSEIDON

POSEIDON (Contemporary Mythos, #5)

BUY IT ON AMAZON

ACKNOWLEDGEMENTS

FIRSTLY, AS ALWAYS, to my husband. You continue to be an inspiration in all my works, even this one, despite your distaste for pirates. LOL. You've always been a natural born leader and Jack Rackham has you to thank for making him a great one.

To my parents, for not only feeding into my Pirates of the Caribbean obsession when it first released, but supporting it and not batting an eyelash when I asked to see it for the tenth time in the theaters.

To AK, I can never express how truly thankful I am that we met all those years ago. I couldn't ask for a better critique partner, friend, and fellow book nerd to have in my corner. Your input and opinions are always top tier for me and I appreciate you tenfold for it. You took the extra time to read this *again* with a big 'ol red pen to make it the best it could be before release when you didn't have to, but you believe in this story, and in me, and I can't thank you enough for doing that. And also, thank you for kicking my butt regarding the blurb. You were right. You always are. LOL.

To Cerys, GIRL, this story has been a long time coming and I sincerely appreciate you letting me bounce ideas off of you, continually keeping me excited, and reminding me to give myself grace amidst a big move and buying my first house while still finishing the first draft. Your alpha reading truly kept me going, friend. Thank you.

To Kristin, I'm so grateful Bookstagram brought us together. Your continued energy whenever you alpha read for me gives me renewed life. Seriously. Your opinions, being an avid romantasy reader yourself, were invaluable and I appreciate your support so much!

And finally, to the readers. This story has been on my mind since 2017, but realistically, it's been living in my brain since I was six, having just experienced the Pirates of the Caribbean ride for the first time and meeting my favorite Disney princess, Ariel. This is for all the readers who love mythology, pirates, and mermaids. For those who've searched high and low for a true adult pirate romantasy and not of the "bodice ripper" variety. And for those that shipped Jack Sparrow with Elizabeth Swann before Will Turner.

Drink up, me hearties, yo ho.

ABOUT THE AUTHOR

CARLY SPADE is an adult romance writer who has been writing since she could pick up a pencil. After the insanity of obtaining a bachelor's and master's degree in cybersecurity, creating worlds to escape to still ate at her very soul. She started writing FanFiction (which can still be found if you scour the internet), and soon felt the need to get her original ideas on paper. And so the adventure began.

She lives in Colorado with her husband and two fur babies, and revels in an enemies to lovers trope with a slow burn.

Find her online:

WWW.CARLYSPADE.COM